SOLEIL, TOO!

by

Larry Bonner

Also by Larry Bonner

Soleil Tangiere

SOLEIL, TOO!

by

Larry Bonner

All rights for the trademark and trade style Soleil Tangiere™ are wholly owned by Larry Bonner and Tangiere International, LLC.
ISBN: 0692224327
ISBN 13: 9780692224328
Library of Congress Control Number: 2014909396
Soleil, Too! Delray Beach, FL

For Stephanie, Too!
Better an honest devil than a lying angel—

SAPPHIRE EYES

The sky was blue: crackling, diamond bright, lung chilling, crystallized azure blue.

Coming over and around the white crest of the steep hill, the two skiers looked like tiny, colorful stick figures in yellow and red and white, leaning and swaying as they left double tracks in their shimmering wakes of powdered diamonds.

They were tracking left and right, suddenly lifting off the snow in small jumps and then making quick, straight schusses, and then leaning into wide turns that left plumes and arcs of white glitter in the frosted air. The wind played steady background themes of icy breaths and whispers, and their skis added quick sandpaper notes to the frosty symphony of movement and sunshine and light.

Far above and to the left of the hurtling skiers, a white, bubble-shaped tram slowly traveled up its double cable system on the spectacular run from the resort town of Engelberg to the summit of Mount Titlis.

The view from the cable car was awe-inspiring: from there, the world was a panorama of glaciers, steep valleys, and secret lakes nestled in the wide, white arms of the snow-covered Swiss Alps. The quickly advancing *pas de deux* of the two tiny skiers below was a charming, living punctuation mark on the magnificent landscape.

Coming to the end of the run, the two ran through clots of other skiers and tourists, ducked as they passed under a pair of ski-shod feet passing above on a lift, and then skillfully swooshed up to the ski station to sudden, standing stops. The young man quickly pulled off his red helmet, lifted his goggles from his dark eyes, and looked at his companion.

Her sun-yellow helmet came off, and an explosion of straight, corn-silk blond hair fell to the shoulders of her white jacket. She pulled off her gloves, then her goggles, shook her head to free up the rest of the hair, looked at the young ski pro, and smiled.

The white smile held breathless happiness, but the eyes ruled the day—deep, shimmering sapphires that mirrored the clarity of this place, of this moment. Stefan wasn't immune to her eyes. They couldn't be denied.

"What do you need me for? You don't need an instructor," he said in German, his breath condensing in the cold air. "You ski beautifully. Obviously you are not a beginner."

They shed their skis and poles and walked across the snow to the crowded snack bar. The outdoor establishment was built on a reinforced rock outcropping. They found a tiny high-top table against one of the railings. As they sat on tall stools, their eyes couldn't help but be drawn to the fabulous Alpine winter scene all around them.

"I haven't skied in a while," she said in broken German, pushing aside a few blond hairs that had fallen across her face, "and never on an Alp. Where I come from, the skiing is good, but nothing like this. I needed a pro around in case I got in over my head."

Stefan barely concealed a grin. "Would you like to speak English?" he asked tactfully in accented English, the lines around his eyes crinkling slightly. Her German needed a lot of work.

"*Danke.*" Switching happily to English, she said, "I've been in Zurich for months, and I found out pretty fast that German is easy on the vocabulary but brutal on sentence structure. *Unmöglich!* Impossible!"

Stefan laughed and said, "Your vocabulary is excellent." They ordered hot cocoas and looked out over the mountains. Then Stefan said, "Where do you come from, America?"

"Canada. Quebec." Her eyes sparkled and reflected the bright sky.

"Ah, that explains your good skiing."

"Not every Canadian skis. Or plays hockey." Another smile.

They were in Engelberg, around one hundred kilometers south of the outskirts of Zurich proper. Many of her fellow passengers had toted their skis and gear on the train, but she had rented everything she needed when she got to the mountain resort. I'd rather travel light, and I certainly don't need anything else to clutter up my apartment.

"You are living in Zurich?" Stefan asked.

"Yes, at least for now," she answered.

The cocoa came, and they took tentative sips of the scalding-hot bittersweet. There was a period of quiet and then he asked, "Are you staying in Engelberg overnight, or are you returning to Zurich?" He made it sound conversational and without subtext.

"I'm not sure," she answered truthfully, and watched his face. He's handsome and looks to be around twenty-five: two years older than I am. And he's like all pros working in resorts, she thought. He has a familiar vain confidence about his ability to talk to and convince female tourists about all manner of things and activities. Both ski and après-ski, I'll bet.

"The hotels here are filled to capacity. You will need to reserve a room soon or you will find yourself with nowhere to sleep." The pupils of his eyes grew wider by a fraction of a millimeter.

She sighed inside. Boys will be boys.

"Well," she said, making up her mind quickly. "Then we'd better get back on the slopes so I won't miss the last train to Zurich later on. I have to be certain of a bed tonight." She wiped a thin line of cocoa from her upper lip. OK, she thought. I couldn't resist that one.

The rest of the afternoon was ski heaven. For both of them: Stefan enjoyed the ease and fun he had showing her the nuances and techniques of skiing in the Alps. She was an amazingly quick learner with an already strong background, and she was undeniably the most beautiful student he could remember teaching. Ever.

After she had returned her skis to the rental center, he kissed her on both cheeks. His body language was obvious and a bit suggestive. She smiled inside. And out.

When she got on the Zentralbahn for the trip to Zurich, she was wiped out. In a good way. I love being tired like this, and I don't mind being alone, traveling alone, she thought. And this train ride is great—the scenery is fantastic.

And Stefan was nice in a predictable kind of way. If I come back to Engelberg to ski, I'll look him up. Just for skiing. Uh-huh.

I'm happy.

In a little under an hour the train pulled into Lucerne for a fifteen-minute stop before continuing on to Zurich. I should live in Lucerne, she thought, gazing at the classic old city and its lake from the train window. It's like Zurich, but prettier, I think.

And I'll never go to Geneva again if I can help it.

Precisely on time, the train pulled out of Lucerne Station and headed onward to Zurich, an hour away. She watched the scenery flow by and hesitantly pulled an event from earlier this year, 1989, out of the well of her subconscious.

I'm happy now, she reminded herself, except for one thing, and I'm slowly coming to terms with that, too.

The Alpine vista unfolding slowly outside the train window seemed to soften, to take on a haze, as she selected that one thing from her memory and turned it over and over in the light...

She remembered how she had stood on the tarmac at the Geneva Airport with her friend, her lover—the man who had sworn his love to her and had saved her life.

He had promised he would return. Soon.

"I must rush back to you, *da*?" he had quipped in his low Russian accent, the answer being happily obvious to them both. His dark eyes had flashed, and his strong arms had encircled her slim body.

They had kissed long and hard, and then he got on the waiting jet, and it had roared down the runway and lifted off, heading to Moscow, and I couldn't really look at it go, so I turned and left and knew that the bad was all behind me and only good things, my things, *my* decisions were ahead of me...

Then a few days later, on November 9, she had read the headline in the *Neue Zürcher Zeitung*: The Berlin Wall had fallen. And she hadn't heard from Max.

The next day, she tried repeatedly to call him, but could not get through. It was extremely difficult to place a phone call to a country that was imploding.

Katia Koziashvili came out of her sleep with a slight hangover. She had heard a noise in the almost-dark room— someone had quietly closed the door.

"Who is it?" she sat bolt upright in the darkness.

"Max."

"Max?" Her head was still filled with the cobwebs of a vodka-enhanced sleep. "You've come back."

"What are you doing here, Katia?" The deep, familiar voice had an annoyed quality to it.

"Aren't you happy to see me?" This was certainly one of the most-asked questions in the history of less-than-ideal relationships.

"Go to sleep. And then you're out of here in the morning—you have your own place."

Ignoring him, she yawned and stretched her arms over her head. The room was hot from the space heater, and during the night, she had shed her pajama top and was only wearing panties. Her long, dark hair cascaded in shining ringlets over her shoulders and down onto the pillow. "Come here."

Max Stepanov sat on the side of the bed fully clothed, and she leaned over to kiss him. He accepted the kiss but did not return it, and Katia knew instantly from the irritated look in his dark eyes that something was very wrong.

It was late, and outside the closed window, the never-ending background white noise of Moscow was muted.

"What happened, Max?" she said again. "I tried finding out why I hadn't heard from you for so long. I called your boss at Nevsky Nickel and then I tried to reach Vlad at the embassy. Of course, I couldn't reach him. But then I saw him on the television last week at that UN meeting in Switzerland with Gorbachev. Did you know anything about that?" Her mouth turned down slightly at the corners.

He had called her at her Moscow apartment when he had first arrived in Switzerland, only because she had pleaded with him to do so. But since then, it had been difficult to place any calls to Russia—almost impossible. Oh, let's face it: I didn't *want* to call her. Our relationship is over. And now things have changed so drastically.

She's in my life now.

"Kat..." he started to say, and then changed his mind. His ex-girlfriend was no fool. One look at his face told her everything. Her large amber eyes widened in the kind of feline anger for which certain girls from Soviet Georgia were famous. *Da*, she realized in a sickening and obvious flash: it looks like Max has found someone else, some girl in the West. Surprise, surprise, she thought bitterly.

Max stood up and started to mumble something, but then his words trailed off, and Katia decided to wait him out—she wasn't going to make this easy for him.

After a full minute of silence, she said, "What's her name?"

"What? Who?" As soon as he said it, he knew it sounded lame.

"Stop it, you *svinya*, you pig!" Now she was on a roll. When he started to protest, she ramped it up. "Shut up; just shut up! What trampy Western slut turned your head, eh? You're like all men, Max—rotten, selfish—your soul in your crotch! I waited all this time for you and you didn't even call."

Her eyes narrowed. "What, she didn't have a phone by the side of her bed?" She searched around in the tousled sheets for her pajama top. Finally, she found it and hastily put it on. She was unstoppable.

"Are you proud of yourself, animal? You leave the arms of your one true love and the first thing you do when you get off the plane is fall into the private parts of some street-walker? I guess that's what capitalism is all about, eh? Free-market honeypot!"

She grabbed the lamp from the night table and threw it at Max, who was now standing against the wall. He ducked, and the lamp made a loud crashing sound. A pillow flew at him. Then a high-heeled shoe.

A moment later, there was a harsh knock on the wall—one of the neighbors was not happy with the voices and the crashing. *"Zatknis!"* came an angry voice through the sheetrock.

"I bet she was..." Katia continued in a lower voice, but then she suddenly came up short. Oh God, she thought. I get it.

Her amber eyes narrowed to slits.

"Her name, my dear Maxim. What's her name?" she said slowly, her voice dripping venom.

Max looked away and then at the ceiling. He was mortally tired, and what was worse, she was right about some of this. After a moment, he picked up his coat and headed for the door.

With a voice dripping accusation, she went on: "That girl, that Canadian girl at the UN meeting in Geneva—you know, Vlad's little heroine of the USSR? What's her name again? That couldn't be your new whore, could it now?"

Max, his hand on the doorknob, turned and looked straight at her. He didn't have to say anything—his face said it all.

Her mouth dropped open and she cursed herself for being right. Of course.

Of course it was the Canadian girl.

The next morning the onion domes of the Cathedral of the Annunciation in the Kremlin were shrouded in a cold fog that choked the city.

Max had spent the night at the apartment of a friend from work.

Katia had packed and was on the way out of Max's small apartment with her battered rolling suitcase. To hell with you Max, you skunk, you snake. The phone started to ring and she turned from the open doorway, thought for a minute, and then walked back into the apartment and picked up the receiver.

"*Privyet,*" she said curtly into the phone.

"Is Max there...*pozhalustah*?"

Katia did a double take. What?

"Who is you?" she said in bad English.

"Sorry, I must have the—"

"*Nyet*. No." Her mind went into overdrive, and her amber eyes narrowed. Well, well, here's the Canadian woman after all. "Is right number," she said putting happiness in her voice.

"Is Max there?" asked the voice again.

Thinking quickly, Katia said, "*Da*, yes, a moment." Katia turned her face away from the phone and called loudly, "Maxim, darling," to the empty apartment. She held the phone away from her face for a count of ten, and then said into the phone, "He is still in shower. We both need one, if you know what I mean, honey." A conspiratorial giggle.

Then she said, "Is there message?" The sweetness dripped through the phone.

"No." There was a long silence. Then, "Just tell him good-bye," the voice said in a whisper.

"Okay. Bye, bye, honey." Katia hung up, her amber eyes smiling in satisfaction.

In Zurich, 1,800 miles to the west, Soleil Tangiere stood leaning against the wall of her small living room, holding the phone and listening to the dial tone coming all the way from Moscow.

She listened for a full minute, and then carefully placed the phone in its cradle, went into the bathroom, and threw up.

Later on, she went out, slamming the apartment door behind her.

A month went by. No word from Max.

Good. I hope he's happy, Soleil thought.

No I don't.

I don't know what I hope.

But why hasn't he called, even to tell me it's over?

Soleil's office was in a classically Swiss office building on Zurich's famous and trendy downtown street, The Bahnhofstrasse.

The office wasn't large, but it was bright and cheerful. It had a reception area with a desk and, through a second door, Soleil's small but tasteful office.

Yvonne considered the reception area to be *her* office.

Her desk faced the door that opened to the corridor, and from her chair she could see the reverse image of "Tangiere International, AG" stenciled on the frosted-glass window in the door.

Yvonne Goulet was as tall and slim as Soleil was. She had large, intelligent, brown eyes and, at thirty, was seven years Soleil's senior. She kept her shoulder-length brown hair in a stylish bob, and dressed *au courant* when she was at work and usually the rest of the time, as well.

Yvonne had moved to Zurich about two months ago. She wasn't fond of that city, but she wanted to be near Soleil. Having been born and raised as an only child in Geneva, where her parents' and her native French was the lingua franca, Yvonne had a hard-wired disdain for the harsh-sounding German language spoken in this part of Switzerland. No language comes close to the music that is French, she said confidently to herself.

Married once when she was twenty-one, she had divorced her cheating husband three years later and had been single since. *Dieu merci*, no kids!

Yvonne had worked for Soleil's fiancé, Tom Patel, for two years before she had met or even heard of the Canadian woman. Then one day, a cunning and merciless woman bent on destroying Soleil Tangiere had nearly killed Yvonne.

She survived, but her voice had never returned completely. She didn't anticipate that men would find her new low voice attractive, but they did. When Soleil found out that Yvonne had been nearly tortured to death, she vowed her friendship and support to the damaged woman for eternity.

Now Yvonne "worked" for Soleil, but they were really just close friends. The company did some trading business with a few select clients, but now mainly existed as a holding company for the funds that Soleil "inherited" after Patel's untimely and violent demise. Soleil was far more interested in the charitable benefits Tom's ill-gotten gains could be channeled into, rather than in seeking deals with people or businesses of questionable character.

Soleil paid Yvonne a generous salary. In Zurich, a generous salary was a necessity for survival—it was one of the most expensive cities in the world.

The door opened, and Soleil came in wearing tapered jeans and a cable-knit sweater. Her coat was over her arm. Yvonne smiled at her friend. "Hi."

"*Bonjour, Yvonne. Ça va?*"

Yvonne loved listening to Soleil's attempts to metropolitanize her outrageous, native Québécois French, and never missed an opportunity to disparage it playfully.

"*Je vais bien.*" She pushed up her lower lip. "Not bad for a farmer," she said, smiling at Soleil.

Soleil tossed her a classic Gallic look of disdain and said, "*Va te faire foutre!* How's that for Parisian French?" They both laughed.

"Anything going on here?" asked Soleil as she walked into her office.

"Just did my nails. That's all. Now I'm taking a break."

A few minutes later, Yvonne went into Soleil's office and found her standing at the window staring out at nothing. She stepped over to stand next to her. "What are you looking at?"

She saw the crestfallen look on Soleil's face. She picked up on it in a second.

"It's still Max, isn't it?" she asked softly.

Soleil looked away for a moment.

"How long will you wait?" Yvonne asked.

"Until what?" Soleil knew exactly what.

"Maybe you should start dating."

She looked at Yvonne. "I'm way ahead of you."

"*Bon*!" Yvonne was sincerely happy. Soleil needs dates, men...sex. It never fails. Once that ball starts rolling, life returns with a vengeance.

"I'm going back to Engelberg to ski." Her eyes narrowed as she thought about Stefan for a second. "And I'm staying there overnight."

2

HALLWAY

Christmas was coming.

Soleil Tangiere's libido had taken over and started clouding her judgment, but she didn't feel bad about it. Face it: it's my nature. That night with Stefan was exactly what I needed. But emotionally it was nothing—just a kind of nice Christmas present, that's all, she thought. A present for me and a present for him.

OK, she thought, was it revenge sex? Maybe, but so what?

She felt suddenly crestfallen: the bar's been set too high. It's going to be a while until I find a man like Max.

Where are you, Max?

She had spoken on the phone to her oldest sister Camille in Minnesota and made her promise to fly to Switzerland for the holiday. "I'm going to meet Kurt in Chicago first," Camille had said. "He's been lusting after me for weeks, and I think I have to succumb."

"Lusting?"

"Calling twice a day, every day. Same thing."

Soleil had to admit that her sister was probably right. Kurt was a good man who had been in the final phase of his divorce when he met Camille. They had hit it off instantly. God knows, Camille deserves to have a good man in her life for a change, thought Soleil.

Kurt Ballas owned a small commodities trading firm on Wacker Drive in Chicago, and had met Camille at a metals industry convention in New York.

He had instantly fallen for Camille. Her statuesque beauty, glittering hazel eyes, and thick, auburn hair were irresistible to Kurt from the moment he laid eyes on her. And her no-nonsense demeanor and direct repartee were endlessly refreshing. He felt that she was even more striking and desirable than Soleil, who was eleven years her junior and caused men to stop and turn and dream.

A set of bizarre happenings at the metal conference's signature ball had highlighted his whirlwind, three-day romance with Camille. These happenings included guns, murder, subterfuge, and the presence of Kurt's ex-wife, Amanda.

That was two months ago.

Since then, Camille had visited her ex-husband one last time at a medium-security facility in Milwaukee, where he was spending a year and half as a guest of the State of Wisconsin. Over the years, Jake Weston had been a guest many times in many states.

I was looking for closure, and I got it, she thought. I'm glad that cord is finally cut. But sometimes in the middle of the night, Jake's disarming smile comes back to haunt me. *C'est la vie.*

Camille had made great strides in her life in the last few months, and felt that she didn't want to derail her progress by making any more bad emotional mistakes. She had fought her way out of a dead-end life populated by a selection of bad men, Jake being the latest and worst, and she was now, at age thirty-four, on what she had come to think of as her "ascension" to a better life.

Earlier in the year, she had spent time with her little sister in Switzerland and then in New York. She and Soleil had gone through a terrible and terrifying time fighting the people who had murdered their father. *I don't want to dwell on that,* she found herself thinking on a regular basis. *It's too crazy.*

The phone on the hotel room's bedside table rang three times before the slender hand snaked out from under the covers and pulled the receiver under the sheets.

"Mmm...'lo?"

"Hi."

"Hi, Soleil. What time is it?"

"All I know is that I'm seven hours ahead of you. That makes it around 10:00 a.m. in Chicago, I guess."

"Where are you, Soleil?" she asked into the phone, pulling the covers off and sitting on the edge of the bed.

"At work."

"Hold on," said Camille, hearing the knock. "Someone's at the door."

She pulled on a hotel robe and went to the door. Looking through the peephole, she saw that it was Kurt. "What's the password?" she said loudly.

"Watermelon."

Laughing, she opened the door. Kurt stepped inside and was about to hug her when she backed up and said, "Wait. I have to get rid of Soleil."

"Soleil's here?" he asked, a perplexed look on his face.

Camille picked up the receiver and waggled it in front of him. Then she said into the phone, "Kurt's here; gotta go."

"Bye," Soleil said, into her already buzzing phone.

Kurt had made Camille's hotel reservation, and he hadn't seen her since she'd gotten into town—he was in Cleveland on business and had just returned to Chicago that morning.

The Harmon House Hotel was centrally located and not far from Kurt's office on Wacker Drive. It had a huge Chicago history dating back to 1871, and while not as modern as other hotels in the area, it oozed the ambiance of the "City of Big Shoulders." Camille calculated that Kurt wanted her to get a feel for his hometown. OK with me, she had said to herself; I've never been to Chicago.

It had been two months since Camille had seen Kurt, and now that he was standing before her, he looked good— very good indeed. He was thirty-eight, six foot three, and had an unruly thatch of thick, tawny hair that hung forward over his well-worn face.

He had on dark slacks, a cotton shirt, and a light gray jacket. And now he sported a rough new goatee. Hmm, thought Camille, eyeing the stubbly chin—interesting. Kurt's face showed unalloyed joy at the sight of her.

They came together for a long, hard hug and a kiss on the cheek. And then suddenly, a brief but complete kiss on the lips. Camille hadn't slept with Kurt, but for some reason she felt that she already had—maybe it had something to do with the intense emotional whirlwind that they had experienced together in New York.

His eyes crinkled, and he said, "I hope you like this place—it's pure Chi-town."

The room was a suite in classic style: strong mahogany furniture, a small crystal chandelier, and highly polished hardwood floors. It smelled slightly of the same lemony furniture polish used in the hotel's gleaming wood-paneled hallways.

"This hotel's very nice, Kurt," she said, checking to see that the sash of her robe hadn't loosened.

"You sure it's OK, Cami?"

"Of course; it's beautiful." She suddenly felt a bit awkward with what had strangely become an oblique and forced conversation.

After a moment of strained silence: "Cami?"

She tilted her head a fraction and looked into his eyes.

He kicked off his shoes, making him an inch or two shorter and closer to her in height, crossed the few feet of distance between them, gently took her shoulders in his hands, and leaned down to kiss her on the lips.

OK, maybe this is a touch fast, but maybe not, she thought. She suddenly felt as if she were a third person in the room, watching this little romantic drama unfold. She was mildly surprised that she liked what she was seeing.

After letting Kurt do all of the work for two or three seconds, she put her arms around him and returned the kiss in kind. A part of her head tried to remember the last time she had kissed a man like this. Oh hell, it was just *too* long ago, and they both put renewed energy into it.

Outside and down the hall from Camille's room, there was a muted "bing" as a set of elevator doors opened. A slender woman in a tan suit strode into the hall, checked the discreet wall sign that directed guests toward different groups of room numbers, and slowly walked down the corridor. Her brown hair was done up in a perm, and she wore very red lipstick.

She carried a stylish hobo bag, and as she approached Camille's door, she stopped. Checking the hallway for any sign of life and satisfied that she was alone, she quickly removed a gleaming, blued Colt .45 automatic with its very special "no-brainer" bullets from the large purse. She walked carefully and quietly down the hall.

Now she stood in front of the door to the suite with the pistol down at her side. She took a deep breath or two, moved her gun hand behind her back, and with the other loudly knocked three times on the door.

After what seemed like a heavenly long time, Kurt and Camille slowly separated from the kiss and looked at each other.

Kurt decided to go for it. "Do you want to stay in this hotel?" he asked.

She eyed him critically. Decision time.

"What do you mean?" She knew what he meant.

"My place is not far." What a surprise.

"And?" Maybe I'd like to stay *there*?

"Maybe you'd like to stay there."

"With..." Obviously...

"Me."

What a shock.

She looked at him for a second, her lips parted to answer his question, but before words could come out, they heard three loud knocks.

They turned their heads simultaneously to look toward the door.

"Yes?" asked Kurt loudly.

A woman's voice through the door: "Harmon House security. Sorry to disturb you. We need to speak to you for just one moment."

Kurt said loudly, "What the problem?"

"Are you Mr. Ballas?" the voice asked through the door.

"Yes." How did they know I was here? Oh, from the reservation.

The voice: "Sorry for the inconvenience, sir. It will be very brief."

Kurt and Camille looked at each other for a second, both annoyed by the bad timing of the intrusion. Then Kurt turned and started for the door.

As he approached the door, he heard Camille say, "I'll stay at your place, Kurt."

One thing about the Harmon House that hadn't changed since 1871 were its room doors. They were thick, stout oak. Well made. And since the Harmon House was a registered historical landmark as well as being a fine hotel, the room doors were exempt from one building code requirement: unlike room doors in newer hotels, the doors in the Harmon House were not required to open inward toward the rooms.

They swung out into the halls.

"I'll stay at your place, Kurt," Camille had said.

Kurt was stunned. As he reached for the door, he happily half-turned to look back at her, and the joyful surprise on his face made Camille smile. His hand turned the doorknob as his feet, shod only in socks, slipped on the lemony-smelling, polished hardwood floor and all 210 pounds of Kurt Ballas slammed into the door.

The woman on the other side of the door was catapulted across the corridor, her head smacking the opposite wall. The automatic skittered down the corridor as Kurt clumsily exploded out of the room. He toppled toward the woman's unsteady body, and his momentum caused both of them to go down in a tangled heap.

He began to think about how to apologize to the woman when he saw the weapon ten feet down the hall. The woman was desperately trying to close the distance between herself and the Colt, and was fiercely trying to disentangle herself as she frantically crawled and squirmed away from Kurt's heavy body.

Kurt felt suddenly confused, but the sight of the woman making a mad lunge for the gun energized him. He knew he was suddenly in imminent and grave danger. He clumsily pushed himself to his feet and charged at her, but she had beaten him to the gun.

She grabbed the pistol, quickly stood, and deftly side-stepped as Kurt, badly off balance, flew past her, landing heavily on the floor a couple of yards farther down the hall.

He quickly raised his head and looked over his shoulder. What he saw chilled him to the core. The woman, gun in hand, was aiming at his prone body.

"Good-bye," she said in a low voice, and squeezed her trigger finger.

The effect was slightly different from what the woman had expected.

A fraction of a second before she fired, Camille, in a flying tackle, crashed into her from behind and slightly to the left. The woman twisted off balance, and her body whammed squarely against a fire extinguisher bolted to a metal plate in the corridor wall, trapping the gun and her hand between her body and the red metal cylinder.

The finger on the trigger completed its tiny chore.

As Camille hit the floor, an obscenely loud blast filled the world.

The specially prepared, maximum-damage bullet left the muzzle of the gun. It took the slug less than one one-thousandth of a second to rip through the curved front of the extinguisher. It slowed by another microsecond as it covered the six inches of travel distance inside the cylinder, and was by then sufficiently destabilized to explode when it hit the opposite interior wall of the canister.

The effect on the fire extinguisher was impressive. The ricocheting particles of the explosive .45-caliber slug shattered a significant section of the metal tube, and even if the red container had been empty, the resultant blast of metal fragments traveling at approximately the speed of sound would have been a cause for major concern.

But it wasn't empty. It was fully charged with highly compressed propellants.

The combination of the metal slug's particulate explosion and the rapidly expanding compressed nitrogen turned the canister into a grenade.

Camille and Kurt were both on the floor when the fire extinguisher blew up. Camille felt quick, sharp pricks in her right arm, and Kurt experienced similar pains in his legs as tiny particles zipped into them. Their ears felt as if they had been smashed shut, but neither yet realized how lucky they were to be on the floor.

The woman, however, wasn't lucky at all.

She had suddenly become a human bomb in the middle of a roaring cloud of foam.

What was left of the midsection of the woman's body instantly blasted into a scarlet, oozing, foamy frieze on the opposite wall—a nauseating collage of ground up and exploded everything, somewhat reminiscent of a very lumpy, three-dimensional Jackson Pollock painting.

From his "drip" period.

A roaring silence filled the hallway for a few seconds.

The smell of lemons was quickly replaced by something less pleasant.

A whole section of corridor was now a splotchy, foamy white with a disturbing pinkish overlay.

Kurt looked at Camille. His face had lost its color, and he was covered in foam. Finally, he said, "Thanks."

Without taking her eyes from the corpse, and stunned at what had just happened, Camille staggered to her feet. Her hotel robe had just about come off, but she was so drenched in white and red foam that her modesty wasn't compromised. She looked over at Kurt and said dully, "Your welcome."

Kurt rose off the floor unsteadily. They both hesitantly stared at the remains. Or at least what was left intact from the shoulders up.

"Who is she?" Kurt asked, as doors in the hallway began to open. A couple of frightened hotel guests peeked out cautiously.

"I don't know," said Camille. I don't know her, and I don't know why this happened. Her brain was in overdrive. "Who has it in for you, Kurt?" This better not have anything to do with his ex-wife.

He was thinking furiously. I have plenty of enemies in the commodities industry, but to this degree? I have to figure this out, and fast, he thought.

One thing is certain: I never saw this woman before today.

The phone rang.

Huh? What time is it? One thirty in the morning. Where's that phone? Oh, here.

"*Allo?*" her voice was a sleep-filled murmur.

"Soleil?" The voice sounded tired.

"Oh. Cami. Hi. What's wrong?"

"Something bad happened."

Soleil's mind was wooly from sleep, but it cleared quickly.

"What's the matter?" She could hear tension in her older sister's voice, and she sat bolt upright in her bed.

Camille was silent for a few seconds. After returning from the police precinct house, it had taken her only a short time to decide when to tell Soleil about what had happened. There was no question that she had to, but she felt that with all Soleil had been through in the recent weeks and months, the timing may have been off.

But she couldn't wait any longer. And maybe Soleil would have some ideas.

"Someone tried to murder Kurt today in my hotel."

"What?" Oh no. Now what?

"A woman. Kurt and I were together in the room. She posed as an employee, came to the room with a gun, and nearly killed him. The cops say her name was Zoe. Zoe Kimball."

Oh God. "Is he hurt? Are you hurt?"

"We're OK. Exhausted, but OK."

"What did she have against him? Did this have something to do with his ex-wife? Where is she now?"

"Slow down, slow down," Camille interrupted. "Too many questions. We just had to sit through hours of interrogation at the police station, and the last thing I need now is another grilling."

"Sorry, you woke me up. What time is it there?"

"Around six thirty in the evening. I keep forgetting that you're seven hours ahead."

"Where are you now?"

"Kurt's apartment."

Hmm, thought Soleil. Camille..."Where's that Zoe person now?"

Camille looked over at Kurt, who was framed in the kitchen door opening a bottle of merlot. Even though I've tapered down on the booze, she said to herself, we're going to have a glass or two of wine. This has been too much of a day—extenuating circumstances in spades.

Camille said, "It ended badly for her."

Soleil felt a chill on the nape of her neck. The bad times of a few months back came flooding in. "You're kidding."

After a few seconds, Camille said, "Sorry to wake you with this stuff. I just needed to talk."

"Don't worry about it." Soleil stood up. She put her feet into her wool-lined slippers, stretched her arms for a second, and then slipped into the fluffy robe she kept at the foot of the bed. Cordless phone in hand, she padded into the little kitchen, filled a pot with water and milk, and put it on the stove. This is a good time for a cup of cocoa, she thought.

"You sure you don't want me to call back in the morning?" Camille asked.

"It's fine. I'm making some cocoa."

"*Tres Suisse.*"

"*Oui, putain.* Actually, it's Dutch cocoa. Now, what happened?"

Camille gave her the story from the time of the knock on the hotel door to the present moment. As she was telling the tale, Soleil finished preparing her cup of Droste's, dropped in a marshmallow, and went back to sit on the edge of the bed.

"And now here we are in Kurt's apartment," Camille finished up. She accepted a wineglass from Kurt, who had come over to sit by her on the couch.

Silence for a few seconds. "Not a bad apartment for a bachelor," she said to both the phone and Kurt. "You'd hate the mess, Soleil. I don't mind it."

Soleil took a tiny sip of the hot cocoa and whispered into the phone, "His divorce is totally final?"

"Yes, or I wouldn't be here," she said, looking over at Kurt. "Listen, Soleil, is there any way you can find out from anyone in that business of yours what kind of desperate deals are going on in the commodity world today? Specifically with the Russians. Kurt's prohibited from having any contact with them. But *you* can find out because—"

"I don't have any Russian friends," Soleil interrupted coldly. "You know that." She let a layer of icy fog overlay her words.

After a few moments, she sighed and said, "I'll find out what I can." And I know that it'll go nowhere. But I'll try, she thought. "Don't hold your breath."

Then she asked, "What are you going to do now, Cami? Can you still get here for Christmas?"

"Well, the cops would love it if I was to stay here in Chicago, but one of the hotel guests saw everything through the peephole in his door and corroborated our story. The police have no reason in the world to hold us here, and this woman has—had—a long rap sheet. Drugs, prostitution, you name it.

"After what happened today, I want to get on a plane for Switzerland." She looked at Kurt, gave a resigned shrug, and said, "As soon as possible."

"I can't wait to see you," Soleil said into the phone, and meant it.

"Kurt's coming, too." Camille looked at him, and he raised his wineglass an inch or two in a salute.

"The more the merrier."

"Sorry to mess up your sleep, Soleil, but..."

"What, Camille?"

There were a few moments of silence on the phone. Then: "I don't know. I just had to hear your voice. *Bonsoir.*"

Soleil was quiet for a second and then said, "Me, too. 'Night."

Then dial tone.

Soleil stood and walked to her window.

The view was excellent from her small apartment. Zurich was pretty much buttoned up at this hour, with scattered lights across the city and the twin spires of the Grossmünster Cathedral and the green needle of the Fraumünster both bathed in light. I like this city, and I like the Swiss. They take a little time to get to know, and seem a little serious at the wrong times, but they've been nothing but kind to me.

And there's something I want to see—Christmas in Switzerland, in the Alps. And New Year's Eve. I don't know if I'll make Switzerland my permanent home yet, but I want to get through the winter, and find my way—hit my stride.

And by a twist of fate, cruel or otherwise, I have more than enough money.

She felt a chill and pulled on the sash of her robe.

Something's not right about this business with Kurt Ballas in Chicago. Something inside says that the crazy times aren't over—they're just taking five. I have to be careful.

And I don't mind being alone now, but that won't last forever.

I'll make sure it doesn't, one way or the other.

It's up to me.

"Ah, Ms. Tangiere. This is a pleasant surprise." Edward Sierra's voice was clear and precise as it came through the phone. He had immediately switched from Spanish to English when he heard that it was Soleil calling him.

"Hello, Mr. Sierra, how are you? How's everything at Rio Plata?"

"Busy as always."

Edward Sierra worked for Rio Plata, one of the largest mining companies in the free world. They had interests around the globe: aluminum, zinc, gold, and diamond mines. Soleil had done a metals deal earlier in the year with Rio, and Kurt Ballas had helped her with the complicated transaction. It was the first commodities deal Soleil herself had made, and she suspected that Sierra had tentacles that reached to Russia and beyond.

"How can I help you, Ms. Tangiere?" Word had filtered back to Sierra over the past few months about Soleil Tangiere's connection with the Russians. Sitting in his office in Barcelona, he had to admit that he was intrigued.

"Mr. Sierra—"

"Edward."

OK. "Edward, Kurt Ballas has a feeling that someone's gunning for him over a commodities deal. Are you aware of anyone in the business who wants to harm him?"

Sierra blinked. That's an odd, blunt question. He thought for a minute. Then he said, "Off the top of my head, Ms. Tangiere, there's nothing out of the ordinary going on in the mining or commodities business that strikes me." Then he added, "If I recall, the big story happened a few months ago, Ms. Tangiere. Or may I call you Soleil?"

Oh man, she thought wearily. "Sure, you can call me Soleil, Edward. If something unusual occurs or you hear of anything out of the ordinary that might affect Ballas Trading, could you call me? Please?"

"Of course, Soleil." He paused for a minute. "Coincidentally, I'll be in Switzerland in January. Perhaps we could get together for a drink."

Oh boy, she thought, softly slapping a hand across her forehead in frustration. "Sure, Edward. Just call me."

"I will, without fail." Oh boy, he said happily to himself.

She hung up. That hardly helped. All I did was succeed in revving up this forty-five- year-old guy. Well, at least I tried.

Edward Sierra hung up the phone. He thought for a moment, and decided that Ms. Soleil Tangiere owed him one. He'd try to find out who was after Kurt Ballas.

If he couldn't find out, he'd make someone up. He was just dying to meet her in the flesh.

3

THE MIR

Betrayal.
It was like blood.

It pulsed through Max Stepanov's veins and clutched at his heart like liquid fire. It was intolerable, and now Max was ready to do anything, anytime, anywhere.

To get revenge.

And to get out of Russia, as he was promised.

I'm the biggest fool of all: I believed a Soviet promise— the joke's on me.

He stood at the small plexiglass window and stared out at the bleak, charcoal-gray sky. Nighttime was fast approaching, but what did it matter? He almost never went outside the half-dome of the Nevsky installation here at the Mir, except to make the freezing walk to and from the bleak apartment block where he had a cubbyhole-size room with a single bed. He tried to get outside during the noon lunch hour to catch a well-needed glimpse of the weak, December sun. Either way, he had to be bundled head to toe in thermal clothing.

Might as well be in a gulag.

Now he was finishing up his "rounds" in the high-security facility, and was ready to have dinner with the other "execs." Then it would be cards or television or darts. And, of course, drinking. Lots of drinking.

"What's wrong, Stepanov?" his compatriots had said during the first week of his rounds, somewhat resentful of Max's distance. "It's just a few months. Come New Year's Day, you are done. You can run back to your wife, or girlfriend...or both."

But now it was well into the second month, and he was mostly ignored. A sleazy, overweight Mongolian named Gravva had tried repeatedly to befriend him, but Max distrusted him totally.

The only human at the Mir that Max liked was Arkady, one of the special armed guards imported from Kiev, who sometimes drank himself silly with Max, regaling him with slurred stories of his typical, difficult Soviet life. Arkady slept in one of the bunks in Gravva's crowded workers' apartment, but he had nothing to do with the large, greasy man.

The other men understood that Max had a deep, unassailable well of anger that usually made him difficult to be around. Impossible, in fact. The rumor was that it had to do with a woman, but all rumors here had women attached to them in one way or another.

Max looked through the frozen plexiglass window and thought back two months in time...

Betrayal.

He had been back in the USSR all of five days, when he was summoned to his boss's Moscow office at Nevsky Nickel, the giant consortium that controlled a vast web of mines throughout Russia. Max held a high-level position in the company, and he had the rare clearance to travel outside the communist country. He had done so twice in the last few years: an extremely rare occurrence for someone of his age who wasn't an Olympic athlete, a chess champion, or a diplomat.

On his last trip, he had been to Switzerland and New York.

And had fallen in love with Soleil Tangiere.

The big boss at Nevsky's Moscow headquarters was Boris Veshkin.

Veshkin was a tall, ascetic man in his late forties with rheumy eyes, tiny teeth, light, thinning hair, and a hawk's nose. It was a poorly kept secret that Veshkin was certainly a KGB running dog, and that Nevsky Nickel, though it had made great strides toward becoming an international corporation, was too critically important to the State to run itself without tight Kremlin oversight.

That's where Veshkin came in.

Max hated him. Veshkin represented everything that had been keeping Russia isolated from the West for the past three generations. And Max knew that the country was now on the very cusp of a sea change that would leave the Old Guard far behind while the country fell into the chaotic but necessary throes of rebirth.

And it was during this chaos that Max intended to leave. He had been promised that he could defect. The thought of leaving the country in which he'd been raised didn't bother him one bit. And if there was any hesitation at all, it was handily counterbalanced by the euphoria of knowing that he would be heading toward a life with the woman of his dreams.

A week ago in Geneva, his KGB friend, Vlad, had promised him that the powers that be would turn a blind eye should he want to defect to the West.

But now he sat in the Nevsky conference room with Veshkin and heard just one word from his boss's mouth: "Yakut."

"What about it?" Max asked. Uh oh.

The Yakut ASSR, east of Siberia, was an autonomous Soviet republic with a land area the size of Argentina, but a population of less than a million. Almost half of the Yakut lay above the Arctic Circle, and almost all of it was covered with permafrost for a good part of the year. Its harsh environment made it resistant to all but the hardiest of human inhabitants. Even the reindeer that lived in the region had evolved extra-warm coats.

It did have one compelling attraction, however: diamonds.

All Russian diamonds, which represent 25 percent of the diamonds in the world, came from there.

Veshkin looked down at his note pad. "You spent one year there, Stepanov," he read aloud. "That was directly after you finished university seven years ago in 1982. You worked at the Mir diamond mine." His pale eyes looked up from the pad. "Good. What a wonderful coincidence that you happen to have the expertise that we need at this moment. You will to go to Yakut. Immediately."

Max was floored. "Why?"

Boris Veshkin stood up slowly and paced behind the empty chairs that lined the conference table. He thought, Why do you think, Stepanov? Because you know the facility, the installation—how it works, and what makes it tick. The Soviet experiment is finished and Nevsky is going to "go public," as they say at the New York Stock Exchange.

More importantly, you have been out of Russia more than once. You've been to Switzerland twice, you privileged prick, with your damn highly placed friend. God knows what you have hidden in a numbered account in Zurich, eh?

And now, with the Wall collapsing, Russia's becoming the "Wild East." And when *my* plan unfolds, the end of the Wall will pale in comparison. Oh, it's good to be alive.

There must be a God, Stepanov. He brought you to me.

But Veshkin said none of this aloud. Instead, he surprised Max with, "You will be leaving on a special military-controlled Aeroflot flight this evening." He reached down to a pile of paperwork on the desk, extracted a slim folder with the appropriate passes and papers, and handed it to Max. "Might as well call your girlfriend now—you won't have an easy time doing so from the Mir."

What! Max's head was reeling. What's going on? This vermin, this *mudak* has to be joking. Yakut! This evening? *The Mir!*

No, it goes past this vapid troll. I've been used and badly. And as bad as this is, it wasn't *you* who broke his promise to me, Veshkin.

As if reading his mind, Veshkin whispered, "Our mutual friend, the esteemed Vladimir, extends his regards, Max. We discussed your short, upcoming sojourn to the far North at length. He wholeheartedly signed off on it." He showed his small teeth.

Max was stunned. Vlad didn't "sign off" on anything; of that I'm fairly certain, he thought. Vlad had helped me immeasurably with saving Soleil. Why the turnabout? Soviet trust: a true oxymoron, Max growled to himself.

Veshkin is lying, I'm sure of it. But I'm trapped if I'm forced to leave Moscow tonight, he said bitterly to himself.

Veshkin walked over and put a hand on his shoulder. "Now. To your little Canadian friend, Soleil Tangiere," he said in an oily voice. He leaned over and pushed a phone on the desk to within Max's reach. "Go ahead. Call her to say good-bye."

Max's heart felt like it would explode with anger. What did this animal know about Soleil? Hearing her name coming out of his pasty mouth made Max shake with rage. He hadn't been able to get a call through to Soleil since he had returned to Moscow: the ability to make calls outside the country was getting worse, not better, and fast.

And he hadn't heard from her. A voice inside him hoped that she was trying to get in touch with him, but it was truly difficult to make calls into and out of the USSR. Certainly, she has tried to call me, he thought. I'm sure of it.

But now it's going to get far, far worse. Once I'm there, in that frozen shit hole, that'll be it: the odds of getting a call out to anywhere will dwindle to zero. Especially from the secure fortress that is the Mir.

And the only man who could get me out of this is the man who may very well have lied to me: Vlad.

Veshkin calmly watched Max, who sat rock still. "Stepanov, aren't you listening? This line is clear for an international call—a rare commodity now. Go ahead, dial. Tell your girlfriend that you won't be able to speak with her until next year." Veshkin's face had the look that Max imagined he saved for pulling the wings off of flies.

He tried not to glare at Veshkin and slowly picked up the phone. He dialed the international call. It rang twenty times before he reluctantly hung up. Where is she?

"What a shame," said Veshkin, synthetic regret dripping from his mouth. "Sorry. Maybe she went shopping. Now go and pack, Max. A driver will take you to your apartment block and wait for you. And then we're off to the airport."

Max rose and looked at him, but said nothing.

Veshkin smiled and said, "I'll come along for the ride to the airport." His tiny teeth showed for a second. "Bring warm clothes."

Betrayal.

The word had burned itself into Max's soul.

And now he'd been here two months with no way to make a phone call. No way to let Soleil know that he was all right, alive, and thinking and dreaming about her. His heart had never gone through what it was going through now. Every minute of every day was torture.

But at least now he knew what everyone was up to...

Nevsky's high-security diamond facility at the Mir was state-of-the-art. The mine had begun operations in 1955 after kimberlite, the volcanic rock that indicates the presence of diamonds, was discovered in the area. Stalin had ordered the mine to be started in order to supply the Soviets with industrial-quality diamonds. Now, almost thirty-five years later, the pit was one of the largest man-made holes on Earth. It was more than 1,700 feet deep and over three-quarters of a mile in diameter.

Building and digging a mine in the Arctic cold was a daunting task. In order to melt the rock-hard permafrost that covers everything for most of the year, the Soviets used the blasts of jet engines mounted on mobile cranes.

The airspace over the huge mine was off-limits to planes and helicopters, the official reason being that the pit was so huge that downward airflow sucked passing aircraft into the maw. The unofficial truth was that as much as possible, the Mir was a closely guarded state secret.

At the very base of the hole, under more solid rock, was the most impregnable of all secret Soviet vaults, its existence known to only the privileged elite of the Soviet hierarchy.

Excavating every foot of depth was a struggle of men and machines, and many lost their lives in the construction of the Mir. In 1977, the government turned day-to-day operations of the immense mine over to Nevsky Nickel, which had the expertise to make vast improvements in its efficiency, safety, and diamond yield.

And diamonds there were—in 1988, over seven million carats of rough diamonds were wrested from the frozen earth of Yakut, half of which were gem quality or near-gem quality. And Nevsky oversaw it all.

Max had spent almost a year at the installation seven years ago in 1982, and had intimate knowledge of the operation of the enterprise. His duties were at the diamond-sorting facility—the heavily guarded, bombproof dome near the edge of the huge hole.

The sorting facility itself was like a giant vault, the rooms of which contained long, sectioned tables at which sat the sorters—men wearing pale-gray, pocketless jumpsuits and head visors with built in magnifying lenses. Special incandescent fixtures in the ceiling duplicated the coveted north light needed to properly determine a diamond's color.

The sorters were presented with trays of rough, uncut diamond crystals by armed guards who had carefully counted and weighed the stones on each tray. Dozens of counters and sorters, ten-power diamond loupes seemingly attached to their hands, checked, re-checked, and spied on each other.

Nothing was ever stolen. The penalty was the maximum.

The sorters were presented with a set number of uncut diamonds on each tray, most looking like small, dull or semi-clear, irregularly shaped glass bits. Some trays held rough stones that exhibited the desirable octahedral shape of the diamonds that wound up being cut and polished for jewelry. The gems.

A sorter weighed one stone at time, picking it up with tweezers and poring over its features through his loupe. By the time he had examined all of the stones in his tray, he had divided them up into small piles organized by size, color, and clarity.

Cameras dotted the ceilings and walls. Microphones were everywhere. So were the very visible, even intrusive guards in full battle gear, hefting AK-47 Kalashnikovs and an assortment of other armaments.

It was here that Max now spent his waking hours.

He had been put in charge of the gem-quality sorting operation, a position that would normally take thirty years to work one's way up to, but was summarily and very suspiciously bestowed upon him by Boris Veshkin.

"You have the knowledge," Veshkin had told him offhandedly on the way to the airport. "And you want to get it over with as soon as possible, eh?" he had suddenly whispered to him. "Get back home and then sneak to the West to cuddle up with your little Canadian *suka*, huh?"

Max had closed his face, but Veshkin was on a roll: "You imbecile! Fooled by Vlad Putin into thinking you can move about and fly here and there in the West at will. Hah!"

As angry as he was, Max realized that there was probably some truth to what Veshkin was saying: Putin had all but promised him a pass to the West, and now that promise had been pulled out from under him in the worst way.

Veshkin continued in a low grumble. "Now, my friend, you have to trust *me*. Out of the frying pan, eh?" He looked at Max's face and could only guess at the depth of resentful anger boiling behind those dark eyes. Too bad, Stepanov—I hold all the cards here, Veshkin thought.

"You will be at the Mir until the end of the year, Max. During that time, you will stroll around and make sure that that squadron of frozen idiots isn't stealing the Hope Diamond or anything like that. Then you will come back. I'll send you messages from time to time. That's all there is to it."

Max knew that there had to be a catch, and that the catch had to be gigantic. The whole affair sounded as stupid and suspicious as could be; it made no sense whatsoever. The chances were good, he shuddered to himself, that now he would never leave Russia. Maybe he would never leave Yakut.

As the car approached the outer boundary of Sheremetyevo Airport, Veshkin leaned even closer to Max—so close that Max could smell the nauseating lunch that the vile toad had stuffed down his throat in the commissary. His fetid mouth said, "Listen closely and we'll both survive this, Stepanov."

Then he told Max the catch.

As Max was getting out of the car, Veshkin leaned over to him and said, "Merry Christmas, comrade."

And now Christmas was just a few days off, and Max was still there.

At least I'm still alive, he thought. I might die trying to get out of here in one piece. And I might die trying to get to the West. And I'm trapped into following Veshkin's orders—his outrageously dangerous plan. Suicide. But it's the only way out of Yakut, out of the Mir. Out of the frozen asshole of the world.

Arkady, the guard, had come by to drink a little, but had to go on his vault shift deep below the surface of the earth.

Now Max sat on his bed in the cold, tiny room in the near darkness and drank vodka straight from the bottle. Then, as he had every night since he had gotten to this place, he thought of her.

He spoke to her: Don't wait for me, Soleil, my love. Go and live and enjoy your life. I know you will; I pray you will. Just thinking about you makes my life tolerable, livable, until...until, I don't know.

But as long as I breathe, I'll love you.

That love is my treasure. He touched the center of his forehead. I keep it here in my secret vault that no one can breach, that no one can take away—whatever they try to do.

The thoughts and memories of you are beyond price, beyond value.

Max realized that the bottle was empty and had been for a while. He wasn't sure how to feel about that.

Good-bye, Soleil.

For now.

4

SINS

The priest passed through the sacristy door and walked across the quiet transept of the church. It was the middle of the morning in the middle of the week, and he was so certain the church was empty that he didn't bother to do the quick scan of the pews that was a subconscious part of his daily routine.

He was looking forward to his daily three-block walk to his favorite bakery. *I would walk thirty blocks for one of those heavenly brioche*, he said to himself.

His thought was cut short when he heard a faint sound. Turning his head, he noticed a lone, unfamiliar, and very attractive young woman sitting in the last row of pews.

She sat calmly, looking straight ahead, and while the priest would not normally approach anyone without a reason, lest he interfere with his or her prayers or reveries, the young woman had a compelling look on her face.

He changed direction, made his way up the center aisle, and stopped at the end of the pew.

She looked over at him and said, *"Guten tag.* Hello."

The priest was happy to reply in English—he had grown up in England and was sent to Switzerland in his late twenties. Now past fifty, he had become a fixture at this little church in the Altstadt, the Old Town section of Zurich.

The young woman was slender and had straight, blond hair, a few strands of which were hanging in front of her startling, sapphire-colored eyes. Although she was twenty-three, she looked younger. She wore a dark blue, high-collared jacket over a cream-colored cotton blouse. A tiny, diamond-studded cross hung on a thin chain between the open top buttons.

"Hello, young lady. I didn't mean to interrupt your meditation, but I thought I saw a questioning look on your face." The priest prided himself on his keen sensitivity to his fellow man. And woman.

She looked at him with a level, kind stare. "Oh, I'm just resting." She pushed the errant hairs away from her eyes.

"This is the best place to rest, both your body and your soul." Stay as long as you like, he said to himself, letting his gaze settle on her face.

The corners of her lips turned up a tiny bit. "I'm reconciling my future actions with my present intents," she said cryptically.

Not knowing at all what she meant, he decided to go off on a familiar tack: "Would you like me to hear your sins—bare your soul, that is?" That sounded strange, he suddenly said to himself. "I mean, do you feel the need to speak about things?"

"What things?"

"Well, this is a place to relieve the burdens in your heart."

She smiled faintly and said quietly, "Sorry, but I'm so far beyond redemption that a confession would be of little use—an insult to God."

What an odd reply from this pretty young woman, he thought. The priest sat down in the pew in front of hers and turned sideways so he could look into her face. He instantly found that he liked looking into it. He crooked one black-sleeved elbow over the back of the pew in front of her.

"Go ahead. It can't be that bad. You can tell me anything." He dipped his chin a fraction of an inch so that his eyes had to look up slightly to continue looking into hers—an affectation he'd found to be an effective communication tool.

She hesitated, but didn't know why. *Isn't this why I stopped here? All right...*

"Very well," she began. "Forgive me, Father, for I have sinned—"

"No, no," he quickly put up a hand. "Without the sanctity of the confessional, this doesn't qualify as a confession—just a conversation. No need for such formality."

She looked at him.

"Of course," he quickly backtracked, "if you want to think of this as a confession, then by all means."

She waited for a moment. Then: "All right. Well, I haven't been to church in months."

"Most of my parish is in the same boat." A small, conspiratorial grin.

"I've used the Lord's name in vain."

"I see. Go on," he urged gently, feeling every inch the kind and wise father confessor.

"I've engaged in carnal activities outside of the bonds of matrimony."

"Please continue," said the priest. "So far, you are very safe." He felt like winking, but instead threw her a cryptic little smile.

"I've caused a few more people to be killed since my last confession."

What? "You've *what*?" Did she say *killed*?

Her sigh was so faint as to be almost inaudible.

Killed? More? What does she mean by killed? What does she mean by *more*?

"Do you want to talk about it?" His cryptic smile had gone somewhere else, and he found himself to be uncharacteristically hesitant.

"In confidence?"

"Yes, of course."

She looked clearly and innocently into his apprehensive eyes. "Swear."

"I swear this will be known only to us and to God," he said quickly and launched his hand into the familiar gesture of the cross. "What happened?"

Her eyes gauged his face again, and she took a deep breath. "I killed a policeman in America."

"What?"

"He had it coming. He was directly involved in a conspiracy to murder my father and six other people. I loved my father dearly."

She paused for a moment and then continued, "Then I came to Europe with my fiancé and inadvertently became an involved witness in the deaths of four men at the Geneva Airport."

The priest's mouth started to open, but he thought better of speaking. He shuddered involuntarily when it suddenly occurred to him that he had read about an incident just like that in the *Neue Zürcher Zeitung* a short time back.

She looked into space for a second as if dwelling on an unpleasant memory and then said, "Well, I didn't bring it on any of those people. They were in the process of kidnapping me."

Kidnapping you. Right. "And who are 'they'?"

"One of them ordered the murder of my father."

"Who were the others?"

"All bad men, trust me. Then I wound up involved in the death of my fiancé."

Why am I falling for this prank? I'd better put a stop to it before she gets too carried away. In a stern voice, he said, "This is all a joke, isn't it? Truly, young lady, it is not funny."

"I wish it were a joke." The quiet and sober response rattled him. "Do you want me to go on?" She tilted her head slightly, and a few more strands of hair fell across her face.

After a moment: "Of course."

"My fiancé betrayed me. Badly. And it was only because I was quick that I wasn't tossed from a seventh-floor window." She sat looking at him. "He wasn't as lucky."

The priest suddenly felt a tiny twinge of fear and gulped. "Is there more?"

"After that, two very bad people followed me when I went back to America, to New York. One of them was my dad's last surviving murderer and the son of the man that orchestrated the disaster. The other was his girlfriend. Those two people both tried to kill me. Obviously, they failed."

The priest just stared at her. Her face was calm; her voice, matter-of-fact.

"Then I had to get back to Switzerland to appear at the World Court." Her eyes suddenly seemed be become unfocused for a moment, as if she were lost in a sad memory.

Then she said, "A very good friend cleverly figured out a way for me to avoid being murdered by anyone else, but I was followed by another bad man who tried to abduct me. He shot one of his own henchmen by accident and then he himself was killed when his helicopter crashed into Lake Geneva."

The priest was dumb struck. If he hadn't seen the report of that spectacular helicopter explosion on television, he would have written her statement off to fantasy, as well. As it stood, it was unbelievable. More than unbelievable.

It was frightening.

"Is that it?" he asked meekly.

She was thoughtful for another second. "Yes. No! I also ate a cheeseburger on Good Friday."

Then: "That's it," she said quietly with a shy finality.

He composed himself and cleared his throat. "You're making all this up, aren't you?"

Her eyes narrowed slightly. "No—sorry. If anything, I left out a number of distasteful details."

"And now you are here contemplating how you can repent for your past transgressions?"

She looked down at her hands folded in her lap.

"I came here to rest for a moment. And to think. To think about what I lost, what I gained, and where I have to go from here."

Then she looked up into his eyes, and he thought he saw into her soul.

"And you see, I have a feeling that things aren't quite over yet."

Camille spent the night after their near-death Harmon House experience at Kurt's apartment. Outside the condo's windows, Chicago was a glittering tapestry reflected in Lake Michigan. The soaring Sears Tower was lit up with special red and green lights for the Christmas season.

The adrenaline high and subsequent crash brought on by the day's events had drained them. They promised each other that this definitely would not be the night that they consummated the next step in their relationship. They'd decided that it would have been a wrong move. It just would have been two people wildly relieving the stress of an insane day.

Nope, they'd said, it wouldn't be the right thing to do. It would have no meaning at all. It would just be a release. Just...

They were unstoppable.

Later, they lay in bed recounting the events of the day.

"Soleil doesn't mind that I'm coming with you?" Kurt asked.

"She wants you to come. Maybe she thinks she stands a chance with you. You know, stealing something from her big sister—a big turn on." She rolled her eyes.

Kurt rolled his as well. Changing the subject, he said, "Mind if I spend tomorrow setting my ducks in a row at my business before I fly away? I have to let my two employees know that they need to keep alert."

"Sure, Kurt." She looked over at him. At thirty-four, she was ready to become half of a couple again. Oh, whom am I kidding? she thought. Jake and I pushed the term "couple" over a cliff years ago. The last intimate little chat I had with my ex was through a bulletproof Lexan barrier at a state prison.

It's not that I'm damaged goods or anything. I've finally beaten the bottle—at least to a large degree—thanks to Soleil and Kurt. And whatever happens, Kurt or no Kurt, I've made up my mind that I'm never going back to being a loser. Or someone else's loser, for that matter.

She looked to her right. Kurt's face exuded a sense of calm as he began to doze off next to her.

Kurt. She said the name over in her mind once or twice. Well, Kurt's the real deal, I think. Baggage and all. He has a big-city roughness that I like, and he's taking this new threat with strength, with aplomb, like a man.

Face it, I'm a bit rough myself, or so my little sister has pointed out from time to time. So I guess we're a good fit.

She smiled. At this moment, the term seems particularly apropos, she thought. Yeah.

"Hey, stud." She poked him. He grumbled awake. "One more time."

Kurt made a call to Detective Burnes the next day from his office.

Walter Burnes was the cop who had interrogated Camille and Kurt in turn, and made a quick determination that they had not planned the chaos that had gone down at the Harmon House.

He had treated them with respect, even kindness, and when Zoe Kimball's rap sheet was pulled, it was baldly apparent that Kurt and Camille were the victims, not the perpetrators of the violence

Nevertheless, Walter Burnes was not happy.

"Don't do this, Ballas," the burly black detective had said in a tired voice. "We asked you nicely, with a cherry on top, to be available if we needed you. Can't you just hang around Chicago? Why, the balmy weather alone—"

"Sorry, Detective. Your case doesn't involve us anymore, as far as I can see, and unless you come out to arrest us, we have to go. Mrs. Weston was heading for Switzerland to visit her sister for the holidays when this all happened, and now she's way behind schedule."

Walter thought for a moment. "Hold on a second, Ballas," he said into the phone and rummaged in his desk drawer for a pad and pencil.

"OK," he continued. "Let's have all the details of your little European vacation."

Kurt gave him the flight number, the name of the hotel, and even the address and phone number of Soleil's business.

"Tangiere International. Sounds important," said Walter. Then, in a sober tone, he added, "Ballas, keep in touch. But if I need you, I'll find you."

"Thanks, Detective," Kurt said. "I'll bring you back a Swiss cheese."

"Make it a Brie," said Walter Burnes. He hung up the phone and a second later had a strong feeling that he hadn't seen the last of this case. Or of Kurt Ballas.

Now Kurt and Camille were high.

Thirty-nine thousand feet high to be exact, their Swissair wide-body traveling east at just under the speed of sound.

The plane left from Chicago O'Hare and made a stop at Newark International. From there, it was a straight shot to Zurich. The flight had left in the early evening, and would arrive in Zurich the following day at around noon.

They were seated in first class, and nursed their drinks while they talked about everything. They played the incident in the Harmon House over and over in their minds and in their discussion, but Kurt was stymied as to who might hate him so much as to try to do him in.

"This Kimball woman has a history of extortion," he said. "Maybe this was a shakedown gone bad." The theory sounded tenuous but plausible. They both agreed it was the strongest possibility.

After a while, the talk shifted to Soleil and the rest of her family.

"All six of us were born in Quebec, me being the first," said Camille, ready to give a three-sentence synopsis of the Tangieres.

"I'm the oldest; Soleil, the youngest. She's twenty-three—eleven years younger than I am. We have two sisters and one living brother. Our other brother, Kent, was killed in an accident when he was twenty-two." Her eyes took on a far-off look, and Kurt put a hand on her arm.

"Soleil and I are at the opposite ends of the spectrum, but we're both loners who are more than capable of taking care of ourselves, as you've surely observed. Our other siblings, Rolf, Nanette, and Lana, each left home when they were fifteen or sixteen and are scattered around Canada and the US."

Looking at Kurt, she said, "I'm not going to sugarcoat our family. Soleil is the only one who's straight and true, and I don't lie about things either. But neither of us are angels."

He patted her arm and said, "Better an honest devil than a lying angel, Cami."

She smiled. It was Soleil's favorite expression.

"Kurt, Soleil is going through a tough time, again. Max never got in touch with her after he left for Russia, and she's raw. She may want to hide it, but not from me. She thinks that the two real relationships in her life wound up in betrayal."

Kurt thought for a minute. "She thinks?"

Camille said, "I know that Max is deeply in love with Soleil. I saw it in New York. Heck, he told me in no uncertain terms that she was his whole life." Kurt was staring at her. "I could tell it was the truth."

"I saw it too," Kurt said. "The man was smitten."

She continued, "She called him in Russia, but when she finally got through to his apartment, she caught him in the shower with a girl."

Kurt made a face. "That doesn't sound like Max."

Camille touched his sleeve. Her face was open and serious. "What's wrong with Soleil, Kurt? Doesn't she know what women do to each other?"

Kurt went through a little aha moment. He patted her hand, but his face looked worried. "Soleil will figure it out. She's smart."

Camille eyed him. "Is there a possibility that Max is in trouble? Maybe serious trouble?"

Kurt thought for a second and said, "It *is* Russia."

"Soleil needs us," Camille said firmly.

There was a small shift in the sound of the engines, and the plane began its descent toward Zurich.

"I always wanted to see Switzerland," said Kurt. "And now I can see it with you. Who's luckier than me?"

Camille smiled and knew the answer.

By the time they had cleared customs, it was the middle of the afternoon. Snow was falling gently but steadily.

They grabbed a taxi at the airport to take them into the city. "*Grüezi*," said the driver politely. Welcome to Switzerland. They had slept for six hours on the plane, and felt as refreshed as could be expected, but both had to admit that jet lag was no fun.

A travel agent friend of Kurt's had arranged reservations at the Baur au Lac Hotel, a Zurich landmark. It was fairly close to Soleil's office and had terrific views of the Zürichsee—Lake Zurich.

The hotel was classic Swiss—traditional architecture, impeccable service, a superb restaurant, and beautifully appointed rooms. Their suite seemed especially luxurious after the long flight.

Camille looked out their window on the lake and felt a sudden chill. It reminded her of the view from the Grand Hotel Kampinsky in Geneva, where she had spent her last night in Switzerland after Soleil's meeting at the World Court.

Lake Zurich doesn't have a giant fountain like the one in Lake Geneva, she said to herself. Thank God.

As Kurt unpacked, Camille picked up the phone and dialed.

"Tangiere International," said a familiar voice.

Camille smiled. *"Bonjour*, Yvonne!"

"Enfin! La sœur!" said Yvonne. "The sister has finally arrived! How are you, Camille?"

"Tres bien, Yvonne. Is Soleil there?"

In a moment she heard a second phone being picked up.

"Hi, Cami! You're here!" It was as if sunlight had come over the phone. That's why they called her Soleil, Camille thought. Mama and Dad saw it from day one.

"How was the flight? Everything went OK? Are you at the hotel? What are—"

"Soleil, slow down! No human on earth can answer questions as fast as you ask them." She smiled.

"I know. I'm just having fun at your expense." Then: "You're probably a mess from all that flying, so I'm not going to bug you. Let's meet for lunch tomorrow, just us." She gave Camille the name of the restaurant, asked her to meet her there at noon, called her something raunchy in Québécois French, and hung up.

"That was Soleil?" Kurt came in from the bedroom.

"Yep, we're having a girls-only lunch tomorrow. Gives you a chance to get the lay of the land." She eyed him. "*Just* the land, handsome."

She told Kurt where to meet her and when.

"We'll try to keep the yapping down to four or five hours."

"Don't break any old habits for me," he said.

She looked at him for a moment, and then kissed him hard.

5

TOOTHPICK

Eddie Poong hung up the phone and paced back and forth in front of the floor-to-ceiling glass windows. His office afforded him a breathtaking, panoramic view of Victoria Harbor with its hundreds of boats, yachts, and sampans.

He stared straight ahead and shook his head as if telling all of Hong Kong and the rest of the world spread out before him that it was wrong and he was right. His brother, lounging in a white-and-chrome Barcelona chair in the office, watched him pace with mild interest.

"Who was that?" his brother finally asked, unable to get enough clues from Eddie's side of the conversation, which primarily had been a long silence sprinkled with some "whats?" and "uh-huhs."

Without looking away from the windows, Eddie said, "That was Gravva on the special phone. I knew he'd get through eventually."

Three Tit clapped his hands slowly. "Very good. Finally. What's the status?"

"His balls have frozen off his body."

"Who cares? What does he have to say about the shit-eating dog?"

"The dog will soon be visiting his mule," said Eddie.

Three grudgingly acknowledged his brother's prescience. "I have to give it to you. You nailed it."

"I always nail it." Eddie harrumphed. I told you so, Three, Eddie thought. The behavior of a jackal is just too predictable: he follows a few steps behind the mortally wounded water buffalo until the beast falls. Then he moves in and starts tearing at the small chunk that he wants.

Witness the jackal Veshkin's variation on that theme: he's skulking along behind the expiring beast that is the Soviet Union so he can rip his piece of fat from its belly before it collapses on him and kills him.

Which it will. That's another one of my predictions.

Eddie continued, "The dog, Veshkin, has planted his mule at the mine. He's ready to make his move. I'll bet it'll be before the first of the year."

"*Gong hey fat choy*. Who am I to argue with the guru?"

Eddie glanced over at his brother and grunted.

Eddie and Three Tit Poong were twins, age forty. Some women might consider them handsome—but in a somewhat frightening and wild way. To say they were "rugged" would be a kindness. It was a little worse than that. These men were crafty, shrewd survivors of a world of hurt and a life of pain, and they were very beaten up.

The two orphans bore the scars of a life that had started in the streets and the gutters of Tianjin, where luck, guts, and their necessary loyalty to each other were the only things that kept them from certain doom. As the hard years went by, they grew into the inseparable and formidable team that they were now.

The map of their young lives had snaked across Asia, finally landing them in Hong Kong, their adopted home base. That was a dozen years ago.

The public face of their business enterprise, Poong Brothers Happy Dragon Import & Export, was, of course, a front. The name itself was a generic caricature that served as a blinder for stupid Westerners who cared little about understanding Asia. To the casual observer, it presented itself as a common, shabby Asian company that exported something or other, and imported money—lots of money.

But their not-so-casual "clientele" knew exactly what they did—what they traded in, bartered for, extorted, and stole: diamonds.

Their ruthlessness was legend among the lowest elements of the international gem trade, and they aimed to keep nurturing that legend and their happy position in the status quo.

The Poongs relied on their almost preternatural sense of survival and swift, proactive precaution. They knew how to fly beneath the radar of corrupt foreign governments and taxing authorities, and to carefully cultivate delicate but hugely profitable relationships with the voracious local criminal *hongs*—mobster organizations that cherished their notoriously ferocious "business" methodologies.

The Poongs perpetually owed much to those organizations, but were known to never renege on their word. Of course, reneging on anything with those people would be suicidal.

The name Three Tit gave people pause.

The moniker referenced one of the physical differences between the twin brothers, which came about when Three was a teenager. In a heated encounter with a Kwong gang member, Three had been shot in the precise center of his chest, chipping his breastbone and leaving an indelible, round scar.

It was a strange and laughable name to the uninitiated, but of course, no one ever felt like laughing in the presence of Three Tit or Eddie unless invited to do so.

While Three Tit considered himself to be the more aggressive of the two, he cautiously conceded that his temper could, at times, be detrimental to the brothers' manifold business endeavors.

Eddie considered himself to be the smarter brother, and over the years had learned perfect English, overlaid with the stuffy British accent endemic to Hong Kong.

Eddie rummaged in a pile of papers on his desk for some smokes, found a crumpled pack of Dunhills, jabbed one into his mouth, and lit it with a heavy crystal lighter.

Three was lounging in the designer chair, noisily moving a gold toothpick around in his mouth. His voice had the same rough, ruined timbre as his brother's had.

Of course, I'm way handsomer than my poor brother, Eddie, thought Three. And when it comes to sheer masculine power, I'm rated as one of the ten most fearsome warrior merchant-princes in Asia. Every whore in Kowloon knows *that*.

The toothpick explored his teeth at a measured pace: click, click.

Gravva Gleb had begun work at the Mir installation six months ago. Originally a midlevel smuggler in the employ of the Poongs, he was born in Novosibirsk, but had spent most of his life in and around Ulan Bator in Mongolia.

Gravva had an earned reputation as a sneak, and before the Poongs came into his life, he had a sweet little deal ratting out low-end Chinese spies to the Russians and vice versa. Even he had to admit that he had caused great misery for and probably even the deaths of scores of basically clueless peasants on both sides of the fence.

Well, it's them or me. That was his motto.

After a few years, his "hobby" was getting a little too dangerous. The gods had smiled on him then, and he hooked up with the Poongs. Under their protection in the early eighties, he found a new niche in the gem- and diamond-smuggling game, which he called "transport."

Earlier in the year, he had volunteered to try to secure a job at the Russian diamond mine as a well-paid-for favor to the Poongs. After many well-placed payoffs and based on a barely true resumé of diamond expertise, a carefully prepared but completely false local history, and a mountain of forged papers, Gravva finally got a sorter's job at the Mir.

Heavy and slow, Gravva Gleb had a head start on acclimating to Yakut with built-in fat layers and a steady, even metabolism. He was confident that he could beat the cold weather.

After less than a week in Yakut, he was freezing his balls off.

Eddie and Three Tit had zeroed in on the Mir diamond mine as a target for their latest masterpiece for good reason: they had been pointedly warned that if they ever set foot in the African subcontinent again, (especially South Africa, Zimbabwe, Namibia, and Sierra Leone), they would be summarily executed in spectacular fashion sure to entertain the bored and destitute local population.

They decided that it would be prudent to heed these warnings—the gentlemen who had issued them were not the type of men that one would want to anger. In fact, Hong Kong wasn't far enough away.

I'm tough, thought Three Tit. But not suicidal.

As diamond specialists, there was only one other place to go—the USSR. It was the opportunity of a lifetime, and Eddie and Three weren't going to be left out.

"Imagine," Eddie had said to Three. "That whole damn country is a runaway train roaring down a track that ends on the edge of a cliff. There's going to be chaos for at least a year, maybe many years to come. A well-positioned 'operative' can get stupid rich, stupid fast. That has to be us." Three liked the word "operative."

And we're the diamond specialists, so there's only one place we have to be: the Mir.

They had paid Gravva fifty thousand US dollars up front to become an innocent fixture at the mine. He was their eyes and ears at the remote installation and had been promised another fifty, plus a share of the profits on anything he could purloin in the future. A heist wouldn't be easy, but it was possible. When he wanted to be, Gravva was more resourceful than he looked.

Then, a few months back, the Poongs had learned something new. Boris Veshkin, the appointed head of Nevsky Nickel, the company that managed the mine from its base in Moscow, had begun working on his own masterpiece. Eddie, certainly the genius that his brother considered him to be, had guessed it just right. He had predicted something like this would happen.

They had learned that Veshkin had just purchased two large safety-deposit boxes in a Swiss bank's vault. Not for his *pirogies*, the Poongs laughed to themselves.

How they learned this important fact was totally illegal.

The Poongs' private Swiss banker in Zurich was Mr. Oscar Menschel at the Zürcher Suisse Bank. Mr. Menschel, stiff and formal and prim, prided himself on his devotion to the bank and its depositors. Also on his devotion to the generous, illegal stipend that the Poongs paid him for a monthly list of new depositors and the details of their private transactions.

After all, the Poongs rented four large safety-deposit boxes in the ZSB that held a major portion of their cash and diamonds. They also maintained three numbered cash accounts in that institution, with deposits totaling twenty-seven million US dollars—90 percent of their liquid assets. They needed to know who their neighbors in the quiet Swiss vault were. One can't be too careful.

Three Tit tossed the gold toothpick around his mouth with his tongue, and its clicking was the only sound in the silent office. Eddie watched the boat traffic in the harbor through the big windows—powerboats, ferries, sampans, yachts. The familiar sight never failed to soothe him. He was in his element. His mind roamed...

Veshkin, Veshkin. You're a jackal, but a smart one, reasoned Eddie. You're planning on ripping off the Mir; that's obvious—it's where the diamonds are.

And you won't do it yourself. You sent someone there in case something goes wrong; in case a wheel comes off. And I bet I know where you're going to meet up with your loot, Boris.

Well, my borscht-slurping friend, there are no guarantees in life, and we have our own fat little someone at the Mir.

The Poongs' fat little someone had been doing a wonderful job keeping track of the happenings at the mine. There was certainly enough time in the day to spy and scheme and dream. And most importantly, Gravva had given Eddie the name of Veshkin's mule.

Max Stepanov.

6

DIRTY FROG

The church bell had already rung the noon hour. Soleil stood on the sidewalk in front of the restaurant in anticipation of Camille's arrival.

Under a tailored, navy-blue pea coat, she wore her favorite oatmeal-colored, cable-knit sweater over a white T-shirt. The toes of her black, high-heel boots peeked out from the slightly flared bottoms of her trim-cut jeans. Her heels brought her up two inches to a touch over five foot ten.

A light wind tousled her straight, blond hair, and she kept running a hand across her face to correct the situation.

She was one minute late. A block from the restaurant, workers were digging up the street for a new phone cable system, and the construction crew, dressed in work clothes with reflective green tape on their helmets, had almost come to a standstill as Soleil Tangiere picked her way across the temporary wooden planks that crossed the broken-up concrete and the cable trench in the street.

One of the pipe fitters, a man with a stubbly, unshaven chin, looks kind of cute, she said to herself. She didn't break her stride, but her little wave and smile broke his. He said loudly in German, "*Hallo, Schatzi*! My name is Lars! You want to go for a ride in my new toy?" He pointed at a bright red Alfa Romeo two-seater parked at the curb between two backhoes. Boys being boys, she said to herself.

"*Vielleicht später,*" she said, smiling at him. Maybe later. But not likely.

Now it was 12:02 and the bells had stopped ringing.

She consulted her watch for the third time (I *am* becoming a Swiss!) and looked up to see a familiar figure coming toward her a block away. She immediately recognized the confident aplomb in the posture and walk. It made her smile.

Like Soleil, Camille Tangiere Weston didn't know she was beautiful.

But she was.

Camille wore a warm, cinnamon, high-collared suede jacket over an olive man-tailored shirt and a jean/boot combo that was similar to Soleil's. The colors worked perfectly with Camille's thick auburn hair and hazel eyes. When she saw her younger sister, she picked up the tempo of her self-assured walk by a few beats. In a moment they were hugging.

Though separated by eleven years to the day, Soleil and Camille believed that they looked like sisters to anyone who cared to study them. And on this outstanding Swiss afternoon, with the brisk, cold air raising androgen levels and triggering all kinds of reproductive stimulants in the gonads of men far and wide, many did indeed care to look.

A couple of men walking by immediately slowed down. The women they were with didn't, and pulled angrily at their boyfriends' jackets. Let's go. Now.

The Zeughauskeller, which started life as a Swiss arsenal in 1487, was a fairly large restaurant. Its dining room seated two hundred and its walls were decorated with medieval weaponry, illustrations of ancient Zurich noblemen, and enough traditional Swiss motifs to satisfy tourist and native alike.

Ornately beamed ceilings, large Palladian windows, bronze statuary, and a hand-painted grandfather clock dominated the dining area. A small army of waiters and servers whisked flagons of beer and steaming plates of traditional Swiss food to seriously hungry patrons, all imbibing, eating, and conversing at sturdy wooden tables.

They were led to a table for two near one of the windows.

A pink-faced, middle-aged waitress dressed in a black blouse and red skirt was suddenly there. She handed menus to Camille and Soleil. *"Willkommen! Bier?"*

A minute or two later, they were sipping from their monstrous glass steins. After a minute of menu studying, they finally settled on a traditional lunch featuring a variation on the ubiquitous homemade sausage-and-potato concoction that everyone else around them seemed to be eating and enjoying.

"'Bye. So long. Good-bye," said Camille.

Soleil looked at her sister. "Good-bye, what?"

Camille put a wistful look on her face and said, "I'm bidding farewell to any hope of losing or even maintaining my weight on this trip. I forgot that I'm back in the land of massive food."

"Oh, cut it out. You can eat anything here. I just thought you might want to get back in the swing." Soleil took a sip of beer and ran her tongue over the foam on her upper lip.

"The fat swing."

"Watch it, Kiddo," said Camille ominously.

"Tell me about Kurt," Soleil said.

Camille looked in her eyes. "About what part? What do you want to know? How far along we are? How I feel, how he feels, or about what's going on? People gunning for him in hotels?"

Soleil liked watching Camille talk. It reminded her of times gone by, of her life as a child and a teenager in Canada—of both hating and worshipping her eldest sister at the same time. The eldest who had the least time for her when they were younger, but wound up being the closest to her in the end.

"How do you think he feels about you?" she asked just as Camille was putting a forkful of food into her mouth.

Camille shrugged. "Umph-phm," she said around a mouthful of potato concoction.

"Ugh. You're disgusting, Cami. How do you keep a man interested with that 'chew-and-show' thing going on?"

Camille swallowed, took a haughty sip of her beer, and said, "Play your cards right and one day I'll teach you. Until then, *va te faire foutre!*"

"*Pute a cinq cennes!*" Soleil shot back.

"Dumb Canuck."

Neither could control her laughter.

Camille thought for a minute and said, "It occurs to me that in English, you never even say 'damn' or 'hell.' What's with the dirty frog?"

"Only with you, Cami. You bring out the worst in me. *Termes d'affection.*"

Camille knew it was true. She took another sip of beer and said, "Kurt." She restarted. "Well. You met him. You seemed to like him."

"Those were very stressful circumstances. But he really seemed to like *you*." Soleil half-closed one eye. "More than liked."

"Look, the biggest hurdle with Kurt will be his kids and, by extension, his ex-wife, Amanda. I can see it coming, but it doesn't faze me—I think he's worthwhile. Honest, direct, kind." She looked at Soleil. "Worthwhile men often bring difficult histories along with them."

"Have you met his children yet?"

Camille shook her head. "No, and that's something huge."

Soleil suddenly saw a rare seriousness come into Camille's eyes.

"Soleil, I'm going to try to make this work. It won't be easy, but I really feel he's been put in my path for me to stumble over. And besides, when have I ever run away from a challenge?"

"Genetic, I guess," Soleil said.

"For you and me, maybe."

Soleil didn't hesitate: "Go for it. You deserve happiness, and you deserve it now. I like Kurt, and I can see he likes you. I saw that when we were in New York."

After a few quiet moments, Camille gathered her thoughts and said, "What about Max?"

Soleil looked at her plate and fiddled with her fork.

"Max is gone."

"Soleil," Camille began. "You never spoke to him, did you?"

Soleil's fork played with a sprig of decorative parsley.

"I really don't want to talk about it now, Camille. Maybe later."

"Don't you know what that Soviet *putain* is doing? She's playing with you—this is the oldest con in the world. And you of all people should know that." She looked into her sister's deep blue eyes.

Soleil looked back. "Of course I know that. But Camille." Her face softened a bit. "He hasn't called me in two months." Camille started to say something, but Soleil held up a hand.

"I know. Don't you think I'm worried? Don't you think I know that he may be in trouble? Serious trouble?" She put her fork down carefully on her plate.

"Cami, I've tried everything short of trying to get into Russia myself, but it's impossible. And even it were possible, I wouldn't know where to begin. I made a hundred attempts to call, but the one and only time I got through to anyone, it turned out to be that woman." She set her jaw. "And she *was* in Max's apartment. And, no, he doesn't have a maid."

"Soleil, he saved—"

"My life. Oh God, Camille, don't I know it? And I'm sure he was in love with me, but listen—sometimes men think that they're in love with a woman, but they're really in love with showing a woman what they can do, what they can accomplish. It's what makes them men, good men. But sometimes a woman is just the mirror of a man's actions." She paused and sat back, and her shoulders sagged half an inch. "Oh, I don't know."

Camille felt like throwing her beer stein at her little sister: "He loved—*loves* you, Soleil. Everyone saw it. You know it."

"Stop." Soleil looked down at her hands in her lap and hardened her voice. "I was fooled once, badly. No, not badly; almost fatally. You have to understand that I won't stop my life now over Max. I love him and will until the day I die, but I'm twenty-three. How much of my life should I devote to a man who is absent? Whom I haven't heard from?"

She sighed audibly. "I might as well just grieve for him and move on, Camille."

When she saw her older sister start to open her mouth, she said with unmistakable finality, "I've made up my mind."

There were a few seconds of silence. Fair enough, thought Camille. For now.

"Now eat," Soleil said, decisively slamming the door on the topic. "You *grosse vache!*"

Daggers flew at Soleil from Camille's eyes. "Now, let's talk about Christmas—Christmas in the Alps."

An hour later, after finishing off a deceptively large amount of food, they split the check and left the Zeughauskeller. They began walking side by side up the street.

"At least we're in Switzerland," said Camille, idly watching peoples' faces as they strolled by. "Everyone seems so much calmer and buttoned-down here."

Kurt was getting the lay of the land.

He had gotten up at around eight and showered and dressed as quietly as possible. Then he had tiptoed into the bedroom, leaned over the bed, and kissed Camille's forehead. She "mmm'd" for a second and turned over in her sleep. Kurt walked back into the suite's living room, gently closed the bedroom door behind him, grabbed his coat, and left.

At a corner table in the hotel's Pavillon restaurant, he ordered a light breakfast that consisted of a pastry and coffee served in elegant European style. *I could get used to this,* he thought. *Classy. There'll be plenty of time for bacon and eggs and pancakes when I get back to Chicago.* He asked for an English copy of the *Financial Times,* and it was brought to his table in seconds. *Impressive.*

A half hour later, he was outside.

Kurt didn't mind the December cold. *I'm from the Windy City anyway,* he thought to himself as he walked along the edge of the crystal-blue lake on the promenade. *This is nothing, easy—no wind. Clear, crisp sky and those wild Alps in the background everywhere you look. What a beautiful city.*

He had brought along another cup of coffee in a takeout cup and felt an attachment—a swift and unusual affinity for this place. Kurt was surprised by the sudden emotion.

It hit him that this was the City of Money. Kurt was the kind of man who was driven by responsibility, as good men often are, and for him that responsibility manifested itself in the making of money. He wasn't inclined to be maudlin or overly introspective about it—it just was him.

He wandered up the Bahnhofstrasse and at first was amused by the metal tracks sunk into the center of the streets for the electric trains that made their precisely timed rounds through and around the city. But after a few minutes, it became perfectly apparent that the system was profoundly efficient and got everyone where they wanted to go safely and quickly.

This place runs like a Swiss watch, he thought. The whole city is geared to a quiet, clean efficiency. Like a well-run bank.

Kurt walked for hours, which gave him time to think about Camille.

She's the polar opposite of Amanda, he thought. Positive and self-assured. But not in the way that some women build themselves up with fixations on appearance and possessions to convince themselves of their worth.

No, Camille's the real deal. She's completely comfortable in her own skin, and doesn't mince words or shape them to manipulate, cajole, or fool people. And she's been through a lot of hard knocks.

Kurt asked himself the same question that he had been asking for years: what was I thinking about when I married Amanda?

Answer: what every other shallow, stupid, young dope like me in the trading pits was thinking—arm candy. Well. Stupid to marry a Snickers bar for the way she glitters in public as if she's a possession that reflects your own shaky self-worth. What an ass I was. Still am in a lot of ways, I guess.

And it's taken two years of legal hell to extricate myself from her.

He thought about the kids. How it had taken those two years to come to terms with what should have been an obvious fact: that staying married for the sake of the children was a mistake—a mistake that many warring, unhappy parents made, and a sin that he had almost committed.

I should have known better then. I do now.

Kurt and his younger sister had come from a war zone of a family. Their parents hated each other. It was dysfunctional and destructive, and his fondest wish as a young boy was for his mother and father to split up and live in different houses so there would be peace. Kurt's parents' "mature" decision to remain married "for the kids" finally took the whole family over the edge.

Kurt had left at sixteen and never returned. I wonder if any family is ever normal, he thought as he walked the Zurich streets.

Before he realized it, it was after noon. He pulled the small piece of paper from his pocket. On it he'd written the name of the restaurant at which Soleil and Camille were having lunch. He'd arranged with Camille to meet there at 2:00 p.m. They should be finished with lunch and their girls' talk-a-thon by then.

He began walking toward that area of town but suddenly came to a halt.

What? Kurt looked left and right, and then turned to look back. He had a sudden and strong premonition that someone was watching him, following him. He walked over to the nearest building and leaned against the wall for a few minutes, watching the passersby.

Must have been a ghost, he said to himself. Or, more likely, a case of paranoid jitters left over from what happened in Chicago. He shook his head, put a slight smile on his face, and continued walking.

7

ALFA AND OPEL

"Everyone seems so much calmer and buttoned-down here," Camille was saying.

They had just come out onto the street in front of the Zeughauskeller and begun walking. "It's as if nothing crazy ever happens in Zurich."

She looked at Soleil. "Geneva, maybe. But Zurich? No."

Soleil was about to agree when they spotted Kurt walking toward them a block away. They each put up an arm and waved in unison, and even from a distance they were able to see Kurt's broad smile. In another minute they had all come together.

"Hey, Soleil!" he gave her a huge hug and lifted her a few inches off the ground. He hadn't seen her in two months—since New York.

"Down, boy," Soleil said, laughing. "Save it for my old, *very* old sister, here."

Camille growled at Soleil, and Kurt set her back down and kissed her cheek. Her eyes on Camille, she pointed at her other cheek, and said, "Right here, handsome. This is Europe, remember?"

He gave her another kiss, and Camille said, "OK, OK, I knew I shouldn't have asked him to meet us here in the red light district."

Laughs all around, and they started walking up the block. "Let's go to my office. It's not far," said Soleil. "And speaking of loose ladies, Kurt, you've never met Yvonne." She gave Camille a look, and half-turned to Kurt, winking broadly. "You'll like her."

Camille smacked her hand to her forehead. "Sheesh, why did I bring him to Europe? I could have just left him back in a gentlemen's club in Chicago for all the good you're doing me, sister dearest." Soleil and Kurt laughed.

They began the ten-block walk to Soleil's building, and Kurt said to Soleil, "Camille told me about Max. Whenever you'd like, maybe I can help you, Soleil. I'm not sure..."

But Soleil's attention had suddenly zeroed in on something else. A green Opel sedan had appeared out of a side street a block ahead and was moving slowly toward them. It was the only car on the street, as this section of the Bahnhofstrasse was an automobile-free zone dedicated to the electric trams.

But there was more. Why's that car giving me bad vibes? she wondered. The driver is looking for someone. Why do I think it's us?

Suddenly the car was alongside them, and to her horror, Soleil saw the round muzzle of a gun's silencer through the open side window. The driver, a young Asian woman with straight black hair, had the gun extended in her right hand. Before Soleil could open her mouth, she saw the black tube jerk. From her left, she heard, "Ahh!"

Kurt Ballas twirled around violently, tried to get his feet to compensate for the motion, but tripped and fell awkwardly to the ground. The cloth of his coat at the shoulder was shredded, and blood began to seep out of it. He got back to his knees, and Camille was instantly on him.

"What?" she yelled. "Again?" The bullet had come so close to Camille's face that she had felt a hot flash across the bridge of her nose an instant before she saw Kurt fly to the ground. If the bullet had been an inch off course, she would have been killed.

She knelt over Kurt.

"I'm all right, I'm all right," he was saying. But the pain in his shoulder was beginning to blossom exponentially. He gritted his teeth and knew that "all right" wasn't exactly accurate—it hurt like hell.

Passersby had already begun to stop and gawk, and one or two began talking at Kurt and Camille in rapid-fire German. A man wearing a beret ran into a nearby store, obviously to use the phone to call the police.

Camille shrugged out of her jacket and tore a large corner off the bottom of her shirt. She jammed it up under Kurt's coat to staunch the flow of blood.

She turned and said, "Damn it, Soleil. I thought we left all this behind us in Chica..." But she was talking to the air.

Soleil was gone.

The car had accelerated, made a fast right turn, and disappeared around the next corner.

Soleil instantly had broken into a run, nearly knocking over a group of pedestrians as she took off after the car.

"I know something you don't, you bitch," she said to herself. "The street you just turned down is closed at the end of the block. It's under construction."

The Opel made the turn and sped down the short block.

The driver turned around in her seat to check whether she was being followed. A second later, she turned back, looked through the windshield, and in sudden panic and disbelief, saw the sawhorses, wooden barricades, and "*Warnung!*" signs blocking her path.

She immediately slammed on the brakes, but it was too late. The Opel crashed into the wooden barriers, loudly splintering them and sending pieces flying in all directions. Construction workers and pedestrians jumped out of the way.

The front of the car bounced into the trench where the work crew was laying the phone cable and crashed to a stop. She put the car in reverse, and the front drive wheels spun as the car rocked while she tried to get traction.

One or two workers in hard hats hesitantly approached the car, but in a matter of seconds, the car screeched backward, bounced heavily into the street, and the driver put it into gear. She steered it over another pile of rubble, finally reached the other side of the trench, and blasted the car away from the scene.

That's when the woman with the blue eyes, blond hair, and the pea coat ran straight into Lars.

"OK, Lars," she said breathing heavily at the stunned pipe fitter. She had nearly knocked him over, and she now held both of his arms as she faced him. "Let's go for that ride in your toy!" She looked over at his red Alfa Spider. "Key in it?"

"*Vas*, what?"

He was flummoxed and tongue-tied, and Soleil didn't have a second to spare. "The key, *der schlüssel*, Lars—is it in your sexy little red car or not?" She was still breathing hard from her run down the block. "*Ja? Nein?*"

Lars was stunned and he stuttered out the word *ja* before he could calculate the long-term wisdom of parting with that little bit of knowledge.

Soleil quickly kissed him as hard as he had ever been kissed on his mouth, but before he could rally his voice, let alone his other senses, the beautiful girl was at the car, then *in* the car. Then the car was moving, and then...she was gone.

With his car.

Lars could only stand there with a very stupid look on his handsome, stubbly chinned face.

Driving was certainly not the best way to get around in Zurich—it's an older city, where the people are reliant on public transportation and their feet.

But on this cold, gloriously clear day, as Christmas was rapidly approaching, the good and orderly citizens of Zurich were hosts to a traffic anomaly that would be remembered in the city for a very long time.

The green Opel roared east and screeched loudly around a corner, as the black-haired driver concentrated on finding a way out of the city.

She roared through a stop light, narrowly missing a woman with a baby carriage in the intersection, and swerved wildly, forcing other angry pedestrians to dive for cover.

Her eyes were intent on the road in front of her, but her normal composure had come undone, was shattered by the events of the last three minutes. She knew this: if she didn't disappear—*disappear right now*—she'd be dead within twenty-four hours.

I have a big, big problem, she thought. The target still breathes.

This is the second time it's happened. At least that Zoe Kimball woman in Chicago had the good sense to check out when she screwed up. Now, I'm a dead woman walking. Failure is not an—"

Her thought was cut short when something smashed loudly into the rear of the Opel, knocking it roughly across the oncoming lane and forcing it onto the sidewalk, up against an HSBC Bank. The car left a green stripe along the front of the building, and she wrestled the wheel back into line, downshifted, and swung the car back into traffic.

She looked in her rearview mirror, and her heart rate instantly rose.

A red Alfa Romeo was a few car lengths behind and closing. At the wheel: Soleil Tangiere.

OK, the driver said to herself, her black hair down in front of her face. I'm taking this into my own hands now. That bitch is toast.

She stomped on the gas pedal and quickly cut in front of one of the large, electric trams that was making its efficient way down the center of the street. She flung the Opel across its path with inches to spare. There was no way the Alfa in pursuit was able to make the turn without being squashed by the heavy train-like vehicle.

Safely on the other side of the long tram, the Asian woman peeled off into a side street and gunned it. At the next corner, she hung a right.

Good, she thought. Now I can get behind the Tangiere woman. Then it will be all over, and I can get the hell out of here.

Soleil was nervously working the wheel, the clutch, and the brakes, and thought she had stopped the Asian woman's car until that stunt with the tram. Now the Opel was nowhere to be seen, but Soleil kept driving as fast as she could in a widening spiral of streets, hoping to come upon the green car and its driver.

I had to do this, Soleil thought tensely. As dangerous as it was, it was a no-brainer to take this course of action—to go after her.

It looks like Kurt survived—I hope it was just his shoulder. I think it was. But I have to go after that woman, or the next time whoever was trying to get Kurt wouldn't miss. I've got to catch her so we can find out what's happening once and for all.

She turned left at the next light, accelerated as quickly as she dared, and scanned the traffic on the street in front of her. And it's got to be now, she said to herself. I can't rely on the poli—Bam!

Her head crashed back into the headrest as the Opel plowed into the rear of the small Alfa. Soleil's car was instantly flung straight toward a delivery van, and she wrenched the wheel over at the last second to avoid a head-on collision. She thought she was home free, but the front of the van clipped the rear quarter panel of the Alfa, and Soleil lost control of the red sports car.

The Alfa spun onto the sidewalk and ricocheted off the front entrance of a Credit Suisse, smashing the bank's front doors into a twenty-foot tall explosion of glittering glass that blew into the lobby and out onto the cars and pedestrians in the area.

The engine shut down, and the car rolled back out into the street. Soleil shook her head and spotted the Opel up the block: it was slowing down to make the next left. She reached for the key, started the motor up, popped the clutch, and screeched off in pursuit.

Soleil got to the intersection, swung her damaged Alfa around the corner, and then quickly stood on the brakes— the Opel was a hundred feet up the crowded block, and the Asian woman was already halfway out the driver's door with her silenced gun aimed at Soleil.

As pedestrians began to scream at the sight of the gun, Soleil ducked her upper body sideways and down across the shifter and the passenger seat. A loud *"chunk-whack!"* sound came from the windshield directly in front of the driver's seat where the bullet had penetrated, instantly making a spider web pattern, and from the plexiglass rear window, which it blew completely out of the car as it exited.

I was wrong, Soleil realized. This girl doesn't care if she's taken alive.

Soleil peeked over the dashboard, her heart pounding, and saw the Asian woman aiming again. She said a silent prayer for the innocent bystanders and drivers all around her, put the car in gear, mashed her foot on the accelerator, and roared directly at the woman and her green car.

Another bullet ripped through the top of the windshield frame, and a small shard of glass cut Soleil's right shoulder. I don't care, she told herself. This has become way too crazy, and it has to end now, this second.

One second later, Soleil rammed the red Alfa into the Opel at a sharp angle. The green car scraped up onto its side, and the driver, her arms and legs akimbo, flew in an arc over the car and landed with a smack on the windshield of a Mercedes traveling in the other direction.

She bounced, somersaulted off the hood of the large car, and landed on the street. A Fiat, its driver trying valiantly to stop, rammed into her and pushed her body up on the sidewalk, where if finally came to rest face down in front of a UBS Money Center office.

Soleil sat shaking in the driver's seat of what was left of the steaming wreck that was Lars's Alfa and breathed for a few seconds. Then she looked at the pandemonium around her and the two destroyed cars. Where's the driver? I have to get to her.

She got out of the car and quickly made her way over to the clot of people that was starting to form around the body. Soleil got down on her knees and said over her shoulder, "Give her some room! And call the police. *Polizei.*"

Amazingly, the woman was moving and had pushed herself over so that now she was lying on her back, one hand bent at an odd angle under her body. Her shoes were gone, and her black blouse and jeans were in tatters and soaked with blood. A red, smeared pattern was forming on the ground beneath her.

Soleil leaned over and looked into her narrow, angry, glazing eyes.

"Please," she whispered in English. "Please, why are you trying to kill Kurt Ballas? What do you have against him? Who sent you and that other woman to do it?"

The Asian woman stared at her, and her mouth moved. Soleil saw that she was trying to say something.

"What's your name?" said Soleil. "Please, who are you?" She leaned over a little more so her ear was at the woman's lips.

Then she heard the woman say, "Furoma."

"Your name is Furoma? Or is that who sent you do this?" Soleil asked softly.

Again, the one word, "Furoma," and then a rattling breath came out of her mouth, and it seemed as if she collapsed in upon herself. Soleil knelt by her side and felt helpless. She's gone, Soleil said blackly to herself. Finally, she slowly stood up and turned away.

There was a crowd of people around her now, and she knew that in a moment or two the police would be...

Suddenly there was a collective gasp from the crowd. Soleil swirled to look down at the Asian woman, who was still lying on her back. But now she had the silencer-shod automatic in her fist. It had been clutched in her hand behind her back where no one had seen it.

Soleil froze as the injured woman stretched out her arm and brought the ugly silenced muzzle to bear on the center of Soleil's chest.

Then the woman turned her hand with the gun, put the muzzle of the silencer in her own mouth, and pulled the trigger.

Everyone jumped back from this shatteringly new, instant red mess on the street.

Only Soleil hadn't moved. Her eyes were wide.

A few seconds later, the whooping sound of approaching sirens broke the stunned silence.

8

LUMPY SHORTS

Cold blasted the Mir.

Frigid ice balls rammed almost horizontally into the reinforced dome of the sorting facility, making an unholy racket that even the layers of poured concrete insulation couldn't entirely silence.

Gravva was watching from his chair at the sorting table. At the other side of the main gem-processing room, the tall, pale man spoke to the mule, Stepanov. The slightly shorter but broader and younger man was silent. Even from this distance, Gravva saw that Max could barely control the contempt he had for the obviously brazen and self-important Veshkin.

Well, it looks like the time is upon us, just as Eddie Poong predicted, Gravva thought. Veshkin has shown up. He must have flown into the nearby army base from Moscow this morning to load up Max, his pack animal. And I'm here to kill the animal and steal his pack. Eddie has the plan in place to get me out of this hellhole and south to Mongolia and Ulan Bator. Once there, he and his three-breasted mongrel brother will supply me with everything I need to start the rest of my very luxurious, very warm life. I really have to be careful once I reach Ulan, but one thing I do know is that Eddie's genius will get me out of this frozen hell—and with more money than a prince.

Gravva raised his right hand with his forefinger up, a signal to the ever-present armed guards that he was going to the bathroom, and then rose and walked as close to Veshkin and Stepanov as he could without looking conspicuous or suspicious.

As Gravva passed the two, he realized that Veshkin was keeping his voice too low to be heard. Max glanced up, but he was too involved in the conversation to acknowledge Gravva.

In the men's room, Gravva considered his next move. All I have to do is stick with Max and keep showing him that I'm the stupid, harmless, fat man who is no threat at all; that I'm his friend, he thought. And when the time comes, I'll know. I'll be able to tell when he's suddenly ready to bolt, Gravva thought. And I'll be in my element. Diamonds are such great contraband. They're so nice and small and light, and often the rough stones look like worthless crap. Fools everyone. This should go along nice and smoothly. I'll make it happen.

And when it's over, even if the wolves don't finish off Max's body, no one's going to bother looking for it out in the tundra where I'm going to dump it. They won't find what's left of him until late in the spring. If ever.

By then I'll be in Costa Rica, Gravva thought as he buttoned his fly.

Ah...Costa Rica. He almost hummed to himself as he went back to his sorting table. From the corner of his eye, he saw Max and Veshkin leaving the room. He knew where they were going now.

The ice balls kept ramming at the dome.

"Here it is, Max, my dear *tovarich*," said Veshkin, his moist, fetid mouth a few inches from Max's face.

Max stood with Veshkin in the small cubicle with its recirculating air and felt claustrophobic. There was no sense in saying a word, Max thought. I'll just watch this *pizda's* face carefully for any unsaid facial clue that he might have missed. Hell, Veshkin's mouth *looks* like a *pizda*.

He and Boris Veshkin had made their way to the most secure part of the Mir complex—the underground vault. It was buried two hundred feet below the pit bottom, almost two thousand feet from the earth's surface at the lip of the mine. It made Max uncomfortable, but it made Veshkin bold.

That must be it, his big surprise, Max said bitterly to himself as he watched Veshkin heft the clumsy red-and-white-striped object a few times, smiling and chortling. Finally, he tossed it into Max's hands.

"My dear *tovarich*," he repeated in a hearty voice. "Go ahead, Max, try it on for size."

Max pulled at the corners of the bumpy, cloth object and saw that it was some kind of a strangely shaped pouch or a pack.

He knew immediately what the bumps were.

Sewn inside were diamonds. And from the feel of those lumps, they were likely the cream of the crop. Veshkin was the boss—he could requisition any diamond in the mine for a vault transfer. Of course, this transfer wasn't going to be to another vault. At least not another vault in Russia.

He felt the lumps again. These must be worth millions— many millions.

As if reading his mind, Veshkin said plainly, "Just ten diamonds. Big ones—over fifty carats each." His pale eyes glittered.

Max turned the package this way and that and then suddenly realized what he had to do with this object. "This isn't..."

Veshkin laughed aloud. "Yes, of course it is, dear Max."

OK, Max said to himself, here's a clue right here: the man's slowly losing his mind—if he hasn't lost it already.

"These are your new Fruit of the Looms, my boy. Your new Jockeys."

His grin is weird as hell, thought Max.

"You just put on these fashionable...uh...briefs like you do your underwear and walk around anywhere you like. Sitting down will, I admit, be painful. But Max," he said, his grin getting even wider, "I don't give a *dermo!*"

Max gave a *dermo*. Hiding diamonds in a lumpy pair of underwear? The man's a sadistic loon, he thought. I could try to hide diamonds a lot deeper than my underwear, and they would still never leave this secure installation. This was his plan?

As if reading his mind, Veshkin said, "Oh, take away that doubting look from your face, Max. The underwear is just an extra layer of precaution. Who would steal your shorts, Max?"

If he thinks I'm going to wear this thing, he's *sumasshedshiy*, Max thought.

"Don't think about cutting those shorts open to take anything, Max. I won't accept delivery if the...uh...item is tampered with. Just do your little chore." Veshkin's voice suddenly became blandly serious. "With my help and Nevsky's clout, you are just going to walk on out of here."

Max doubted that. "Why don't you just take it all yourself, now?" Max asked, his fists flexing. Enough of this idiocy, he said to himself.

"Look Stepanov, there's a chance something may go wrong." Suddenly Veshkin was speaking rapidly with as much menace as he could muster. "This is Russia. What *can* go wrong, *will* go wrong. And if that happens, who's going to take the fall, Stepanov? You, of course."

He paused for effect and showed his small teeth. "And that fall will be fatal if it happens. Fatal." Another repellent smile. "I will be waiting at the end of your little trip, Max. Safe and sound. If you get yourself killed before you get to me, well, at least I will be alive and happy. So do precisely what I say, exactly what I request—no, *command*—you to do. And, hopefully, you will live." He raised his head so that he could look down at Max over his nose. "Live to cuddle up with your capitalist *pizda*, Soleil."

He stopped suddenly, as if gathering his thoughts. After a few seconds, he added, "I can't stand you, Max. If it weren't my diamonds you're carrying out for me, I'd find a way to have you executed, killed right now. You piss me off with your sanctimonious honesty and fake loyalty, while all the while you're just like the rest of us—looking for a way out."

Max stood still and calm and waited for more. Yes, Veshkin was losing it. Big time.

Finally, Veshkin said, "Well, you'll get your way out. You'll deliver my diamonds to me in Europe, and then you're free." Veshkin turned his face away from Max, glanced at the diamond pouch, and said, "Put it on, donkey."

Something hit Max in the back of his subconscious. There was something here he didn't know. Something that he was sure he *should* know. He pulled his thermal pants off and wrestled the idiotic thing on. Veshkin looked at the ceiling. Max felt like ripping the man's head off.

After Max had put on the badly fitting and ridiculously annoying boxers and gotten the thermals back on, he said, "Done." He had managed to push the lumps around through the material so they made a rough line around his waist. Any lower and it would have been downright dangerous.

Veshkin grinned again and said, "I don't know about *you*, Max, but I'm going to my new home for Christmas time. You're lucky—you get to stay here a bit longer and freeze your diamond-wrapped ass off. But oh well! Them's the breaks, as the bourgeois Americans say."

He looked hard at Max, went serious again, and said. "In five days, Max, a Sukhoi Su-15 Interceptor will touch down at the army base two miles from here. You will be waiting for it on the runway at 8:00 a.m."

Max was shocked. What?

Veshkin continued, "Take nothing away from the mine. Nothing. Of course, you will be wearing your nifty new underwear. At each checkpoint, you will show this." Veshkin reached into his pocket and extracted some papers and a laminated card. "This gets you past the X-ray room, as well."

Max looked at the photo of himself on the card. It also displayed the official Soviet clearance codes and an embossed gold hammer and sickle.

"You will not be searched leaving the Mir. You will board the plane with the pilot at 8:00 a.m. and it will fly to Ljubljana in Slovenia. Then you will make a quick change of plane to the Nevsky jet, and then continue on to Switzerland. I've arranged all the proper justifications and paperwork for your, er, itinerary. The Swiss government will be apprised of the flight and will allow you to land at Zurich airport. Just in time for the New Year." He slapped a passport and more papers into Max's hand.

Then he pushed his finger into Max's chest and tapped it along with each word: "I...will...be...waiting." He stared at Max and finally let all of his madness flood his eyes. "Do as I say and I won't kill your girlfriend."

Then Veshkin tossed him another odd sneer and reached behind him to knock on the cubicle door. A uniformed guard, who looked a bit drunk but was festooned with enough guns and ammo to conquer a small country, opened the door. The three walked to the elevator at the far end of the hall. Max looked at the guard, his drinking pal, Arkady, but couldn't read his face.

They had to change elevators twice—the extreme depth of the vault made it impractical to have a single, half-mile long elevator. Finally, the last set of doors opened, and Veshkin walked briskly down the hall toward his two personal, armed bodyguards, who were waiting in their thermal clothing. When he reached them, he turned to look at Max and smiled with his little moist teeth.

"Good-bye, Max. Happy Christmas."

Max thought that if he had a gun now, Veshkin would be dead.

Then Veshkin turned, a door opened and closed, and he was gone.

Max stood staring after him. Arkady, who had accompanied them in the elevators, swayed slightly at his side.

The first chance I get, Max said to himself, I'll make sure that Boris Veshkin gets what's coming to him. He looked at Arkady, who seemed as if he was about to topple over, and said, "Go sleep it off, my friend."

Arkady nodded, put his hand on Max's shoulder for a moment, and then walked away to do just that.

Gravva Gleb couldn't believe his good luck.

And I owe it all to vodka, he thought. Hell, most Russians owe everything they have, and don't have, to that wonderful drink.

Take this Arkady idiot, my stupid, sometime roommate here at Ice Station Vodka. At his post, he's a ferocious-looking guard with enough guns and ammo hanging off him to sever his spinal cord. I almost never see him, as his duties are all over the clock, but I'm glad that fate assigned me to Arkady's room when I came to the Mir.

When we're both here in this crappy, crowded room, which isn't all that common an occurrence anyway, all I have to do is pass a liter of vodka to Arkady while he's lying in his upper bunk, and by the time it disappears down his gullet, he's magically transformed into a newscaster.

And today's news was *really* news, Gravva thought happily. Finally, something about Max Stepanov.

Arkady stunned Gravva with his slurred version of what had transpired deep in the Mir's vault.

When he was done trying to extract as many details as he could before Arkady passed out, Gravva rubbed his hands in glee. Ooh, life was grand! For the next five days of Christmas, Max Stepanov would be walking around with his crotch all aglow. Ha! This made it easier than easy.

Now, Gravva could use a little of that vodka, himself.

Gravva reached under his bed and extracted another bottle. He called Arkady's name but the man in the upper bunk had already passed out.

Good. Sharing sucks. He twisted the top off the bottle and drank.

The next day, Gravva made the call.

After the work shift ended at 5:50 p.m., he walked nonchalantly past Max, who was conferring with a sorter at the second table over. He calmly walked out the only door in the sorting room and directly into X-ray, as the diamond-checking room was called.

It was in this room that workers were searched for even the tiniest diamond that a less-than-honest sorter might decide to purloin. Some of their searching methods were state of the art; others, a bit more primitive.

Passing, as always, with flying colors, Gravva then went into the ice room, as the place for coats, hats, boots, and insulated clothing of all kinds was called.

Donning his usual mountain of outdoor clothing, he finally got to the air lock, which was a double-doored cubicle that allowed the men to exit into the Arctic air.

Once outside under the diamond-sharp stars in the early Arctic night, he made his way quickly to the apartment block where he shared his small room with Arkady. But he didn't go through the regular entrance door. Instead, he looked cautiously left and right and then ducked around the side of the building.

A few dozen feet along the wall of the structure, he stopped near a drainpipe that he used as his marker. He got down heavily on his knees, reached his hand into a one-foot-square hole below the snow line and behind the metal pipe, and worked a plastic-wrapped package out of its hiding place. He slipped the football-sized package into his thermal insulated parka.

In his room, he locked the door and pulled the package from his inside his coat. How on earth had the Poongs gotten this thing out here? he asked himself. He carefully removed the plastic in which he had wrapped it the three previous times he had used it and caressed it lovingly.

It was a phone. A military-grade portable phone that worked by piggybacking on the radio frequencies that it could pick up with the long antenna that Gravva pulled out of its Bakelite casing. The phone's reliability was spotty near the Arctic, but with persistence and time, Gravva could call almost anywhere in the world.

It took a few minutes. There was a world of static and wrong connections, but finally, his call went through.

Eddie picked up the phone. It was nine o'clock in Hong Kong, and the harbor, the skyline, and the flotilla of water-craft were ablaze with a million lights. Eddie stood by the window and looked intently at his brother.

"The diamonds are in possession of the courier, Stepanov, in his underwear," Gravva's scratchy voice came over the phone.

Eddie's eyebrows went up. "Underwear, you say?"

"He has a specially made pair of Jockey shorts with the stones sewn into it."

"Hold on a minute, Gravva," Eddie said. He turned to Three Tit and said, "Stepanov has the diamonds in his under-wear." After three seconds of silence, both brothers exploded in laughter. When Eddie finally stopped laughing, he said to Gravva, "Stop messing around. Where are the diamonds?"

After listening to a minute or two of explanation, Eddie began jotting notes on a pad on his desk. Finally, he asked Gravva to give him the details of the hand-off.

"Why do you need that?" asked Gravva. "I'll have the diamonds. He'll be dead. And my escape route is overland. What difference does it make if you—"

Eddie interrupted him sharply. "Because I have to know everything. It's for your own safety."

Gravva gave him the information about the military jet and the arrival and departure times at Yakut, Ljubljana, and Zurich.

Then Eddie said, "Don't forget anything now—anything! You'll terminate Stepanov on the evening before his scheduled departure, December 28. At midnight, you have to be at our prearranged checkpoint with the stones. Your transport will absolutely be ready to pick you up. When you arrive in Ulan Bator three days later, we will be there."

Gravva's heart rate picked up. This was it! The beginning of his new life! "I'll be ready, Eddie. Stepanov will see Christmas, but not the New Year."

"Good," said Eddie. "Good luck." He hung up.

He looked at Three Tit and said, "Merry Christmas. We're almost there."

Three Tit was thoughtful. "We have to be in Ulan Bator on New Year's Eve. Do you think Gravva can really pull this off?"

Deep down, Eddie had huge, grave doubts about Gravva. But he said, "Three, all he has to do now is stick to the plan and deliver the goods. We'll hold up our end—we're the Poongs." He looked out the big window and took a deep breath. "Of course, we might convince him to take a slightly, er, smaller percentage, seeing as how our expenses have proved to be so high on this endeavor. As chief negotiator, I'm sure you have a strategy in mind."

Three Tit chuckled. "It will be a win-win solution, Eddie."

"Correct. I win and you win."

Three Tit nodded. He was still smiling, the glinting gold toothpick sticking out of his mouth reflecting his good mood.

Win-win.

Click-click.

9

GIRL TALK

Soleil didn't move. Her eyes were wide with a mixture of frustration and confusion.

In a circle around the badly damaged body, people were talking, whispering, and yelling. Some were crying. Why on earth did this woman just kill herself? Soleil could only stand there in disturbed wonder.

It took less than two minutes for the police and emergency medical vehicles to descend on the scene. Three police officers in their short, black, down-filled jackets with POLIZEI emblazoned on the backs in white letters, converged on Soleil and escorted her a few dozen feet away from the center of the confusing mêlée.

The three started to ask a torrent of questions in rapid German, which Soleil had some difficulty following. One officer finally realized that she was having a hard time and switched to French. "Please, mademoiselle, if you would accompany us to the station house," he said.

Can I refuse? Soleil thought dismally.

An hour later, she found herself at the Zurich Cantonal Police headquarters in the Kasernenstrasse. She was escorted into a plain room and seated at a table opposite Inspector Ulrika Sonnenreich.

The inspector was in her late thirties, a tall, striking blonde, whose looks were a stunning credit to her Norwegian origins. Her powder-blue business suit was well tailored to her figure. Probably drives the young male officers at the station insane, thought Soleil.

From her office door, the blond inspector had watched the three officers bring the disheveled but startlingly pretty Canadian woman up to the main desk and saw the looks from two dozen police officers' eyes. She had been secretly relieved that the officers had someone new to look at, someone else they could silently ogle for a change.

Now Soleil sat across from her at the table in the small interrogation room.

When Soleil had taken her first look at the inspector, her heart sank. She instantly knew that she would be spending the night behind bars. More than one night, probably. Not only was this woman likely the queen of the station house, but Soleil knew that she had probably stolen a chunk of her thunder when she'd walked into the building.

Vanity has nothing to do with it. It was just what it was. She'd had that problem with other women before. She hated it, but it happened sometimes. Soleil could see it in the inspector's face and body language. If it was going to come down to a catfight—well, that cat had the keys to the jail. It was not a very promising position for her to be in.

"You speak German, Frau..." the inspector said slowly in German, consulting some notes on the table in front of her. "Frau Tanger?"

"No." Soleil wasn't going to give her the satisfaction of correcting her. And she was not going to make this any easier for her than necessary.

Ulrika looked levelly at her. In English, she said, "You are in a fat mess, as they say in America, Frau Tanger. You will tell me what happened now?"

Soleil was further assessing the situation and decided how she would play it. "I'm Canadian, not American, as you know."

Ulrika flashed a perfect smile. "You don't know what I know, Soleil *Tangiere*."

This is why I have problems with some cops, Soleil thought wearily: games on games.

The inspector looked down in her lap and smoothed her skirt. Then she looked back at Soleil and said, "You just killed someone. I don't think you understand how much—"

"I didn't kill anyone," Soleil interrupted her.

Ulrika leaned forward. "Two dozen witnesses—"

"Saw the woman put a gun in her mouth and pull the trigger. Sounds like a suicide to me."

Ulrika was about to say something when the phone on the table rang. She picked it up on the first ring. "*Was wollen Sie?*" she barked into the phone. "*Ich bin beschäftigt!*" What do you want? I'm busy!

Chill, inspector, Soleil said to herself, keeping her eyes dead level on the woman's face. You should have stayed home at this time of the month if it's that bad. *Ulrika.*

As if reading her mind, the inspector glared at Soleil while listening to whoever was on the other end of the phone call. Her mouth turned down in obvious disapproval. After a minute or two, she hung up, rose from her chair, and started to pace the room.

"That was our chief. He has reminded me to inform you that you will now get a lawyer. If you cannot afford a lawyer, the Canton of Zurich will appoint one to represent you." She looked down and gave Soleil a power-trippy look.

Soleil gave one back, pulled the phone on the desk closer, picked up the receiver, and said to Ulrika, "How do I get an outside line?" More faces back and forth.

In a tight voice, Inspector Ulrika Sonnenreich instructed her how to make the call.

Soleil said, "*Danke!*" Then, under her breath, she added, "For nothing."

She dialed her office number, and thankfully, Yvonne picked up on the second ring.

"Yvonne, I'm at the police station. There's been a big problem—someone tried to kill Kurt on the Bahnhofstrasse, and now I need a lawyer."

Yvonne was stunned. "Is Kurt all right?"

"I don't know. I think so, but there's no way for me to find out."

"Why do you need a lawyer if someone tried to kill Kurt?" She didn't wait for Soleil to answer, as it suddenly hit her. "Oh." Oh, Soleil.

"Yvonne, please call Monsieur Deshautels in Geneva. You remember him?"

Inspector Ulrika Sonnenreich, who had been pacing in front of the table, came to a stop and slowly turned her head to look at Soleil.

"*Oui*." Yvonne remembered him. Henri Deshautels was the chief inspector in Geneva who had helped Soleil in the recent past. When she had gotten involved in a violent situation, he had not only helped her—he had saved her life.

Yvonne sighed. But this wasn't good. Even though Henri was a married man in his late forties, he had been and probably still was deeply infatuated with Soleil. And when he had saved her from falling to her death in Geneva, he figured he owned her. Thank God, Soleil had known how to handle that. Deshautels had power, and Yvonne hated men who used power in that way.

Soleil was speaking. "Tell him I'm in police custody and ask if he can please call the chief of the Zurich Cantonal Police. And tell him I need a lawyer—he knows every Swiss criminal lawyer in the country."

"That's a lot of asking, Soleil." But Yvonne knew that Deshautels would certainly do it. And he would absolutely come running from Geneva to be by her side. And then by her front, and then her back, and...

"What if he's not there?" Yvonne asked. "If he cannot pick up the phone or is on a vacation?"

Soleil was running out of options. "Then you'll have to find me a lawyer. A good one. Thanks." She hung up and looked at Ulrika, who had been listening. What on earth? she suddenly asked herself. The inspector's face had changed radically.

Finally, the woman said, "Henri Deshautels? Of the Geneva police?"

"Yes."

"How do you know him?" Ulrika asked. There was a forced nonchalance in her voice but certainly not on her face.

What's going on? Soleil asked herself. The atmosphere in the room had changed suddenly and palpably. On instinct, she said, "He helped me once. He did me a favor. It was earlier this year."

Ulrika sat down heavily in her chair on the other side of the table. Her distress was palpable. "I'm sure he will try to do the same now." She stared into the middle distance. "Oh, I'm certain he has a whole stack of favors for someone like you."

She knows him, Soleil said to herself. And more than that, she *knows* him.

I see.

"What's wrong?" she said softly to the inspector. In a second, Soleil had morphed from adversary to confidante. She realized that she had been far too nasty. "What happened, Inspector?"

The woman looked at Soleil. "Nothing."

Soleil's intuition wouldn't be stopped. "He injured you, didn't he?"

Ulrika's face registered surprised shock. "How do you know that?"

"Because I know how some men injure women. Most men don't, or at least don't mean to. Some men are hurtful just by being their frustrated, aging, insecure selves. Mix in a little official status and power, and you have a very flawed man. Henri Deshautels is one of those men."

Ulrika looked at her and felt a mild shock. Could this actually be an accomplished and obviously beautiful woman who is willing to understand the complications and pains that I have to go through every day? Did I finally find another woman who seems to be like me but isn't caught up in the one-upmanship race that other good looking women automatically enter into with me?

She tried to put her police voice back on. "Frau Tangiere, you are being detained for possible complicity in the death of an unidentified woman on the streets of Zurich. Endangering the lives of...innocent passersby. Possible theft of an automobile. Breaking every traffic code in...in..." She came to a stop. Her eyes were moist, and she rubbed them angrily with one hand.

"It's all right, Inspector." Soleil sat calmly, both hands on the table in front of her. "What happened?"

What am I doing? Ulrika said to herself. Why am I doing this? I have a job and this person is a suspect. What...

As if reading her mind, Soleil said softly, "You can tell me about this because I know this guy, this man Deshautels." She paused. "Get it off your chest. For both our sakes."

Ulrika looked at her strangely for a few seconds. Then she decided to take a chance.

"I knew him when I was a patrol officer in Geneva. He was my boss." Soleil saw a look of agony on her face. "He was married, and we, we..."

Oh. "You don't have to finish. I can guess."

Ulrika looked away. "No, you can't guess."

There was silence for the better part of a minute. Soleil thought the conversation was over. Then Ulrika said, "Henri Deshautels is the father of my child."

Oh. Soleil hadn't a clue how to react. She looked away and then back. "Does he know?"

The inspector looked anywhere but at Soleil. Finally, she said softly, "Yes, of course he does. It was only after the fact that it was finally revealed to me that he was a family man. I would never have gotten involved with him had I known. When I confronted him, he implored me, begged me on bended knee to keep quiet. For the good of his 'real' family. He cried like a baby for the sake of his four other children."

Her eyes hardened, and she looked down. "I could destroy that family, but I don't have the heart. I don't want to hurt children. But over time, I've gotten to hate him, hate his weakness, his hypocrisies, and the lack of responsibility he's shown to both myself and my—our—daughter."

She pursed her lips. "Basically, he just ran away." Then she said, "He's conveniently forgotten and ignored her. Better for me."

There were a few beats of silence. Then, quickly gathering up her emotions, the inspector looked straight at Soleil and said in a low voice, "But now, now you are bringing him here. To this office. To jump into your life, while I've been committed to holding him at arm's distance from mine. And there's no conceivable way that you could know how difficult it's been up until now."

Her lips compressed into a thin line for a few seconds, and then she said, "I despise that man, and now you are about to inflict him on me. Thank you very much, Soleil Tangiere."

A heavy blanket of silence settled on the room.

Then Soleil saw the bitter sadness trapped deep behind the inspector's eyes, the bleakness that lives in the back of a woman's mind when she has been decimated by a man and can't or won't fight back. Even if she is a police inspector.

She's alone in this mess, Soleil thought. She could use one female friend.

Soleil reached across the table and put her hand on Ulrika's. She thought that the police officer would pull it away, but she didn't. "No, I won't bring him here. I won't do that to you."

She pulled the phone back toward her and dialed out again while Ulrika watched in stunned silence.

"Yvonne, it's me again."

"Oh, Soleil, I just hung up with Camille. Kurt's all right. He's in the hospital, but the wound is not serious. She wanted me to tell you that."

Soleil felt as if at least one weight was lifted from her heart.

Then she said, "Did you get Monsieur Deshautels on the phone yet?"

"I left a message with someone at the Geneva police station. I said it was urgent that he call, nothing more. I just left a phone number, that's all."

Soleil sighed and looked at Ulrika. "When he calls back, tell him you had made a mistake. I don't want him involved in this."

"What? He's certainly the only one who can help you."

"Yvonne, please do as I ask. Now, can you please see if you can get ahold of Camille again and try to find me a lawyer?"

Suddenly she felt a hand touch hers. She looked at the other woman. "Wait; hold on a second, Yvonne." She put her hand over the receiver.

The inspector's pained eyes told her all that she needed to know. "You will not need a lawyer. Not today." She nodded at the phone in Soleil's hand.

"Yvonne, never mind," Soleil finally said into the phone, not taking her eyes off the inspector's.

"Soleil, are you all right?"

"It's all right, Yvonne. I think the police are going to let me go."

Then she hung up the phone.

It was after seven when Soleil finally let herself into her apartment.

She placed her purse on the small kitchen counter, made sure her window blinds were closed, and quickly stripped out of her dirty clothing. Boy, do I need a long shower, she thought.

She walked into the living room and flipped on the wall switch.

The five-foot-tall Christmas tree lit up, dripping of tinsel, crystal decorations, and dozens of tiny lights. On the top was a crystal angel. Soleil inspected the tree and made a few small adjustments.

She stood back to take it in and was satisfied. Her tiny diamond cross on its thin chain glittered on her chest as she stood in the light of the tree. She said a quick, silent prayer of thanks. Thank you, God, for life. For letting me be alive and free after a day like today.

She crossed the living room to the bathroom, wrapped a towel around herself, and went over to the phone to listen to the messages on her answering machine.

One of them was from an attorney. Lars's attorney.

She pursed her lips. Well, that was quick.

The lawyer's serious German voice stated with ominous precision that the car was worth fifteen thousand Swiss francs—around ten thousand dollars. Now it was rolling garbage. "You will reimburse my client immediately or will be subject to severe consequences," he said. She jotted down his number. Next message.

"Soleil, it's Stefan. I will be in Zermatt on Christmas, but I'll be thinking of no one but you. I won't be able to call you because I will be wrapped up in family activities. Happy Christmas." Yeah, you'll be wrapped up in activities with someone, Stefan, she thought. Next.

"Hi, Ice Queen, it's Aimee. Hope you're having a Merry Christmas and you're not knocked up yet. Brenda and Izzy say hi. And Tango says woof. 'Bye." Soleil smiled to hear her friend's Brooklyn-accented voice. I'll call her on Christmas, she thought. I'll call everyone on Christmas. Next.

Camille had left a couple of messages. Kurt was in a semi-private room at the University Hospital on the Rämistrasse. He'd lost a fair amount of blood, but it was a flesh wound—nothing was broken, and there were no internal injuries.

"Kurt put up a stink when they told him he'd have to stay overnight. But the hospital insisted. He said if he was on the first floor, he would have climbed out the window," Camille said. "Call me as soon as you get this message. I hope you're all right."

Soleil smiled and dialed the operator. She got the hospital number and finally was connected to Kurt's room.

"Hello?" It was Camille.

"Hi."

"Where are you? Are you all right? I thought you were dead."

"Nope. Still breathing."

"Yvonne said you were with the police. What's happened?"

Soleil realized that Camille had been terrified that something had happened to her. She said gently, "The woman who tried to shoot Kurt is dead. I'll tell you more when I get to the hospital. I'll be there in an hour."

"No, don't come, Soleil. The hospital is throwing me out now anyway. How about we get something to eat?"

"Sure," said Soleil, and gave her the name of a small restaurant around the corner from her apartment. "See you in an hour? I badly need a shower first." She glanced down at her shoulder. It was smarting from a small cut made by the ricocheting windshield glass.

"No problem," said Camille, and hung up.

Soleil started to walk into the bathroom, but saw that the tiny light on the answering machine was still blinking. She must have missed one more message.

She pressed the play button. A faint static came over the phone that lasted for around half a minute. Then she heard a dial tone.

Something else to worry about? she asked herself.

Soleil sat in front of her oldest sister and a bowl of French onion soup.

Fewer than a dozen people were eating in the restaurant, and the two women were grateful for the peace and privacy.

"I had no choice. She was shooting away, and it was her or me," Soleil told Camille.

"You didn't feel like ducking or hiding like any sane person would, did you, Soleil?" Camille knew that was a lost cause.

"If I did, I stood the risk of losing her and then worrying about her finishing the job on Kurt. There were also a lot of pedestrians standing around. Someone could have gotten hurt or worse."

Camille blew on a spoon of the scalding soup. "You did good, little sister."

Soleil's face hardened slightly. "Camille, that girl was crazy. Who would have guessed she would kill herself? What or who was she so afraid of? And most of all, why are these people trying to hurt Kurt?"

Camille said, "Kurt's been wracking his brain about it. He's pretty certain now that some business he did a while back may have inadvertently had an impact on a large Asian commodities deal that has since gone sour. He thinks it's a long shot, but possible."

"Asian?" said Soleil. "The woman with the gun was Asian. Could be connected."

Camille's interest picked up noticeably. "I don't know, but that's an odd coincidence. I'll tell Kurt in the morning when he's released from the hospital. I wonder when the police will be able to identify her?"

"They're working on it."

Camille looked at Soleil strangely. "How do you know that?"

"When I was in the police station, the head inspector on the case gave me as much information as they had up to that point."

"What did you do to him, Soleil? I thought they would have thrown the cuffs on you."

"It's not a him, it's a her. They were going to, Cami," Soleil said. "But the inspector is a woman who knows Henri Deshautels, and she afforded me a professional courtesy." That was the truth, she thought, in a convoluted kind of way. I can't tell Camille the whole story—I gave Ulrika my word that I would stay silent.

Camille didn't underestimate the resourcefulness of her little sister. She watched her playing half-heartedly with her soup. Tomorrow's Christmas Eve, thought Camille, and Soleil is all alone.

I know Soleil is really missing Max terribly. She could protest all she wants, Camille thought while watching her sister's face, and she can throw her body around once in a while in frustration, but I know she wants him here. She never really let him go.

I need to do something.

"Listen," she said. "I'm picking Kurt up at the hospital in the morning. We need to stay together. Let's do some Christmas shopping to distract ourselves from today's events."

Soleil started to protest, but Camille would hear none of it. "I don't know about you, but I haven't done any Christmas present shopping yet." She took a spoonful of soup. "Have you?"

As a matter of fact, she had. But she wanted to be with Camille and Kurt—*someone* on Christmas Eve. And the one person she really wanted to be with wasn't there. Where was he?

The question that she had carefully buried in her subconscious surfaced for a brief, stark second: Is he dead?

Camille saw the bleak sadness behind her sister's eyes. She said forcefully, "And I also have an idea for tomorrow evening."

She told Soleil, and Soleil had to admit that it wasn't bad.

10

BLADES AND TEARS

It was the day before Christmas, and all along the Bahnhofstrasse, the shoppers were imbued with the kind of yuletide spirits that warm the hearts of all merchants under heaven.

Kurt had accompanied them to the toney boulevard but bowed out of the shopping excursion, claiming that he needed to be away from the prying eyes of the recipients of his imminent purchases.

"He's going to the hotel after this," Camille said to Soleil and Yvonne as Kurt went off down the street, checking the store windows. "He wants to spend some time on the phone with his kids. When his ex-wife Amanda heard about the mess in the Harmon House, she tried to get a restraining order to keep him away from his children. She claimed that his presence was a danger."

Soleil and Yvonne exchanged looks. Camille said, "I know. At the moment, it turns out that's somewhat true. What a mess."

Soleil turned to Yvonne. "By now you understand the risks you're taking being around a Tangiere girl. Never a dull moment: restraining orders, car crashes, guns. Yesterday, I nearly wound up dead, in jail, or extradited to Canada. Or all of the above." In a low, conspiratorial voice she added, "You sure you don't want to run while you still have a chance?"

"*Quelle blague.* What a joke, Soleil. In these?" She looked down at the five-inch heels on her boots.

Camille interjected, "OK, let's go, *chiennes.* Christmas is coming."

They were bundled against the cold, but the colored lights and the crowded streets helped cheered up the three women. Soleil was feeling well. She could breathe again.

But as they walked past Cartier's window, something caught Soleil's eye. It was a tiny card bearing flowery calligraphy. It rested against a small display with an engagement ring on it. The card said, "*Frohe Weihnachten! 4.00-carat makellos. Aus Siberien.*"

Under the intense halogen display lights, the flawless, four-carat, pear-shaped Russian diamond exploded with clear, pure, white flashes of light. For a moment, thoughts of Max came flooding into her head, but after a few painful seconds, she forced them back into the dark.

Where are you, Max? she thought.

The sky was almost dark when they met on the shore of the lake.

It was getting very cold, but they didn't mind. Camille and Soleil were used to it. This wasn't even chilly, thought Soleil.

Before they'd arrived, Kurt had asked if they could skate well. "Kurt," Camille had said to him, "Repeat after me: Can-a-di-an."

Soleil had laughed.

The skate-rental kiosk was ablaze with Christmas lights and crowded with men, women, and children in colorful parkas, gloves, and knitted Christmas hats. Strings of colored lights bedecked the trees and spanned the poles stuck at intervals in the ice, indicating the safe skating boundaries.

Music was everywhere as an army of skaters swirled on frozen Lake Zurich under the Alpine stars.

Soleil, Camille, and Kurt were lacing up when Yvonne and a young man walked up.

"*Ay, salut,*" said Soleil when she saw her.

"What language is that?" asked Yvonne, eternally amused by Soleil's Québécois patois.

"*Ta gueule!*" Then Soleil looked at the young man standing next to Yvonne. He smiled and said, "*Bonsoir.*"

Yvonne looked at him and said, "This is André."

He nodded to the little group, and Soleil and Camille exchanged puzzled looks. André looked to be around twenty—ten years younger that Yvonne.

Yvonne saw the girls' looks and said, "André doesn't speak English, or German, for that matter. He's on holiday from Grenoble." The kid grinned and nodded a little. He had light-brown, shaggy hair and innocent brown eyes.

He said something to Yvonne, and then she said, "He's alone on a Christmas holiday here in Zurich, and I invited him to skate with us. He's very good, he says."

"You don't know how to skate, Yvonne," said Soleil evenly.

"*Oui*," said Yvonne perfunctorily. She looked at André. "Now I learn." She pulled André off toward the rental kiosk.

Kurt said to Camille, "In a few years, my son will as be old as André."

"Leave it alone, Kurt. Yvonne's just having fun. Look how much younger I am than you are." She poked an elbow in his side.

Kurt smiled and wisely withheld comment.

"*Ciao*," said Soleil, and she disappeared into the crowd of skaters.

Three hundred revelers skated on the lake as Christmas Eve blossomed around them. As Soleil smoothly flew in a wide circle along with the crowd, she realized that someone was skating alongside her.

He was around six feet tall, slim, and fit, and he had thick, dark hair and deep-green eyes. He wore a navy-blue windbreaker and dark slacks, and a white scarf trailed behind him as he glided easily among the other skaters, keeping up with her.

Soleil glanced at him and thought that he was some kind of skating pro or maybe a fashion model. She speeded up and began weaving between the slower skaters. He had no problem keeping up, and after ten minutes or so when Soleil skated to one of the benches on the shore of the lake, he zipped to a stop right in front of her, his skates kicking up little puffs of crystals.

"Hi," he said.

She nodded, and realized that she liked those eyes.

"Do you speak English?" he asked with a slight accent. That sounds nice, she thought to herself. What is it, British, Irish?

She nodded again and tilted her head.

"May I?" he indicated an empty spot on the bench next to her.

Another nod. He sat down and turned to face her.

"Do you speak at all?"

Another nod.

Grinning, he said, "Very well, I'll do all the talking. My name is Dustin. Dustin Magill. What's yours?"

"Soleil," she said plainly.

"Ah, for a second I thought you were a mute."

"No, no such luck."

At that moment, Camille and Kurt skated up to them. "Hello," Camille said, quickly sizing him up. Dustin gave her a long look back.

Soleil said, "This is Dustin. He's from..." She left it to him to finish the sentence.

"Edinburgh. Can ye na tell a Scottish brogue when ye hear one?" he said broadly with a smile. Soleil liked the smile.

As if on cue, André skated up, half pulling, half holding Yvonne upright. Their perfect timing made the casual introductions quick and easy. Yvonne tilted her head slightly and stared at Dustin for a few seconds.

After a moment, Dustin held one hand out and said to Soleil, "Shall we?"

"Sure." They got up and were immediately scooped along by the circling crowd.

Camille looked at Kurt watching them, and shrugged. "It's easy for her," was all she said.

Yvonne half fell, half sat down on the bench. André dropped down next to her and started babbling in French. Camille saw that Yvonne wasn't paying any attention. Her mind's completely elsewhere, thought Camille.

But that wasn't entirely so. Yvonne looked off in the direction that Soleil and Dustin had gone, and her large brown eyes narrowed. She pulled her jacket tightly around her and finally turned back to her enthusiastic young admirer.

"Do you live here in Zurich?" Dustin asked.

"Do you?" Soleil countered.

They were skating and talking side by side, and bits and pieces of each other's lives were coming to the surface.

Dustin told her that he worked for the Royal Bank of Scotland and had just been relocated to Zurich two weeks ago. He was single and was living in a borrowed apartment north of the city.

"No one around for Christmas Eve?" Soleil asked.

"No. I came here to the lake tonight just to skate and to be around people. I'm glad I found someone to talk to. The Swiss are somewhat cold."

"Well, it helps a little to know German or French, or even Italian in the south of the country. But if you make the effort, you'll see they're wonderful people. And when they get to know and trust you, they're steadfast friends." Her thoughts went to Ulrika Sonnenreich—a case in point.

"Well, now I know you," he said. "But you're not Swiss, are you?"

"I'm a Canadian national living here under a work permit and a special visa."

"Are you going to go back to Canada?"

"Maybe."

They talked awhile longer, and Dustin suddenly stopped and said, "I'm going to go. It's a bit of trip back to my apartment, and I'm sure you and your friends have plans."

Soleil said, "Stay. It's not an imposition."

But he stood his ground and said, "May I call you?"

With a little hesitation, she said, "Sure," and she gave him her phone number. Dustin kissed her cheek, and then he was gone.

She stood looking down at her skates and said to herself, Admit it, you like him. He's steady and handsome and real.

And here.

He'll call and want to go out, and I'll say yes, and one day it won't be a one-night stand like it was with Stefan. It'll be more. I can tell. And if it's not Dustin, someone else like him will come into my life, she thought.

Soleil started to skate slowly with the other revelers, with the music, with the thousands of little lights. At the edge of the crowd, she slowed and then stopped. Suddenly feeling completely alone in a circle of peace, she turned her face upward to the glittering and spangled stars in the clear, night sky.

OK, Max, I guess this is it: Merry Christmas, my love, wherever you are. She could just make out the hazy band of the Milky Way spanning the heavens.

Good-bye, Max, she said to herself, consigning what was left of her hope to the bright stars. I'll never forget you.

Soleil wiped away a tear and skated away.

Four thousand two hundred miles to the east, Max Stepanov sat on a plain chair in his room, staring off into space. He had been planning to spend his first Christmas Eve out of Russia with Soleil. The vodka bottle was a poor substitute.

The underwear with the diamonds was hidden deep within a cutout in his mattress, and he had put it out of his mind for the evening. He would think about it in three days, when he finally got out of there. *If* he finally got out of there.

And if something happens and he could not, he swore to God that he would take down everyone who had put him in that position before he died.

And I will die trying to get to you Soleil, he swore silently.

The thought sounded final—like a prediction or an omen.

He shivered and his eyes glazed with a mixture of sadness and fury.

Outside the drab, frozen, sleeping, apartment block, the Milky Way glittered and spangled above the world, above the spot where the Yakut reindeer usually slept.

But they weren't there. Tonight, the reindeer had gone off somewhere else.

11

PLOW

The Zurich Kloten International Airport was quiet on Christmas day.

There were fewer flights arriving and departing than usual—it wasn't a busy travel time, and Old Gregor sat in his cab in the taxi queue with a Styrofoam cup of coffee on the dash and the morning paper propped in front of him against the steering wheel.

The lead story had to do with American President Bush explaining something about his "thousand points of light" program. Ha, thought Old Gregor. Very inspirational: another politician with a slogan. All politicians should get the crabs. Then they'd get to feel a thousand points for themselves.

He glanced up and saw a couple walking out of the terminal. The man strode up to the taxi stand. Gregor's was the next cab in the queue, so he folded up his paper, put it on the seat next to him, and stepped heavily out of the cab to help them with their luggage.

The man was tall and plain. He looked to be in his late forties: rheumy eyes; tiny teeth; light, thinning hair; and a thin, hawklike nose.

One look at his bulky but inexpensive luggage and his plain but serviceable old coat, and Gregor immediately thought: Lithuania or maybe Estonia—ugh!

But wait. The woman: that was a whole other story.

She too was tall and slim, but she was at least twenty years younger than her companion. Her deep purple, military-cut coat with its high collar fit her well, and as she stood there with her long, dark, cascading hair, a pout on her full lips, and a flash of impatient anger in her amber eyes, Old Gregor made up his mind: Georgia. She's definitely from Soviet Georgia.

The man stood aloof as Old Gregor wrestled their heavy bags into the trunk of the Peugeot cab and then, seeing the two standing and waiting with an air of supreme entitlement, he slowly went around the car to open the back door for them. The couple stood waiting, an imperious look on the man's face, until the door was fully open and Gregor had gestured to them that the seat of their chariot was ready to accept their Eastern asses.

Who would have thought that I would be privileged to transport Russian royalty today? he asked himself with a familiar bitterness. And just think of the royal tip to come. I'm sick with anticipation. Or was that from last night's *blutwurst*?

He got into the driver's seat and said tiredly in German and English, "*Wohin gehst?* Where to?"

His majesty gave Old Gregor the name of their destination, waved a hand in dismissal over the seat back, and turned to speak with the dark-haired woman.

"We have three days, *dorogaya*," he said in Russian. "Do as you're told and you're home free after that." The woman looked out the window as he spoke, barely acknowledging him.

Old Gregor, who spoke fluent Russian, tweaked his previous assessment based on the man's accent. No, he was not from Estonia or Lithuania. This *sobaka* was from Moscow, or at least he had lived in Moscow for a long time. Lucky me, thought Gregor.

Do as you're told, the miffed woman repeated sarcastically to herself, staring out the cab's window. That's laughable. This vile lizard holds my future in his hands for the next three days, but after that, it will be good-bye forever to the filthy weasel.

"Your old friend will be happy to see you, I'm sure," the man said snidely. "Sorry it will be..." he suddenly stopped short and looked at the back of the taxi driver's head. He watched the driver's eyes in the rearview mirror carefully and said, "*Mudak! Yeb tvoyu mat!*" The old man's eyes didn't even flicker. Good, the passenger thought. The driver did not understand a word of Russian.

He turned back to the woman. "Sorry it will be short-lived. Your reunion with your lover, that is. But that's all part of our agreement, isn't it?"

Yes, worm, all part of our agreement, she thought. But what happens to that other woman, well, that's out of your hands, boss man. She just nodded and looked at him with barely concealed disdain.

He patted her hand and said, "When we get to the hotel, we will address other aspects of our agreement." He winked at her with one malevolently suggestive, rheumy eye.

If I don't throw up all over you first, insect, she said to herself behind her thin smile. Ooh, you slimy *zmeya*, you'd better come through with the money you promised me. If you don't...

Twenty minutes later, the taxi pulled up at their destination, and the two waited for Old Gregor to lever himself out of his seat and come around the cab to open the door for them. It took the old man an extra minute or two to heft their heavy bags out of the trunk.

Old Gregor waited as they got out of the cab and then told the man the fare. The prince of the Volga carefully counted out some Swiss francs that he had obtained at the airport and said, "Keep the change," which turned out to be less than fifty cents.

Old Gregor coughed once through his hand as the man turned, and the old taxi driver had the small satisfaction of seeing his snotty spit dribble down the back of the Russian's coat.

Yeb tvoyu mat to you. *Ukol.* Prick.

He watched as Boris Veshkin and Katia Koziashvili walked confidently into the glittering, Christmas-decorated lobby of the Baur au Lac Hotel.

"Merry Christmas, Soleil." It was Dustin's voice with his slight Scots accent.

"Hi. Merry Christmas." That was quick—how long had it been, about twelve hours? She had been folding a small pile of laundry and feeling anything but Christmas cheer. Good timing, Dustin.

"I know this is sudden, but do you have plans for this evening?"

Soleil's mind shifted to automatic, and she was about to give her standard response of "No, not tonight," but something inside her said why not? She said, "My sister and I are doing some things, but I'm free after seven. What did you have in mind?"

Did that sound too fast? Maybe.

"I was going to suggest skating on Lake Zurich, but we've done that. We're running out of things to do. What about dinner?"

"What *about* dinner?"

"Tonight? You. Me."

Something inside her said, Wait. Just wait. God, have I made mistakes with men in the last few years. Something must be missing in my brain that should be putting the brakes on these kinds of decisions.

But she said, "Where?" and thought about those intriguing green eyes.

"Someplace ridiculously expensive and stylish. You name it—I'm new around here."

"I don't know about stylish, but all of Zurich is ridiculously expensive."

"Oh, I'm on an RBS expense account. The sky's the limit."

"Die Kronenhalle," she said immediately.

"What?"

She smiled. The restaurant was far enough away from where she lived so that both would have to take, or at least share, cabs. He didn't have to be too near where she lived. Yet.

"You said the sky's the limit. Well, if you can get a reservation for tonight at the Kronenhalle, you'll be happy to be bumping right up against the sky in that department." She spelled out the well-known restaurant's name for him and gave him the address. Then she said, "I'll meet you there." They decided on eight o'clock.

When she hung up, she had an odd premonition. No. She should call him back. Cancel. She didn't know why, hadn't a clue. But...

Soleil gave up thinking about it—it was starting to hurt her heart. She turned to look at her tree with the Christmas gifts under it.

She was glad that Camille was coming.

The elevator doors in the hotel lobby opened, and Camille and Kurt nearly crashed into another couple that seemed in a hurry to get on. The tall, ascetic man stopped short and the younger woman with him bumped into Camille's shoulder.

"Sorry," she muttered in bad German, and her amber eyes and Camille's hazel ones met for a fraction of a second. No love lost here, girl, thought Camille with mild aggravation. The couple moved apart so that Kurt and Camille could pass. Then the two got on the elevator in silence.

"They were in a hurry," Kurt said as they walked out together through the main hotel doors. Kurt asked a valet to get a cab for him, and a white-gloved hand instantly waved in the air. A taxi pulled up in front of them.

In the cab, Camille asked Kurt, "What do you make of this Dustin?"

"The super skater? Seems OK to me. Why?"

"I saw Soleil's face and how she reacted to him. It didn't end last night—he's going to call her." She looked troubled. "And she'll respond."

Kurt was quiet for few seconds. "It's Max, isn't it, Cami?"

"Yes, it's Max. It's just that Soleil...oh, never mind, Kurt. You're not a woman. You just don't get it."

After another second, she said, "This Dustin seems, I don't know, too perfect."

Kurt looked at her. "Let it go, Cami. He's just a guy who thinks he has a chance with her because his good looks have gotten him places with women before. And besides," he lifted his head slightly to look down his nose at her, "good looks don't count for all that much in *this* case. Being with a Tangiere girl takes skill and brains and toughness and resourcefulness and..."

"All right," she said, her smile breaking through.

The old cab driver smiled. He enjoyed people who communicated plainly and liked each other. Not like Mr. and Mrs. Cheap Communist a few minutes ago. He'd bet this man knew how to tip. He sounded like an American. They both did. When Americans were drunk or in good moods they tipped like it was the end of the world. And his wife, or whoever this good-looking woman was, was certainly keeping him happy.

After a while, they pulled up in front of Soleil's building.

Kurt paid the driver and gave him a twenty-franc note as a tip—more than the actual cost of the ride. The driver touched his cap and smiled as the two walked into the apartment building.

In perfect Russian, Old Gregor said to no one, "I told you so." Then he pocketed the twenty and drove off.

Gravva Gleb's first mistake was a big one. A very big one.

There was no work on Christmas, and even though the USSR was a communist country where God wasn't allowed to apply for a work permit, there were enough imported specialists working at the Mir for the managers to decree December 25 a work holiday.

The sky was already dark at five in the afternoon when Gravva casually walked past the secret hole on the side of the building where he stashed his phone. He came to a dead stop, and his heart nearly came up out of his throat. The area around the hole behind the water pipe looked as if it had been dug out with a sledgehammer.

Gravva realized instantly that in spite of all his precautions, he had been seen.

He quickly looked around and then knelt down. The phone was gone. If he couldn't get it back, he would be unable to contact the Poong brothers.

He straightened up and assured himself that he still had the diamonds, and that was what mattered. As long as I possess them, he thought, I truly call the shots.

That's when he came to a decision that turned out to be a bigger mistake than the first: he decided to alter the timetable. He wanted to get those diamonds now. If he couldn't speak with the Poongs, he would not feel safe waiting the three more days.

As they say in the West, he thought, Merry Christmas. To me.

Unfortunately for Gravva, he didn't know that he was being played.

He knew where Max's apartment was, and he was sure that the diamonds would be stashed there. He returned to his room first but didn't take off his heavy, hooded parka. He wasn't planning to stay for long.

Arkady wasn't in the room, and Gravva was certain that he was still on patrol somewhere in the complex or down in the vaults. Or drunk in a closet. He climbed the short ladder up to Arkady's bunk and lay on his back on the mattress. The bunk bed groaned under Gravva's 290 pounds, and he quickly set to work loosening a wooden panel in the wall, nearly hidden in a corner.

Excellent! He reached behind the panel and pulled out a gun. One of Arkady's many toys was there in his not-so-secret hiding place, just as Gravva knew it would be.

The Makarov PM was a straightforward semiautomatic, and Gravva checked to make sure that the clip was full and a bullet was chambered. He clumsily pushed the pistol into the pocket of his parka and carefully lowered himself back down the ladder to the floor.

He straightened up and quickly organized his thoughts. Taking the gun out of his pocket, he smashed the door lock a few times with the heavy pistol's butt until he heard a part break inside the simple lock's mechanism. There! His answer to Arkady's inevitable future question, "Where's my gun?" Simple: There was a break-in.

He stepped out into the dingy hall, closing the door behind him, and quickly made his way to the front door of the building and out into the Arctic air.

After a frozen walk, he reached Max's building. He had never been in Max's room, but he had visited another worker who was bunking down the hall. Putting his hand on the gun in his pocket, he knocked quietly on Max's door.

"Who?" asked a man on the other side.

"Gravva, Max." He waited for half a minute, and then the door opened. Max stood inside the small apartment with a ferocious scowl on his face. "What is it?" he growled menacingly.

Gravva, thrown off balance by Max's unexpected aggression, suddenly felt his nerve going soft. "I, uh, you..."

The knock on the door had sent Max's adrenaline into attack mode. When he saw the Makarov in Gravva's hand, he didn't hesitate. Max backed quickly into the room, grabbed a lumpy parcel from beneath his mattress, and sprinted quickly past the ungainly Mongolian who had suddenly become far too ambivalent in the intimacy of the small room to pull the trigger.

Gravva was shocked that he was suddenly standing alone, and that Max had taken off with the diamonds. Max was much faster than he was. Think, he said to himself. Where's he going with millions in the middle of the night? Only the apartment blocks are open. The rest of the facility is locked down—seriously locked down.

There's only one place he can hide that is always open and where there is some heat, Gravva reasoned. And it's just a few hundred meters down the road.

Max was already there, and he glanced back to see if Gravva was following. A single guard was sitting in the small shack at the edge of the snowplow paddock, where a dozen machines of various sizes were stored within a Quonset-type metal structure. Similar to a small airplane hangar, the roomy metal building had a large overhead door at one end.

Max walked quickly up to the shack and showed the guard the special laminated pass that Veshkin had given to him. He told the guard that Gravva was right behind him and would be there in a minute. The guard said, "Do I let him in too?"

Max looked at him and said, "Yes."

A moment later, he was inside the metal building.

Gravva carefully approached the snowplow paddock. He felt the gun in his pocket for the tenth time and approached the guard. Looking around, he was about to pull the weapon and shoot the man, but he saw the guard merely wave.

That was his last big mistake—he should have been suspicious of the easy, almost welcome access, but his brain was on overload, and he chalked it up to good fortune.

Inside the silent, dimly lit paddock, the twelve large snowplows were scattered in a random pattern like a frozen heard of giant white dinosaurs. Gravva virtually tiptoed among them, gun out and ready, listening and straining for a glimpse or a sound of Max.

He had almost reached the last huge snowplow that was pointed toward the large overhead door when he heard a whisper, "Gravva." At the exact moment he heard his name, the rumbling motor of the gigantic plow started up, and he saw a human figure hunched in the small driver's cabin above the tank treads and a few feet behind the monstrous plow blade.

An arm and hand came out of the small cabin, loosely holding a package. It looked like a pair of men's Jockey shorts, but very lumpy. As nervous as Gravva was, he nearly laughed.

"Come and get it," he heard a taunting voice over the noise of the snowplow's engine. Then the hand disappeared back into the tiny cabin.

Gravva was mostly shielded by the next plow over, and as he peeked over one of the treads, he came face to face with three objects that suddenly filled the space in front of him.

One object was the portable phone, still wrapped in plastic. The second object was another Makarov, aimed at his head. And the third object was holding the first two objects. It was Max Stepanov.

"Give me the gun. Slowly," Max growled. "And tell me right now who you're working for."

Gravva's brain went into the ionosphere. What! Who's in the snowplow? How?

He wrenched his face away from Max and stared at the small cabin on the plow. Arkady and his Kalashnikov rifle were framed in the small window.

"Up yours!" Arkady yelled out at him with a strange smile on his face. "You fat-ass, murderous *svinya*."

Gravva lost control then and started firing his gun. The first round blasted Max's gun from his hand and barely missed blowing his head off. Max's hand felt as if it had been hit by a baseball bat. He ducked behind another machine. A second bullet zipped within a few inches of Arkady. Max had a clear view of Arkady up in the cab as he started to aim his assault rifle, and he indicated with his hands not to shoot at Gravva.

The heavyset man was now frozen in fear behind one of the plows, and Max slowly worked his way to the other side of the giant white machine. Coming up behind Gravva, the noise of his footsteps drowned out by the loud snowplow, Max broke into a run and tackled the large man.

Gravva managed to hold on to his gun, but now he and Max were wrestling in front of the rumbling plow's blade.

Then Arkady put the huge machine in gear.

The plow started moving inexorably forward, and Max and Gravva were immediately pushed down onto the hard-packed snow and out through paddock's huge overhead door. The plow blade itself was almost six feet high, and the two grappling men scrambled and fell and rolled and got up and were knocked over again by the relentlessly advancing, curved blade. It was as if they were trapped in a half-pipe wave, but instead of surf, there was the gigantic, rounded plow blade pushing, pushing, pushing them forward.

Finally, starting to get dizzy from the mad, pushing plow, Max saw his opportunity.

When Gravva went down once again in front of the blade, Max lunged for the large man's gun and finally wrested it from his pudgy fist. Inexorably pushed along by the plow, Gravva tried to stay upright, and he made a comically unbalanced attempt to wrap his arms around his adversary.

Max viciously pulled on the reinforced, fur-lined hood of the large man's parka. He managed to impale the hood on one of the large, triangular studs that stuck out of the top of the plow blade like a giant, upward-pointing, triangular tooth.

He fell off Gravva, rolled, and was pushed farther along. Finally, he managed to get up, stumble out of the path of the unstoppable blade, and run alongside the giant, white machine.

Gravva was hanging like an overstuffed doll in front of the center of the plow, hoisted by the hood of his ensnared parka. His feet kicked a few inches above the ground, and his arms flailed in the air and banged against the curved plow at his back. Now he was screaming—something about this being Eddie's fault and something about three tits.

Arkady, up in the cab, knew what he had to do next.

It was all part of Max's plan...

The other night Max, in a deep funk, had walked silently under the gleaming stars and had seen Gravva retrieve his plastic-wrapped package from the secret place under the snow and behind the water pipe. He had followed Gravva and listened at the door of his room. He was shocked, stunned. The man had a phone. A phone!

That he was planning to kill Max came as no big surprise. He had heard the muttered names through Gravva's door: Eddie and...what? Three Tit? Who or what is *that*?

Max knew that he had to move fast and think fast.

This morning, he had approached Arkady, the armed guard, and confided in him. Max had laid out the whole truth to the man. He had reasoned that his fate was so fragile and his chance of survival so slim that telling his friend everything about his situation couldn't do much more harm.

He told Arkady that Gravva was going to kill him, so he needed to strike first and find out why and for whom. And until Veshkin had given him his special pass, he hadn't found a way to do it.

But now there was a way.

Arkady had listened carefully. The guard was razor-sharp with a weapon, but almost never sober. When Max told him that he had been ripped away from the one woman in his life that he ever truly loved, Arkady nearly broke down in tears over the typically tragic Russian story.

Then Arkady admitted that he had overheard everything down in the vault and, in his usual nighttime vodka stupor, may have told Gravva things he shouldn't have. He was mortally ashamed—almost physically wounded when he realized the gravity of his drunken betrayal. Max merely put an arm around his shoulder and said, "Forget it, Arkady. You may have done me a favor. Now I can expect my enemies to come straight to me—that is a great advantage."

The soldier in Arkady understood immediately. "And now I also understand the hold that skinny prick, Veshkin, has over you, Max." His eyes glazed. "Your woman, Max. He threatens to hurt your woman."

The knowledge of the stolen diamonds had no effect on Arkady—he was an action man, a soldier—not a hoarder of money or wealth. He was old Russia, pre-Communist Russia—a man a hundred years behind the times and happy for it.

He had spit on the ground then. "I will make this right, Max. I will help you get to the West. I know I will never leave Russia, but I feel that I'm owed some small satisfaction here in my frozen-ass life in the Great Icebox of Yakut."

Then Max told him his plan for Gravva. When he had finished, Arkady was energized: it was right up his alley.

Max squeezed the guard's shoulder and said, "Arkady, if I live to get to the West, I will owe it all to you. What can I promise you in return?"

The guard said, "I will think about it."

"And I will do it," Max vowed. Whatever *it* turns out to be.

"*Chorosho!*" Arkady had said with unalloyed joy.

"Aaeeh!" Gravva was screaming as the plow blade approached the edge of the diamond pit. It was an incredibly long, vertical drop with a vertiginously steep slope all the way to the bottom, one-third of a mile down. At the lip of the hole, it was almost three-quarters of a mile to the other side.

In the dark, the monstrous pit looked like the mouth of hell.

The plow was almost at the edge of the huge hole, and suddenly Gravva felt himself being lifted. Arkady was raising the plow blade, and it was now a good ten feet off the ground. Gravva hung from it like a fat, waving doll.

The ground beneath the waving doll fell away into black nothingness as the huge blade passed over the lip of the pit. The snowplow stopped moving forward when the front edges of its metal treads cleared the edge of the hole. Gravva, hanging over the abyss, looked down into the darkness and screamed again.

Max had been running next to the machine, and now, breathing heavily, he walked up to the edge of the monstrous hole and looked up and out at Gravva.

"Eddie and Three Tit," he yelled at the large waving body. "Who are they?"

Gravva's eyes were wide. His arms flailed madly.

"Who are they?" Max yelled again over the sound of the snowplow's engine. "Tell me, and we'll pull the plow back!"

"They...they're the..." But suddenly and without warning, the reinforced hood of his parka tore away from the rest of his coat, and Gravva Gleb took off like a giant, flying walrus into the Mir diamond pit, his arms and legs waving furiously. His round, writhing body dwindled rapidly in size and then disappeared into the abyss, into the black maw of the frozen asshole of the world.

Max heard the one long shrieking word, "Poooong..."

Then there was just the rumbling of the giant machine under the diamond-sharp stars.

Arkady jumped down from the plow's control cabin and walked up to Max, a strange smile on his face. He stood on the edge of the pit, looked into the darkness, and said, "*Prikolna*! That felt good."

Max looked over at Arkady and breathed the frozen air deeply. Then he looked down into the giant, black hole. "I have to admit, it did feel good," he found himself saying.

So I'm a devil, Max's inner voice grudgingly conceded. A devil with promises to keep.

Arkady looked into the pit for a minute or two and tossed out a few choice curses under his breath.

Then he spit into the darkness, turned to Max, and said, "Now I know what I want from you, Max." His normally vodka-clouded eyes were crystal-clear. Max braced himself for the request that he had vowed to honor.

Arkady looked straight at him and said, "When you get to the West, make love to a beautiful woman. For me."

"I will, Arkady." Max smiled. "I promise."

High above, the stars glittered like diamonds.

Then they climbed up to the small cabin on top of the plow, Arkady turned the giant machine around, and they rumbled off into the frozen night.

12

A REAL MAN

Every table in the Kronenhalle restaurant was filled with talking and laughing people, happy and content and filled with warm holiday bonhomie. Soft music filled the spaces between muted conversation and the clinking of glasses.

"A toast." He held up the slim champagne flute. Tiny lines of bubbles advanced up the inside of the glass.

"To...?"

He paused to consider. Then, "To Christmas, of course."

She picked up her glass and clicked it against his. "Merry Christmas."

They each took sips and set the glasses down. A waiter materialized at the table and politely handed each of them a menu. *"Bon apetit,"* he said, and then vanished.

"You were right, Soleil," said Dustin, perusing the menu, "this restaurant does bump up against the outer limits of an expense account." He showed his straight white teeth.

Must be a whopper of an account, thought Soleil, as she observed his dark Brioni suit jacket over the open-collared Versace silk shirt. Platinum cuff links winked from the precise inch of shirt showing at the ends of his sleeves.

Dustin had been doing his own observing. He was impressed by the rich wood tones of the elegantly under-stated eatery, and his mood was further elevated when he felt the admiring eyes of the other diners on him as he strode behind the maître d' to the table for two. He some-what resembled the Irish actor who had played Remington Steele on American television.

After a few minutes, Soleil appeared at the front of the restaurant and immediately saw Dustin. As she walked between the tables, Dustin realized that he had just been drastically upstaged.

Soleil, head held high as was her way, wore a tai-lored, amethyst-hued dress. The matching earrings were a Christmas present from Camille and Kurt. Her little dia-mond cross hung at the center of her modest cleavage and winked in the low light as she walked confidently on laven-der pumps. Her hair was as it always was—straight, shining, and hanging past her shoulders.

Her only other jewelry was her eyes.

By the time she reached the table, the conversations in the restaurant had dwindled away to a whisper. Dustin stood as she approached, and a smorgasbord of emotions went through his mind. Some of those emotions were as primal as they come.

She gave Dustin's cheek a quick kiss. A white-jacketed waiter, seemingly appearing out of midair, pulled her chair back for her, and she sat down.

Dustin was stunned. He had been delighted with the way she looked the night before at the lake, but now—well! This was the kind of woman with whom he should be seen in public.

And he knew where they were going with their blossoming relationship.

He sat down opposite her and said, "You look beautiful."

"Thanks, Dustin. So do you. I mean handsome, of course."

The sommelier materialized at tableside with a bottle of Taittinger Brut and a tripod with an ice bucket. He expertly freed and popped the cork, handing it to Dustin to run under his nose. Dustin took his time sniffing the cork, and then nodded.

The steward poured three-quarters of an inch of champagne in Dustin's crystal flute and waited while Dustin went through the smelling and tasting ritual. Soleil watched the small pantomime from across the table. Finally, after Dustin nodded his approval, the sommelier carefully filled the two thin flutes, bowed slightly, and backed away.

After they had toasted and ordered their meal, Dustin settled back in his chair, draping one elbow over its back. With his other hand, he massaged the stem of his champagne flute. He looks like a model, especially in that pose, thought Soleil. Very handsome.

"I'm glad we met," he offered. "This restaurant was an excellent choice, Soleil. I checked it out—it's one of the highest-rated restaurants in Europe." He grinned through his chiseled jaw and Soleil thought she was at a fashion show.

"You said no limit to the price, Dustin. I didn't want to disappoint."

"I doubt that you even know *how* to disappoint, Soleil," he said.

She breathed a quiet laugh and looked into his eyes. "Everyone knows how to disappoint, Dustin."

She was mildly surprised when Dustin seemed shaken by her innocent parry. What's that about? she wondered for a second.

"Tell me about yourself, Dustin," she asked, knowing that most men appreciated that question. Of course, it had the desired effect.

Soleil nodded and smiled, and her face showed her interest at all the right moments as Dustin enthusiastically reeled off the inventory of his thirty-year life.

Born in Edinburgh, father a barrister, mother a hospital administrator, educated in London and New York, got a job at Barclay's through a family friend, and then was "bought" from that company by the Royal Bank of Scotland, where he was on an accelerating fast track as a rising star in the bank's European global mergers and acquisitions division.

"Hence, my latest assignment to Zurich," he said. "At first I balked at the move, but since yesterday, I'm thanking my lucky stars that it happened to me." He tilted his head slightly and locked his green eyes with Soleil's blues.

"No wife?" asked Soleil. "No lassie back in Scotland, crying into her tartan until your return?"

He chuckled. "No, no wife. Not yet. And as to heartbroken lassies in Scotland, well, they'll live." Then he said, "And what about you? What's your story?"

She took a forkful of salad and chewed thoughtfully for a minute. Then she said, "Well, I was born in Quebec. That's in Canada, y'know."

He rolled his eyes and she smiled.

"Anyway, I was born in Quebec, the youngest of six children, finished high school, and went right to work at a mine."

"Mine?"

She sighed inside and said, "It was in Montana. My father worked there too, but he was killed in a cave-in."

Dustin gave her an "I'm sorry" look.

"Then I went to New York and worked in the jewelry business on Forty-Seventh Street for a couple of years with some lovely Jewish people—they sort of took me in when I needed a little help."

"Are you Jewish?" Dustin asked with a strange look on his face.

"No, I'm Catholic." What was that look? "And not a very good one, I'm afraid. What about you, Dustin?"

After a brief pause, he said, "I'm an agnostic. And one who knows that when religion is brought up in a conversation, it's time to turn to another topic."

Soleil shrugged. Fair enough. "In New York, I met and got engaged to someone. I came here to Europe with him, but we're no longer together." How's that for making a pretzel of the truth? she said to herself. "I stayed here in Switzerland."

"What do you do here?"

"I have a small business. It started out as a metals trading firm, but now it's a holding company."

"Now, that's interesting," he said.

What, she said to herself, suddenly defensive for no discernable reason. It was boring up to now, Dustin? Typical male, she thought. Mention metals and trading, and they perk up. It must be a testosterone cue or something.

"Tell me about the metals," he said with enthusiasm.

"There's not much to tell, just that I learned how large deals are made and who the big companies are that make them. Dustin, I'm really not very involved in that anymore."

He looked a touch crestfallen, but then said, "All right, be cagy if you must." He smiled and said, "Now you tell me—any boyfriends or fiancés I should know about?"

He looked expectantly into her eyes, picked up his champagne flute, and took a sip. Soleil noticed that he had long fingers with perfectly trimmed nails.

A breath seemed to catch in her throat, and she had a sudden memory of another hand holding a wineglass. But that hand had much thicker, rougher, stronger fingers with heavy, worn, square nails—the hand of a bricklayer or a laborer or a farmer—the hand of the man who had saved her, who loved her.

Max's hand.

God, I missed Max's hands, she thought.

She shook her head for a second as if to rid it of the unwanted, bittersweet memory that had rushed in uninvited. She had promised herself that she would move on.

"Well?" asked Dustin, breaking into her reverie.

"Oh, I'm sorry, Dustin." What did he want to know? Oh, yeah. "No, no boyfriends or fiancés—at the moment." A smile. Again: I have to move on.

"That was a lot of thinking," he said. "You're sure, now?"

She nodded. Then she picked up her glass and said, "To new friends."

After taking a sip, she said, "Where did you study in New York?"

"What?"

"You said you were educated in New York. What school, what college?"

He hesitated for a second. "New York University."

"Oh. In the Square?"

"Pardon?"

"You know, Washington Square. C'mon Dustin, how long ago were you there?"

"Oh, right, sure." He focused his sexiest stare at her. "I was distracted. You know how distracting you are." Up came the almost empty champagne glass and then the attentive sommelier was suddenly standing near the table again, holding a second bottle.

"I think I've had enough champagne, Dustin. At least for now."

Dustin signaled the sommelier to leave the bottle anyway in the tableside ice bucket. "I'll work on it," he said.

I like him, she thought, even though he has a touch of the "me" virus. I guess it's not fatal, and someone so good-looking, well, it happens.

And he seems like he's accomplished, very accomplished for his age. And I've never seen a man who dresses so well, keeps himself so perfect: every hair in place.

And he likes me, there can be no doubt. I can deal with good looks. The women at some of the tables in here haven't taken their eyes off him, but that's easy to handle.

She took another sip of champagne. I guess I should be feeling pretty good about myself.

She shrugged inside.

Dustin was the perfect gentleman for the rest of the meal. When they were done, he retrieved their coats from the check booth, and they walked out into the starry night.

A Mercedes with a driver was waiting across the street. "What an expense account!" Soleil quipped when she saw the car and driver.

"May I drop you at your door?" Dustin asked.

"No, Dustin, not tonight. I don't mind walking, and after that dinner, I could use the exercise."

He seemed deflated. "I'll cover my eyes when we get close to your house. I won't look—don't tell me where you live. Whisper the address to the driver."

Soleil sighed inside. "Dustin, we just met. I like you. I'm sure we'll become good friends." She moved a step closer to him and kissed him on the lips. He tried to make it last, reaching his arm out to put it behind her back and bring her closer to him, but she had already pulled back.

"Call me," she said. "Good night, Dustin." She turned and, in a moment, was gone around a corner.

Dustin stood at the side of the Mercedes, a raft of different emotions floating across his mind. Finally, he got into the car and told the driver to take him back to his apartment.

He watched out the window as the lights of Zurich passed by.

I'll call you, Soleil, he thought. And I'll sleep with you too. Soon. And after that?

I guess you'll just have to leave it to me.

"Hello, Ballas."

Kurt recognized the voice instantly. He had spoken to Walter Burnes from his hospital room in Zurich, and Walter had been all ears. "Morning, Detective. How's the Windy City?"

Burnes found the matchbook he was searching for, glanced out the window at the early morning snow falling on Chicago, and lit his first Camel of the day. "I have something new on Zoe Kimball, and I want to share it with you."

Kurt looked over at Camille, who had just come out of the bathroom. She was dressed in a black-and-white ski outfit. Kurt had made light of his quickly healing shoulder and was determined to try skiing while they were in Switzerland. Camille had protested for a minute or so, but then deemed it useless—the man was a man and he knew his limitations, so they had decided to travel to Engelberg on Soleil's recommendation.

"Sure, Walter. Go ahead," Kurt said into the phone. Why not be on a first-name basis? he thought.

Apparently, the familiarity didn't bother Burnes. "We combed the woman's records and her past associations. Not a pretty list of accomplishments or friends."

He paused for a moment, as if gathering his thoughts, Then he said, "We found something of interest in her apartment. Money. A lot of it."

"What?"

"Yeah, Kurt, I suspected all along that someone paid Zoe Kimball to kill you. She seemed to have had no other reason. You're lucky you're alive." He paused for a second, and then he said bluntly, "You still don't have any idea who might want you dead?"

"No," Kurt said with bitterness. "Maybe it was drug money. You said she had a bad history."

"Yeah, maybe. But there was something strange about the money."

"Strange?"

"It wasn't dollars. It was like a money buffet: German marks, British pounds, and French and Swiss francs. The equivalent of twenty thousand dollars. It appears as if this chick was heading for Europe, Kurt." He paused. "Europe, where you are. Coincidence?"

"I don't know, Walter." Then he said, "If it's that important, I can come back to the States. I was only going to be here a short while longer anyway."

This guy's just an unlucky schmuck who's hated by some very bad guys, Burnes said to himself. Ah, what the hell. "No, stay there, Ballas. But please, if you think of anyone or anything that I need to know about, call me, right?"

"Sure, Walter."

"And don't forget to bring me back a Swiss cheese."

"Brie," he reminded the detective, and hung up.

Yeah. Burnes held the Camel in front of his face between two thick fingers. Brie.

"Someone gave that woman European money," Kurt said to Camille. "Whoever wanted me killed is somewhere in Europe, lives here. If he was in the US he would have just paid her in dollars and left the currency transactions to her."

After a reflective moment, Camille said, "I need to make a phone call."

"Hello."

"Hi, it's me," said Camille. "How did it go last night?"

"Good." Soleil was about to leave her apartment and now was glad she had picked up the phone.

"That's it? *Good*? Don't even try it. You'd better give me a massive amount of details, down to the label on his tie..."

"He didn't wear a tie."

"Really? At that fancy restaurant? Hmm. He looked like he knew better."

"He was dressed beautifully—better than I was."

"And...?" Camille pushed.

"And I like him. He's a pretty nice guy."

"Did anything else happen?"

Soleil sighed. "Yes, Camille. Right there in the restaurant on Table 12. We stripped naked and went at it between the salad and the main course. Some of the other customers complained when the dishes from our table went flying across the room. Next stupid question?"

"That's a no, right?"

"Right."

"But you *are* seeing him again?"

"Is there any way this conversation can take a different course?"

"Yes. I had an idea." She told Soleil about what the Chicago detective had told Kurt. "When I heard that the dead girl had a big hunk of European money in her apartment, I thought you might call your inspector friend and ask if she found something like that in the Asian girl's place. If they did, it would tie them together, and maybe bring us closer to getting answers."

Soleil's eyes widened a fraction. "*Très bon*! Good idea! You should have been a cop."

"I've had enough to do with them via my associations with Jake and the other fine gentlemen who've passed through my life before Kurt showed up."

"I'll call the inspector now. Are you still going skiing?"

"We're leaving now. Have a nice day with Remington Steele."

It was useless to pursue that line of patter, so Soleil just said, "Have fun," and hung up. She looked up the inspector's phone number in her little address book and dialed.

The call had to be transferred once or twice, but finally the familiar voice came on the phone. "*Ja*?"

"Hi, Ulrika, it's Soleil Tangiere."

"Oh, hello, Soleil. I only have a minute."

"I found something out that might help your investigation into the dead Asian girl." She told her what Walter Burnes had said about Zoe Kimball and the European payoff money.

Ulrika Sonnenreich listened and jotted down notes with great interest. When Soleil was done, Ulrika said, "We found out that the Asian woman's name is Li Hua Chung. She had been living alone in a small apartment here in Zurich on a monthly lease since the beginning of November. We were lucky to have found out this much so far."

Then she said, "And yes, we found the equivalent of twenty thousand US dollars in her apartment in various currencies, as you describe. Soleil, you just tied the two together. Thank you."

"Don't thank me. My sister suggested I call you with this information." Then she gave her Walter Burnes's name at the Chicago Police Department. Ulrika said she would call him as soon as she hung up.

"I would also like to talk to Mr. Ballas again." The Zurich police had questioned Kurt in the hospital, but he had been unable to come up with anyone who wanted him dead. "Can he come to the station to speak with me? Just a few questions, now that we have your new information."

"I'll ask him. He's out of Zurich today, but he'll be back tomorrow. As I've told you, he's my sister's boyfriend. Whatever she asks of him, I'm sure he'll do."

"Thank you, Soleil. And thank you for your rare consideration the other day. If you need me for anything, let me know."

They said their good-byes, and Soleil hung up the phone. She suddenly had an odd, vague premonition.

Something in that short conversation had pricked her subconscious, but try as she might, she couldn't bring it to the surface. It'll come to me, she thought. These things always have a way of circling back into my mind.

She shrugged, grabbed her coat, and left the apartment.

When she got to her office and opened the door, Yvonne was there, which was no surprise.

So was Yvonne's barely-out-of-his-teens friend, André. Surprise!

"Hi," said Soleil, giving Yvonne a questioning look. "Hi, André."

"Allo!" He grinned and shrugged around a bit with his hands in the pockets of his voluminous camo pants. The back of his green, hooded sweatshirt had a rough stencil of Michael Jackson moonwalking across a giant white glove. Yvonne stood next to him, a slight look of guilt on her face.

"Oh, sorry if I'm interrupting something," Soleil said with laughter behind her eyes. "I'll just go out and come back in a while. What—two, three hours, Yvonne?" Her glorious smile filled the office.

André looked from Yvonne's face to Soleil's. Then, his eyes drifted slowly down Soleil's body to her shoes, across to Yvonne's feet, and up to rest on the front of her half-open blouse. *Sensationnel!* he thought. I may not understand ze English, but I know ze chick heaven when I fall into it!

Soleil looked at Yvonne and then at André and then back at Yvonne. "Really?"

Yvonne couldn't hide the sheepish look on her face. She said to André in French, "Time for me to go to work. Maybe I'll see you tomorrow. Maybe."

He rolled his eyes at her, and at Soleil. Then he whispered something in Yvonne's ear. She scowled at him, walked behind her desk, and rummaged in her bag. Then she handed the man-child a few francs.

He kissed her on both cheeks and left.

"Really?" Soleil asked again, after the door had closed.

Yvonne quickly regained her dignity. "*Jaloux?* That means 'jealous' in French, just in case you don't speak that language."

Soleil was about to hurl a particularly raunchy Québécois epithet at her when the phone rang.

Yvonne gave Soleil a smug little smile, picked up the phone, and said, "Tangiere International." She listened for a few seconds, said, "One moment, please," and pressed the hold button on the phone. She turned to Soleil and said, "Dustin Magill."

So soon? Soleil said to herself. Why the rush?

"Should I tell him you're not here?" asked Yvonne.

"No, no, I'll talk to him." She went into her small office, sat down in her desk chair, and picked up the phone. "Hello."

"Hi, Soleil. I know, it's too much, too soon, but—"

She interrupted him. "Dustin, I think it is."

"I agree completely," he said in a rush. "And I don't want to see you tonight, but I just wanted to know if you'd like to see Tina Turner."

"What?"

"Tina Turner. She has a concert scheduled here in Zurich this Saturday night, and I have two tickets. Will you go with me?"

Oh. She liked Tina Turner. And she was getting to like him. "You don't want to?" she said.

"Don't want to what?"

"You don't want to see me tonight?"

Silence for a minute. "Is that what I said?"

"Yes."

There was pause on the other end. "I didn't think you wanted to go on another date so soon."

"I didn't say a date. I'm going to be at the lake again tonight to skate. It's my new form of exercise. That's all. If you're there skating too, maybe I'll see you." She waited a moment. "Otherwise, it's on for Saturday night."

"What time will you be at the lake?"

She told him and hung up.

She turned and saw Yvonne leaning against the door-frame. She was shaking her head.

"What?" said Soleil.

Yvonne came into the room and sat down. She looked at Soleil for a minute. "Remember what happened to me in Geneva?"

Soleil was suddenly shaken. "You mean Fiona?"

Yvonne nodded. She had been tortured and almost killed by a woman named Fiona who was bent on Soleil's destruction. Soleil had felt responsible from that day forward.

"What about it?" Soleil asked.

"When that woman came into your office that day looking for you, I immediately sensed that something was wrong—even before she opened her mouth. It didn't take long for me to be proven right."

Soleil waited. She thought she saw where this was going.

Yvonne went on. "When I saw this Dustin the other night, I had a similar kind of feeling."

Soleil began to protest, but Yvonne overrode her. "No, no, don't. I'm sure he's just fine—a good man, perhaps. But sometimes I sense things in the air, like that day I saw Fiona." She looked at the floor. "I'm sorry. I can't be silent about something that I feel might hurt you. I can't."

Soleil saw that a tear was about to drop from one of Yvonne's eyes. I'm lucky, she thought. I'm lucky that Yvonne cares—lucky that she's alive today. She said, "Thanks, Yvonne. I don't see that in Dustin." She shrugged and went on, "But look at my record with men. Horrible." She sighed. "I'll be careful, I promise."

But Yvonne was too distressed to stop. "I don't know. I'm just afraid for you, Soleil. And..."

"What, Yvonne?"

She hesitated and wiped her eyes. "Max."

Soleil's shoulders sagged. "What about Max?"

Yvonne lowered her eyes.

Soleil continued, "I know. Everyone thinks I should just either fold up and die or enter a convent. Let me tell you something, Yvonne." She started to feel her own emotions rising quickly and getting the better of her. "Let me tell you something. If, just *if*, Max can't call me for any reason, or *if* he's found someone else to love, or if *anything*, I know this one thing: he wouldn't want me to be unhappy, to be alone, to dwell on him. He would want me to live."

Yvonne looked up. "That's because *he's* the real man," she said quietly.

Soleil felt frozen. Why couldn't everyone leave her alone about this? Nothing, no one could help her about Max.

"Oh, damn it, Yvonne! Don't ever mention Max to me again!"

She stood, quickly gathered her purse, and walked out. Yvonne heard the door to the corridor slam.

"Max *is* the real man," Yvonne repeated to herself, sitting alone in the office.

"Oh, yeah, baby, oh yeah—you are a real man! Oh, baby, grrrrr!"

"Wait! No, no, you're not doing that exactly right!"

Katia Koziashvili stopped bouncing up and down on Boris Veshkin. Now what? Now what does this nauseating snake want me to do?

"Move a little there!" he ordered.

"Where? Here?"

"*Nyet, pizda*," he said, pushing her roughly.

"Here?"

"Yes, there."

Oh great, she said to herself. How's *this* going to work? Yechh!

"You're not saying it!" he growled.

"Oh, sorry." *Mudak*. "Oh, Boris! You're such a man, such a real man. Yesss! Ooh! Ahh!"

"That's more like it."

Katia questioned how low a filthy slut she had really become in the name of freedom, money, and revenge. This gross worm had better pay me everything he promised or I swear, I'll cut off *his* worm and stomp on it with studded boots.

"Say it more, Katia. Say it more!"

"Real man. Ahh. Ooh."

Later on, after the worm was snoring like a chainsaw, Katia took a hot shower, dressed, and went downstairs. She needed a long walk in the cold air.

Yechhh!

"Where is he?" Three was not a happy man.

"I don't know, Three." Neither was Eddie.

The Poong brothers hadn't heard from their man, Gravva, in almost three days. They couldn't call the military phone lest they give themselves away, and by now, he was to have murdered Max Stepanov, stolen the already-stolen diamonds and be ready to rendezvous with his transport at midnight on the outskirts of the Mir.

Gravva had the only phone.

And he hadn't called.

Eddie and Three had a sinking feeling that they were screwed. There was a chance the phone went dead or went missing, Eddie had theorized, but inside he was already on Plan B. He paced around Three's living room.

Three Tit Poong's house clung precipitously to the hillside off Magazine Gap below Lugard Road on Peak Road, high above Hong Kong. It was hugely expensive when he bought it ten years ago in 1979, and was worth a small fortune now.

Though he could easily be mistaken for someone of garish tastes, especially when it came to women, Three Tit had a hidden side—he loved art and its manifold expressions. One of those expressions was his gorgeous house.

Three paced with Eddie inside the modern living room, which was a study in rare woods and finishes and subtle lighting. It lacked the flamboyant dragon and flame motifs, which tended to dominate contemporary Asian interior design. Here and there, delicate jade sculptures posed on slender alabaster columns, their exquisite artistry and craftsmanship highlighted by precisely aimed halogens mounted in the ceiling.

The brothers stopped pacing and stared out the living room window at the spectacular view—the lights of the city and harbor spread out below them in all their glory.

Three looked at Eddie and suddenly felt tired. Tired and angry. His mind wandered to his two daughters, both in their teens, who lived on Taiwan. Sporadic attempts to keep in touch with them were routinely thwarted by their respective mothers, and lately had been ignored by the girls themselves.

His daughters had learned to despise him, and he couldn't completely blame them. Three was not one to pretend that he was someone or something else, and being a good father was far down on his list of personal accomplishments. He knew that his other interests superseded family—it was just his way. But sometimes in the middle of the night, he would wake up in a sweat and feel the yearning for his daughters pierce the armor over his heart.

One day he might change; he should change. He would see...

He caromed the gold toothpick around the inside of his mouth and eyed his brother again. Eddie had never married and had no children. At least none that he knew of. Who was better off?

Click, click.

"The big question now," Three broke his reverie. "The big question is: what happens if Gravva doesn't reach Ulan Bator?"

Eddie kept looking out at the view. In every cell of his body, he knew it was over for Gravva.

He turned to his brother. "The moment our transporter can get to a phone, he'll call us, whether Gravva is with him or not. That should be very soon."

Eddie turned and sat down heavily in a chair. That idiot Gravva. All right. Time is flying. He said to Three Tit, "Let's go to Zurich. Now."

Three nodded, stood up, and walked into his bedroom. He picked up the bedside phone and started making travel arrangements.

Ten minutes later, their transporter got a call through from outside the patrolled boundaries of the Mir. Gravva Gleb never showed, he said.

In fact, he was dead.

Round and round the skaters went.

"You don't mind that I showed up?"

"If I didn't want to see you, I wouldn't have told you I'd be here."

He maneuvered around her in a circle as they glided along.

They made small talk and skated fast and then skated slowly and finally almost came to a standstill on the ice. He put his arms around her waist, and they slowly twirled in one spot. He focused his green eyes on her sapphire ones and very slowly brought his lips close to hers.

She looked inside herself once at the chaos in her soul and then she kissed him. They nurtured and explored the kiss while the wave of skaters drifted past them.

Afterward, when they sat on a lakeside bench unlacing their skates, Dustin said, "Where would you like to go after this?"

She looked at him with a slight smile and said, "My place."

He smiled, and his green eyes shone.

"And *you're* going to *your* place," she said.

His face fell. "But I..."

She put a finger on his lips and said, "Not tonight, Dustin."

He started to say something, but she said, "Maybe tomorrow night. Just not tonight—let's give it one more day."

"One more day, and then I'm yours?"

She looked at him. "No. Maybe." She shrugged noncommittally.

On the way back to his apartment alone, he said aloud, "Oh, Soleil Tangiere, there're no 'maybe's about it." There was a strange smile on his face.

A lump of coal.

That's all that phone is to me, Max thought with anger.

Without a code sequence, he couldn't make any calls at all, and there must be a million possible combinations. And Gravva must have had that sequence memorized—he and Arkady had searched the room and found nothing.

Max was walking in the brutal, frozen wind from the sorting facility to his small apartment for the last time; his thermal coat felt heavy and oppressive. The idea that tomorrow he might be in the West, in Switzerland, was counterbalanced by the feelings of dread about what lay ahead in the next twenty-four hours.

He let himself into the apartment and unceremoniously got into the small bed.

This is where I've ended up, he said bitterly to himself.

The end of the line.

Tomorrow, I will either be in the West. I will finally be my own man again...

Or I will be dead.

A snowmobile driven by a silent, heavily bundled driver with a Kalashnikov slung over his shoulder met Max at the outer perimeter gates of the Mir at 6:00 a.m.

After flashing the laminated pass that Veshkin had given him, Max got on the backseat of the machine and they headed directly to the military airstrip two miles west of the mining installation. Light snow was falling from the still-dark sky. The driver dropped Max off at the base's manned security gate. Max produced the special card again from his coat pocket and was directed to a small building at one end of the seemingly endless landing strip.

Inside, three soldiers asked him to remove his insulated parka and almost all of his other clothing and don a flight suit, complete with an oxygen helmet. In the men's locker room, he took off the diamond shorts and jammed them into one of the suit's zippered pockets. No way was he going to sit in those things for four thousand miles.

He sat at a metal table with the three soldiers, who went over the things he had to know for the flight. There were just a few. They were mostly concerned that Max touched nothing unless he had to eject from the plane. In that case, he would probably die anyway. The soldiers laughed. Max didn't. Everyone smoked.

At eight o'clock, he heard the whining sound of an aircraft and the soldiers who had been sitting and smoking with him rose and escorted him outside to the edge of the airstrip.

The Sukhoi Su-15 Flagon Interceptor was the sleekest aircraft Max had ever seen. It was sixty-five feet long, with a small cockpit peeking from the top of its long, tapered fuselage. Below the cockpit on either side were huge, rectangular air intakes, and below the tail at the back were two giant, blackened side-by-side exhausts.

Surprisingly warm in the insulated flight suit, he climbed the wheeled ladder and was helped into the plane.

The three soldiers scoured the plane, made maintenance checks and conducted their refueling procedure.

Max jammed himself into the single seat in front of the pilot, and the ejection lever between his legs was carefully and menacingly pointed out to him. He was told that if he had to pee, he should just pee. Great, just great, he thought.

A soldier checked Max's oxygen one last time, the cockpit canopy was lowered into place by its servo motor, the pilot behind him tapped his shoulder and showed him an upraised thumb, and the plane lurched forward toward the end of the snowy airstrip.

At the end of the runway, the plane turned, and Max saw the double line of lights converging ahead in the distance. In his earphones, he heard the pilot's cheery voice. "OK, Max, hold on to your lunch," and for the first time in his life, Max learned what the term "blast off" really meant.

He had the terrifying feeling that a giant hand had slammed him back in his seat, and the ground lights on either side of the cockpit instantly became two unbroken red lines. Suddenly, he was violently upended—it felt as if his feet pointed straight up at the sky and the already heavy hand pushed even harder.

Before he could decide whether to yell or to pray or to try to pass out, the plane rolled viciously to the left and kept rolling, the earth and the giant black pit of the Mir were below, now above, and now below again as the pilot had his fun of the morning. Max fought with everything he had to keep from throwing up. He thanked God that he hadn't had a bite to eat since yesterday afternoon.

In no time flat, the jet was at almost 50,000 feet and traveling just under the speed of sound. They would have flown twice as fast, but only high-priority military planes with nuclear payloads got permission to go supersonic over land in the Soviet Union.

The crystal-clear sky he was flying through was starting to lighten on the horizon, and above, through the clear canopy, a billion stars blazed.

After an hour, just as Max was finally getting used to the ride—actually starting to enjoy it—the plane suddenly felt like it was plunging, and in ten minutes, it was on the ground at the first of two army bases where it had to land for refueling. Its range between fill-ups was only 1,800 miles.

Finally, after two more heart-pounding takeoffs and landings, the needle-nosed jet was on the ground at the Ljubljana army base in Slovenia. It had taken just over six hours to travel almost four thousand miles.

The canopy tilted up, and a soldier helped a shaky Max down the ladder. The miraculously bored-looking pilot tossed him a final thumbs-up, and Max headed to a waiting UAZ-469, the Russian equivalent of a jeep.

He was handed a bag with his clothing and his ID, and after changing into his diamond-filled jockeys and civilian clothes in an unmarked barracks, he was unceremoniously hustled back to the UAZ.

"Where are we going?" he asked the driver.

"Real airport," was all he got from the taciturn corporal behind the wheel.

Max was silently jubilant: the Ljubljana airport. Maybe there'll be a phone there that has international capabilities. Maybe.

He must call her.

And then—he scarcely breathed—and then: the West.

13

BLINKING LIGHT

Camille wasn't one to hold back her opinions.

"It's your life, Soleil. It's just that—"

"It's just, what, Camille? I appreciate your concern, and I love you for it, but sometimes you lack limits."

"I just have a bad feeling about Dustin. So does Yvonne."

They were walking on the street near her office, and Soleil was feeling better. She was looking forward to the afternoon and evening, and nothing was going to derail it. She was not sure where it might lead, but she wanted to find out. Maybe that was her downfall, but it was what it was.

Soleil had asked Camille to do a little shopping with her for her apartment. She knew that Camille and Kurt would be leaving after New Year's Day, and she wanted to make the most of what time was left. Kurt had taken a cab to the police station to speak with Inspector Sonnenreich, which left the two sisters with a chance to talk.

"I like Kurt, Camille. A lot," Soleil said to change the subject. "He's quiet and strong, and what you see is what you get." She skirted a small snow pile on the sidewalk.

"I'm falling for him, Soleil. Too bad I had to wait thirty-four years to find him. But now that I have, I'm not going to let him go. When we get back to the States, we're going to move in together. And that feels good."

"It looks like he's crazy about you." Soleil eyed her. "And I'm not going to tell you to 'be careful' or 'take your time' or anything like that. You know what you're doing. I can't get inside your head."

"All right, touché, I get the point."

They walked a block or so, and Soleil said, "How'd Kurt do with the skiing yesterday?"

Camille laughed. "You should have been there! He insisted on skiing, despite his shoulder, so he went out onto the kiddie slope. He was all arms and legs flailing around, falling on his butt. The little Swiss kids who were zooming by him like pros were cracking up. He became 'the Kurt Show' for them. Hysterical."

Camille rolled her eyes. "And then Mr. Macho suggested we try something harder, so we took the cable car to the top of Mount Titlis. One look from the summit and he decided to take the tram back down the mountain." She paused. "I skied it, of course."

"Of course."

"Oh, by the way. Do you know someone named Stefan?"
Soleil stopped in her tracks and looked at her.

"He skied down with me while Kurt took the tram." Camille narrowed her eyes and gave her younger sister a look. Soleil just stared at her.

"A real good skier." She made the comment sound off-hand. "When we got to the bottom of the run, he made a pretty tempting pass at me—said he reminded me of someone he knew." Another look. "I let that hot, young man down as gently as I could, Soleil. Then Kurt showed up." A happy little grin. "And then we left."

Camille raised her eyebrows and, in an exasperated voice, said, "Stefan?"

"Come on," said Soleil. "I don't know what you're talking about." She pointed to a café across the street. "Let's get some cocoa. After that I'm going to meet Dustin."

Camille shrugged and then nodded. "Whatever you say, Soleil."

Three Tit Poong was about to murder his brother.

That was because Eddie Poong was about to murder everyone else—a dozen passengers, a few of the flight attendants, even the pilots.

Everyone.

Eddie knew this was bound to happen, but he didn't care—he had no control over himself when he had to endure the torture of flying. He loathed it.

It wasn't any particular incident on the fourteen-hour, nonstop SwissAir flight from Hong Kong to Zurich that set him off. It was just that Eddie was a natural, dyed-in-the-wool aerophobe—scared to death of any kind of flying—and the worst airline passenger in Asia, as Three was quick to point out.

He was sharp and clever on the ground, but once above ten thousand feet, Eddie became a brain-dead, out-of-control force that no one wanted to reckon with.

Eddie could never sleep on a plane—could never contemplate that possibility. In fact, he woke up his brother three times just to annoy him. How can that dog with the third eye in the middle of his chest sleep like that? Eddie thought. He could sleep through a typhoon. Dog.

The most harrowing part of the flight for Eddie was its last hour or so. He felt as if his body was exploding from the inside out with nervous, itching, excess energy and raw, animal fear. He growled at anyone who even deigned to glance at him.

Fortunately for most of the passengers and crew, he and Three Tit were in the first-class section in a row consisting only of their two, plush seats. Nevertheless, Eddie managed to make a frightening nuisance of himself to everyone else in the front of the plane.

When the large jet landed in Zurich and he was finally able to deplane, he shoved his way to the front exit door, almost knocking over three hapless passengers who'd had the temerity to get to the exit first.

A moment later, he was off the plane.

With complete disregard for where he was or where he was going and oblivious to the angry cries of the people he shoved out of his way, he virtually charged out of the terminal after a nerve-racking harangue with the customs agent, who, after one look at this maniac, made sure to take his precise Swiss time.

Now Eddie Poong stood under the terminal overhang breathing in lungsful of cold Swiss air. He looked left and right and realized that his brother wasn't with him. He started to get a grip, breathe a bit slower. After five minutes, he turned and walked back into the terminal and nearly collided with Three Tit, who was carrying their two small suitcases. Three had had no problem politely clearing customs with both of their carry-ons.

But he was not in a good mood.

"*Bèndàn!* Idiot!" Three growled at Eddie. This wasn't funny. His brother may be a smart, dangerous, murderous, ruthless, unstable maniac, but Three was not afraid of him. Never was, never would be. That's what makes us work well together, thought Three.

And of course, Three considered himself to be the smarter brother and the handsomer one. Every whore in Kowloon knew *that*.

Without giving Eddie a chance to reply, Three barreled on angrily. "We're in Europe. *We're* the *laowai* now. Don't make it difficult, at least not for me. I don't give a snake's rectum what you do to yourself on a plane, but don't embarrass me here on the ground." He stuck his gold toothpick in his mouth, and it commenced its annoying little click-clicking routine across his teeth.

Eddie screwed a dangerous look onto his face that said, "You're a dead man," but it fazed Three not a bit. Three reached past his brother and opened the back door of a cab that had pulled up in the taxi queue behind Eddie's back. The old driver slowly came around to take their luggage, which he deposited in the trunk, while the Poong brothers settled into the backseat.

Three gave Old Gregor a slip of paper that said "Baur au Lac."

That hotel should just *give* me one of their cars, Gregor said to himself. It seemed like the whole damned UN was showing up that week and staying at that hotel. Gregor just couldn't wait to see what kind of tip the Chinese delegation in the backseat would fork over. *Dermo!*

Eddie had finally reverted to his old self. He calmly said, "We have to find Veshkin before he gets to Max Stepanov." Three looked out the window.

"Then we have to go get our diamonds."

Three's toothpick picked up speed.

Click, click, click.

"Give me money."

The slim hand was extended across the small, round table in the clean and pleasant café. "A lot. I earned it."

Boris Veshkin had to admit that Katia had done some "work," but he felt that she had gotten at least as much ecstatic pleasure out of it as he had. Why should he give her money for *her* pleasure? Well, to be the brutally fair person that he was, it *was* part of the deal.

He hesitantly reached into his jacket pocket, extracted a roll of Swiss francs, and started carefully counting some out. Katia's slim hand quickly grabbed the entire wad, and it instantly vanished below the table.

Before Veshkin could object, she leaned over as close as she could to him, her amber eyes blazing, and repeated, "I earned it." *Really* earned it, you slime.

Boris gave her a sour look, but he resigned himself to the happy fact that he would soon be so incredibly rich that he could buy this whole café, this whole *city*, and not bat an eye. Let the little *shlyukha* have the crumbs. She had a short shelf life ahead, anyway.

He thought about the future and chuckled. Boris Veshkin is here! Watch out world. Now *I* call the shots.

Katia looked at him. She figured that she was ready for the main event—the reason she was there, aside from being a blow-up doll for that lunatic.

On the plane from Moscow, Veshkin had explained that Katia's lucky pass to the West would continue only as long as she held up her end—if she did just what he told her to do.

Boris needed the deck massively stacked in his favor. The success of his plan required every small edge he could get, and he had to have leverage against any unforeseen problems. So he had pulled strings to find, and then bring Katia, who also had to, uh, perform things for him on demand. Nice! He grinned inwardly.

He would make sure that Max saw Katia and that he understood the game: if Max tried to cross him in any way, his ex-girlfriend would never be seen alive again. He grunted. Max was too easy. He had a conscience, which was a net negative in their world.

And Max's lucky association with the Tangiere woman added an extra layer of implied retribution if the threat to Katia wasn't enough. Max would just have to keep silent for the rest of his life, or take responsibility for the deaths of one or both of the women.

Any way you slice it, Veshkin said to himself, Max's ex, Katia Koziashvili, was a dead woman. Man, I'm tough and smart, Veshkin thought.

And soon, I'll be very, very rich.

Soon, I'll be in Los Angeles, thought Katia.

When this is over, the next time you see me, Boris Veshkin, it will be in a movie theater, and I'll be the one on the screen, not the one bending over your lap from the next seat.

She would change her last name to Kozh. *Katia Kozh*—a perfect stage name! If she'd been able to sleep and scheme her way out of the USSR, she figured that she could take a similar path to Hollywood, if necessary.

She sighed inside and thought about her rough young life in Tbilisi in Soviet Georgia. How her father drank himself to death. How her uncle had abused her as a child. How she had to use every ounce of her brain and then her body to get the hell somewhere else, anywhere else, when she was old enough.

She had made it to Moscow on the favors of a variety of unsavory men and had finally met Max, the only decent man she'd ever really known.

But she had been on a trajectory that had not included the decent or the kind, with whom she had no experience— no leverage. Inevitably, their relationship had fallen apart.

When she tried to get back on track with him, had waited for him to return to her, it was too late.

She cast her eyes around the small café and put those thoughts aside.

This place, Switzerland, was nice in its own way, but now her goal was to get to America, the land of—

She suddenly put the emergency brakes on her train of thought. She had been idly watching two women at a small table on the other side of the café having cocoa when something flashed in her head: she knew one of them!

Yes, the younger one, the blonde. Katia had seen her before. Could she be in the movies? Was she an actress?

At that moment, the woman glanced Katia's way. A second later, she returned her attention to her auburn-haired companion. No recognition had registered on her face.

Veshkin, watching Katia's eyes, said, "What?" He started to turn in his chair.

"Oh, no, Boris, nothing. I was, uh, was looking for a waiter. This coffee is cold."

Veshkin turned the other way and made a "more coffee" hand gesture at a server.

How do I know that woman? Think. Who do I know in the West? No one. Not a single...

Wait a minute.

Well, well.

Her mind flashed back to the day she had been watching the small television in Max's Moscow apartment. Pravda TV had been covering Gorbachev's speech at the World Court in Geneva. At the end of the speech, the Canadian woman had been called up to the podium.

The Canadian woman who had stolen Max.

And now here she was, in this café.

She looked quickly at Veshkin.

"What? What is it Katia?" he said, perplexed by her distracted demeanor.

"Oh, nothing Boris." She started to smile.

"Just nothing."

"No one. Just no one."

Kurt had wracked his brain to think of anyone who wanted him dead. He had been thinking about the problem every day since Zoe Kimball blew herself to bits in Chicago.

Inspector Ulrika Sonnenreich sat behind her desk, across from Kurt. When he had come into her office at the police station, she had quickly appraised him with her eyes and liked what she saw—tall, rugged, self-assured. If he weren't involved with Soleil's sister, well, who knew? But he was.

"What about your business transactions? Have you been stepping on the wrong toes, Mr. Ballas, as you go about your commodities deals?"

"Kurt."

"Yes, Kurt."

"Nothing that would lead to this. I think."

Camille, laughing, had pointedly warned Kurt to "keep it in your pants" when he had left that morning for his meeting with the inspector. Soleil had described Ulrika's raw Scandinavian charms to her, and Camille thought that a little extra fear of God couldn't hurt.

To be forewarned is to be forearmed, Camille said to herself, though she was confident that Kurt wasn't that kind of guy. Of course, she didn't know what kind of woman this inspector was. She'd better keep her "inspecting" verbal, not physical.

"We've been working on tying the known associates of Li Hua Chung to Zoe Kimball's, but have so far come up with nothing," Ulrika was saying. "The only solid clue remains the identical baskets of mixed currencies in the possession of each of them at the time of their deaths. I cannot believe that's a coincidence."

"I don't know, Inspector—"

"Ulrika."

"Ulrika. I don't know. I'm out of my depth here. I had my office in Chicago send over a list of all my customers and associates who I did business with over the last couple of years. I pored over it and thought I was onto something when I found that one of our metals deals had adversely affected an Asian company's profits. But it wasn't anything large enough to make that company or anyone there to go off the deep end."

"Kurt, according to Soleil, Li Hua Chung called out a name before she shot herself. 'Furoma.' Do you have any idea who Furoma is?"

Kurt shook his head, no.

The inspector looked off into space for a minute.

"What about your girlfriend, Camille? Is she angry with you? Murderously angry?" Ulrika said it with a barely concealed smile on her lips.

Kurt chuckled. "If she was, she wouldn't have missed. Certainly not twice." He looked at the inspector. "Besides, both times she was nearly caught in the cross fire herself."

"You're a dangerous man to be around, Kurt Ballas. Does it have something to do with living in Chicago?"

"Maybe, Ulrika."

She nodded and flipped the pad on her desk closed, tilting her head to indicate she was finished.

They both stood up. The inspector came around the desk. She held a card out and leaned back slightly against her desk. "Call me if you think of anything else."

He took the card and smiled. "Sure, Ulrika."

He shook her hand and left. She looked at the floor.

What am I missing here? she asked herself silently.

"You're missing part of your brain, you know," said Camille.

"Yeah, the part that says, 'Don't listen to your sister.'"

"No, you're missing the little gate in your brain that stays closed until you've thought things through. I call it the 'man gate.'"

"Uh huh. And what about *your* man gate, *pute a cinq cennes*?"

"Mine costs more than five cents to open, thank you. Five dollars is more like it."

"Ha!"

"Anyway, I can't believe you're falling for Dustin's pretty face. It's not like you."

They had been walking from the café, and Soleil stopped on the sidewalk and took Camille's hands in hers.

"Camille, I need a solid man. A one-night stand like the one I had with Stefan was a reaction to anger and hurt, and I don't want to make that mistake again."

Camille looked at her with understanding.

"And as for Dustin," she went on, "for the last time—I'm going to continue dating him. More than dating. He's easy to be with, and he's smarter than most. It's different, and I like it." Camille started to protest. "And yes, it's going to go beyond holding his hand. That's it. Now please, Cami, respect my privacy."

Camille sighed and hugged her sister. Then out of the corner of her eye, she saw a tall familiar figure walking toward them.

"Hi, Kurt," said Soleil as he came up to them and kissed her on the cheek and Camille on the lips. Soleil teased, "I'm glad you just did that in that order."

"Don't pay attention to Soleil. She's in love." Camille squinted at Kurt. "And speaking of love, I hope that Scandinavian she-wolf at the police station kept her paws off you and vice versa."

"Don't worry, Cami," he said smiling. "She's not having my baby or anything like that. It was just the facts, ma'am."

Camille gave him a dubious look.

He turned to Soleil. "Are you joining us for dinner tonight?"

"Sorry, Kurt. I have plans."

Camille chimed in: "They're going museum-hopping."

"Is there any way to shut you up?" asked Soleil.

Kurt laughed. "Have a good time. And say hello to your new boyfriend. Maybe tomorrow we'll all go out."

"That sounds nice." Soleil threw an unreadable look at her sister.

Camille put her arm through Kurt's and said, "C'mon, handsome, explain to me how police woman tried to put you in cuffs."

They walked off chuckling.

Now Soleil was running late—she knew Dustin would be waiting for her at the museum.

"He's not listed as a guest, but I smell him. He's here."

Three Tit and Eddie were riding up in the elevator to their room. They had calculated that there was no way they could get to Max before Veshkin did. Only he would know Max's exact arrival time. Therefore, they had to find Veshkin first, get Max's schedule out of him one way or another, and then have a clear shot at the diamonds.

Eddie had just come from the front desk and, after ascertaining that a Mr. Boris Veshkin was not on the guest list, he had tried to describe him to the concierge. Though Eddie had never seen Veshkin in the flesh, his picture had been faxed to him from Herr Menschel's office at the ZSB bank. Nothing like having a bought-and-paid-for Swiss banker on your side, thought Eddie.

A young trainee at the desk thought he had seen someone check in that fit the description, but said he had arrived with a woman. "A good-looking woman, too," the kid had added.

"That was Veshkin," Eddie said to Three. "I'll bet you a thousand, HK."

"US," said Eddie, and they shook on it.

On the way to the elevator, they passed a tall man with tawny hair and a new goatee. When the Poongs got into their suite, Eddie said, "Do we know him? That tall guy in the lobby?"

Three thought for a second. "Not likely. I never saw him before." His toothpick clicked. "Besides, they all look alike to me."

"Who, whites?"

"Hotel guests."

"You're an idiot."

Three went to a window and looked out on the frozen lake. "How are we going to find Veshkin?"

"Simple. According to Gravva, Max Stepanov was to have left the Mir today. It's doubtful that he will be here until late tonight—it's a huge trip, and he has to cross borders. Veshkin will have him come here. He'd never risk meeting him in public, in an airport. He's Russian, full of secrets."

"I hope you know what you're doing, Eddie," said Three, a touch of nervousness in his voice. "We can't afford to miss Veshkin."

"Don't worry. He's here. And we won't."

Ljubljana was the capital and largest city of Slovenia.

And since it was closer to Europe than most of the Soviet Empire was, the people in Ljubljana's streets seemed to be carrying glimmers of optimism in their pockets at the end of 1989. It was the most widely acknowledged secret in their world that the USSR was stumbling, and when it finally heeled over into a ditch, Slovenia would quickly run free. The last three generations of Slovenes had been waiting for that chance.

But their airport was a mess. A commercial carrier with forty passengers aboard had skidded on landing a half hour before Max and the taciturn corporal had driven up to the terminal. The plane nearly flipped over and caught fire in the exact center of the landing strip. The passengers had been evacuated safely, but the wreck was unmovable, and the heat of the inferno had damaged the runway.

Within the terminal, which was in the process of a major repair project, chaos reigned.

All Max knew was what the corporal had told him on the trip from the army base: the Nevsky Nickel corporate jet would be landing at 4:00 p.m. to fly Max directly to Zurich Kloten International Airport in Switzerland.

And he wouldn't let Max out of his sight until he was on board.

Now there was a bonfire on the Ljubljana runway, and the Nevsky plane was still in Moscow, cooling its jets until it received clearance to take off and get to Slovenia.

Max had to cool his jets, too.

According to Veshkin's orders, he had to stay glued to the armed corporal, who seemed to be eternally pissed off, especially at Max. He literally went to the bathroom with Max, and as the day turned into night, Max was on the verge of going for the soldier's gun and shooting him.

They had spent most of the day in the airport administrator's cramped office, where the corporal kept harassing the already inundated administrator to determine when the runway would be cleared and the Nevsky jet could land.

It was eight o'clock at night when they got the word—the plane would be there at seven the next morning to pick up Max.

Max and the corporal wearily walked out of the terminal to return to the army base where they would be forced to spend the night. When they arrived at the UAZ jeep, the soldier swore: one of the tires had gone flat.

Since this was the USSR, the spare had a flat as well.

They walked back to the terminal, and the corporal used the administrator's phone to call his base for a replacement vehicle. Max knew that could it could take half the night to get a requisition for another UAZ to be driven out to them.

"I'm going to sleep," Max said, the exhaustion of the day too overpowering to ignore. The airport administrator had left his office, and Max stretched out on an uncomfortable couch against the wall and was instantly asleep.

A few minutes later, the corporal shook Max gently. Getting no response, he left the office to find the men's room.

The instant the door closed behind him, Max was up and on the phone. He tried an international dialing code first and came up with a bad series of harsh clicks and disconnects.

Then he dialed a direct line to Nevsky Nickel in Moscow and entered a series of codes that he had often used to make international calls. He kept one eye on the door. If the corporal walked in and saw him making an unauthorized call, Max didn't know what his reaction would be. This soldier wasn't very bright, and he kept his gun very visibly hung on his canvas belt.

Then, suddenly, he heard the ring tone. Please answer, please answer, please be there, Max prayed. After four rings, he heard, "Hi. This is Soleil. I can't pick up the phone, so leave a message. Thanks, *danke, merci!*"

When he heard the voice over the phone, his heart felt like it was taking off for outer space. Oh, Soleil, I'm so close.

At the sound of the beep, he started to leave a message. Less than half a minute later, he heard fast footsteps. The door swung open.

The corporal was suddenly in the room, looking to the left and right, but Max was obviously fast asleep on the couch, exactly where he had left him. The soldier grunted, pulled off his jacket, and settled into a chair. In a few minutes, he was snoring.

Max lay on the couch counting the minutes until the next day.

Until Soleil.

They met at three o'clock at the Kunsthaus Museum and discovered that they had something else in common—art.

Dustin did a little showing off about this Impressionist or that modernist as they strolled through the cool corridors and halls. He was floored when Soleil began speaking about almost every painting they passed with impressive knowledge.

"How did you learn all this?" he finally asked as she was commenting on a Cézanne.

"For two years, I lived just one block from the Metropolitan Museum of Art in New York. I spent a lot of weekends exploring the museum. Also the Museum of Modern Art on Fifty-Third Street during my lunch hours. I like art." But not in the way some New Yorkers can be snobs about it, she thought. I like it because, well, because I just do.

Dustin doubled down on his efforts to show Soleil how much he knew about art and artists, and she started to realize that he was very competitive—even when it wasn't necessary. Well, he was a man, after all, she thought.

They had an early dinner at a restaurant near the museum and talked on and on. Dustin asked Soleil about her family, and she gave him bits and pieces. At one point, he said, "Camille seemed very nice. You're very close, aren't you?"

"We weren't always. But this year we bonded, and I'm happy we did. I love her. She's my best friend in the world."

Dustin smiled. He poured her a glass from the expensive bottle of Chateau Petrus, and then he asked if he could accompany her home.

This time she said yes.

Soleil opened the door and they both went into her apartment. Dustin asked, "Aren't you going to lock it behind us?"

"Not necessary," she answered. "This place is completely safe—very boring."

Dustin looked around for a few seconds and said hesitantly, "This is very nice. It's..."

"I know, it's a little small," she finished his sentence. "But I'm on a month-to-month lease, and this is really all I need."

She showed him the small kitchen and the living area.

"What's in there?" he gestured at a doorway. "The bedroom?"

She nodded. Yep, Dustin, that's the bedroom. Stay focused. We have time.

He poked his head inside and looked at her neatly made bed and the few bright paintings she had on the walls. He looked at one that showed a woman with a white parasol alone in a small rowboat on a lake with lily pads. "I know this painting," he said.

She stood in the doorway and said, "It's a copy of a Claude Monet that's in the Metropolitan in New York. I loved it when I discovered it there and bought this copy when I moved in here."

He stared at the painting. "The woman in the painting reminds me of you: alone and happy to be so."

Very clever, Dustin. "Maybe," was all she said.

He crossed the small bedroom and took her in his arms. Then he kissed her deeply. She tasted wine on his lips from dinner, and she was sure that he tasted it on hers. She suspected that there was no turning back now.

She gently pushed him off her, emotions bouncing inside her head like agitated molecules, and said, "Not yet. We have all night."

"I doubt I can wait that long."

"You might want to take your coat off," she said, smiling. "Here, give it to me."

He shrugged out of his expensive Armani cloth coat and handed it to her. Under the coat, he was wearing a dark-blue, Burberry crew-neck sweater.

He followed her through the living room. Her resolve twisted and turned with a combination of want and indecision. He watched her as she hung his coat in the small closet near the apartment door—a narrow closet that she almost never used.

"Let's have another glass of wine," she said suddenly, and went into the small kitchen to retrieve a bottle that she had been saving for...for what? Or should she say for whom?

Dustin sat on the couch in the living room, and in a few moments, she was back with two large, full glasses. She sat next to him, and they clinked their wineglasses in a toast. "To tonight," he said.

Fair enough, she thought—to tonight.

He put down his glass and kissed her deeply.

She thought she might have found a man who might be more than a one-night stand—someone with whom she might really have a future.

She guessed she'd finally moved on. She guessed.

They parted, and she picked up her glass again. He picked up his, and they clinked happily, and her full glass of wine shattered into a million pieces.

"Damn it!" Dustin yelled, his Burberry sweater suddenly a sodden mess. The crotch area of his pants was even worse.

"I'm sorry," said Soleil, already on the way into the kitchen for wet towels and anything else that might help.

When she rushed back into the living room, Dustin was standing, pulling the sweater off. The light-blue shirt he was wearing underneath was ruined.

"I've got to get these off," said Dustin, feeling the wine all over his skin beneath his clothes. "Could I use your shower for a minute?"

"Sure." She quickly fetched a towel from the bathroom and turned her back as he stripped in the middle of the room. "Don't worry about the clothes," he said. "We'll deal with them later."

She heard him go into the bathroom and close the door.

Well, he's here, she thought.

She stood in the living room and heard the water being turned on in the shower. The tiny light blinking on her phone's answering machine caught her eye. But she'd listen to the message later. After.

She went into the bedroom and looked thoughtfully at the bed. All right, she said to herself again. All right.

She glanced back out the bedroom door. In the living room, the tiny light went blink, blink, blink.

She stood still.

Don't listen to that message, she told herself.

No. Listen to it.

She walked slowly into the living room and put the tip of her finger on the "play" button. She looked back at the bedroom.

No, I won't.

Then, from some deep well inside her, a small voice insisted, "Listen to it."

She let her finger push down on the "play" button.

"Soleil."

It was Max.

14

SLITHER

Boris Veshkin was panicking.

He had decided to check on Max's progress, but events had quickly deteriorated.

It took an hour to get a line to his office in Moscow. Finally getting through to the department that handled the Nevsky jet's schedule, he was told that Max Stepanov would not be arriving in Zurich until the next day. According to Nevsky, there was some kind of screw-up in Ljubljana, but Boris's own office wasn't sure what was happening. To Boris's mind, the reports of the reasons behind the delay were sketchy and vague.

At this stage of the game, the plan was almost complete. Why take any chances? he thought.

A visit to Ms. Tangiere was imperative. It was time for Boris to take out an insurance policy, as they said in the West.

He'd better take control of Max's little friend, Soleil Tangiere, before Max got to Switzerland.

Three Tit had found Boris Veshkin.

Eddie was right again, he said to himself. He had smelled the Russian rat in the hotel, and sure enough, he and some hooker were staying in a room on the floor below the brothers. *Diu*! He was an ugly bastard—his amber-eyed, big-breasted *dai boh mui* must surely be taking big money to be with him.

Three and Eddie had set up their observation post at the Rive Gauche bar off the Baur au Lac's lobby. Sitting at a small table partially hidden behind a pillar, they had spotted Veshkin and Katia leaving the hotel around eight o'clock. Three had quickly dropped some money on the table, donned sunglasses in a somewhat feeble attempt to disguise himself, and they were now walking a half block behind the couple in the freezing cold.

"We look like damn drug dealers," said Eddie, referring to the sunglasses at night.

"Yeah, but we don't look like Chinese," said Three. "Unfortunately, we stand out here."

"Too bad," said Eddie, and he ripped the shades off his brother and jammed them into his coat pocket, right next to his Beretta PX4 semiautomatic pistol.

They followed the Russian couple through the cold streets for what seemed an interminable amount of time. Finally, they watched as Boris and the woman stopped in front of an apartment building and looked up.

"This could be it," said Eddie. "Stepanov and our diamonds are probably inside this building."

They quickly crossed to the far side of the street and stood watching as Veshkin conferred with his amber-eyed *dai boh mui.*

"Yeah, this is it," said Three Tit Poong.

She stood stiffly, not moving a muscle, the volume on the answering machine set to low. She could feel her heart beating.

"Soleil." His deep voice with its slight accent sounded rushed and intense. And welcome.

"*Lyubov moya,* my love, I have only seconds. I was sent away a few days after we parted and have been held in a secure facility like a prison in the Arctic. Yesterday they let me go, and I'm returning to Zurich, but there's so much danger. Soleil, trust no one you don't know. No one. I'm in Slovenia now and will be in Zurich tomorrow. Don't try to meet me, I'll find you. Please be careful.

"I love you."

Then the answering machine beeped and was silent.

Soleil slowly pressed the off button on the machine. Then she touched the small diamond cross that hung on a thin chain on her chest and stared intently at the phone.

"Ahem."

She quickly turned at the sound.

Dustin stood in the bedroom door.

A towel tied at the waist was his only article of clothing.

"Go ahead," said Veshkin, standing in front of the building. "The name on the panel will be Tangiere or Soleil Tangiere.

Ah, my prayer has been answered, Katia reflected with growing excitement.

"When someone answers the intercom, make something up to get yourself into her place," Boris was saying. "Improvise. I want you to go and get the girl."

My pleasure, she said to herself.

She walked up to the directory panel on the outside of the building's lobby door.

I really hope that woman's home, she thought.

Dustin stood in the bedroom door, fingering the knot he had made in the towel to keep it from falling to the floor.

Soleil stood absolutely still and hoped that her face wasn't showing the range of emotions that were caroming around in her head. How long had Dustin been standing there? Did he hear that message? The volume was very low, but she was not certain.

Sensing that something was off kilter, he said, "Who was on the phone?" He just stood there, a few feet in front of her.

Some seconds went by, and then she said, "Dustin..."

"What?"

She suddenly sat down on the couch. "Dustin, I don't know if I can do this now," she said slowly. Her head was reeling from the message.

"What? Why?"

"I just don't think I can."

She watched his face carefully and waited for his next question. He was not doing a very good job of hiding his feelings, and she saw that this was not good news. His face was telling it all.

Finally, he said, "I don't understand." Then he looked at the phone. "Who was on the phone?"

She was afraid to look away from his face for even a second. What should she do? Tell him that she can't sleep with him now because a voice that she hadn't heard in over two months suddenly said, "I love you?" That was pretty cruel.

But now I can't, she thought. I just can't.

"Who was on the phone?" Dustin repeated.

Soleil saw that he wasn't a happy man at the moment. She reached for his hand.

It took Katia just a few seconds to find the button with the label, 6-B Soleil Tangiere.

Who would have thought I would have the great good fortune to confront the bitch? she thought. And confront her I will—by myself. Sorry, Boris.

Katia stood at the panel of buttons outside the lobby doors of Soleil's building and looked back at Veshkin standing on the street. He gave her an impatient hand signal that said, "Go ahead."

She gave the button a long, insistent push.

Soleil reached for his hand, and the intercom bell in the kitchen rang.

They both turned to look. It was a long and loud ring.

She walked slowly into the kitchen and pressed the button on the wall intercom. She looked through the door at Dustin in his towel. He was not a happy man. "Yes?" she said into the small box on the wall.

But there was no answer. Could it be someone just pushing all of the buttons in the building in hopes of getting in?

That had never happened before—this was Switzerland. But there was always a first time.

She turned from the intercom box. Dustin stood behind her in the kitchen in his towel. She said, "I think the best thing is to get dressed now, Dustin."

They walked into the living room.

"I don't know what's going on, Soleil, but..."

"It's just too soon, Dustin. That's all. I'm sorry if I've sort of rushed this—"

"Rushed? C'mon, Soleil, who was on that bloody phone?" He began quickly picking up his wine-soaked clothes, and the tone of his voice was ominously aggressive.

Soleil suddenly saw a side of him that she didn't like—his angry side. But before she could say another word, his question was answered.

"Yes, who was on phone?" The woman's voice came from behind them. They both whirled and looked at the open apartment door.

A tall brunette with amber eyes stood in the doorway. She wore a short, fake-fur jacket and had a gun in her hand.

Dustin's hands immediately went up in the classic gesture of surrender, and his towel immediately went down in the classic grip of gravity.

"Well," said Katia to Soleil in a thick accent. "Looks like you waste no time since Max is gone, honey." Looking at Dustin in the nude, she added, "No time at all."

Soleil knew who she was instantly. The voice and the accent were unmistakable: Max's girlfriend. Or ex-girlfriend. Or who knows what she was, except she was there with a gun, and she was angry, and Soleil was in trouble.

Bad trouble.

When Katia had pressed the intercom button outside the lobby, she had gotten no answer. But a moment later, quiet and reserved Herr Kleinschwanz, who lived on the seventh floor, happened to be leaving the building with his dachshund, Jagg.

The plain, middle-aged man saw the striking woman's smile through the building's glass outer doors and the "I forgot my key" motion she was making with her hands. He pushed the door and graciously held it open for her. She swept into the building and stopped for a second as Jagg started barking madly. Herr Kleinschwanz pulled on Jagg's leash, but the dog kept yelping.

Katia ignored the yapping black wiener dog and calmly got into the elevator. She pressed six, Soleil's floor, and took the gun from the inside pocket of her fur jacket.

And now, here she was, Katia said to herself: Max's Canadian whore and some well-hung stranger, obviously having a good time. "Sorry to be interrupt," she said in her fractured English. She waved the gun, signaling for Dustin to move away from Soleil.

Soleil's brain was in overdrive. What was this woman doing here? Did she come here to meet Max? Did she come here to *kill* Max? Or me? Or both? What does she know that I don't?

She glanced over at Dustin, standing nude on the other side of the room. He had lowered his hands a bit and seemed to be stunned.

"D-do you mind if I put on some clothes?" he stuttered at Katia.

Katia raised her chin and said, "Quick. Then leave us." She waved the gun at Dustin and gave him a look she reserved for road kill. "If you trip over a snake named Veshkin downstairs, tell him to wait for me. I won't be long." She turned back to Soleil.

Dustin was in his wine-sopped pants in a flash, frantically pulled on his sweater, and then he rushed past Katia before she could react any further. In seconds, he was out the apartment door.

You have to be kidding, Soleil said bitterly to herself. Thanks, Dustin. How brave you are when it comes to the crunch. But there was little time to let Dustin's hasty exit bother her.

"Sorry, Miss Whore, but you are having to answer questions." Katia held the gun straight out at Soleil. "You stole my Max, not that you haven't been busy with other mans."

"Men," Soleil shot back reflexively. She saw the hint of confusion in the Russian woman's eyes and tried stalling for time, now that the only man in the room had taken off liked a scared rabbit.

"You will leave Max alone," Katia hissed. "Or I will—"

"Katia." The voice came from behind her. Without lowering the gun, Katia turned her head toward the door.

Boris Veshkin stood in the doorway, a strange look on his face. He, too, had found a way into the building.

Rapidly reaching new heights of paranoia when Katia went into the building, Boris realized that he couldn't trust her. Whom was he kidding? She would probably betray him as well. He must do this himself.

When she saw Boris, Katia's face registered confusion and hatred. She swung the gun from Soleil to Veshkin to Soleil again. "Stay out of this, Veshkin," she hissed in Russian.

Boris was surprisingly fast, and he covered the few feet between them in a flash. He viciously grabbed the gun, held it one hand, and slapped Katia hard across the face with the other. She brought her hand up to her mouth and felt blood. His face was contorted in anger—why did she say his name? Not good at all, Katia, he said to himself in a rage. Not good.

He quickly turned back, but Soleil was moving like a blur. In a second, she was out the door of the apartment and sprinting down the short hallway, making for the exit to the stairwell.

Veshkin ran into the hall, looked both ways, and saw the stairwell door swinging closed. He charged at it and pushed it open. He heard Soleil's rapidly diminishing footsteps and peered over the open well at the center of the spiral staircase. He strained to see either feet on the stairs or a hand on the railing below him, but saw neither.

Suddenly he heard a slam. From above. He looked up quickly. The stairway ended two floors above him.

Veshkin took two steps at a time, and in a matter of seconds, he was at the door at the top of the stairs. It had a security bar that had to be pushed to open it. He waited and listened. Nothing.

Two landings below him, a door opened and closed. He looked down and saw Katia's face looking down and then up from the railing. The hell with her, he said to himself. He would deal with that crazy bitch later. He carefully pushed the door open.

He was on the roof.

There was a single light above the door to the stairway. The ambient glow of the city faintly lighted the rest of the roof.

A ten-foot-tall brick cube containing the elevator motors and machinery dominated part of the roof. Brooms, a red-handled shovel, and some pails were arrayed against the enclosed brick box. A variety of vents and ducts poked up at irregular intervals across the roof and the structure that housed the top level of the stairwell. A low brick wall, not more than two feet high, formed a barrier at the edge of the roof.

A foot of snow from the last snowfall blanketed the roof. A woman's small shoeprints curved away from the door at which Veshkin stood and disappeared behind the elevator cube. Easy enough to follow, Veshkin said to himself.

But he didn't feel like wasting time or playing games. He stood where he was and said loudly, "Ms. Tangiere, we are needing to talk."

The only responses were the faint city sounds from the street, eight floors below.

"I just am saving your life, Ms. Tangiere." His Russian accent and mangling of the English language would have been comical if his intentions hadn't been transparently deadly.

"No you aren't," said a voice suddenly.

He whirled—the woman's voice seemed to have come from behind the stairwell. He felt the gun in his pocket and pulled it out.

"That woman was going to kill you," he said loudly. "Did you not see what happened?" Veshkin was confident. This Soleil certainly didn't have any kind of a weapon. In fact, all she wore was a light dress. And it was cold up there.

Quiet for a half a minute. Then her disembodied voice said, "What are your intentions?"

That's an odd question, Boris thought. Somehow, she was moving around the roof without his seeing her. Now it sounded like she was behind the elevator cube.

"When are you meeting Max? And where?" asked Boris.

Silence for a few seconds. Then the voice said, "Don't you know?"

Boris whirled again. How was she doing that? Where was she now?

"No, I don't," he replied.

There was silence for over a minute, and then the voice said, "I know who you are, Mr. Veshkin."

Damn it, Veshkin said to himself. That stupid Katia. Now this Soleil woman has become a threat. A very real threat.

"You're the top man at that metal company Max works for."

Soleil was now far to his left. She was flat on her stomach on the ground and up against the low brick wall that served as the building's railing. When she had come out onto the roof and seen the snow, she had instantly remembered the game she used to play with her brother, Kent, when she was a child. It was called Slither.

In a foot of snow, I can slither all over this roof, she thought with determination. I can sort of burrow through it, and as long Veshkin stays where he is, he's not going to see me. I don't have a coat, so I'm as low to the ground as I'm going to get. This whole roof is a carpet of snow with good hiding places and I don't mind being down on the ground like a snake. It's so darn cold, but better cold than dead.

She lifted her head an inch or two above the snow and saw Veshkin moving carefully away from the stair door. He was making for the elevator cube. Yeah, he wants to talk? she thought. I'm supposed to believe anything this guy says? I don't think so.

"I repeat, when are you meeting Max and where?" he said loudly.

She slithered along the wall and worked her way back behind the elevator enclosure. Suddenly Veshkin ran forward, kicking up snow as he quickly reached the concrete structure.

Soleil jumped up and ran around the other side of the elevator cube. She headed straight to the spot where the brooms, the shovel, and the cleaning paraphernalia leaned against the wall. She quickly bent down and grabbed the metal handle of one of the pails.

The pail, full of snow, was startlingly heavy. She whirled in one spot, pulling it up with both hands. Then she swung it in an arc around her and let it fly at Veshkin, who had just appeared around the corner.

The heavy pail crashed into his solar plexus, but Soleil was moving too fast and was too determined to get back to the stairs to turn to see the results. She ran straight to the stairway door, intending to get inside and somehow lock Veshkin on the roof. But at the last minute, the door swung open, and Katia ran out, crashing into Soleil. The door closed behind her.

The two women immediately went down in the snow. Soleil quickly got to her knees, pushed Katia's face down into a low snowdrift, and took off across the roof.

"There's no way out, Soleil." Veshkin was clutching his stomach where the heavy pail had hit him. He stumbled after her through the snow, his gun drawn. She ran diagonally across his path toward the railing. Suddenly, a monstrous shot rang out. Surprised by the huge noise, Soleil slipped and grasped the low brick wall for support.

She turned and saw Veshkin, with his smoking gun pointing toward the dark sky. Her shoes slipped in the snow again and she half fell. In a moment, Veshkin was just ten feet away. He lowered the muzzle of the gun until it was pointing straight at her.

There was nowhere to run or hide, and she was kneeling in the snow, freezing in her thin dress, her wet, frozen hair hanging in front of her face. God, am I sick of people pointing guns at me, she thought.

"Why are you trying to kill Kurt Ballas?" The words came out slowly, and her body began to shake. Might as well take a stab at it—keep his mind off shooting for a few more seconds.

"Who?" It was suddenly obvious that Veshkin had no idea what she was talking about. Then his eyes took on a frighteningly determined look. "Is your last chance."

Soleil slowly stood, pushed the hair out of her face, and looked directly into Boris Veshkin's outraged, squinting eyes. "Drop dead." Her voice was shaking from the cold.

"Sorry, is you who is now to be dead," he said and aimed the barrel of the gun directly at Soleil. "Back on your knees."

No, I'm not getting on my knees for you. Or anyone, Soleil thought. She stood in the dark, frozen air. Her sapphire eyes blazed. She touched her little diamond cross and said, "Go ahead. Go ahead and shoot an unarmed girl, coward."

Over Veshkin's shoulder, Soleil saw the stairway door open.

A low, dark shape streaked out of the opened door and made its way madly through the snow. It growled and leaped and clamped onto Veshkin's leg. The man yelled and hopped in confusion.

Soleil watched Veshkin swatting at his leg and suddenly realized what she was seeing. Herr Kleinschwanz's dachshund, Jagg, was growling and chewing on the man's calf. Blood sprayed across the snow from his pant leg. He tried to hit the low-slung hound with a fist while keeping his gun trained on Soleil, but only succeeded in smashing his own ankle and making things worse. "Let go!" he screamed in Russian and kicked his leg madly.

"Hey, *mudak!*" The shout was surprisingly loud.

Veshkin's head whipped up and around in response to the voice. Someone behind Boris had the red-handled shovel and was swinging it in a fast arc. Jagg's jaws opened and the little dog backed away a foot or two. The flat blade of the heavy shovel was moving so fast when it hit Veshkin in the face that its impact sounded like a car crash.

The gun dropped from his hand into the snow, and he took two huge, off-balance, backward steps. The backs of his legs hit the low roof railing, and his arms flew out to his sides. Then he toppled backward over the low wall, closely resembling a professional swimmer at the start of a very difficult reverse high dive into eternity.

One second later, Boris Veshkin was no longer on the roof.

Soleil stared at Katia, who was breathing hard and was still holding the shovel. The Russian woman's amber eyes smoldered with a strange mélange of contempt, hatred, triumph, and relief.

Soleil looked down at the panting dog rapidly wagging his tail, and then turned and walked unsteadily to the low railing. Herr Kleinschwanz came up beside her. So did Katia. The three looked over the edge of the roof and down toward the street below.

After a minute, Soleil turned to face the man. "Hello, Herr Kleinschwanz." She knew him from the building. He was a quiet man, and everyone in the building knew Jagg. The man looked at Soleil with hesitant eyes and then leaned down and picked up the excited dog. He made a short bow and said in German, "*Guten Abend,* Frau Tangiere." Good evening.

He was a timid, fearful man who lived alone, and he had long ago trained his beloved dog to smell guns and gunpowder as a kind of protection for them both. When Katia had passed him in the lobby earlier, Herr Kleinschwanz had watched as the dachshund went crazy. She has a gun, he said to himself. At first, he didn't want to interfere—it was the classic Swiss way of butting out. But after taking the dog on his usual evening walk, he let Jagg into the stairwell, and the dog had climbed all the way up eight flights of stairs to the roof in search of the gun he had smelled.

At the top of the stairs, Herr Kleinschwanz had opened the door and let Jagg out just in time. The dog had saved Soleil's life.

So had Katia.

Katia looked carefully over the railing. Well, this changes things, she said to herself. Her face hurt from when Veshkin slapped it and from when Soleil had pushed it into the snow. She turned to glare at Soleil, who glared back.

Now Katia's face was a frieze of hot, female emotion, and she took a final look down into the street below. Her lower lip was split, and a thin line of blood ran to her chin, but she didn't seem to notice. She had finally had enough of that *ublyudok*, that bastard, and his filthy ways. For all the resentment she held for the Soleil woman, she couldn't watch that piece of garbage kill her in cold blood.

I'll get my own revenge on Soleil, she thought. When the time is right.

"Herr Kleinschwanz," Soleil said to the quiet man. "Are you going to tell the police?"

The short man was cradling his dog in his arms, tickling its belly. He looked up at Soleil and then at Katia and thought about his quiet life with his only love, his long little dog. Would the police take my Jagg away? Well, I will not allow it. Never.

After a moment, he shook his head, and said, *"Nein. No."*

Soleil believed him. *"Danke,"* she said.

Katia walked unsteadily to the stairway door, which Herr Kleinschwanz had wedged open with a loose brick. She turned from the doorway, cast a final glance at Soleil, and then went through the door and down the stairs.

Herr Kleinschwanz tickled the dog's belly for another minute, looked at Soleil, and said in German, "Come. You will freeze to death."

Then the shivering young Canadian woman, the middle-aged Swiss man, and the very content dachshund went to the stairway door, and a moment later, they were gone.

"It's too damn cold."

Eddie and Three Tit Poong had crossed the street and were now in front of Soleil's building, sitting a few feet apart on a bench made of thick wooden slats. Three Tit's breath was a frosty cloud in front of his face. So was Eddie's.

Eddie said, "Patience, Three. All we have to do is wait. Veshkin has to come downstairs soon. Probably with his girlfriend. When he does, he'll either have Max or have the diamonds with him. Then we move in on him. Or them." He smiled.

Three, shivering, said, "I hope it's soon." He saw his brother tap a cigarette from a pack of Dunhills and put it between his lips. "Here. Need a light?"

Three Tit pulled his gold lighter from a pocket, flicked it open, and Eddie started to lean across the bench toward the tiny flame.

Dustin rushed out of the building through the lobby door.

He quickly passed two Asian men sitting on a bench, looked frantically around, and finally found a pay phone on the next block.

Stupid for me to hang around and be killed back there, he thought. That Russian woman was insane, and I'm not going to be a dead innocent bystander. He fumbled a credit card out of his wallet and dialed the operator. After giving her the number, it took two minutes for the overseas call to go through. A man's voice answered, "Yes?"

"Let me talk to the chairman. It's Dustin Magill." There was silence for a minute or two on the other end of the phone. Dustin was shivering in his sweater. His coat was upstairs in Soleil's apartment, but he would just have to abandon it—there was nothing in it anyway, he thought.

Finally, a gritty voice said, "Hello, Dustin." It was the unmistakable voice of the chairman.

Dustin quickly recapped the events of the evening. When he came to the name "Veshkin," the chairman interrupted his nervous, run-on sentence.

"Boris Veshkin was there?" The chairman sounded incredulous. "At Soleil Tangiere's apartment?"

"Yeah, who's he?" Dustin felt safe in dropping the phony cultured voice he had been using for the last week.

There was another long silence on the phone.

"Who he is, is no concern of yours."

"By now he may have killed Soleil. If that's happened, what about my job?"

More silence on the phone. Then the chairman said, "Did you have sex with Soleil Tangiere yet?"

"No."

A moment of silence, then: "Well, that was part of our contract, Dustin. You had to have—how do the Americans say it?—'closed the deal' with her before you terminated your target. Or targets, I should say."

"Yeah, but—"

"There are no buts, Dustin. For some reason, everyone on this project has so far wound up dead. Except you." A pregnant pause. "So far."

"Whaddaya want from me? I've done everything you told me to do up until now." Dustin was way off balance.

"Up until now," the chairman repeated thoughtfully.

Dustin gulped and listened nervously as the chairman said, "Leave Soleil Tangiere to me from this point forward. If she's still breathing." There was a heavy, sarcastic sigh freighted with a subtext of menace. "Oh, Dustin, Dustin. When you need to get something done, evidently you have to do it yourself."

After another moment the chairman continued, "I want you to follow Veshkin closely and let me know what he's doing. You can do that, Dustin, can't you?"

Dustin's fear was slightly assuaged. "Sure. Yeah."

"Keep me informed of his whereabouts."

As the words were coming through the phone, Dustin looked down the block and saw a man's body zooming down the side of Soleil's building.

Dustin couldn't move. You've got to be kidding, he thought.

Finally, without taking his eyes off the scene unfolding before him, he said into the phone, "I think Veshkin has just left the building."

Boris Veshkin's body blasted between the Poong brothers and literally exploded when it hit the bench between them. Eddie and Three were catapulted into the air by the seesaw effect of the heavy wooden boards of the bench, which were flung in all directions by the impact.

The brothers both fell back to the ground on their rumps and were instantly splattered with blood, splinters, and tiny little pieces of Boris that had whizzed out in a wide arc when he whammed into the well-made Swiss bench.

Eyes wide and completely stunned, both brothers suddenly felt nauseous. They shakily stood up at the edge of the quickly spreading mess. A variety of gore dripped off them and what was left of the bench. Then they slowly backed up. As tough as they both believed themselves to be, this was pushing the envelope.

They didn't notice the amber-eyed woman who walked quickly out through the glass door of the lobby. She merely glanced with an open disdain at the body of Boris Veshkin—sprawled, mangled, and smeared across the ruined bench and the snowy sidewalk. Then she determinedly walked away down the street.

Neither did the brothers take notice of the handsome man in a wine-soaked sweater watching wide-eyed from a pay phone one block over.

Finally, Eddie said, "Well, Veshkin's here."

Three Tit, cigarette forgotten and his hands shaking like mad, rummaged in his pocket and found his gold toothpick. He put it in his mouth.

Click, click, click, click, click...

15

THE FREE WORLD

The engines of the Nevsky Nickel corporate jet wound down in a descending whine.

A Zurich Airport employee in a small electric vehicle wheeled a metal staircase up to the plane. The door near the front of the jet opened, and in a moment Max Stepanov, his dark hair uncombed and his almost-black eyes squinting in the morning sun, came down the steps and stood on the ground of the Free World.

He looked to the left and right and flexed his fists. Standing on the tarmac in his wrinkled, slept-in clothing; dark, thermal-insulated jacket; and dirty shoes, Max nevertheless felt new life flowing into him. No one on earth would force him to leave the West again.

He had wound up tossing and turning on the lumpy couch at the Ljubljana Airport, but thankfully, the Nevsky jet was on time from Moscow the next morning to pick him up. He had barely nodded a good-bye to his dimwitted companion and had almost run up the steps onto the plane. He was traveling as lightly as it comes, with just the clothes on his back, his passport and papers in his pocket, a few Swiss francs, and the insipid diamond Jockey shorts. Which moron thought that up? Veshkin, of course, he reminded himself with rhetorical sarcasm for the umpteenth time.

Nevsky used its Gulfstream jet to ferry big shots to points around the world where a Soviet military aircraft would cause too much of a stir and/or too much paperwork and a security nightmare. But Switzerland had a forward-thinking, neutral attitude toward international commerce of all kinds. Two neatly dressed customs agents met Max at the terminal access door. They asked him a few perfunctory questions and then quickly gave him clearance. *Willkommen in der Schweiz*! Welcome to Switzerland.

His name was on their arrival roster for the previous day, but they had verified the one-day delay, found all to be in order, and stamped his passport. He walked into the terminal.

After crossing the busy concourse, he emerged at the front of the terminal into the cold, clear air under a sparkling, blue sky. He spotted a sign with an arrow that indicated a taxi queue, and turned to walk in that direction. He looked ahead and stopped in his tracks.

She was there.

Standing where anyone arriving at the airport would have to go to get a cab, was Soleil Tangiere.

She was wearing a high-collared jacket over a sweater and slightly flared jeans. The light, steady wind and the morning sun seemed to be sprinkling icy glitter in her gently blowing hair.

She stood in profile and then, as if sensing he was there, she turned and saw him. He was fifty feet away, and busy travelers and passengers crisscrossed incessantly between them.

He could see her eyes from where he stood, see the flashing sapphires that had melted his heart, and prayed that she still loved him. Well, she was there, but that proved nothing. I know her, he thought. She could just as easily be here to say good-bye as to say hello.

She saw him—saw his stocky, solid stance, his shrewd confidence even through the crowd. His dark eyes held hers.

In an instant, she knew there was a reason things had worked out this way, and that reason was simple. Now she realized the true quality of the love she had for him. Seeing him standing there wiped out all of her doubts, all of her well-thought-out hesitations.

He walked to her and stopped a few feet away.

They looked into each other's eyes for what seemed an eternity.

Finally, he said, "Hello, Soleil."

"*Privet*, Max," and a second later, they were in each other's arms.

The people milling and walking and speaking around them seemed to fade into indistinct muted shades—murmuring ghosts in a pale landscape—while Soleil and Max came into crystal-sharp focus in each other's eyes.

Finally, they parted, but their hands remained touching. He couldn't stop looking at her, and her sapphire eyes bored into him like blue lasers. "Where were you?" she asked.

"A place without a phone. The worst place in the world."

She squeezed his hands.

He felt disoriented, light. But a cloud seemed to cross his face. He said seriously, "I asked you not to meet me. It's very dan—"

"Boris Veshkin is dead."

Max's mouth stopped in midword, and he stared at her. "What?"

"Your horrible boss. He's dead."

"How do you know?"

Soleil's eyes narrowed. "Katia killed him. She threw him off my building."

"*Katia*?" What? *What*? "Threw him off your building?"

"Veshkin came looking for you. And it seems as if Katia came for me." She stopped talking for a moment. Then she asked, "Do you still love her?"

"I never loved her," he said.

Soleil looked at him and said nothing. Either I believe him now or I don't, she thought. Huh! Boy, am I an expert at this—look at my reading on Dustin and just about every other man in my life. With the exception of Max, I have a lifetime batting average of zero.

Finally, she said, "The last and only time I was ever able to get through to Russia, Katia answered the phone and said she was taking a shower with you."

"That was a lie." He looked away for a moment, profoundly frustrated. Then he said, "She was once my girlfriend, before I met you. When I returned to Russia after you and I met, she had taken up residence in my apartment on her own initiative. I threw her out. You must have called her when I wasn't there, and she lied to you. She's jealous."

"She saved my life when she killed Veshkin," Soleil said. "I'm not sure why."

Max stared at her in disbelief.

She thought, this isn't the time or place, and after a few seconds, she wrinkled her nose, smiled, and said, "Let's go. You stink! A shower is in your future."

Max kissed her again, and they walked toward the next cab in the queue.

"Cigarette?"

"Thanks." Her amber eyes took him in. She had seen him somewhere before, probably here at the Baur au Lac. She was sitting at the Rive Gauche bar off the lobby, nursing a Perrier and thinking about the future, when he sat down on the barstool next to her. Since it was still morning, he ordered himself a bloody mary.

He tapped a Dunhill out of a pack and handed her his gold lighter. She lit the cigarette herself, placed the lighter on the bar, and squinted at him through the smoke.

"Where are you from?" he asked.

She looked at his rough face and pitch-black, Asian eyes.

"West of where you're from," she said in her heavy accent.

"And you're Russian," said Eddie Poong. "A Soviet." It wasn't a question.

She took another drag on the cigarette, pointed it at him, and said, "Hong Kong?"

"How did you know?"

"Your English. It is so good that you are coming from Hong Kong."

And your English is a typical Russian mess, he said, laughing to himself. He just eyed her.

After a minute, he said, "I met your friend."

The two slender fingers lifting the cigarette to her mouth paused for a brief second. Her lips pursed, which made the thin cut on her lower lip sweat a tiny drop of blood from where it had been split the night before. Eddie thought that was very sexy.

"Friend?"

"Boris. Veshkin."

She took another drag, blew the smoke upward, and said, "Not anymore."

He nodded. "Not...any...more," he said slowly as if turning each word over in his mind.

She looked at him closely and said, "What are you wanting from me?"

Eddie took a sip of his drink and leaned toward her. She could smell the cocktail and the cigarette on his breath. He said, "Boris owes me something." His face came closer still. "Do you have it?"

Katia heard a faint clicking noise and turned on her barstool. A second Asian, seemingly a clone of the first, stood a few feet behind her. He wore a tailored suit similar to Eddie's, and a gold toothpick was rapidly traversing his teeth, making a ridiculously annoying clicking sound. He sat down on the barstool on the other side of hers and pushed his body toward her until she felt completely bracketed by the two brothers.

She squinted at Three and then turned back to Eddie. "Hokay," she said. "A Chinese sandwich with Russian dressing. What happens now?"

Eddie shrugged. "Tell us what you know about Veshkin. Everything."

She looked back at Three Tit and knew that she was in trouble once again. These guys are the real deal, she said to herself. The real bad deal.

"All righty, boys," she finally said, and told them what they wanted to hear.

Yvonne answered the phone on her desk. "Tangiere International."

"*Ay, salut.*"

Soleil's voice was a welcome sound.

"Soleil, you really ought to learn French," she began to kid her. But suddenly Yvonne realized that there was a new tone to her friend's voice. "What's going on?" she asked.

"Two things you might want to know: *Première*, Dustin is gone."

"*Vraiment?*" Really? Good. Very good. "Don't expect me to cry any big tears now, Soleil."

"I don't."

"What happened?"

"He ran away after he put his clothes back on."

"Eh?"

"It's a long story. And *deuxième*...Max is here with me."

Yvonne carefully thought about her next response. The news immediately thrilled her—though she had met Max just one time, she had seen how his personality was a perfect complement to Soleil's. And his love for her seemed to be pure.

But, even with this good feeling, Yvonne instinctively felt that she should hold back a little for Soleil's sake. The girl had such an abysmal, even dangerous track record with men. She didn't know what to say, so she just stayed quiet.

"Yvonne?"

"That's good news, Soleil."

"That's it? Just good?"

"Oh, Soleil, I just think you should be cautious and slow now, with any man. Even with Max."

"When you hear what happened to him, your doubts will fade away, Yvonne." Soleil was grateful that Yvonne cared. "If you have to know just one thing, it's this—Max was in a place where he could not escape, not make a call. Nothing. That he's here now is a miracle."

"Well then, *c'est magnifique*." Her fear for her friend evaporated, and she smiled. "So. When can I see that hunky man?"

"Later. He's had a long, rough trip. He fell asleep in the cab from the airport. I just wanted you to know he came back."

"You made my day. I'll see you later, maybe tonight. Of course, I have to put on something *très sexy* to wear when I see him."

"Don't even think about it. See you later. *Ciao*."

"*Au revoir*, as people who can speak French say," Yvonne taunted.

They both laughed.

Camille and Kurt stood with Soleil on the street.

They had come to see Max, but Soleil asked if they could meet her downstairs—Max was sleeping.

It was unseasonably warm and brilliantly sunny—a veritable heat wave for a December 29 in Zurich: forty-seven degrees Fahrenheit.

Most of the sidewalk had been cordoned off with bright orange tape. The epicenter of last night's excitement had been mostly cleaned up by the police, the detectives, the coroner, and all the other components common to law-enforcement departments around the world.

A large pile of red-splattered wood that was once a bench now lay against the building. Leaning against the wall next to the wood was the tall, blond figure of police inspector Ulrika Sonnenreich. Her eyes were tired.

She said to Soleil, "Why am I standing in front of *your* building? Are you involved in this? What are you doing, Soleil?"

Soleil shrugged. "Nothing."

Ulrika looked at Kurt, then Camille, and then back to Soleil. "You don't know this unidentified man who we had to scrape off the street?"

Soleil shook her head noncommittally.

Ulrika sighed. "He jumped or was pushed off this building. Probably pushed. My boys found a gun on the roof in the puddles of melted snow. It might have been his. We're checking it out."

Soleil, Kurt, and Camille all shrugged at her and at each other. Ulrika pushed off the wall, took Soleil's elbow, and walked her across the street.

"Look," she said, stopping and turning to Soleil. "I like you. I like your brother-in-law—"

"Kurt's not my brother-in-law. Yet."

"OK. But Soleil, I have to know—off the record—is this dead man the one who's been taking shots at Kurt?"

"I don't know. I really don't." That was the truth.

"Why here? Why *your* building?"

Soleil shrugged and said, "Ulrika, if this was the man who was after Kurt, well...I guess he got what he deserved. One thing you can be sure of—I certainly didn't kill him."

Ulrika's frustration was almost palpable, and she wasn't certain that Soleil was being totally forthcoming. But she decided to give her a pass. Again.

Soleil looked up at the sky for a second and felt a sense of relief. Maybe this Veshkin *was* the one who was after Kurt. If so, the threat had been lifted. She looked back at the inspector and said, "OK, what do you want me to do?"

Ulrika looked at her for a half a minute. "Nothing. Hang around. Don't leave town, et cetera, et cetera."

Soleil smiled. "I'll try," she said. She looked across the street and saw Camille and Kurt bending down, petting the little dachshund named Jagg.

As Ulrika's police car was pulling away, Max came out of the building.

"You're awake," said Soleil, going over to him for a kiss. "I was going to let you sleep until next year."

"Not a chance," he said, looking tired but happy. "And miss this beautiful day?"

"Max!" Camille was on him in a moment, and Max's smile was nearly as big as hers was. Lots of kisses from Camille, until Kurt said, "Hey, hey, Max—that's *my* job."

He grabbed Max in a bear hug and kissed his cheeks in the Russian way. Max said to the taller man, "You're growing a beard now, Kurt. Very nice—very Soviet."

"Very Chicago," corrected Kurt with a smile. "Where've you been, *tovarich*?" He tilted his head toward Soleil. "Your girlfriend here's been—" Camille's elbow smacked into Kurt's belly.

"Kurt, how about giving Max a chance to breathe?"

Soleil said, "Speaking of breathing, we have to go buy this Russian bear some new clothes and right now, before he starts to smell like the gulag again." She sniffed dramatically.

"It's a custom of the far north," Max began. "They don't shower with water. They use—"

"I don't want to know," Soleil interrupted. "Come on." She grabbed his hand and the foursome walked up the block toward the Bahnhofstrasse.

When they reached the trendy shopping boulevard, Soleil shooed Camille and Kurt away and methodically ran Max through a half dozen men's fashion stores.

In less than two hours, the two were loaded down with an armload of shopping bags stuffed with thousands of francs worth of the best men's clothing money could buy. Max was going through profound culture shock with the transition from the barren living at Yakut to the immense embarrassment of riches in Zurich. I can deal with the shock, Max said to himself, as long as it's in the right direction—East to West.

Hefting his share of the shopping bags, Max asked Soleil, "How much do I owe you?" They were waiting for the next tram.

"A million."

"Dollars or francs?"

"Kisses," she said.

"That I have," he said and kissed her. "You're going to charge interest?"

"You know it."

A few minutes later, the tram came to its precise stop, and they stepped on. Through the window of a woman's shoe store across the street, Katia Koziashvili, who now thought of herself as Katia Kozh, watched them carefully. She paid for her shoes with some of the cash that Eddie Poong had given her, and left the store.

Nice to see you, Max, she said bitterly to herself. All of the sympathetic thoughts that she had started to cultivate about Soleil Tangiere had been placed on hold: Max is here. I'm here. Soleil is here. One too many.

Katia turned a corner and walked two blocks to where Eddie said he would meet her. Arriving at the spot and not seeing him among the pedestrians, she began to get impatient and was about to walk off when she was startled by the sound of a car's horn. It was parked in the street not ten feet from her.

Eddie was at the wheel of a brand new, black Porsche 911 Turbo convertible. The top was down and Three Tit sat in the passenger seat, his sunglasses reflecting Katia standing above him with the sky and the tops of the low buildings behind her.

He opened the door and levered himself out of the low-slung car. He reached over and pulled the back of the passenger seat forward to allow her to squeeze into the tiny seating area in the back. Eddie sat behind the wheel tapping on it impatiently and playing with the sport car's shifter knob.

Katia, her short skirt catching every little wind gust, swung her long legs into the car and Three Tit enjoyed the sight of her trying to get comfortable in a seat that was obviously designed for people under the age of three. Katia, seeing his obviously lascivious grin and leering wink, momentarily entertained the possibility of saving herself a lot of grief and becoming a lesbian.

As they drove to the hotel, Katia said, "Where did you get this car?"

Eddie leaned back slightly without turning his head. "Porsche."

"You *bought* it?" She was surprised. Didn't these guys say they were going back to Hong Kong as soon as possible?

"We bought it for you," said Three Tit.

"Sure you did."

Three turned around in his seat. "A trade, Katia. Get us the diamonds, we give you the car."

"Can you give me money instead? Why do I need a car?"

Eddie said above the noise of the wind, "My brother is kidding around. I can't get this model in Hong Kong, so I'm going to have it shipped to me when we're done here. Until we leave, it'll come in handy." He slowed down and stopped the car at a red light. "And we'll give you money. Don't worry. Just do your part."

Katia wondered if there was a single man left in the world who would want her for who she was, not what she could give to him. Since Max, it seemed like the answer was no. Maybe she *should* become a lesbian...

She looked idly at two women walking across the intersection. After a minute of trying to get excited about it, she gave up.

"What in the world?" Soleil couldn't believe it. This was sick. What were they up to in Russia, those perverts? She held the diamond shorts at arm's length.

"Don't ask," said Max as he came into the living room. He was wearing new everything—shirt, pants, shoes, and especially underwear. He looked like a new man.

When Soleil had determined that the time had finally come to broach the topic of his two-month disappearance, he had handed her the odd bundle and said, "This is it—the long and the shorts of it."

"Short," she corrected.

"No, shorts. I know what I said."

Now she stood in the living room holding the lumpy Jockeys. He took them from her and set them down on her coffee table. In his other hand, he had a knife and a small white dish towel that he brought in from the kitchen.

He carefully made a long slit in the shorts and shook the contents onto the towel. Soleil looked on with interest. Hmm. Eight, nine...ten stones.

And one—what is this thing?

She held up an object. It was the size and shape of a rectangular soda cracker and was made of dull, bronze metal with gold and plastic edges. On one side was a label with Cyrillic lettering, some numbers, and a tiny red hammer and sickle.

She handed it to Max. "What does it say?"

He peered at the writing and numbers and then turned it over a few times in his hands. "Not much. It's mostly scientific stuff and a string of numbers."

Soleil said, "If that Veshkin character sewed it in with the diamonds, it must have had value to him." She thought back to last summer when that awful key had come into her life. She hated this. Why did she think that that stupid computer chip, or whatever it was, was worth more than the diamonds?

Soleil held one of the stones up to the light. "Max," she said. "These are very nice diamonds. But I guess you knew that."

The sun was streaming in her window. The uncut octahedral crystal she held up between her slim thumb and forefinger was larger than the other nine. It was rough but colorless. She studied it closely and moved her hand a fraction of an inch. A rainbow of light refracted off its surface and danced on the wall behind her.

She looked at Max. "How much does this weigh?"

Max admired the question—it was the right response from someone who knew something about diamonds. "I was told that each of these weigh at least fifty carats."

She peered at the one stone that was obviously larger than the others. It was a little over two inches long, and she hefted it in her palm. Then she said, "Max, this big one must weigh close to an ounce. That's over one hundred carats. Even though this hasn't been cut yet, this one stone will be worth a fortune when it is." She held it up to the light.

She looked over at him said, "Ouch! These must have really hurt."

"I shifted them around as best I could, but yes, they were very annoying," he said with an exaggerated look of pain on his face.

She placed the stone down with the others and pushed the lot of them around on the dish towel with one of her fingers. "Whom do these belong to, Max?"

"The Mir. I think. But I'm not bringing them back. Boris Veshkin organized this theft, and he used his power to order me to the Mir and to blackmail me into being the putsy."

"Patsy."

"Thank you. He took abusive advantage of his high position. And of his knowledge of my need to get to out of Russia—to get back to you."

Guilt suddenly flooded into Soleil's heart, but she felt that now wasn't the time to tell Max about how she had almost abandoned him in favor of the coward, Dustin. Or about her revenge tryst with Stefan. No, she wouldn't tell him yet. But soon.

She picked up the strange computer chip and said, "Do you think we should throw this out?"

"No way, Soleil." He suddenly frowned. "Oh, sorry. That sounded weird. I didn't mean for it to come out that way."

She gave him a miffed look.

"OK," he continued. "Don't throw it out. Knowing Veshkin, there's got to be some valuable information stored on that chip. I have a feeling that one day soon someone's going to miss it—maybe more than the diamonds. We'd better keep it in a safe place."

She pointed at the group of dully gleaming stones. "What about these?"

Max picked up one of the diamonds. "Soleil," he said, "there are more diamonds in the Mir than you can count. All Veshkin had to do was make some small changes in their computer, which he had full authority over, to make these ten stones disappear." He looked at her. "Now *he's* disappeared. For good."

They were silent for a moment. He nodded at the stones. "They may never be missed."

Soleil leaned back on the couch and seemed deep in thought. "Problems seem to follow us everywhere, don't they?" She looked at Max.

Catching the hint, he said, "Where did Katia go?" He knew he would have to address this problem.

"I don't know, Max. She's probably still in Zurich. She must have come in with some kind of visa or passport or something. I certainly haven't seen her since—well you know, since the incident on the roof."

Max pushed Katia to the back of his mind next to the other loose ends that he knew would have to be tied up in the near future. And I will tie them up, he thought with determination. Now that I'm here, anything can happen.

Soleil picked up the largest of the stones again and peered at it in the light.

"I have an idea," she said, and reached for the phone.

The old man turned the corner at Sixth Avenue and West Forty-Seventh Street, and walked halfway down the block, a brown paper bag in one hand.

He pushed open the glass doors of one of the many jewelry exchanges that jammed the famous "Diamond Way," as tourists called this street. This was the exchange where his tiny business reposed along with one hundred other "booths" or micro businesses, ten feet on a side, consisting of a few glass counters, a jeweler's work bench, and a safe.

And there were, in turn, dozens of exchanges, thousands of jewelry businesses in the three-square-block area bordered by Fifth and Sixth Avenues to the east and west, and Forty-Sixth and Forty-Eighth Streets to the north and south.

West Forty-Seventh Street is one of midtown New York's most distinct commercial neighborhoods, and since the Second World War, the area had been one of the primary centers of the global diamond industry, alongside London, Antwerp, and Bombay.

The old man, easily over seventy and very bald, muttered for the ten-thousandth time that he was too old for this, as he walked past a dozen other booths and finally came to his. The small, tasteful sign on his counter said, Gutthelf Fine Jewelry. Two women stood behind the waist-high glass counters.

"Where've you been?" the older heavyset woman behind the jewelry counter asked. She reached over the counter to take his coat, which she folded and placed on a chair.

"Here, Brenda," he said, sticking his hand in the brown bag. "I got you..." A dramatic pause, then: "Danish!" Out came the hand with the pastry on a square of wax paper.

He handed his wife the Danish and looked over at the striking young woman standing next to her. "And for you, Aimee..." More drama and finally the hand came out again. "Éclair!" He handed her the soft yellow cake with white cream oozing out of its center.

"Thanks, Izzy," said Aimee. She was twenty-four and at least a head taller than Brenda was, especially standing in her newest pair of trendy, mile-high shoes. "You always come through."

She smiled a radiant smile that offset her latest hairstyle—a dramatic sweep of dark hair coming down one side of her face while the rest of her hair did some kind of crazy jig on top of her head. Oy, thought Izzy, looking at her. Youth.

He gave Aimee and Brenda their Styrofoam cups of coffee from the bag and leaned on his counter. He looked around at the business going on around him.

Not bad, he thought secretly to himself. This was a pretty good Christmas season—we sold some nice jewelry.

The only downside was that we lost Soleil last summer, but...he turned and looked at Aimee, who was munching on her éclair. But Aimee is a doll, and she's really taken up the slack. And, like her Canadian predecessor, she's a beacon, a magnet for the men coming in to buy gifts for their girl-friends and wives.

He sighed. Sex sells, as they say in the Talmud.

The phone rang in the booth. Aimee tried to swallow her bite of pastry, picked up the phone, and said through the mouthful of éclair, "Gutthelf's."

"Hi, Aims. Merry belated Christmas."

Aimee nearly choked. She swallowed the rest of the mouthful and said, "Soleil? Hey, Ice Queen! How're the Alps? Have any good downhill runs lately?"

"Is that Soleil?" Brenda asked, her plain, kind face breaking into a smile. "Here, Aimee, give me the phone."

Aimee smiled and handed the phone over to Brenda. "Soleil, how are you?" she said. "We miss you. What are you doing? How's—"

"Wait. Hold on, Brenda, catch your breath." Soleil was smiling. She loved these people—they had taken her in, no questions asked, after her father was killed, and brought her back to the world of the living when she was almost dead. They had nursed her back to health and given her a home and a job in the jewelry business.

They talked for a few minutes, and then Soleil said, "Is Izzy there, Brenda? I need to ask him a question."

Brenda handed the phone to her husband, who was impatiently waiting to talk to Soleil.

"Solie?" he said into the phone. "How are you, my love?"

"Fine, Izzy. I miss you—I miss kissing your bald head, so I use a cantaloupe as a substitute."

Hearing this, Max looked over at Soleil and rolled his eyes. She stuck her tongue out at him.

Izzy laughed. "What's up Solie? What's happening in your life?"

"I need to ask you something, Izzy. A jewelry thing—a diamond thing."

His old face got serious. "Shoot," he said.

"OK. I have some rough. Large rough."

"What kind of rough?" Izzy asked, not realizing that they had both started talking "diamond," a language of its own.

"Big. One piece over a hundred carats."

Izzy whistled under his breath. "From where? South Africa? Botswana?"

"Nope."

"Don't tell me Sierra Leone. If it's from Sierra Leone, I don't want to know. The problems there—"

"No, Izzy. It's from Russia."

"What? From Russia? That means it's outside the reach of the Syndicate. But I've never heard of rough larger than five-caraters coming on the market from Russia. You have to be mistaken."

Soleil looked over at Max. "No, Izzy. It's from Russia. And it's gorgeous."

Izzy looked over at his wife and Aimee. "What are you doing with that rough, Solie?" he said into the phone.

"I'm going to need someone to look at the stone. Just the one piece."

"You need a cutter, you mean."

"Right. A cutter would be the only one who could give me a good idea of what I can get out of the stone—how many diamonds, what quality, and what sizes and shapes could be cut from the single crystal. That's all I want to know."

Izzy scratched his chin and said, "I won't vouch for any cutter here in New York. This place is a rat's nest of incompetents, fumble-fingers, fakers, and thieves. A job like that—an evaluation for a stone like you describe—you have to take it out of New York."

"I'm ahead of you, Izzy. I need to know if you can vouch for a good cutter here in Europe. If anyone should know, it's you, Izzy."

Izzy did know. He had a few old friends who had fled the Holocaust when he had, and settled in Antwerp and Amsterdam, two of the major diamond-cutting centers in the world. Now their children had become merchants and cutters in the arcane and closed world of diamonds.

Izzy hoped that Soleil knew what she was doing. Where on earth did she get a hundred-carat rough? A hundred-carat *Russian* rough?

"I can vouch for a few," he finally said.

He gestured for Brenda to hand him his Rolodex. He flipped through it and pulled out a few cards. He read the names and phone numbers to Soleil: old-time, honest friends in Amsterdam and Antwerp whose families were entrenched in the business. She wrote them down carefully.

When he was done, Soleil said, "Oh, Izzy, thanks so much. You don't know how much you've helped me."

"My pleasure, Solie, my love." Something suddenly struck him. "Wait, Solie. I forgot one cutter. Hold on a minute." He turned the Rolodex to the letter Z. One old card was there—one old card for one old man. Izzy looked at the one word in faded pencil: *Zvi*. Next to the name was a phone number. Izzy wondered if he was still alive.

"Solie, write this down." He gave the name and number to her. Then he said, "This is the man you should see with your Russian diamond. He's an old friend, and the most expert of them all. And I trust him completely."

"Where is he, Izzy? Amsterdam or Antwerp?"

"Neither. He's in Italy."

Soleil looked over at Max and mouthed the word "Italy." Max shrugged and nodded.

"You want I should call him and tell him you'll contact him?"

"Could you?"

"What do you think, my sweet girl?" said Izzy. "Of course." He rubbed the bridge of his nose between two fingers to cover for a sudden tear in his eye and said softly into the phone, "Come visit us soon, all right?"

"I will. I promise."

"Wait," he said, "Aimee wants to—"

Suddenly Aimee was on the phone. "When are you getting your skinny Canadian ass back here, Soleil?" Aimee's dark eyes glittered. "There're fifty or sixty guys waiting to hook up with you. And that's just on *this* block."

Soleil looked at Max. "Oh, I have a guy right here, Aimee. You'd like him."

"Huh! *One* guy? Borrrring, Soleil!"

She eyed Max. "Yeah, he's boring, I guess."

Max leaned over to tickle her.

"Gotta go," Soleil said, giggling, and hung up.

Gotta go.

To Italy.

16

FUROMA

The crystal-blue of the sky was starting to take on the darker shading of late afternoon.

"This is going to be easy if we all keep our heads," said Eddie Poong.

The Poong brothers were back at the hotel bar with Katia. Three Tit had come up with a boatload of clever reasons why they should have this meeting in their suite upstairs or, better yet, in Katia's room. But Katia was smarter than that.

"*Nyet*, you horny little lizard. No."

So here they were at the bar.

Eddie was sketching out his rough plan: Katia had to play along and be a "dangerous Russian mafia-type woman," whatever the hell that was. What a couple of morons, she thought.

She listened half-heartedly as Eddie said, "And that's when our jockstrap full of diamonds will be delivered to us on a silver platter."

He suddenly realized how weird that sounded.

Again, Katia thought, Morons.

He looked at the woman's face. "Soleil and Max both know you. Intimately, one could say. So here're some new details you need to know." He pushed a piece of paper down the bar to her.

Katia's eyes narrowed as she read it. This was it, she silently vowed. This was the very last thing she would do for people like this. But she was trapped again, stuck. Without big money or some kind of connection, her options were limited. She looked up and said resignedly to Eddie, "All right. Yes."

Then she looked around at Three, who had pushed his barstool a couple of inches closer to hers and was smiling with what he thought was seductive innuendo. "No," she said to him plainly.

"All right," Eddie said. He reached into his pocket and pulled out a fat wad of bills. He peeled off about an inch, handed it to Katia, and said, "Here. Go have a good time tonight. We'll meet you in the lobby tomorrow at 9:00 a.m. Be prompt."

Katia silently put the money in her purse and got off the barstool. She nodded at Eddie, threw Three Tit a pissed-off, not-in-a-million-years look, and walked out of the bar.

Three watched her backside as she walked off, and then moved over to her vacated barstool. Eddie scowled at him and said, "You too. Give me some space. Go get laid or something. You're embarrassing."

Three shrugged. He said to his brother, "You sure you just don't want to move in on the Soleil woman's apartment and take the diamonds? Just *take* them?"

Eddie looked at Three with scorn. He loved his brother, but subtlety wasn't his strongest suit. Nor was thinking ahead.

"Three," he finally said. "What do we look like? A couple of criminals?"

Yvonne stood in front of Soleil's open door.

"*Bonsoir*," Soleil said, throwing a haughty look at her friend.

"Oh, how nice. You're learning French," Yvonne said as she swept into the apartment. She was wearing a short black dress with a wide, matching belt, and black pumps. Her dark hair matched her large eyes.

"Aren't you a bit overdressed for dinner?" Soleil asked.

"Compared to you? *Certainmente*." She looked her friend up and down. Soleil was wearing a blousy white shirt over tailored jeans and her favorite black high-heeled boots.

"Where's André?" asked Soleil, closing the door behind her.

Yvonne turned to Soleil. "Back in Grenoble. His Christmas holiday is over."

"Back to Mommy and Daddy for little André, I guess." Soleil cast a judgmental eye on Yvonne. "Cradle robber."

Yvonne narrowed her eyes and smiled. "You just don't understand me—my female needs."

"What you need is to get a grip on your hormones! How old was he anyway, eighteen?"

"Irrelevant," she said. Then suddenly, "Max!"

Max had just come out of the bedroom wearing a new, navy Italian suit jacket that had fit him well off the rack.

He wore an open-necked white shirt and a pair of designer jeans. The other suits he had bought were being tailored to fit his stocky, muscular frame.

Yvonne went over to him. He put his strong hands on either side of her waist and easily picked her up a few inches off the floor. She hugged him while kicking back one leg and quickly kissed him on the mouth. Soleil stood by with her arms crossed in front of her chest.

"Yvonne! Hormones? Remember?" she said, hooking her fingers in the back of Yvonne's belt and pulling her off Max. Max let the woman down and he made a beatific face and shrugged at Soleil.

"Max, I'm so glad you're here," Yvonne said, plainly appraising him from top to bottom. She was truly happy to see Max. She had only met him that one time in Geneva, the day before he had to return to Russia. She had instantly seen that he and Soleil were a perfect fit.

And now she was having fun with this little back-and-forth.

Soleil shook her head from side to side with exaggerated tiredness. "Give it up, Frenchy," she said to Yvonne. "You're out of your depth." Soleil went to stand next to Max and loudly whispered in his ear, "You will forget everything that happened in the last thirty seconds," and snapped her fingers.

"I doubt it," he said, winking broadly at Yvonne.

The intercom bell in the kitchen rang. Soleil went over to it, spoke for a second, and pressed the access button on the small box. She turned back into the room and said, "Camille and Kurt are here. They're on their way up."

"Great, I'm famished," said Max.

His joy at being here with Soleil overrode the profound weariness that was the product of his two months at the Mir and the last few crazy days. He'd better ease up on the drinking from now on, he reminded himself. Like every single other soul at the frozen mine, Max had unconsciously become heavily dependent on vodka—cheap vodka—to stay sane and to stay warm. He was already craving a drink.

But he had done that before. It wouldn't be easy, but he owed it to Soleil to cut out drinking. He owed it to both of them.

The door opened and Camille came in, followed by Kurt. They were also dressed in a dinner-casual way.

Kurt said, "Hi, Yvonne. Wow, nice dress."

Soleil said through clenched but smiling teeth, "OK, that's it! Why don't I just stay here, and all you guys go out with Yvonne?"

Everyone laughed, and Camille said, "Chill out, Soleil. Remember, its two Tangieres against one Goulet. She doesn't stand a chance."

"Don't bet on it," Yvonne parried.

"C'mon, let's go eat," said Camille in her usual direct way. "I'm starving."

"I'll get your coat, Soleil," Max said, and went to the small hall closet that Soleil almost never used. In a moment, he came out holding a men's Armani cloth coat. He looked at Soleil. "Whose is this?" he asked innocently.

Soleil suddenly caught her breath.

She was stunned—the coat was Dustin's. He had left it in that closet when he fled in fear the other night.

Her eyes went from the coat to Max's face. I can't lie to him. I just can't.

Max looked at the coat folded over his arm and noticed the corner of a piece of paper was peeking from one of the pockets. He pulled it out. It was a photograph.

Max looked up. "This coat must be yours, Kurt."

He flipped the photo so everyone could see it.

It was a perfect portrait shot of Camille.

Camille, a confused expression in her eyes, looked quickly from the photo to Soleil. She was about to say something but then thought better of it.

The room was silent.

Max's eyes narrowed for just a second, and he said, "Keeping anymore of your clothes in Soleil's apartment?" He threw Kurt a conspiratorial look. "I hope Camille knows about this."

Kurt smiled uncertainly and started to say something, but Camille was digging her fingernails into the palm of his hand. Finally, he muttered, "You've got nothing to worry about, amigo."

"Let's go," Yvonne interjected brightly, covering her sudden nervousness, and successfully defusing some of the confused tension in the air. Her eyes slid toward Soleil.

All Soleil could do was nod. No, this isn't right, she thought. I have to say something to Max.

She went to the bedroom closet to get her coat, and Max followed her. She quickly turned to look at him, her eyes searching his, her heart beating fast.

He looked at her for a second, and then leaned in and gave her a feather-light kiss on her lips. He whispered, "Whatever." Then another kiss. "Later."

She nodded, and they went back into the living room.

In a minute or two, they had all left.

The photograph of Camille lay on the coffee table.

They were in the Zeughauskeller, where Soleil and Camille had eaten lunch the day that Kurt was shot.

The popular restaurant was packed at the dinner hour, and they were lucky to have gotten a table. Kurt's outrageous tip to the maître d' hadn't hurt, either. The five sat at a table positioned between two of the large Palladian windows.

Max was bombarded by questions about Russia from Camille, Kurt, and Yvonne, which he answered between bites of food and sips of his Pellegrino. He was dead serious about going cold turkey with the alcohol, at least for a while.

Soleil was quiet and mostly listened. Her soul was troubled, and she wondered how this day would finally end.

What could she say? Later that night, she would have to come clean with Max. She would have done just that back at the apartment, but everyone was there and it would have been worse than awkward. And Max seemed to be fine. So far. All she could do was wait to get back home, alone with him, and see how it played out.

She sipped her beer and toyed with her schnitzel.

At the table next to theirs, an older couple accompanied by three young children were eating and talking. They were obviously seniors taking their grandkids out for dinner. The kids were a bit on the loud side, and Soleil overheard their grandfather lay down the law:

"Settle down," he said to them in German. "We are in public. You children must be quieter for the sake of the other people in this restaurant." He pointed to himself, "*Und für*

Opa." And for Grandpa. Then he pointed to his wife. "*Und für Oma.*" And for Grandma.

Soleil's eyes suddenly went wide.

What? Soleil said to herself. What did he say?

Für Oma.

For Grandma.

Furoma. That's what the Asian woman had said before she killed herself on the streets of Zurich. *Für Oma.* For Grandma.

Oh, no.

The picture of Camille in Dustin's pocket exploded in front of her eyes.

In a blinding flash of horrendous intuition, it all came crashing together in Soleil's mind.

She pushed back her chair and quickly stood up. The conversation at the table came to a halt, and everyone looked up at Soleil's shocked face.

"Soleil," Max said, quickly getting up from his chair and putting his hands on her shoulders. "Soleil, what's wrong?"

She was staring off into space and almost shaking. Then she looked down at Camille, who was sitting at the table, her mouth open in surprise.

Camille?

Für Oma.

Oh my God.

He stepped out of the old-fashioned cab in front of the gleaming, stainless-steel skyscraper and wished he were anywhere else.

The hour-and-a-half flight had seemed longer than it was, and there was no joy in it—just one part annoyance mixed with three parts of fear. This had become a real mess, Dustin Magill kept saying to himself. A real, dangerous mess.

Dustin gave his name to the guard at the lobby desk and was told to sit on one of the low couches against the wall. Someone would be down to fetch him. Outside the two-story-tall lobby windows, the sky was darkening. He had never liked this city. In fact, he hated it.

In a few minutes, a burly man in a dark suit came out of an elevator and gave Dustin a "come with me" signal with his hand. Dustin rose, walked over to him, and the two got into the elevator. The man was silent as he took a key from his pocket and inserted it in a lock next to the button for the thirty-third floor. He turned the key, and they went up in silence.

The elevator door sighed open, and Dustin followed the man to the door at the end of the corridor. A discreet plaque said, "Chairman." Directly beneath the plaque was a logo: the letters *CM* in a modern, intertwined motif.

The man opened the door and allowed Dustin to walk through it ahead of him. He followed Dustin in, and then took up a position with his back against the door.

The room was large, but stark, with a single desk in the center and no chairs. An entire wall was comprised of floor-to-ceiling windows that presented an impressive view of the city of London—Parliament, Big Ben—the works. On one of the walls hung two pictures incongruously framed in old-fashioned, flowery, gilt frames. Each was of a man, and they were obviously related. One looked like the father of the other.

A strange contraption on large wheels stood in front of one of the giant windows. Dustin had only seen it once before—the other time he had been here and was recruited by the chairman for his delicate task. At the time, the chairman was delighted that Dustin Magill had been referred to this office with his impressive resumé: actor, petty thief, minor extortionist. Murderer—just once, but he was ambitious...

The contraption was a motorized wheelchair, and a highly unusual one at that. Attached to it were myriad levers and monitors that allowed its operator to not only get around on almost any surface, but to keep track of heart and respiration rates, blood pressure, and other critical body functions. It was a mobile life-support system for its operator, who sat at its center.

"Hello, Dustin," came the gritty, dusty voice of its operator, the chairman.

"Grandma," said Dustin Magill.

Delores "Grandma" Clooney, at age ninety-two, was the undisputed owner, operating officer, and chairman of the board of Carrington Metals.

The London-based company was a major player in the world of PGMs—the platinum group metals—their mining, fabrication, and marketing. And, thanks to Grandma, the company was the premier expert in the bribery, payoffs, blackmail, extortion, and murder that came with conducting illegal business deals in the undeveloped, despot-run countries across Africa, where those metals were mined.

To be fair, not all the nefarious credit should go to Grandma.

It was a family tradition, a dynasty—a hierarchy built on the dirtiest business tactics conceivable, affording Carrington Metals a strong global foothold in the platinum and palladium markets. "The ends justify the means" was the solid family motto.

Her son, who called himself Philip Smythe, president of the company, (his picture was the one on the right), had inherited her flair for organizing and executing the dirtiest, most illegal and amoral deals imaginable.

And Smythe's son, John Clooney, executive vice president (the dashing young fellow in the picture on the left), had been following in his father and grandmother's footsteps.

But it had all come crashing down a few short months earlier.

Grandma's poor son, her only son, Philip, had been crushed, chopped in half, and then fricasseed in his Audi at the Geneva airport.

Then, adding insult to injury, *his* son, her one and only, wonderful grandson, John Clooney, was tossed forty-five stories to his explosive death in New York.

Her legacy, her family line was wiped out. Completely.

Who was to blame? Grandma had posed that rhetorical question to herself. Well, it was painfully evident, blatantly obvious. The facts were the facts. The same person had thwarted their dark and ambitious plans to steal the key to the Soviet Union's vast bullion hoard.

It was Soleil Tangiere...

Grandma's eyes began to glow. How did that Tangiere woman manage to keep eluding her wrath? Did she have a guardian angel? There was no doubt that her luck *would* run out one day—angel or no angel.

Well, the time had come. It was time to end her. She had lived too long under the same sun that shone down on Philip and John's graves.

She looked over at a stack of dollars, francs, German marks, and British pounds on her desk and nodded at Dustin, who was standing before it.

She lifted a wizened hand and waved it at the money. "Go ahead; it's yours." He picked it up hesitantly and then shoved it in his jacket pocket.

Grandma rolled closer to him. He hadn't been able to get over how tiny the woman was. The chair was almost too large for her. Her intelligent eyes, surrounded by layers of reptilian skin, shone at him.

"Two of my employees, now deceased, have failed to inflict a single ounce of pain on Soleil Tangiere, Dustin. All that money down the drain." Her voice was like a dry wind blowing over the Sahara.

Dustin shifted his weight from one foot to the other and waited.

Grandma used a wizened hand to control the pitch and yaw of the chair. She turned again and said, "Go back to Switzerland, Dustin, and wait to hear from me." She waved a claw-like hand.

"And please, young man." Her face suddenly twisted into a horrifying mask of madness, and her dry voice turned into a sandstorm. "When I call to tell you to pull the trigger, you will pull...the...trigger!"

"Max," Soleil said shakily. "Come outside with me."

They got their coats, and in a matter of a minute, stood outside the restaurant on the Zurich sidewalk. She hadn't spoken; she just stared straight ahead. After a moment, she whispered Camille's name.

He had his arms around her. Finally, he felt her pull away slightly. She looked into his eyes. She was coming back. Max had never seen anything like it.

"Max."

"Yes, Soleil?"

"That Zoe woman in Chicago whom I told you about, and the Asian woman here in Zurich. They weren't trying to kill Kurt. They were being paid to kill Camille."

"What? What are you talking about?" He was profoundly worried for Soleil.

She was shaking and felt a vertiginous sense of unreality. "Max. If someone wanted to hurt me, *really* hurt me, there's really only way they could do it. They would try to hurt the people I love."

She looked steadily into his eyes. "That someone hired those...assassins to kill my sister to hurt me, and Kurt wound up in the line of fire."

She looked at the ground. "Kurt wracked his brain trying to figure out who had a strong enough motive to kill him. He kept coming up empty. Why didn't I see this?"

She looked up at Max. "That bullet that hit Kurt's shoulder here in Zurich. It came within an inch of Camille's face."

A tear shook in one of Soleil's eyes and then ran quickly down her cheek.

"And as for Dustin, he—" She stopped suddenly and looked anywhere but at Max.

"Who?" he asked.

She looked quickly into Max's eyes. Then she slumped toward him. She couldn't do this now. She couldn't lose him now.

"Max. I have to go home."

"Of course." He guided her back through the restaurant's door, but Camille, Kurt, and Yvonne had their coats on and were on their way out to help.

Soleil looked at them and said, "I'm OK."

She looked at Camille and said, "Be careful, Cami. I don't believe everything is solved at all, and all of us are still in danger."

Camille looked at her with deep concern. Then she nodded her head uncertainly. "Sure, Soleil, of course." What on earth had gotten into her? Camille wondered.

Max had the maître d' call for a cab, and in less than two minutes, it pulled up in front of the restaurant. By then, Soleil was almost back to her former self. She kissed Camille, Kurt, and Yvonne good night and got into the backseat. Max sat next to her and took her hand in his.

She looked at him. "We have to talk."

17

ABOUT ANGELS

Soleil was feeling better, but she hadn't been able to organize her thoughts or figure out how to handle this new situation yet. And the first thing she wanted to do was straighten everything out with Max. Now. For better or worse.

Max hung their coats in the closet, next to Dustin's, and he looked at the expensive garment for a moment. He closed the narrow closet door and turned to find Soleil standing in front of him.

"We have to talk," she said, and pulled him by the hand into the living room. She sat down at one end of the couch and waved her hand at him in a silent invitation.

He slowly sat down on the opposite end of the couch and looked over at her. "This sounds serious," he said.

She hesitated for a moment, gathering her thoughts. "At least you're here now." She looked at the floor. "That is, if you decide that you want to be."

What's she getting at? Max thought. Acting oblique and indirect wasn't in Soleil's repertoire. "What's wrong, Soleil? What do you want to talk about that's so serious that it's chased the sunshine off your face?"

He's such a Russian, she said to herself. His turn of phrase is odd and corny, but so attractive. "A lot has happened since you left," she began.

"No kidding." He smiled.

"Some of it has to do with us—you and me."

"You found someone else," he said glibly. Then his face fell. Looking at her, he suddenly realized that what he had just said was accurate, or at least partially accurate. Her hesitation was classic, he said to himself with bitter sadness. Clearly.

And in spite of his toughing it out at the Mir, in spite of his wishing and praying for her happiness, now when it came down to it, it was still crushing.

He looked over at the photograph of Camille that was still on the coffee table. After a moment, he said, "It's not Kurt's coat, is it?"

Soleil shook her head.

His face asked, Who?

"Max..." She knew that no matter how she said it, it would hurt; it would sound trite and insufficient and selfish. And it would likely break them apart. But at least it would be the truth. And better an honest devil than a lying angel.

"Max, when I thought you were with Katia, I figured that you had changed your mind—that coming back to me, back to the West, was too difficult and not possible." She looked at the rock-hard expression on his face and knew that what she was saying was woefully lame and inadequate. "And you had someone else. I thought that it wasn't worth it to you."

She fidgeted for a moment, but the words stumbled out. "I was angry and felt...well...I just felt that you had immediately started on a new life far away. A life without me.

"I had tried to call so many times. None of the calls I was able to make to Nevsky Nickel were answered. Nothing. I even tried to get a visa to travel to Russia, but it was impossible, what with the political chaos. And then I got Katia on the phone."

"So you gave up." Without waiting for her to reply, he said, "I would have too." God knows what else Katia had said to her—she could be ruthless, he said to himself.

"A few days ago, I met Dustin. That's his coat." She turned her head in the direction of the closet for a second. "He left here in a hurry the night Veshkin was killed, and now I know why."

Max looked across the room, then out the window, and then at Soleil. "You made love with him?"

Soleil shook her head. "No, but it was close."

"So that's it?" Max asked, an odd sense of relief beginning to assuage his ambivalence toward the situation. "That's all?"

She shook her head. "There's more," she said quietly.

Max's sense of relief sank beneath the waves. He just looked at her.

"I had revenge sex." It was almost a whisper.

"Revenge sex?"

"I was angry after the 'I'm-in-the-shower-with-Max' call, and I took it out on you. And on some ski bum named

Stefan." Boy, that sounded really bad, she thought. *I wish that I could hide under this couch. And then die.*

Oh, damn it.

She suddenly stood up and glared down at him, a few straight, blond hairs falling in front of her face. She had finally hit the wall. "Am I sorry? No! I'm not sorry! Why should I be?" She paced in front of him. "The man I loved was somewhere in Moscow taking a shower with some Russian *putain*, and he hadn't had the decency to call to at least say 'good-bye.' Damn you, Maxim Stepanov!" Her eyes blazed like two blue suns.

He looked at her from the couch. After a minute, he slowly got up and said, "What is '*putain*'?"

She turned her back on him and said, "OK, go. Just go! Get out! Don't stay here! If I were you I'd—"

His arms came around her waist from the back, and his mouth was near her ear. "You don't have to yell," he whispered. "All that vodka sharpened my hearing over the last couple of months."

She turned in his arms to face him.

He looked at her with a serious expression. "Soleil. I have some news for you."

"You're leaving me now?"

He gave her an exasperated look. "The news is that you are not an angel. If you were, I couldn't love you, because I don't have wings either. If you knew what I did up at the Mir, you would surely throw me out right now."

She gave him an inquisitive look. He quickly said, "No, there were no girls in the Arctic, except the female reindeers. But in order for me to escape that hell, I had to do some bad things. Awful. Not worthy of someone who you love."

Her eyes searched his. "You would never do anything to hurt me, though." It wasn't a question.

"And that's exactly what I know about *you*, Soleil. That's why I love you."

He held her, and her arms went around his neck, and she pulled him closer.

Their eyes spoke for them then, and reaffirmed that there were no angels in the room.

Soleil carefully opened the small, chamois bag into which they had transferred the rough diamonds, and let them fall on the dresser top.

Were the diamonds alive, they would have reveled in the soft light.

Having been in the quiet darkness of the Arctic ground for half a billion years, they would have rejoiced in the pure colors and subtle tones of the living; the loudness and the quietness of those walking the earth; the insistent beating of a million hearts...

Soleil knew instinctively that sound and light and love were the intermingled colors on life's palette. She thoughtfully lined the diamonds up in a single row on the dresser top near the window and appraised them from a few feet away. Then she walked over to Max, who put his arms around her.

I'll never leave again, Soleil, his heart said silently to the woman in his arms.

I'll never doubt you again, Max, her eyes told his without a word spoken.

Never.

They kissed...

Later, the city's light coming through the window flowed through the diamonds, casting a line of refracted stars on the bed's headboard. The stars flickered on and off intermittently in concert with the movements and the muted but earnest sounds:

"Yes."

"Mmm."

"Does that...?"

"No."

"Yes?"

"Here."

"Mmm."

A sharp intake of breath.

"OK."

"*Da.*"

A long exhale.

"Un hnnn."

"Yeah."

"Oh!"

"Don't, yes, do."

"Was that...?"

"Mmm."

"Yes."
"Yes."
"Soleil."
"Shh."

Later on, the diamonds hoarded whatever tiny flashes of light they could, as the soft sounds of secrets and truths swirled in the still air below their spangled reflections:
"Leaving?"
"*Nyet.*"
"Until...?"
"Never."
"And?"
"Is this revenge?"
A breath.
"Maybe."
"Soleil."
A breath.
"Yes?"
Three seconds.
"Try."
"Always."
A breath, a moment.
"Yes."
"Mmmm."
"There?"
"Yes."
Then:
"Yes..."
Never?

Always.

And toward morning, the line of diamonds was surrounded with the insistent eternal whisper of two lovers whose light breathing mingled in the stillness of a clear and dreamless sleep.

The diamonds hadn't moved, but everything around them—the light, the sounds, the love—was in constant motion in the room, in the world, in the pulses and the heartbeats of all who were living on that day.

18

HEAT WAVE

Vlad stood in the vault two thousand feet below the frozen surface and felt like killing someone.

He had used his special clearance from the Kremlin to requisition a Tupolev Tu-22m supersonic swing-wing long-range bomber to fly him at almost twice the speed of sound over land from Moscow to the Mir.

The futuristic fighter jet then proceeded to experience an engine malfunction midflight and was forced to land at a remote airstrip a thousand miles east of Moscow.

Classic Soviet inefficiency came to the rescue. The plane finally had been repaired, but now Vlad was running over thirty-six hours behind schedule. He had lost a day and a half since his meeting with the general secretary.

In a violent frame of mind, he was listening to the lame excuses and terrified explanations from anyone and every-one as to how someone had executed the theft from the vaults. The Mir's twenty senior managers were jammed into the small room.

One of the vault guards, Arkady, stood at attention in the back of the room, loaded with enough weaponry to bring Czechoslovakia to its knees. Arkady quietly tsk-tsked as, one by one, everyone in charge was stripped of his position and power at the Mir.

The expression "heads will roll" seemed very appropriate, Arkady said to himself in bemusement as he watched Vlad's purge unfolding in the room.

Then there was the heated debate over the ongoing investigation into the body discovered at the bottom of the diamond hole. In its spectacular fall, it had been smashed and mangled beyond anything resembling a human. All that was left was an extra-large parka wrapped around what looked like the rearranged remains of a freeze-dried water buffalo.

The frozen-solid buffalo was finally identified as one Gravva Gleb, a Mongolian who, Vlad reasoned bitterly, had no real business being at the Mir. Unless, of course, he was some kind of a spy who slipped right by these shit-for-brains morons who ran this place.

Vlad and the dangerous-looking KGB agent who had accompanied him had ripped through everyone who thought he had seen anything else out of the ordinary in the last six months, but he wasn't hopeful.

At one point, Vlad shouted to the cowed and nervous managers around him, "You incompetent fools!" He stabbed a finger toward Arkady. "This lowly guard here probably has a better grip on managing the Mir than you do!"

He walked up to Arkady, who stood at rigid attention. "They should have put *you* in charge. You look smarter than all of them put together."

"Thank you," said Arkady through tight lips, keeping his eyes front and center and trying hard not to belch. He hoped this jacked-up People's Commissar didn't smell the vodka on his breath.

Vlad learned three startling pieces of information:

One: In addition to the locus of his world-class headache—the disappearance of the irreplaceable chip that had been stored in these "impregnable" vaults—ten large, rough diamonds had also gone missing. Their value was many, many millions of dollars.

Two: Boris Veshkin had been there less than two weeks ago. Vlad knew him too well. He was a grasping, greedy, murderous paranoid, which was why he had been sought out and promoted to the position of manager of the large Soviet enterprise, Nevsky Nickel, which operated the mine.

And three: Max Stepanov had also been there.

Max?

What had *he* been doing there? Vlad was mystified and horrified all at once—Max Stepanov was his friend. Max had helped Vlad immensely with recovering the key that had led to Vlad's meteoric rise in the Soviet hierarchy over the last two months. And he had saved that Tangiere woman's life at the same time.

And Vlad had promised Max freedom, a clear avenue to defect to the West.

But again, what had he been doing at the Mir? Helping Veshkin? *Max*?

Vlad knew that he must find Veshkin and Max. Now.

He gestured to his KGB companion, and they swept out of the vault. They headed for the elevators to the surface and then got on the snowmobiles that took them to the waiting bomber.

There was a full minute of dead silence after they left the room.

Then Arkady stood silently while the Mir managers, as if on cue, began shouting and yelling and blaming each other all at the same time. In another minute, the argument had devolved into a fistfight.

Arkady stood by calmly and retreated into his memories: The night with the plow was the most fun he'd had in a long time. Thanks, Max, he thought.

One of the Mir managers crashed onto the floor in front of him, his nose broken and bleeding, but Arkady didn't care. He reached into his pocket for a cigarette.

He hoped that Max remembered what he had asked him to do. Max, my friend, he thought as he lit a match, I hope you didn't forget to make love to a beautiful woman when you got to the West.

He held the match to the cigarette dangling from his lips, drew the deep, satisfying smoke into his lungs, and confidently knew that Max wouldn't renege on a promise.

Spasibo, Max! Thank you!

They had awakened early to the sound of the phone ringing. Soleil had reached across Max to pick it up. "Mmm?"

"Soleil, are you all right?" said Camille, in a worried tone.

"Um hm."

"Oh, I get it."

"Um hmmm."

"Meet us for breakfast at the hotel?"

"Unhh."

"About 8:30?"

"Unh hm."

Finally, too frustrated to continue playing the "mmm" game, Camille said, "See you soon, and please—try to remember what galaxy you're in."

"Mm."

"Delores Clooney wants me dead, but tortured first."

It was 8:30 and Soleil was sitting next to Max at the Pavillon restaurant in the Baur au Lac Hotel. Camille and Max sat facing them. Though the mood was serious, through the windows, the view of the sparkling lake under the azure sky was inspiring.

Soleil had a croissant in one hand and watched distractedly as steam rose from her cup of cocoa. Outside, the sun was glorious and a welcome rarity in this part of the winter—tomorrow was the last day of the year.

"Soleil," Max said. "I'm going to put an end to it. That vicious *babushka* is worse than insane—she's insane with a lot of money." He was silent for a moment. "That Asian woman was so fearful of Grandma's punishment that she decided to skip the agony and shoot herself. *Dermo!*"

Soleil shook her head. "You're not going to do anything, please, Max. I want to go to Italy to visit Izzy's friend. We should get out of this city for a while." She took a bite of the croissant. "I thnk wsh shlg."

"Is that French?" Max said blandly.

She gulped and said, "I think we should all go." She looked for a response from Camille. "All of us, even Yvonne. If bad people are trying to catch up to us, why make it easy for them?"

Max couldn't argue with that logic. He smiled. Most of the smile had to do with the previous night, and Soleil could see it—it was obvious. She smiled as well, but mostly inside.

"And Dustin," she said, taking a tiny sip of the cocoa. "Dustin was Grandma Clooney's third and worst hired gun. He came after me first to become my lover and then certainly planned to kill Camille in front of my eyes. And then me."

Camille looked into her cup of coffee and marshaled her thoughts. "What's it going to take to stop that lunatic? It sounds like a case of pure psycho revenge on steroids." She thought about how lucky she and Kurt were to have survived the first two attempts on her life. "I'm not looking forward to the third time being the charm."

"I have an idea," Kurt said suddenly. "You guys enjoy your breakfast. I'll be back in a few minutes." He excused himself and walked out of the restaurant.

"Not an original way of skipping out on the tab," Max quipped, looking after him.

"Where's he going?" asked Soleil, but Camille merely shrugged.

After five minutes, Max said, "Maybe he got lost." He excused himself and walked out of the restaurant into the lobby.

Ulrika Sonnenreich stood in front of the fax machine in the precinct's communication room, held up the sheet of paper, and narrowed her eyes.

Now a Russian big shot had hit the Interpol list of most critical fugitives and was believed to be in Europe, most likely in Switzerland. Not likely anymore, she said to herself. Now it was confirmed. The fax of his photo was an exact match for the man who had blown a perfectly good bench to bloody splinters on the street in front of Soleil Tangiere's building.

According to this report, there likely would be a numbered account at the ZSB.

She stood up and went to get her coat.

She would follow up on that immediately. But she was not anxious to do what she knew she would have to do after that.

You're my only real friend, Soleil, she thought. Give me something to keep me from arresting you.

Kurt finished arranging for a rental car at the front desk.

They needed to have wheels. Soleil was right—it was time to get out of town for a while. Bullets flying in the street, people flying off buildings. It was a good idea to drive into Italy—at least they could avoid flying.

The hotel was more than pleased to satisfy Mr. Ballas's simple request. A Mercedes 300 sedan would be delivered within an hour. Kurt's outsized cash tips to the staff helped him immeasurably.

While he was standing at one end of the front desk, filling out paperwork for the rental, two Asian men and a statuesque brunette strode up and stood next to him. One of the men addressed a hotel clerk in British-accented English.

"Have them bring our car around. The name is Poong," he said.

The clerk, who was far more proficient in German than in English, said, "Herr Pong, to help you I would be happy." The clerk picked up a phone and asked for the black Porsche to be brought around immediately. He put the phone down and said, "Your car is now in the front being brought, Herr Pong."

"That's *Poong*," Eddie said loudly and irritably, and the three strode out the front door of the hotel.

Kurt turned back to the paperwork, but he was startled to see that Max had just walked up. Max's face was white, and he was looking after the three people who had just left. "Max, you OK?" Kurt asked.

Max wasn't OK. He had come out of the restaurant looking for Kurt and had overheard the loud conversation at the front desk. When he had heard the word "Poong," he felt like his insides had turned to stone. He'd looked at the two Chinese men, and when he saw the woman with them, he literally froze. *Katia*.

He flashed back to the night that Gravva had fallen into the Mir diamond pit. Max had yelled over the rumbling of the plow, trying to find out who had been the man's controller, who had ordered Max's death.

Then Gravva had screamed his last word: "Poooong!" as he disappeared into oblivion.

And now, here in the Baur au Lac Hotel in Zurich, their room probably just down the hall from Camille and Kurt's, were the Poong brothers themselves. With Katia.

"Max," Kurt repeated. "Are you all right?"

Without answering, Max walked slowly to the side of the large front doors and peered out. Neither the brothers nor Katia had seen him.

A black Porsche convertible had just been brought under the *porte corchère* at the front of the hotel. Katia was climbing awkwardly into the backseat while the Asians looked on. In another minute, they were all in the car and had driven off, the top of the convertible down in this unseasonably beautiful weather.

Max stood there for a full minute before he noticed Kurt standing next to him. "You know them?" Kurt asked.

Max looked at him and said, "I do now."

"Poong?" asked Soleil Tangiere.

"Eddie and, er, his brother," said Max.

"What's the brother's name?" asked Camille.

"Huh?"

"Do you know his brother's name?" Kurt was curious.

Though Max was a plain speaker and by nature socially competent, he couldn't find a way out of this one. He looked down at his cup of coffee and said, "Three Tit."

Soleil made a face. "What?"

Max looked to Kurt for help, but the Chicagoan just threw him an odd look.

"Three Tit?" Camille asked loudly. "What kind of name is Three Tit?" A few guests having breakfast at a nearby table looked over, their faces registering mixed emotions, none of them good.

Max looked at Soleil, who had a vaguely disgusted look on her face.

Finally, Max said, "All right, now that we have that behind us, all I can say for certain is that they're the ones who sent someone to the Mir to kill me. And I'm certain that's why they're here in Zurich." His brow furrowed. "I don't believe in coincidences."

Camille looked at Soleil and said, "Don't you know any normal guys? You know, guys who go to work, watch the game on TV, and tinker with the car?"

Soleil gave her a look, took a sip of cocoa, and shook her head. "Nope." Then she added, "Do you?"

Kurt said, "How did this Katia woman wind up with them?"

Soleil put down her cup, looked at Max and said coolly, "Yes, Max. How *did* this Katia woman wind up with them?" She was understanding and all that, but now her lover's ex was running around Zurich with a couple of murderous Chinese mobsters. Camille is right, she thought. Maybe I'm a magnet for this kind of thing. Maybe I should have been a nun.

Max said, "Veshkin got her out of Russia. She had to have come here with him."

And it made perfect sense, Max said to himself. The bastard was going to use Katia to make sure he came through with flying colors and delivered the diamonds. Then, most likely after killing Max if he could, Veshkin certainly would have had to kill Katia.

Camille said, "OK, but why is she with these Poong brothers?"

"Odds are they met her in this hotel." Max cast his eyes around the restaurant. "Knowing Veshkin, he would have stayed here—it's the finest hotel in the city. I guess these Poong people are of a similar bent."

Kurt said, "I saw them here yesterday as well. And the woman." He turned to Camille. "Maybe we should switch hotels."

"Better yet," said Soleil, "Now that we have a car, let's get out of town."

19

BANKER'S HOURS

Herr Oscar Menschel stood sideways to better behold his tight, slim figure.

He was in front of a large mirror in his upper-floor office at the Zürcher Suisse Bank, quietly reveling in his status as the quintessential—the *ultimate*—Swiss banker.

Ach, what man wouldn't want to be me? he thought. At only forty-two years of age, I have attained huge and impressive stature here at the ZSB, and my fortunes grow by the day—by the minute—in so many ways.

He loved his dark gray, pinstriped, three-piece suits and was convinced that the rimless reading glasses that were perpetually perched on the end of his thin nose gave him the air of a sophisticated mover, shaker, and insider in the world of secret money.

Herr Oscar Menschel knew a lot about secret money, and even more about the people who stashed it in his bank.

He knew Boris Veshkin. He knew Eddie and Three Tit Poong. And he certainly knew and remembered quite well Frau Soleil Tangiere.

But he didn't know Katia Koziashvili, now calling herself Katia Kozh.

Through one of the windows between his office and his reception area, he could see her sandwiched between Eddie and Three Tit on a visitors' couch. The Poong brothers had made an appointment just a few hours ago, and Oscar was anxious to see them.

Anxious was a particularly appropriate word, he mused, loving his own knack for keen observation. The lack of couth and odd habits that followed the brothers from the Far East *were* a bit disturbing, he conceded with distaste, but those peccadillos were easily overlooked. The Poongs were truly such wonderful clients. They had several safe deposit boxes at the bank, kept a running cash minimum of over twenty-five million US dollars in commercial accounts, and had a credit line of twice that.

And, of course, there was the monthly "accommodation" that was sent to Menschel personally at a drop box—payment for lists of current and past clients and their transactions. They had been easily and steadily bribing Oscar to violate his depositors' privacy—a transgression so gigantic and heinous in Switzerland that if he were ever caught, he would never see the light of day again. Guaranteed.

And that's why his hush money was so huge. But Oscar had rationalized early on that it was just a perk that came with the moniker "Swiss banker *par excellence*." He just couldn't refuse that harmless and impressive income stream.

Now there was a woman with them; quite a beautiful one, at that. Exotic, he said to himself, was the appropriate word. Well, he shouldn't be keeping them waiting. He pressed an intercom button on his phone and ordered his secretary to show them in.

They filed into his office, and the men shook hands. Menschel was all smiles. Eddie and Three gave him grudging grins. He took Katia's hand and gave it a clumsy kiss. She smiled demurely at him.

"Please sit," said Menschel. "Coffee?"

"No," said Three Tit, dropping into a chair and placing his gold toothpick in his mouth. "We're sort of in a hurry. Oh, by the way." He waved his hand in Katia's direction. "This is Ms. Katia Kooz."

"Kozh," corrected Katia. "Katia Kozh." She smiled sweetly, her amber eyes large and innocent. Oscar Menschel liked those eyes. His reading glasses slipped a millimeter further down his nose as he smiled back. "Please have a seat," he said as he gallantly pulled a chair over for her.

Then Menschel looked at Three Tit and said, "To what do I owe the pleasure of your visit?"

Eddie had been watching Menschel closely. What an easily manipulated, preening peacock, he thought to himself. He decided to remain standing and got right to the point. In his high-end British accent, Eddie said, "I want to ask you a favor."

Menschel didn't like the look in Eddie Poong's eyes. It was a look that obviously had been cultivated in a world that Menschel had never inhabited. It carried a hooded, lazy, gutter-smelling threat laced with contempt that rattled the quintessential Swiss banker in his three-piece suit.

"Favor?"

"According to our files, you have a safety deposit box in the bank belonging to someone named Max Stepanov."

Menschel mentally shrugged. The name was vaguely familiar.

"Can you check and see if he has been in this bank in the last week?" He gave Menschel a look.

Oscar went around his desk, located a floppy disk in one of the drawers, and inserted it into a slot in his big, new, beige Compaq computer. Then he typed for a moment on the keyboard and consulted the green letters on the black screen. "Yes, we do have a safe deposit box in that name. It was opened in 1988." Then he shook his head. "No, he hasn't been in the bank recently."

Eddie, not at all impressed by the futuristic technology, continued, "We are staying at the Baur au Lac." He pulled an envelope from his inside jacket pocket with his room number and the hotel's phone number written on the front. "If this man tries to access his box—if he sets foot in this bank—I would appreciate it if you would call me immediately."

"Immediately," Three repeated from his chair. Click, click.

Eddie pushed the envelope at Menschel, who gingerly took it and felt the bulge of cash within.

Three Tit nodded at Katia, who then said, "Immediately," in a breathy, postcoital-sounding voice. That was enough to put Oscar totally off balance.

Eddie glanced at his brother, and nodded a "let's go." Three reached over, took Katia's hand, and they both stood to leave.

Eddie planted himself in front of Menschel one last time and said, "Max Stepanov. If he sets foot in this bank, and you don't call me immediately, I'll get...I'll get snippy." Then he stepped back a pace or two, glanced at Katia and his brother, straightened his jacket, and said, "All right, then. Cheerio, Oscar! Good day!"

He strolled out of the office followed by Three. Katia turned to Menschel, walked back to him, put her mouth within an inch of his ear, and whispered in her husky Russian accent, "When Eddie says 'snippy,' that means he will kill you."

He could feel her breath in his ear, and his eyes went wide.

"Will snip off balls first. Did you know that?" She quickly nipped the tip of his earlobe with her front teeth.

Menschel looked into her amber eyes and tried not to gulp.

With one of her fingertips, she pushed his rimless glasses a bit higher onto his nose, and a few moments later, Katia was gone.

All that was left was the quintessential Swiss banker.

She hung up the phone and wheeled over to the windows.

Delores "Grandma" Clooney had gotten a very interesting call. Her well-paid and deeply embedded contact in the Moscow government had told her a startling piece of news in three fascinating parts:

Part one: Boris Veshkin was dead. Killed in Switzerland. Too bad. Boris had been feeding information to Grandma for years about Soviet mining forays into African nations. She had used that information to generate massive, blood-soaked profits for her company, Carrington Metals. Now, it seemed, he had become a master thief.

Part two: He was in the middle of defecting from the USSR and having his stolen items carried out of the Mir when he was killed right in front of Soleil Tangiere's building. Her eyes narrowed. Am I to believe that *that* was a coincidence?

Part three: Max Stepanov had been Veshkin's hapless—probably blackmailed—courier, the man taking all the risks. He was to deliver a stolen computer chip of immense value to the now dead Veshkin in Switzerland.

The chip. If the devious Veshkin had done this to steal the chip, it must be of the highest—the ultimate—importance. It seemed like the kind of thing the Russians would certainly pay a massive fortune to get back, Grandma almost sang to herself.

She wondered what was on it.

Dustin was exhausted from flying to London and then flying back to Zurich. And his phone had been ringing when he had walked in the door. He held the phone and listened carefully without saying a word. Finally, he nodded and said, "Yes, ma'am," and hung up.

A half a million dollars if he did.

His head blown off if he didn't.

Hmm. Now, which should I choose?

Dustin tossed the sarcasm around in his head and threw his overnight bag onto the bed in his rented Zurich apartment.

Grandma had given him his new instructions. They were fairly straightforward. He was to retrieve the computer chip from Max Stepanov, Soleil Tangiere's boyfriend, in any way necessary.

He was to kill Soleil Tangiere as soon as said chip was in his possession, preferably killing Max and Camille in front of her eyes first, making it as painful as possible for the poor dear.

He was to deliver said chip to Grandma.

"Do not fail," she had said. "If you do, you will surely die."

Man, he said to himself, whistling softly, that old bird has totally gone over the edge. But she has the power and a boatload of money. And when it came to money, she never reneged on a promise of payment.

He could do this chore.

After all, Soleil Tangiere was just a girl.

Yvonne Goulet had an easy job.

Tangiere International did very little business. It didn't have to.

When its founder, a commodities trader named Tom Patel, formed the company, a large part of its profits and funding came from less-than-straightforward dealings and from dirty kickbacks and payoffs.

Some of that dirty money had come from Carrington Metals; specifically, through Philip Smythe, the deceased son of Grandma Clooney. Patel + Company, which was originally in New York, had moved to Switzerland two years ago. Tom Patel had been seduced by Smythe's schemes, by money, and by the selfish high of running shady international deals.

Aside from money, he had little else to show for his low activities, which included his insincere love affair with a naïve, rural Canadian girl, herself on the run and seeking justice for the murder of her father. It was almost two years before Soleil discovered his secret office in Geneva, among his other duplicities.

When Tom was killed in a struggle with Soleil in Geneva, she discovered that her name had been put on the company checks, in the company books, and on the company accounts without her knowledge or permission. She had been stunned to find that she had been exposed to a myriad of huge problems that were not of her making.

But she also found that she had clean title to and possession of Tom Patel's bank account at the ZSB. When Soleil went to Zurich to inquire about the checkbook, she learned from Herr Menschel that it was certainly her property, and that there was a considerable amount of money in it: over fifteen million Swiss francs—around ten million US dollars.

Rather than take the money and run, Soleil decided to rename the business Tangiere International, rent an office in Zurich, and continue it. She had learned about metals and diamonds in New York, and was in no hurry to return to Canada or to the United States, reasoning that there were bad forces there that might still want her harmed or worse.

Caring little about having millions, but energized by being a player on the "boy's only" international commodities scene, Soleil funneled the considerable money she was making in the trading business to women's shelters and other charitable causes in Switzerland and Canada. Soleil had a special place in her heart for women who had been abused by men. And now she could really make a difference.

Only Yvonne knew the extent of Tangiere International's charitable endeavors, and Soleil had sworn her to silence. Yvonne was Swiss, and secrecy was almost genetic for her.

Soleil wanted as much anonymity as she could get. She had learned that a woman gets a lot farther when she flies under the radar. And, she's generally safer.

The office was closed that day, but Yvonne had come in search of her wallet. It had gone missing, and André had come to mind as a suspect.

But when she opened the top of drawer of her desk, there it was.

When the phone rang, she debated whether to answer it. Then she picked it up.

"Is Ms. Tangiere available, please?" It was a man's voice with a British accent.

"I'm sorry, she's not in the office. Who is this, please?"

"Are you expecting her today?" the man asked, ignoring her question.

Her defenses up, Yvonne said, "Who is this?"

"I will call back," said the man, and the phone went dead.

She replaced the receiver and stared at the phone. A small voice inside her said that a whole new world of trouble was right around the corner.

She dialed Soleil's apartment, but got the answering machine.

I'd better find Soleil, she said to herself as she left the office.

And the sooner, the better.

Kurt liked the white Mercedes.

It was solid and fast and a credit to the obsessive German engineering for which the brand was famous.

He and Camille were taking a short ride around town. They both wanted to get a last look before they left the next day with Soleil and Max. They had all decided to spend one night in Engelberg before going on to Italy.

"When do you have to get back?" Camille knew that Kurt had to return to Chicago, to his business. And she sensed that he wanted to spend a little time with his kids—a common condition with all good parents who are away from children for a while.

There will always be that challenge, thought Camille. She watched Kurt and knew that she was up to it. She tried to get a glimpse into the future, but at the moment, everything seemed up in the air.

"I might fly back when we get to Italy," Kurt said. "Business will be getting into gear after New Year's Day. I want to be with you all the time, Cami, but I have get back to see if the walls are still standing at my business."

He looked over at her. "But I won't leave until I'm sure that you and Soleil are safe and all of this trouble is behind us."

"As for your business, Kurt, if the walls have collapsed, you'll build them back up," Camille said. "There's no doubt about it. You're that kind of guy."

He smiled at the confidence she had in him. What a woman, he said to himself.

A few minutes later, they drove back to the Baur au Lac.

Getting out of the car, they noticed the empty black Porsche parked close to the hotel's entrance. Camille and Kurt walked casually through the lobby. They didn't see the Poongs or Katia.

They were about to get into an elevator when Camille put her hand on Kurt's arm. "Let's get a cup of cocoa," she said. "Soleil's got me hooked on it."

"Sure," said Kurt, and they walked into the bar off the lobby.

They were still sitting at the small table in the bar thirty minutes later when two police cars pulled up in front of the hotel. Three officers and Inspector Sonnenreich, obviously in charge, strode to the front desk and then to the bank of elevators.

Kurt and Camille looked at each other. "Let's stick around a little longer," said Camille, and she ordered another cocoa.

Ten minutes later, the elevator doors opened, and Ulrika, the three uniformed cops, and the two Poong brothers came out of the elevator and walked quickly across the lobby. Kurt and Camille could see that the two were not happy.

Kurt said to Camille, "Those were the Poong brothers."

Camille shivered. "I know the type," she said, thinking about some of the rougher associates of her ex-husband, Jake.

As she watched them leaving the hotel, she said, "I wonder if Soleil had anything to do with this. Where are Soleil and Max anyway?"

"I'm not sure," he said.

And where was Katia?

Herr Menschel had been in the midst of fawning over a wealthy and very paranoid client from Argentina when the inspector strode into his outer office, ID in hand. Ulrika had quickly shown her badge to the secretary, walked to the door with "Oscar Menschel" emblazoned on its plaque, and opened it.

Menschel was at first outraged, but when Ulrika walked in purposefully and said, "Cantonal Police, Herr Menschel. Sorry, but this is urgent," his stomach did a somersault.

The nervous client nearly fell over himself making an almost comically quick exit from the banker's office. Ulrika watched him dispassionately as he mumbled and stumbled through his hasty departure.

Turning to Oscar, the inspector said, "I'm here about a murder...one of your clients, Boris Veshkin."

Menschel's eyes were wide.

"And to make matters worse," she continued, "I've received a disturbing fax from Interpol."

Interpol? Menschel gasped to himself. He knew it—the Poongs. Trouble times two. Horrible, horrible clients.

"As you know, a capital crime in this canton trumps local secrecy law, and time is of the essence." She walked over to Menschel. "Please sit," she said, almost pushing him down into his office chair.

Menschel grabbed the arms of his chair, and Ulrika paced back and forth in her black, tailored suit, towering over him. "Who were the two Asian men and the woman meeting with you here in your office an hour ago?"

"What?" Oscar's cool charm had left the building. "I... what?"

Ulrika had been having the bank watched on a hunch, because it was common knowledge that foreigners invariably visited their hidden accounts at these secretive institutions. That's what Switzerland is for, she thought dryly.

Menschel's face had become frozen in a rictus of fear. He would have thought that the inspector was beautiful when she was angry if she hadn't been reducing him to a quaking emotional wreck.

She looked at his chalk-white face and leaned over him. His reading glasses dropped off his nose and into his lap. He reached for them. "Get your hands out of your lap," she said. Then she smiled enigmatically and said, "Let's go to the station now."

That was the last straw for the quintessential Swiss banker. He sang like a tiny bird in a cuckoo clock. Wearing a three-piece suit.

"X marks the spot." Max and Soleil were standing on the street, looking at a new metal bench that the city had quickly and efficiently installed to replace the wooden one that Veshkin had destroyed in his fall.

Soleil said, "That's where Boris bought the farm."

"The farm?"

"It's an American or English expression. It means 'died.' I don't know why."

"Soleil!" Yvonne was walking rapidly down the street toward them. When she reached them, she seemed out of breath. And scared.

"Yvonne, what's wrong?" asked Max.

Before she could answer, Soleil said, "Come on, let's go upstairs." She took Yvonne by the arm.

On the next block, hidden behind a pair of sunglasses, Dustin was watching as the three went into the building.

In her apartment, Yvonne told Soleil about the odd phone call she had gotten at the office. "The British accent made me very nervous. At first I thought it was Dustin."

Max frowned at the mention of the name, and Yvonne gave him an "it is what it is" look. "But then, well, I don't know, I'm not sure. The voice, the call, it just got to me. Then I called you, but you weren't here."

Soleil walked over to her phone and saw the little light blinking on the answering machine. She pressed the button and listened to Yvonne's message. When it ended, Yvonne, who had been listening as well, said, "Is my voice that deep?"

"Everyone agrees its *très sexy*." Max smiled, breaking the bleak mood.

"Almost everyone," said Soleil.

Yvonne put her nose in the air and struck a pose.

At that moment, the phone rang.

Soleil picked it up. "Hello?"

She listened for a minute or two, only interrupting the caller with an "OK" or an "uh-huh." Finally, she said, "*Danke*," and hung up.

She turned to Max and Yvonne. "That was Inspector Sonnenreich. They took the Poongs to the cantonal police station for questioning about Veshkin's murder. She doubts that anything will stick to them, but she has the authority to keep them there overnight."

Max looked skeptical.

"Apparently these Poongs are big shots in Hong Kong—dirty big shots. Did you know that, Max?"

Max's face became hard. "I think I heard of them once or twice at Nevsky, but never had any contact with them. What I do know is that they sent a man to the Mir who they contracted to kill me. There can be no doubt about that."

Soleil went on, "According to Ulrika, the Swiss police pulled a report on the brothers, and they're considered extremely interesting to Interpol and other global police organizations. They seem to be perpetually on the edge of the law." She looked at Max. "And they specialize in diamonds."

Max returned her look, and then glanced at Yvonne. Soleil had told Yvonne nothing about the diamonds, and she was glad for that. Yvonne's involvement with Soleil in the recent past had almost gotten her killed. Soleil didn't want a repeat of that performance.

Max's intention was to stash the diamonds and the chip in a safety deposit box at the ZSB, which he had obtained on his first trip out of Russia in 1988. At that time, he had secreted some personal items in the box in anticipation of the day when he would be able to leave the Soviet Union.

But now things had taken off on a new trajectory. Soleil had hidden the chip and the stones in an empty cocoa tin in a kitchen cabinet. She would take them out before they left tomorrow.

Max decided to change the subject. "I think we should try and have a good time. You know, let it all hang loose."

"Let it all hang out," Soleil corrected.

"Oh. Thank you."

Soleil looked at Yvonne. "Ever since he returned from Russia, I spend half my time correcting his English."

"Huh," said Yvonne. "I spend the other half correcting *your* French."

"OK, everyone, chill out," Max said, happy that the blush was back on the conversational rose. "Why don't we just go out and have a good time tonight? Tomorrow will take care of itself." He looked at Soleil. "Let's go dancing."

Soleil's face lit up—she loved that idea, loved his attitude. And it was smart—why sit around worrying about things that were not in their control? What was the expression? Living well is the best revenge? Too true, Max.

Yvonne liked the idea too. She turned to the handsome Russian. "*Bon*, Monsieur Max, let's go dancing."

Soleil said, "I'd better get something to wear."

That was another idea that Yvonne liked.

20

ROAD TRIP

Katia Kozh wasn't a morning person.

When the phone rang in her room at the Baur au Lac at 8:00 a.m. on the last day of the year, she tried her best to ignore it. Finally it stopped, only to start ringing again two minutes later. She knew who it was, and she knew that she was not going to like it.

She reached over for the phone, picked it up, and whispered, *"Da?"*

When she heard Three Tit Poong's voice, she knew she was right—she didn't like it at all. If these Poongs weren't controlling her money and passport, she would have found a way to be out of Zurich a long time ago.

Maybe she even would have found a way to get to Hollywood.

Three Tit didn't waste much time on pleasantries. He immediately said, "Can you drive?"

"Yes," she said, running her tongue around the inside of her mouth. It tasted like the bottom of a birdcage.

She had sat in the hotel bar until three in the morning, knocking back mojitos and waiting for one or the other Poong to show up. Finally, she had had enough sense to throw in the towel when her internal gyroscope told her to drag her body into the elevator and get up to the room before she pitched off the barstool.

"Yes, I can drive. Why?" She yawned.

"Go down to the valet, get our Porsche, and come pick us up at the police station."

Katia squinted into the middle distance and tried to think if there was anything worse in the universe than what he was asking her do right now. She concluded there wasn't. "Give me a few minutes."

"Get a pencil." He gave her an address and directions, which she scribbled down on a hotel pad. Then he said, "Hurry." He hung up.

Katia's head fell back on the pillow. She mumbled a curse in Russian, but she knew that if she fell back to sleep, she probably would be murdered for it.

Welcome to the West, she grumbled as she slid out of bed.

One floor above Katia, Kurt was on the phone ordering some coffee and rolls to be brought up to the suite. Camille, fresh from the shower, came into the room wrapped in a hotel towel. Her hair hung down in thick, wet, auburn ropes.

He turned and looked at her. I don't want to go back to Chicago, he said to himself.

"Give me the phone," said Camille, throwing Kurt a look designed to neutralize any lingering testosterone-laced thoughts from the night before. "Let's get this show on the road." She picked up the phone and dialed out.

"Did I wake you?" she asked Soleil, who picked up the phone on the third ring.

"Not really. I've been up for a while. A little bird has been pushing me to get an early start. Russian bird."

"We'll pick you up at ten?" Camille said it loud enough for Kurt to hear.

He nodded; no problem.

"Sure," said Soleil, "we'll be downstairs. I'll call Yvonne."

Soleil's call definitely woke Yvonne, but after a moment, she felt the anticipation of the day ahead energizing her. "*Bon.* Can you pick me up?"

"*D'accord.*" Sure.

Eddie and Three Tit had spent the morning on the phone to Hong Kong, where it was already late afternoon, that city being eight hours ahead of Zurich. They had been dealt a devastating blow and were now trying to stop the hemorrhaging of their carefully crafted but illegal businesses, and save their lives at the same time.

Evidently, Oscar Menschel had disclosed their interest in Max Stepanov to the police, and that had branded the brothers persons of extreme interest. And not only in Switzerland, but now, thanks to Ulrika's quick and clever calls and faxes—everywhere.

Damn it, Eddie thought, holding back panic.

The only positive aspect of the mess was that the Swiss couldn't hold them. There wasn't a shred of physical evidence linking them to the death of Veshkin.

Eddie was furious and had made a single call to Hong Kong to his extremely well-paid lawyer. The inspector had tried her damnedest to keep them there, but the flood of calls that had inundated the police station from Eddie's raft of lawyers, both Asian and European, spelled out the word "release," which Ulrika Sonnenreich reluctantly had signed off on first thing in the morning.

Now, in the beautiful, Swiss morning light, the brothers stood at two phone booths across the street from the police station making numerous, idiotically expensive credit-card calls to Hong Kong while they waited for Katia and their car. They owed a boatload of money to a boatload of bad people, and now they couldn't pay. Herr Menschel's weakness had seen to that.

Eddie and Three Tit now thought of Oscar as a dead banker walking...

Though Ulrika had failed to keep the Poongs in jail, she *was* able to freeze all of their accounts and vault boxes at the ZSB under the edict of an Interpol "most urgent" request. This freeze would be in effect until a Swiss judge could review the case.

Then the inspector informed them with a smile on her face that the judge would certainly have the freeze lifted. Hopefully, by April. Of 1997. Oh, and don't leave town, she finally said, knowing full well that her words were falling on deaf and panicked ears.

Most of the Poongs' money was in the secure safety of the ultra-private, legendary Swiss bank, the ZSB. And now it had been effectively frozen well into the distant future.

This wouldn't work for them. It was a fatal situation for Eddie and Three Tit. Cash flow—huge cash flow—was their lifeblood. They had never owed as much money to their criminal associates as they did now. If the Poongs couldn't raise a lot of money, and fast, they were, in any language, dead.

But they did know where a small fortune in diamonds was: right here in Zurich. With Max Stepanov and Soleil Tangiere.

We'd better get those diamonds right now, Eddie said to himself, visibly shaken from the little chat he had just concluded with Mok Ng, the head of the deadly criminal Tung Kwon Lok Triad in Kowloon. Mok, after listening to Eddie's sob story, swore to five different gods that if Eddie didn't come up with the money he owed to the syndicate, he could expect to be reduced to Poong Krispies in short order.

Where was Katia with his car?

Kurt had appointed himself driver, and Max got into the passenger seat after gallantly holding the back door open for Soleil and Camille and throwing their bags in the trunk. They were in fine spirits, and there was no way they could ignore the incredible beauty of this last day of the year.

As Kurt guided the Mercedes up the block, the phone rang in Soleil's empty apartment. After five rings, it switched over to the answering machine. A frustrated voice spoke into the machine, saying, "This is a message for Max, Max

Stepanov. When you get this message, please stay at Ms. Tangiere's apartment. Don't leave. It is imperative that you wait for me."

There was click and then the hang up.

The entire message was in Russian.

Vlad.

"Where the hell have you been?" Eddie was almost hopping on the sidewalk in freak-out mode when the black Porsche pulled up next to him.

"What? What's wrong? Here's your car. Better late than never." Katia had actually enjoyed the trip to the police station with the top down. These Swiss men looked conservative, but boy, did they appreciate a girl in a convertible, she said to herself.

Eddie stood on the street fuming. He literally pulled Katia out of the driver's seat and practically threw her into the small backseat before he got behind the wheel. His brother sat in the front next to him, and they took off, wheels screeching, heading for Soleil Tangiere's apartment building.

The Mercedes proved itself once again when Yvonne joined the group.

Camille stepped out of the car, and Yvonne got in to sit between Camille and Soleil. The three slender women discovered that the wide car gave them plenty of room. Yvonne looked left and right, made a joke about sandwiches, and they were off.

Kurt said, "Does anyone know where we're going?"

Max, a map folded in his hand, said, "Of course."

Getting into Soleil's apartment wasn't pretty.

Katia was incredibly nervous even being in the neighborhood again, and it took them ten minutes to finagle their way into the building.

Their next stop was the basement, where the maintenance man had a small office. The gun to his head and its implied death threat handily convinced him to unlock Soleil's apartment. Then it took another few minutes to tie him up with strips of sheets ripped from her bed and push him into Soleil's bathroom.

It began to dawn on Katia that the Poong brothers were running on fumes and fear, making a million mistakes, and as such, her life was in serious danger.

As the Poongs went crazily through everything in the apartment and growled at each other incessantly in Cantonese, Katia sat down heavily on the couch.

Something on the coffee table caught her eye. She reached out and looked at the piece of paper, read it, and called out, "Eddie. I think you might want to see this."

The two brothers turned as one. Katia was holding a sheet of paper with Cyrillic handwriting on. "It's in Russian," she said. The Poongs were silent.

She suddenly smiled. It was in Max's handwriting.

"Well?" said Three.

"This is a confirmation number for a hotel reservation for tonight. Max must have left it here."

The Poongs looked at each other. "Hotel?" said Eddie. "What hotel?"

Katia stood up. "We'll need a map," she said. That's when she looked over and saw the light on the answering machine going blink, blink, blink.

Switzerland was a small country.

The distances weren't vast, but the Alpine terrain made it more efficient to travel by rail than by car. Soleil knew this, and she had never felt the need to own a car during her time in Switzerland, even though she was a good driver.

It just hasn't been important. So far.

Their final destination was Como, the gorgeous city on the Italian lake of the same name just southeast of the southern tip of Switzerland. But they agreed to take a detour.

It took them about two hours to reach Engelberg. They had decided to spend New Year's Eve in Engelberg for practical reasons—the record-shattering warm weather was wreaking havoc with the skiing season, and the accommodations were no problem. Now, on short notice there just were no decent places to stay in Lugano or Como until after New Year's Day.

Engelberg, on the other hand, was easy. Waves of skiers, frustrated by the warm weather, had flown north like migrating birds. Three suites at the luxurious Terrace Hotel? No problem. No discounts, but no problem. Skiing? Not good, too warm, but they weren't concerned.

There was another reason they chose Engelberg—Soleil knew the resort, and Camille and Kurt had spent a day skiing there. She reasoned that if anything bad was following them, at least she had a little familiarity with the surroundings. And she was still in Switzerland.

They had driven south, skirting Lake Zug and winding down through Emmenbrüke to Lucerne, where they stopped for coffee (and cocoa) at a café that had thrown open its doors to let the glorious weather in.

Max took over the driving after Lucerne, and they continued down to Sarnen, where they turned east and began the difficult but spectacular drive up through the mountains and glacier that led into the Engelberg region. Max had never felt the need to drive a car as slowly and cautiously as he did on that road—it was a concrete snake that coiled back and forth on itself as it climbed one mountain and descended the next, and then climbed again, one side perpetually open to seemingly bottomless drop-offs.

And this was in warm weather, when the pavement was clear. In the snow—forget it! No wonder everyone took the train directly to Engelberg station. Driving this road was slightly crazy.

After the heart-stopping drive through the mountains, it was early afternoon when Max pulled up in front of the large and immaculate hotel.

The impressive Terrace Hotel had 170 rooms, each with an amazing view of Engelberg, the Titlis glacier, and the surrounding peaks. It was up the mountain above the village of Engelberg, and had its own private funicular railway, making it easy to get from the town to the hotel.

This is what Switzerland is all about, Max said to himself as a valet handed him a green claim ticket.

As they walked into the grandiose, neocolonial-inspired lobby, Yvonne was looking around ardently.

"Let me guess, Yvonne," said Soleil, a hand on her arm. "You're searching for twenty-year-olds." Yvonne shrugged and threw Soleil a saccharin smile.

Soleil laughed with her friend. But inside, she had a strong feeling that something was catching up to her. The events of the last two weeks weren't over by a long shot, she reminded herself. She shuddered.

The three suites weren't cheap, but the moment Max walked into theirs, he vowed to stay a few extra nights. Here he was, in this amazing place with Soleil. This was truly paradise. Italy would have to wait a day or two longer. Soleil stood beside him looking out the window and read his mind.

"We should stay for more than just one night," she said with conviction.

Eddie Poong was running out of curses.

He was driving the Porsche at about ten miles an hour. They had been following a wobbling panel truck up and down the mountain road for the past hour. Every time Eddie thought he had an opportunity to pass it, another car came around one of the blind curves from the opposite direction. At this rate, they wouldn't get to Engelberg until next year, he thought bitterly.

In a way, he owed the truck something. The road was a twisting, outrageously challenging one, even by Swiss standards. There were dozens of tight hairpin turns that had become famous for claiming the lives of drunk, sleepy, or inattentive drivers.

He looked at his brother in the passenger seat. Three was silent for a change—he must be gritting his teeth into dust, Eddie thought. Even the toothpick was nowhere to be seen. He looked in the rearview mirror. Somehow, Katia seemed to be enjoying the torture.

They had hurried back to the Baur au Lac, gotten their things together, and then made a reservation at the Edelweiss Hotel, down the mountain from the Terrace Hotel in the town of Engelberg. New Year's Eve, now less than twelve hours away, was screwing everything up. The Poongs decided that they would wait until the early morning to finish their plan. It was a simple plan, but the brothers conceded that at least two people would have to die. Maybe more.

Oh well, Three said to himself. Now it's them or us. No-brainer.

Eddie could have his stupid car. Three was not driving back down this mountain. He was going to take a train.

Soleil and her party met in the lobby and took the hotel's private train, its funicular, down into the village. There were still plenty of tourists and locals enjoying the amazing weather, and the excitement over the impending New Year was infectious.

The Terrace was holding a huge, come-as-you-are outdoor New Year's Eve dance and party that night, and Soleil had been keeping her fingers crossed that they would all get to midnight without any more crazy incidents.

As they walked the crowded streets and wandered in and out of shops, Camille's mind started to wander. At first, she hadn't understood how Soleil could adapt so easily to Switzerland, but it really could be a dreamland.

Let's be realistic, though, Camille said to herself. She looked up at Kurt, who was obviously having a great time, and sighed inside. Better Chicago with Kurt than the Alps alone.

Soleil, a yellow-and-white knit cap holding her hair in place, discreetly watched her sister and saw that she was happy. If anything good had come of all this so far, it was that Camille had finally found someone to love. Now Soleil had just one thing left to do: get rid of the people who were after her and Max.

She suddenly felt a bitter truth invade her heart: She had run out of ideas.

As each hour passed, Katia regretted her forced association with the Poongs more and more.

She was becoming unstable and rabidly ambivalent. She was ready to bolt on any pretext one minute, and then suddenly determined to see it through to the end a minute later. She would have bailed already if not for the three forces that kept her bonded to the now frantic brothers...

Force A: She was a Soviet citizen alone in the West with the soon-to-be-worthless, two-week special visa, supplied by Veshkin. When that ran out, any country could and would extradite her straight back to the Soviet Union.

Force B: She had finally comes to terms with the fact that she both loved and hated Max Stepanov at the same time. He was the only man she had ever known who wasn't a total *pridurok*, a douchebag. Maybe she should have turned around and tossed Soleil off the roof after Veshkin. Maybe.

And Force C: The Poongs would hunt her down and kill her if she tried to leave them before they got their diamonds.

But now it was clear that the Poongs weren't going to let her leave for *any* reason, and since this morning, their insanity had skyrocketed to a whole new level.

To play it safe, they didn't even get a separate room for Katia. They had rented a single suite in the Edelweiss Hotel—better to keep tabs on her. And now, even the beautiful scenery all around her couldn't lift her spirits.

Tomorrow, she said grimly to herself.

Tomorrow, something has to give.

The Terrace Hotel and the entire town of Engelberg were in full celebratory mode as midnight approached. The lights from the Christmas celebrations of a week ago were reignited and blazing, the hotel's disco was overflowing with music, laughter, and noise, and on the building's signature, monster, outdoor terrace, the party was at full throttle.

Everyone was dressed in jeans, ski clothes, parkas, and a multicolored smorgasbord of hats, caps, and scarves of all kinds. Tables of hot and cold food were lined up on the terrace. Beer and wine flowed like mountain streams, and the view of the lights in the valley and the town below was nothing short of spectacular.

Good thing we had time for a little rest this afternoon, Yvonne said to herself, as she led her latest companion to the railing, where Max had rounded up some barstools and everyone was eating and drinking.

"This is Joe," Yvonne said happily, putting her arm around a muscular, six-foot-tall young man in a gray parka with a big, red number fourteen on the back.

At least this guy was a little older than André was, Soleil said to herself. By maybe six months...

"Hi," Joe said uncertainly, taken by surprise by the group of four. Then he instantly relaxed, smiled, and showed his big teeth.

"Joe's American," Yvonne said with an unmistakable bit of pride in her voice. "From Ohio," she added, beaming.

"Uh, Columbus, really," he said. Joe was out of his element but didn't seem to mind. He was on vacation with a dozen of his college football buddies from Ohio State and was making the most of a Swiss ski holiday. Until now, the skiing had been less than cool, but suddenly here was this super-hot French chick drinking beer with him. Whoa! Touchdown!

Yvonne watched Joe and leaned into Soleil. "This is exciting, *oui*? I've never been with an American before."

Soleil studied Joe, who was suddenly deep in conversation with Kurt, probably about football. Dispassionately appraising him from afar, she said to Yvonne, "Want some tips?"

"*Bien sûr*," she said hesitantly. Of course.

Soleil took a sip of her beer, put on a professional air, and said, "OK, first off, try as hard as you can to keep little Joe here from getting hammered."

"Hammered?"

"Drunk. That could happen quicker than you think. Once he's over the line, he'll be as useful to you as overcooked escargot. Messy, stupid, embarrassing."

"Oh."

"Now, at some point he's going to try to have sex with you." She glanced at the big clock on the wall, which said 11:37. "Probably before midnight."

Yvonne frowned, but Soleil was unstoppable.

"He's probably here with at least a dozen of his friends, since the Joes of the world are, sorry to tell you, generally timid, unsure of their masculinity, and utterly inept socially until they're intoxicated. That's why they travel in packs. They all tend to look, sound, and drink more or less the same, and they're far more bonded to each other than to women. So keep in mind that you're dealing with a hoard of Joe clones lurking in the background."

Yvonne looked at Soleil nervously, but Soleil was having too much fun. "Now, if after all I've told you, you still want to have sex with Joe, tell him you like the Ohio State Buckeyes."

"What are those?"

"But if you want to dump him quickly, tell him your favorite sport is soccer and you have two kids." She looked over at Joe, who was walking away from Kurt. "That's it. Here he comes. *Bon chance.*"

"Hey, *Eevonn!*" said Joe, walking up to her in a state of ecstasy. "Kurt, here, can get me super tickets to Bears games anytime—for *free!*" He looked back at Kurt with a monster, good-buddy smile. Kurt nodded and shrugged. Camille desperately tried not to grin. Soleil sat on her barstool impassively with her arm in Max's.

"*Tres bien,*" Yvonne muttered to herself. She looked to Soleil for help, but got a plain, vanilla stare. Then she turned to Joe and smiled hesitantly. "Sorry, Joe, ze only sport I like is ze soccer. I take my leetle ones to ze games all ze time."

Soleil leaned and whispered something to Max.

Max got up from his chair, stepped up to Joe, and in the broadest Russian accent he could muster said, "Heppy New Year, Mr. Joe. Is nice to meet you. I buy you drink now, *tovarich*?" He put his arm around Joe's shoulder and guided the confused, hesitant, but suddenly relieved Joe across the crowded terrace to the bar.

Yvonne sat on Max's chair. "You are lucky, Soleil," she said to her in French, "to have a built-in bouncer."

"How old is this Joe?" Soleil asked her.

"Twenty-one."

Soleil narrowed her eyes. "There is definitely something wrong with you."

A half dozen TV screens had been set up on the huge terrace so the crowd could watch the New Year countdown. As the last minutes of the year ticked away, suddenly a live camera view of the Eiffel Tower flashed on the screens.

New York was several times zones behind Switzerland, and the ball on the top of the Allied Chemical Building in Times Square in New York wouldn't begin its descent for six hours. Switzerland was in the same time zone as Paris.

Camille and Kurt stood with their arms around each other. "Here we go, Cami," Kurt said. "New year, new beginning." In spite of the events of the last two weeks, Camille couldn't remember when she had felt so good or so optimistic about her life.

Max and Soleil stood looking into each other's eyes, close but not yet touching. "How do you say 'Happy New Year' in Russian?" she asked.

"*S novym godahm.*"

"That's a very hard language, Max."

"So is English."

On the TV screens, the Eiffel Tower was alive with its rapid-fire light show, and thousands of people could be seen jamming the Paris streets. Suddenly, the tower lit up fully and white bands of light began going black in the countdown sequence.

Everyone chanted the descending numbers:

"Ten...nine...eight...seven..."

Max leaned over and said into Soleil's ear, "*Ya tebya lyublyu.*"

"Six...five...four...three..."

"I love you too, Max."

"Two...one...zero...Happy New Year!"

The terrace went crazy with intense kissing and yelling and noisemakers and champagne corks popping. Suddenly, fireworks and skyrockets from the town down the mountain screamed as they climbed in the night sky and flowered into bright chrysanthemums of loud, echoing explosions in the cold Swiss air.

Through their deep kiss, Soleil said silently to herself: let this last. Let this last tonight and tomorrow and for whatever time destiny has planned for us.

Then she shifted her eyes and saw that Yvonne was kissing a man with a sparse new beard and long hair. Soleil laughed. She didn't want to know.

From above the mountain, the crowded terrace looked like a living, breathing, ocean of people radiant with that unique happiness and joy that infects New Year's Eve crowds.

In Paris, the *Tour Eiffel* blazed in a frenzy of a thousand lights and a forest of synchronized fireworks.

And as the world relentlessly turned in its twenty-four hour rotation, and the New Year was born over and again in its global progression through the time zones, the calendars of man all became fresh and new.

The Nineties had begun.

21

MORNING

Kurt Ballas was up early.

He hung up the phone and stared at the floor. In spite of all the legal agreements and fought-over schedules, he felt awful having to wish his two kids Happy New Year over the phone rather than in person. At least Amanda didn't interfere with this phone call, he said bitterly to himself. Though his rational mind said this was the best anyone could do under the circumstances, the man inside still felt guilty as hell.

It was a few minutes after seven, but midnight had just happened back in Chicago. He and Camille had danced and celebrated until after two in the morning. Now Camille was fast asleep, and Kurt wasn't going to wake her this early.

He put on a pair of jeans and a sweater, grabbed his tan North Face jacket, and went down to the lobby.

He was surprised at the number of people up and about at this time on New Year's morning, but spirits were high, and the mind-blowing vista of the white Alps under the cerulean-blue sky outside the tall windows was electrifying.

He got a Styrofoam cup of steaming java at the small coffee shop in the lobby and walked out of the hotel. The air was colder than it was yesterday and he had heard talk in the lobby that the "heat wave" would end that evening. He stood in the bright morning light admiring the view, and then he walked past the valet station and down the drive that circled the hotel before it began zigzagging down the mountain.

He stopped to take a few sips of his coffee as the hotel's funicular from the town below arrived and disgorged its passengers. Kurt waited for everyone to get off, and then boarded the private train to ride down to the village. It would be a while before anyone was awake. When he got down to the town, he would get on the Rotair gondola and take in the view from the top of Titlis Peak. It was a great way to spend an hour in that glorious place. And when he got back to the hotel, he would wake Camille. They would have something to eat, and then they would pack.

Arriving in town, Kurt stepped off the small train and bumped against one of the people waiting to get on—a man in a yellow ski jacket, black knit cap, and wraparound sunglasses. "Sorry," Kurt said automatically without looking at him. The man, equally disinterested, grunted and got on the funicular. On his way up to the Terrace Hotel, the man took a gold toothpick from the pocket of his yellow ski jacket and put it in a corner of his mouth.

"Hi."

"You're already up?" Max said, coming awake in a second. Soleil was standing in the bedroom door, pulling a white cable-knit sweater over her shirt. She was wearing jeans and snow boots.

They had partied and danced until two in the morning and then gone back to their suite, where they fell asleep quickly. That's another thing I like about Max, she thought. He doesn't insist, doesn't push at the wrong times. He can read me and he respects what he sees. I'm lucky.

And I read him too. It's easy because at heart, he's a simple man—he's dedicated to one main driving force: survival. Getting away from the USSR and living through the mess at the Mir are admirable accomplishments in anyone's book.

He puts most men I've met to shame. And now he's not alone. He has me.

But they still had unfinished business to take care of.

"I was going to surprise you with some cocoa and a brioche from downstairs," she said.

"Oh, don't let me stop you," he said, yawning. "Surprise me. I'll be right here."

"Be back in a bit," she said. Then she was out the door.

Max knew that he couldn't fall asleep again, not in this place, on this beautiful day. He got out of bed and went into the bathroom to shower and shave. In the steamy heat of the shower, he reflected on the two worlds he had inhabited within the space of one week—one hell, the other heaven. His resolve to remain in the West at all costs strengthened.

He thought of his small apartment in Moscow, one of thousands in its dingy block, and how even though he had advanced dramatically at Nevsky Nickel in the last few years, he was still considered fodder for the Soviet machine. And at the Mir, he had been blackmailed and nearly killed and was, by now, certainly a confirmed enemy of the State.

He dressed quickly. He was about to pick up his jacket and surprise Soleil downstairs when he heard a light knock on the door. "Soleil?" he asked through the door.

"Yes," came the light, happy answer.

He pulled the door open, and without looking, turned to grab his ski jacket from the back of a chair. He turned back to the door. "I was going to surprise you—"

"You were going to surprise me, Max?" said Katia Kozh, lightly kicking the door closed behind her. She stood with her feet apart, her amber eyes ablaze, and a large automatic in her two fists, which were extended in front of her. "Oh, *chorosho*, I love surprises."

Max's heart forgot to beat for a second, and he stood rock still, his ski jacket in one hand.

"You look well, Max. How do they say it in the West? You look like a hot hunk." Daggers of light flashed from her amber eyes.

Max said nothing and watched her every move.

"I missed you, my darling," she said in Russian. "At first I thought you died from a venereal disease you picked up from your Canadian girlfriend, but Boris Veshkin informed me otherwise."

She moved carefully, keeping her back against the wall until she was clear of the door. If anyone came in, she would have an instant, clear shot.

Max knew that whatever else she might be, Katia was tough. She could be ruthless, and she loved breathing. He could not assume that she would make any mistakes. And he was sure that the gun had a full clip.

"Yes, poor Boris," she was saying. "He was a dangerous, powerful, repulsive man, you know, Max? And he was your boss on top of it! Typical Soviet hierarchy, eh?"

Max's eyes shifted slightly to the door.

"Oh, don't worry about your little Miss Quebec, Max. I saw her downstairs, chatting away with some woman. They looked like they were about to kiss each other. You sure can pick them, my love."

Max edged an inch to the side to get Katia used to movement, but she was too sharp. "*Nyet*, Max. Move a little more, and I'll shoot you. You know that, darling."

"Soleil said you saved her life," Max said as blandly as he could.

Katia nodded and smiled. "Ah, it's true. I saved her, I did." Her eyes narrowed. "I saved her for this moment, Max."

And then the door to the suite opened.

"If it involves another teenager keeping you awake all night, I don't want to know," Soleil was saying to Yvonne.

She was surprised but pleased to find Yvonne downstairs in the hotel coffee shop, munching on a croissant and sipping coffee from a mug. Yvonne beckoned her to sit down at the small table off the lobby. Soleil walked to the counter and ordered some pastries and cocoa to take up to Max in the room. Then she went over to Yvonne's table and sat down.

"So, you think I slept with Joe and his football team last night, eh?" Yvonne said as she patted a dot of butter on her croissant.

"Maybe not the whole team..."

Yvonne had danced with a number of men, including Kurt and Max, and had gone to her suite around 2:00 a.m. She had been slightly inebriated, but happy to fall into the warm hotel bed. It will be a happy new year after all, she'd thought as she dropped off to sleep.

But the higher altitude of the resort had given her a headache, and by six thirty, she was awake and dressed and downstairs in the lobby. She had watched the sun rise over a break in the mountains and felt that this was the year that she would find a man for herself. A good man like Max or Kurt. It was time, she had said to herself with Gallic certainty and determination.

Now, as she and Soleil laughed about Joe and the football team, they were too involved in their conversation to notice Katia walking slowly past the coffee shop, glancing sharply at them, and then disappearing across the lobby to talk with someone.

"Have you seen Camille yet?" Yvonne asked, changing the subject.

"Oh, my sister won't be up for hours, I'm sure," Soleil said. She turned in her chair and saw that her cocoa and pastries were waiting on the counter.

She brought the cups and paper bag back to the table and said, "Can you do me a favor? I'm going to the front desk to see about extending our stay. You don't mind taking these things upstairs to Max, do you?"

"Are you kidding?" Yvonne said. She got up, smiled at Soleil, picked up the food, and went to the elevator. Her hands were full, so she asked the man in the yellow ski jacket with the gold toothpick in his mouth to press the button for her floor.

"Sure," he said.

The door to the suite opened.

Yvonne nearly fell into the room, followed immediately by Three Tit Poong in his garish yellow ski jacket. He was twisting one of her arms around her back, almost breaking it. Her face was white with fear and shame. Three had a duplicate of Katia's Ruger .45 pressed up against Yvonne's neck. He kicked the door closed behind him.

He looked at Max for a few seconds and then said one word: "Diamonds." It was a command. Max looked at him and then at Yvonne's terrified face.

Max mind was in overdrive. He said, "In my jacket pocket."

Three's toothpick clicked. "Give," he said, pushing the gun harder into Yvonne's neck. She cried out and looked beseechingly at Max. She said in French, "Tell him to fuck himself, Max." She glanced at Katia. "Both of them."

Max understood her, but said nothing. Katia looked at Yvonne and said to Max, "This is Soleil's girlfriend, isn't it? Don't tell me you all—"

"Enough! Business only," Three said harshly to Katia. Max noted his dominance over her but said nothing. His overriding thought was to get Yvonne out of the room, out of this mess. And he silently prayed that Soleil wouldn't walk in and that and bullets wouldn't start flying.

"Jacket. Where?" Three said, impending mayhem dripping from the words.

Max tilted his head toward the closet. "Black jacket, inside pocket." He would let them have the diamonds, if that's what it took. They weren't his anyway. It would be a very small price to pay if everyone walked out of this. And where was this *svinya's* brother, the other Poong?

Without taking her eyes off Max, Katia moved to the closet, opened the door, and reached into the inside pocket of Max's black jacket. Her hand closed on the chamois bag, and she returned with it.

Three said, "Open it."

She undid the drawstring on the little bag and the ten diamonds rolled out onto the low coffee table. One was considerably larger than the others were, but they were all sizeable. Worth millions, thought Katia, instantly.

A bronze and plastic computer chip fell out along with them.

"What's that?" Three said, eyeing the chip.

"Your mother," said Max bluntly.

Three Tit said to Katia, "Aim your gun right here." He pointed his gun at Yvonne's forehead. "Right here at our new little insurance policy."

Katia swung the Ruger around to aim it between Yvonne's eyes as Three took a fast step at Max and swung his gun in a tremendous arc. It crashed into the side of Max's head with a loud crack, and Max went down. Blood started to seep onto the carpet.

Yvonne gasped and tried to claw at Three, but in a moment, both Katia's gun and Three's gun were pointed at her head. Not taking his eyes off Yvonne, Three rifled the unconscious Max's pockets and pulled out the man's wallet. He was about to stuff it into his jacket when a square of green paper slipped out of it and fell to the floor.

The car claim stub.

"Katia," he said, and held it up to her. "Call for Max Stepanov's car." Katia's eyes blazed. She instantly understood what was happening. She picked up the hotel phone, said she was Mrs. Stepanov, and asked if their car could be brought around, please. She read off the stub number. "Immediately, please, we are very late," she added and hung up.

Max, his brain making a monster effort to remain conscious, heard Katia calling for the car on the phone and inadvertently grunted. Three leaned over him and smashed his gun on the side of his head again. Max lay still, and more blood flowed.

Three Tit quickly swept the diamonds and the microchip back into the small bag, stuffed it into his ski jacket pocket, and said to Yvonne, "Go."

Yvonne looked at Max's bleeding body with horror but knew she had no choice. Then she looked into the eyes of her abductors and suddenly felt lost and alone.

A minute later Katia, Yvonne, and Three Tit Poong were out of the room and in the elevator.

Eddie Poong had covered his ass.

Sorry, dear brother, this is how it has to be, he had said to himself as Three Tit and Katia walked out of their room at the Edelweiss.

You and Katia will get the diamonds, and if you have to kill everyone in sight, so be it. And then kill Katia, if you please, Three Tit.

Go up to the Terrace Hotel on that private train and fetch the stones. Do it at 7:00 a.m. while everyone is still sleeping off the New Year festivities. I will come with the car at 8:00, pick you up, and we'll leave for Zurich.

But Three Tit, Eddie had said silently to himself, if you screw up, well, I'll still be down the mountain. So sorry. This has become the low point of our lives, and I owe it to both of us to live, no matter what. So I'll be there after you've done your part and have the diamonds. I'm sure you're able to handle this. But if you're dead, I'll improvise...

Now I can leave with my diamonds, Three said to himself joyfully as he pushed his gun harshly into Yvonne's spine. Katia was pressed up against Yvonne in the empty elevator, her own gun aimed at Yvonne's navel. Katia's other hand was jammed against the "close door" button on the elevator panel, ensuring that no one else would get on before they got to the lobby.

Eddie, my brilliant brother, Three said fatalistically to himself. I know what you're doing.

If you were willing to send me on this dangerous errand, then I've earned everything, all of it. I've even improvised with a new addition—a hostage. I'm not going to go back to

Zurich. No, I'm heading for the Austrian border. Once there, I'll dump Katia's body and the French girl's. Then I'm gone. We'll meet back in Hong Kong.

And if this doesn't work out, I'll see you in twenty years, Eddie. Or maybe in the afterlife.

The hotel was extremely accommodating, and the woman behind the front desk cheerfully extended their stay for another night without a problem.

Soleil thanked the young woman and went to the bank of elevators. She waited for a moment, and a set of elevator doors opened. She stepped inside the empty elevator and pressed the button labeled "five."

When she got to the fifth floor, she knocked on the door of the suite. "It's me," she said, but not too loudly. She was sure that everyone else on the floor was still asleep. It wasn't even 8:00 a.m.

Getting no response, she fished in her jeans pocket for her copy of the key, turned it quietly in the lock, and stepped into the room.

The doors of the elevator that Three, Katia, and Yvonne occupied, opened in the lobby a minute after the doors of Soleil's had closed. Three had impressed on Yvonne in no uncertain terms that he himself was ready to die if she alerted anyone at all to their little drama. "And before that happens, you will be dead, and I promise, *promise*—so will Soleil Tangiere."

The three walked close together across the lobby. The hotel guests who were up and about were interested in being outside in the glorious weather and paid them no mind. Yvonne wracked her brain for a way to alert someone to the unfolding crisis, but in less than thirty seconds, they were standing in front of the hotel.

Katia handed the green car stub to a valet. The pimple-faced kid said, "*Ja*! Your car is waiting," and waved his hand at the white Mercedes that had just been brought around the front of the building.

Nice car, thought Three.

"Max! Max!" Soleil was beside herself.

He was lying in a pool of blood, and she instantly bent down and put her ear to his chest to listen to his heart. After a few seconds, she heard the clear, rhythmic beat. Thank you, God.

She straddled him and pushed down hard with both hands on the center of his chest. After a few hard pushes, Max moaned and his eyes opened. She wiped her bloody hands on the front of her white sweater. Then she jumped up, took a pillow off the bed, and positioned it under his head. She saw the giant bruise and the vicious cut on his temple. The bleeding had mostly stopped. A hesitant feeling of relief began to come to her.

"Max, what happened? Who did this?"

He was fluctuating in and out of consciousness, but finally managed to whisper, "Poong, Katia. They took Yvonne. The diamonds. Our car."

The effort to speak took its toll, and he passed out again.

Soleil inhaled one huge breath, thought furiously, and then jumped up to grab the phone. She pushed the button for the front desk. When someone answered, she said quickly in bad German, "A man is injured badly in Room 512. Get the police, ambulance, hurry!"

She knelt quickly at her unconscious lover's side and whispered, "I'll be back, Max."

In another few beats of her heart, Soleil Tangiere was up, out of the room, and racing down the corridor.

Katia pushed Yvonne into the backseat, her gun never wavering. Then she quickly got in after her.

She said, "Sit over there," indicating that Yvonne should push herself up against the other rear door. Reading the woman's mind, Katia continued in her bad English, "If door opens at any time, I will hear, I will shoot, and you will die before hitting road. For sure."

Yvonne spit at her, and Katia hit her quickly in the ribs with the gun before training it on her face. "Stupid," she said.

Yvonne settled back in her seat, hatred in her eyes.

Three Tit got in behind the wheel and put the car in gear. He looked in the rearview mirror and saw Katia seated directly behind him and Yvonne in the seat next to her.

"Anything at all, Katia, just shoot her," he said.

This may be good-bye, Eddie, he said to himself as he bent over the wheel and drove away.

The elevator door hissed open. Soleil pushed past a startled couple and sprinted across the lobby. She ran out the main entrance, hurried past the valets, and pulled up short as she saw the taillights of the white Mercedes disappear at the end of the long, curving driveway. She looked left and right and at the valets—no help there.

What do I do?

22

BLACK AND WHITE

Hans Petzenfelder was at the top of his game.

The happy young man guided his shiny, new, red Yamaha FZR600 motorcycle to a careful stop at the valet station.

Ja, I've always loved Engelberg, he said to himself. I love riding in the mountains. And I love this unseasonably wonderful weather. What luck that I have a chance to ride on this perfect day to conquer that challenging road. I love it!

He was dressed in new, black leather pants and a matching jacket, which he also loved. On his head, his bright red helmet was the same color as the gas tank, fairings, and fenders of his powerful machine.

He put the sleek, red motorcycle in neutral, placed one foot on the hotel driveway, and swung the other over the bike. He walked a few steps away from his new mount and turned to gaze lovingly at it for the tenth time that day. He had left the engine running so he could stand there for a few moments admiring his living, breathing, perfect posses-sion. He might even be treated to a few words of envy and jealousy from the valets, he thought. He was sure that he would be.

So powerful and impressive, he thought as he gazed at his trusty red mount. So perfect.

I love perfect.

When he finally turned his face from the bike, he imme-diately saw the girl. She had on slim jeans, snow boots, and a white sweater with—was that *blood*? She was standing a few paces away. Her legs were apart, her hands were on her hips, and her blond hair was blowing in the light wind.

She was looking straight at him.

He froze. It was her eyes that threw him. They were not only the most unusual shade of blue he had ever seen, but they seemed to hold a promise: an alarming, exciting prom-ise. And coupled with the way she was standing there, more than a hint of sex.

He smiled at her uncertainly, and she immediately walked right up to him. She reached up and put one arm around his neck, snaked the other around the small of his back, and kissed him hard on the lips. *Really* hard.

After a few seconds, she backed away from him, ran the tip of her tongue across her lips, and said in a sultry voice, "You wouldn't mind if I climb on?" She backed up another step, and her eyes frankly took him in from top to bottom.

Hans Petzenfelder was stunned. *Really* stunned. Before he could open his mouth or move a muscle, she had turned and was at the motorcycle. To the delight of the staring valets, she expertly swung a jean-clad leg over the bike and gave her lower body a quick shake to get comfortable.

Then she bent low over the café-racer-style handlebars, put the bike in gear, and let out the clutch. The engine roared, and the rear wheel suddenly spun loudly in a cloud of tire smoke.

Hans was paralyzed in his jacked-up state of confusion, and the valets' already wide eyes opened even farther at the screech of the smoking tire. Everyone froze in various states of wonder, awe, and lust.

Five seconds later, Soleil and the motorcycle were gone.

Three was nailing the accelerator and zigzagging through the pretty town of Engelberg as fast as he could. He narrowly missed some pedestrians who were dressed in classic mountain-climbing gear and leading a brown-and-black Saint Bernard on a leash, but the cliché didn't register in his mind.

Directly behind him in the backseat, Katia was holding the gun on Yvonne and wondering how this would end. She had been waiting for her chance to see Max, even if it was for one last time. To kiss him or kill him? Her eyes narrowed. She was not sure.

But after that...what?

Over the last two days, she had been calculating a dozen ways to get away, but when she finally saw the diamonds, everything changed. They were huge and worth more money than she could ever spend. They were freedom—*unlimited* freedom. And now they were a few feet from her in Three Tit's pocket.

OK. Simple. All she had to do was wait until they stopped somewhere. Then she would quickly kill Three Tit, take the diamonds, and go.

Oh, and kill the French girl, too.

But could she do it? Just shoot him in the back of the head? Or kill this girl the same way? She shook her head for a second. Ah, face it, she told herself. I couldn't even let Veshkin shoot Soleil. I just don't know...

Then, as if reading her mind, Three said loudly, "Don't get any ideas, Katia. Eddie will be meeting us at the bottom of the hill. Stick with us, and you'll reach Hollywood." The gold toothpick in his mouth clicked loudly along his teeth. "Anything else will be hazardous to your health."

Three was too busy cajoling and lying and cursing and clicking and driving to notice a small red flash appear in his rearview mirror.

A few hundred yards more and the Mercedes was almost out of the town of Engelberg and onto one of the most winding, twisting, and dangerous roads in the world. Three had been energized since he saw the diamonds, and now he felt he was up to the challenge. I'm a great driver, he said to himself—and face it, an overall badass dude.

Every whore in Kowloon knew *that*.

It was still unseasonably warm, around forty degrees, but Soleil was freezing. She consciously kept reminding herself to keep her legs away from the hot exhaust pipe even though its warmth was tempting.

"Thank God for this sweater," she thought. Though it was splotched with Max's blood, it was a heavy, wool knit with a high turtle collar, which offered at least a bit of protection against the windblast. Her hands were numb, but there was nothing she could do about that. Her whole body was cold.

She was confident on the bike, having learned to ride in her teens on the twisting roads around her Canadian hometown. A few high school boys had bikes, and they had fought for the privilege of teaching Soleil to ride. She had loved it.

Now the Alpine air was pummeling her relentlessly as she and the red motorcycle roared through town in hot pursuit of the white Mercedes. The Yamaha was powerful and had a low center of gravity. It loudly and deftly maneuvered around cars and other obstacles as Soleil tried to close the distance.

But she wasn't sure what she would do when she caught up with the white car.

"Improvise," she said through her clenched teeth as the bike whooshed over a short rise and went airborne for a second or two.

Eddie Poong swung his black Porsche along the curved hotel driveway and came to a screeching stop in front of the valets.

He put the convertible in neutral, pulled up on the emergency brake, and got out of the car.

A silly-looking man in a leather outfit was sitting on the curb holding a red helmet in his lap and crying like a baby.

Four young valets were chortling and laughing to each other and making obscene gestures behind the crying man's back. One was laughing so hard tears were coming down his cheeks.

Eddie quickly had a stroke of intuition. He grabbed the arm of one of the useless valets and said angrily in English, "What's happening here?"

The hapless kid whom Eddie had in his grip didn't understand, but another valet heard the menacing question and tone and stepped up to answer him.

"Ah, a super-hot *fraulein* just tricked this *dummkopf* into stealing his motorcycle." He looked down and pointed at Hans. "He is so stupid! But she was so *hot...*"

Eddie's stomach started to churn. He put his face in the kid's. "Did you see another man like me? *Ein Chinesischer mann?* Eh?"

"Oh *ja*, I thought you were him. Are you brothers?"

Eddie almost growled. The valet continued. "He left a few seconds before this all happened with two *other* hot girls in a white Mercedes."

This kid thinks everything is "hot," thought Eddie. He needed some hot answers and now. "Which way did the Chinese man go? Did he say anything to you?"

The valet pointed to the road down to Engelberg. Where else was there to go? *Dummkopf.*

"The girl?" Eddie continued in a heated voice. "What happened to the girl on the bike?"

"The hot girl?"

Eddie just glared at him. The valet continued, "*Ja.* Like I said. The hot girl twisted the crying man's *schwanz,* got on his motorcycle, and took off after your Chinese brother."

Great. Just great, thought Eddie, sizing it all up in a second.

"The whole thing was..."

"Yeah, I know," said Eddie, bolting for his car. "Hot."

"*Ja.*"

Eddie jumped into the convertible, put it in gear, and roared off, tires smoking.

Three was driving as fast as he dared as he pointed the car down the serpentine mountain road. This section of Alpine passes was internationally rated as one of the most dramatic, scenic, and dangerous roads on the planet. The cars he passed coming from the opposite direction were slowly and carefully clawing their way up the challenging and sometimes terrifying roadway.

He glanced in the rearview mirror at the two women in the backseat and then saw the quick flash of scarlet on the road behind them once again, before it disappeared behind a curve. Hmm, a motorcycle. If that rider catches up to me, Three thought, he'd better be careful. With a car like this on a road like this, his life is in my hands.

Three gave the car a little more gas.

Now Soleil was out of the town, and she poured it on.

The Yamaha screamed through the thin, crystal-clear air as she crouched as low as possible and leaned deeply into one of the many S curves in the serpentine road. The concrete ribbon twisted over and back on itself dozens of times on its descent into the valley half a mile below.

She came out of the first hairpin a bit shaky, but she quickly straightened out her line, and knew she was getting the hang of it.

She marveled at the tremendous power between her legs and blipped the throttle a few times on a straight section of the road to get acquainted with the motorcycle's abilities. Brrrrrp! Brrrrrp! She held on tightly as the fierce accelerations almost pulled her backward off the bike.

She carefully smoothed out the throttle and zeroed in on the white Mercedes ahead of her.

To help him concentrate, Eddie had Mötley Crüe blasting through the car's speakers as he pushed the Porsche as hard as he could. He had the roof down, and the cold wind, whipped into a little maelstrom in the interior of the car, was only a mild irritant. He felt exhilarated, and he knew he was tough—tougher than Three was—and now he reveled in the howling open-air chase in the mountains.

He had to get to Three. He obviously had the diamonds, a hostage, and the stupid Russian girl. And he might have set his own agenda, and that just wouldn't do.

And that must be the Tangiere girl up ahead on the red motorcycle.

When I catch up to her, I'll have the opportunity to watch this nice car of mine send her and that bike flying off the road, crashing through a guardrail, and tumbling a thousand yards to the rocks below. That would be the high point of my day.

His right foot pressed harder on the gas. He was closing on Soleil. And the bike was an easy target for his three-thousand-pound rocket.

Haliaeetus albicilla, the white-tailed eagle, was a rare, but not unknown visitor to the Alpine skies. This particular male was slightly off his usual course and was now riding an unseasonably pleasant thermal about three thousand feet above Engelberg and the Titlis glacier.

The large, brown-and-white bird incessantly scanned the ground below for food as he silently wheeled and turned in the crisp, azure sky.

Now he was distracted by movement on the cement ribbon far below—the gray concrete serpent that turned back and forth on itself as it wound around the mountains and snaked into the steep valley. *Haliaeetus* naturally understood when prey was being hunted, and his evaluation of the scenario playing out on the roadway below was surprisingly accurate:

The large white prey was being chased by a small, red, two-wheeled hunter. In its dangerous preoccupation with its target, however, the red hunter was likely unaware that it was, in turn, being stalked by a black predator, which was slowly closing in from behind. *Haliaeetus* was unable to anticipate the method by which the small red hunter intended to strike at its white prey, but he did not think it had any chance of succeeding.

Even a bird knew that a motorcycle was no match for two cars...

Soleil's biggest problem was what to do when she finally caught up to Three.

It was problematic at best if her only intention was to stop him. But it became a bleak conundrum when she realized that she had to save Yvonne, if she was still alive.

Please let her be alive, she asked the howling wind through her clenched teeth.

To make matters worse, the freezing wind was unbearably distracting, but she dared not slow down for a moment.

She bent low to the left and launched the bike into the next hairpin turn. As she was coming out of it, she glanced back and finally saw the low-slung black Porsche. It was a short distance behind and above her, coming quickly down the previous switchback, and it looked like it was closing the gap between them.

She got a fast glimpse at the driver and almost retched: it was the other Poong.

Soleil took her hand off the throttle, touched the spot on her sweater beneath which her little diamond cross was hanging, and then she and the roaring motorcycle blasted faster down the zigzagging Alpine road.

Two Vespa motorbikes from Frankenhöffer's Bakery in the next valley were slowly making their way up the winding pass.

Old Frankenhöffer's sons had convinced him to buy the two Vespas for deliveries on sunny days instead of using his old pickup truck. The old man loved his sons and finally gave in to their pestering on the subject. Why not? If it won't increase business, at least maybe it will save on gas. Smart kids.

The two sons of Frankenhöffer, both in their late teens, guided their small motorbikes with élan. They rode abreast of each other up the spectacular Alpine roadway, playing a not-so-smart game in which they separated to opposite sides of the road when traffic from either direction went by them. The lack of guardrails anywhere on these roads added to their excitement. They thought their game was daring and hilarious. Other motorists didn't.

The flat platforms over the rear wheels of their motorbikes each carried a precariously tied and taped, four-foot-high tower of boxes containing an impressive variety of Frankenhöffer's German pastries to be delivered up the mountain to the hotels in Engelberg.

Neither young rider had an inkling of what was about to descend on him around the next turn.

A suddenly increasing roar filled their ears, and in a flash, Three's white Mercedes barreled around the blind hairpin turn and headed straight for them. The boys quickly separated to opposite sides of the narrow road, and the Mercedes swerved between them, missing one of them by only two or three inches. The Vespa wobbled violently in the car's draft, and its teetering tower of boxed pastries leaned over toward the center of the roadway.

As the boxes began to topple, Soleil suddenly roared around the turn in hot pursuit, saw the collapsing tower of cakes, angled slightly to the right to avoid being hit by it, and decided that she had to nail it or be caught in a hailstorm of strudel.

She didn't see the second Vespa on the opposite side of the road until it was almost too late. She put out an arm to shield her face, but it smacked into the second pastry tower. As both motorbike riders lost control, the two towers of boxes crashed into each other in midair a split second after Soleil's red Yamaha rocket zoomed between them.

That's when Eddie's Porsche whizzed into the tornado of shredding cardboard boxes, caroming cakes and flying pastries. The avalanche of airborne baked goods was violently sucked down into his convertible's interior.

A half-dozen ring-shaped *baumkuchen* splatted into the passenger seat along with a hailstorm of *franzbrötchen*, which instantly disintegrated, becoming a tornado of swirling crumbs.

Dampfnudelen, lebkuchen, schneebällen, and *pfeffernüssen* filled the tiny area behind the front seats for a moment before the pastries exploded in the strong eddy of wind that was coming over the top of the windshield.

Eddie ducked as he was pelted by *bethmänchen, spritzgebäck,* and a large *gugelhupf,* all of which messily smashed onto the dashboard, steering wheel, and center console.

It was when a large, rectangular *zwetschgenkuchen* whammed into Eddie, enveloping his entire head in shortcrust dough, that he finally lost control of the car.

The front end of the Porsche started to fishtail and then whipped over the short shoulder between the roadway and the rocky mountain wall. A headlight exploded as the car banged into the wall, and then the Porsche bounced hard and raced backward across the pavement toward the edge of the picturesque, one-third-of-a-mile precipice that was the other side of the road.

Trying to push the gooey cake from his face and eyes, Eddie screamed an embarrassingly high-pitched shriek as the Porsche's rear wheels, still in gear, fought against the momentum that was taking its driver and his cargo of tasty baked goods toward certain doom.

"Eeee!" The scream was a surprisingly appropriate counterpoint to the Mötley Crüe lyrics that were coming through the speakers as the car flew over the edge.

As Soleil leaned into the next hairpin, she turned her head to check on the progress of her pursuer, and caught her breath as she saw the black Porsche fly off the roadway into the thin, crystal air.

Three Tit scanned the twisting road through the windshield. He glanced into his rearview mirror and saw that the red motorcycle was close. Was that a woman on the bike? he wondered when he saw the rider's blond hair whipping in the wind.

That motorcycle driver better not try anything stupid, he thought. He was nervous enough, and if she did something dumb, she would become collateral damage—a crumpled, bloody, broken mess at the bottom of the mountain.

Nothing was going to slow him down now.

He held the gun in his lap with one hand and tightened his grip on the wheel with the other.

The Mercedes's tires chirped as he guided the car quickly around the next turn.

The cold was outrageous.

Brrr. Soleil might as well have been naked. She could not remember ever feeling so cold.

She quickly leaned the bike into a hard right along the next curve and estimated that the distance between the bike and the Mercedes was now about ten yards. Through the car's window, she saw the backs of Katia and Yvonne's heads. Thank God, Yvonne was still alive. But she knew that the Poongs would never, ever let her live through this. Soleil had to do something.

And she was running out of time.

She risked looking over to the left and down, and saw that a red-and-white vehicle was slowly making its way up the twisty road toward them. In a few more turns of the road, they would pass it going in the other direction.

Her mind was racing. This may be my last chance, she thought desperately.

First, I have to get in front of the Mercedes.

The wind screamed, the concrete zoomed by under her two flashing tires, her cold hand twisted the throttle further still, and the bike roared.

Eddie Poong dangled over the abyss and held on to the concrete ledge of the road with everything he had. Receding in size quickly below him, the dwindling black Porsche twirled lazily as it plummeted, the sound of its radio and its screaming engine fading fast.

It took almost ten seconds of falling through the clear air before the car finally smashed loudly into a rock outcropping. Its suddenly truncated shape rocketed outward and then bounced down the remainder of the mountain as though it were a tin can tossed down a rock staircase. The almost unrecognizable car finally crashed onto the valley floor, and a second later, the wreck exploded.

An interesting smell of burning gasoline mixed with home-baked pastries wafted up the side of the mountain.

Eddie painfully pulled himself onto the road and stood up. He was breathing hard. For a moment, he relived the last thirty seconds: He had abandoned any hope of saving the car from going off the side of the road. Covered with crumb cake, he had pushed opened the driver's door and jumped out of the machine. As he hit the pavement and rolled, he felt himself following the Porsche over the edge, and he willed himself to grab onto anything to stop his momentum. At the last second, as he slid feet-first over the side of the roadway on his belly, he was able to hook his hands around the slightly raised lip of the rough concrete edge of the pavement.

Now he stood in the road. He shook his head like a dog coming in from the rain and looked around. The panicked anger in his dark eyes was electric. Suddenly, he spotted something to kill.

One of the Vespas was standing on its kickstand on the other side of the road, and the bakery kid stood next to it, slack-jawed at what he had just seen.

"*Lay hoe chun ah!*" You idiot! Eddie's fists were balled so tightly that his arms were shaking up to his shoulders. "*Wo sha ni!*"

The kid understood the murderous intent if not the literal translation of Eddie's death threat, and he nervously started to get on the still-puttering Vespa.

When Eddie slammed into him, the shocked Frankenhöffer boy flew a dozen feet down the road and landed on his back. He gasped for breath, looking up at the blue sky, and then heard his motorbike's engine suddenly rev up.

Eddie nearly ran over him with the Vespa. He gunned the throttle, and he and the scooter wobbled and nearly flew off the edge of the road. In a moment the Vespa regained its poise and Eddie Poong accelerated away down the mountain in pursuit of his twin brother, the diamonds, and Soleil Tangiere.

As Three Tit's car came out of the next turn, a sudden crescendo of noise made his head whip around to the right—what the hell?

With a piercingly loud, whining roar, a red cannonball blasted past the Mercedes through the narrow space between it and the rock wall, trailing a swirling cloud of dust and gravel. It pulled ahead at what must have been a hundred miles an hour.

The driver of the bike was leaning so far forward that the straight, blond hair seemed to be blowing back from the short, low-slung handlebars. A pair of long, jeans-clad legs straddled the machine, burning an explosive image dominated by action and sex into Three Tit's mind. This startling vision would remain in his mind's eye for the rest of his life.

Katia saw the motorcycle roar by and her eyes went wide. It was Soleil, and she was obviously suicidal.

Yvonne took one look and knew instantly what was happening. She inadvertently gasped, "Soleil!" Then she looked from Katia to Three Tit and spat, "*Allez tous vous faire foutre!*" Fuck you all.

But Three Tit Poong and Katia Kozh didn't speak French.

In the next fleeting seconds, the brake lights on the red motorcycle ahead blipped once or twice, and the rider leaned the bike over to the left at a steep angle and quickly disappeared around the next hairpin turn.

It was Soleil Tangier, Three marveled with abject admiration, grinning at the over-the-top bravado he had just witnessed. What a driver.

What a woman.

He took his hand off the wheel for a second, cocked the automatic, and his grin suddenly disappeared.

What a waste.

The sisters of the Kliene Kirche Catholic Church in the valley had been looking forward to their annual New Year's Day brunch.

Every year, weather permitting, on the first of January, the eight nuns would excitedly board the church's old microbus and make their way up the twisting road to the Alpine town of Engelberg for a blessed brunch at an inn with a magnificent view of the Lord's grand creation.

They were singing their familiar and happy litany of holiday hymns as Sister Hildegard, behind the wheel, carefully guided the red-and-white VW up the mountain road.

Soleil blasted around the next turn and instantly saw the VW microbus coming slowly up the hill from the opposite direction. It was coming right at her. She quickly looked back and saw that Three's white Mercedes had not yet come around the last hairpin curve. With a silent prayer, she drove her machine straight at the driver of the VW on a collision course.

That driver had better be good, or this is the end, she said to herself as bits of her life zoomed across the forefront of her mind. Then she gave the brakes everything she had.

The Yamaha, with Soleil hanging on, screeched and slid to a standing stop, blocking the narrow road.

Since one side of the road was a sheer drop, the quick-witted driver of the microbus, dressed in classic black and white, hit the brakes and turned the wheel toward the rock wall to avoid hitting Soleil or driving off into space. The van fishtailed and came to rest sideways, blocking the road mere inches from the red motorcycle and its rider.

The eight nuns heaved a collective sigh when they saw that the young woman straddling the motorcycle had miraculously avoided harm. But when they saw the Mercedes hurtling around the turn and bearing down on them, they all bailed out of the VW like paratroopers.

Soleil jumped off the bike and pushed and pulled the frightened nuns until they were standing in a tight group against the rock wall.

With the growing roar of the Mercedes in her ears, she sprinted back to make the sure no one was left in the van.

Then she threw herself at the black-and-white crowd.

Three Tit flung the Mercedes around the turn, and his eyes opened wide.

Sitting broadside less than a hundred feet down the steep road, a red-and-white van completely blocked his path. A driverless red motorcycle stood on its kickstand at the exact center of the van, and—what was *that*? A bunch of religious fanatics on the side of the road?

Katia and Yvonne took in the scene at the same instant. Katia gritted her teeth and quickly turned her head from the inevitability of was about to happen. Yvonne leaned as far forward and down as she could, braced herself against the seat back in front of her, and waited.

Soleil landed in the center of the group of nuns as the Mercedes hurtled loudly past them.

The first thing that the car hit was Hans's perfect red motorcycle. The barreling Mercedes rammed the Yamaha into the van and just kept going. Then the Mercedes, with the bike mashed into its grille, blasted out the other side of the VW, cutting the crumpled van in half. What was left of the bike exploded out of the wreckage in dozens of flying red, black, and chrome bits, blowing and tumbling and cascading down the roadway.

The heavy Mercedes bounced crazily over and through the wreckage and then fishtailed into the wall, twenty feet past the eight nuns and Soleil.

It seemed to climb the wall for a moment and then, after a long, screeching slide down the pavement, it came to a stop, facing away and down the road.

A moment later, thick black smoke began to pour out of the Mercedes's engine compartment.

The nuns stood crossing themselves like it was the End of Days, but Soleil was already running down the road toward the smoking car. Suddenly, through the smoky windows of the wreck, came the sound of a gunshot.

Soleil slowed down and felt sick—did they just shoot Yvonne? The thought nearly brought her to her knees.

The front of the Mercedes was burning. The driver's door suddenly flew open, and Three Tit Poong erupted sideways out of the door, onto the pavement, and rolled over. Then he pulled himself up, gun in hand, shook his head once wildly, and spotted Soleil.

Without another word, he aimed at her.

She caught her breath and froze.

The sound of the gunshot banged through the clear air.

But it had come from inside the white car. Three's gun fell out of his hand, and he sat down heavily in the road, a red stain spreading quickly on the front of his yellow ski jacket.

One of the back doors opened, and Katia stumbled out. She took two long steps and fell to her knees. There was a cut on her forehead, and blood was running down one of her legs. She looked at Soleil, frowned, and crawled over to Three Tit.

She reached into a pocket of his yellow jacket, pulled out the little chamois bag, and clutched it tightly in her fist. All Three Tit could do was stare at her stupidly.

"Drop it!"

All heads turned.

Eddie Poong was fifty feet up the road behind Soleil, straddling the Vespa, his huge gun pointing at Katia.

Katia had had it. *"Poshel na khuy,"* she spat at Eddie. To hell with all this, she said to herself, her natural instinct for survival having finally run to ground. Before anyone could move, she tossed the small chamois bag over the precipice at the edge of the road. Then her eyes rolled up in her head, and she passed out on the pavement.

Eddie was stunned. He looked at his brother, who had quietly toppled over and was now lying motionless on his back. Then he looked at Soleil, who stood immobile.

"You," he said, and aimed his automatic at her.

Yvonne had been pinned in the backseat when the car rammed through the microbus, but having curled up into a ball, she was more or less unhurt. One of her ankles felt completely stuck. Katia's head had smashed into the back of Three's seat, and she had nearly been knocked out.

It had been a bit of a struggle to wrest the gun away from the dazed Katia in the seat next to her, and it had gone off in the car, grazing the Russian woman's thigh and almost making Yvonne deaf.

Realizing that the Swiss woman now had her weapon, Katia had pushed her door open and was falling out of the car when Yvonne saw Three Tit standing outside the car and aiming his gun at Soleil. She had carefully pointed Katia's automatic through one of the windows and shot him.

She heard a man say, "Drop it!" and she turned her head to look out the rear window. She grimly realized what she had to do.

She twisted around painfully, instantly saw Eddie's murderous intention toward Soleil, took aim through the back window, squinted, and pulled the trigger.

The rear window of the car exploded, and Eddie spun around viciously. Both the gun and the hand grasping it blew off and landed fifteen feet up the road. He screamed, clutching his right arm, and fell to his knees straddling the Vespa. Yvonne opened her eyes.

"*Bon*," she said with satisfaction. Then the front of the car exploded.

The Mercedes rocked violently, but Soleil had already run up to it and was pulling open Yvonne's door.

Yvonne's legs were folded beneath her, and one was firmly stuck under her seat. She dropped the gun and opened her arms for Soleil.

Soleil put her arms around Yvonne and pulled with all her strength, but it wasn't working. Flames quickly started running across the dashboard and the tops of the front seats. Yvonne stared imploringly into Soleil's eyes.

"I won't let you go," said Soleil.

Then Soleil felt arms around her waist, and she was pulled purposefully backward. A loud voice behind her said, "*Eins, zwei...drei!*"

The nuns had formed a conga line, and the combined force of eight well-fed German Sisters relentlessly pulled

Soleil at the waist. Yvonne, her hair about to catch fire, felt something small snap in her leg, and then she was out of the car.

The women fell back on the pavement as the Mercedes whumped into an all-encompassing fireball. The heat blast was immense, and Soleil and the nuns quickly got Yvonne to the side of the road.

"*Merci, chéri*," Yvonne said, looking up at Soleil through the pain of her broken ankle. And then finally, mercifully, she fainted.

Traffic was building up in both directions on either side of the crash.

After a few minutes, a single motorcycle cop threaded his way up and through the honking mess, but hadn't a clue where to start.

His inventory of problems included: one Chinese man in a yellow ski jacket, unconscious and bleeding heavily from a chest wound; another Chinese man in a state of shock, with a hand and part of his arm blown off, and a Vespa motorbike between his legs; one Russian woman with head and thigh injuries, now conscious, but not inclined to communicate in any language other than Russian; one Swiss/French woman with a broken ankle, passed out; one mangled Mercedes Benz 300 sedan, burned beyond recognition; one Volkswagen microbus, torn in half; one unidentifiable motorcycle, pieces flung in a two-hundred-yard radius; eight German nuns.

And Soleil—her chest heaving, her hair wild, her eyes flashing with adrenaline.

She was too wired and hyped up to try talking to the motorcycle cop. Kneeling next to Yvonne, she barely took note of a familiar and insistent sound.

The whup-whup-whup grew quickly in intensity, and in a minute, the motorcycle policeman had ordered the cars that were lining up on the road to try to back away. A white police helicopter with ZKP in blue letters on its side quickly and noisily set down on the pavement.

As the rotors began to slow, a familiar figure jumped out of the machine, ducked below the spinning blades, and made her way toward Soleil, who was kneeling on the ground next to Yvonne.

"I knew I'd find you here," said inspector Ulrika Sonnenreich. Her black police flight jacket compressed her figure, and her blond hair was tucked under a black helmet. She stood over Soleil and surveyed the area. It looked like a battlefield.

Soleil squinted up at Ulrika and said, "Max Stepanov is up at the Terrace Hotel. I left him there in room 512, and—"

Ulrika interrupted her. "I know. Medics already have him in an ambulance and as far I've heard, he's stable, conscious, and will have a big bump on his head for a while."

Soleil looked quickly down at Yvonne. "This woman needs help now." Soleil saw that Yvonne was coming to. She leaned over her and whispered, "Don't move your leg. You'll be fine."

Yvonne moaned and opened her eyes. She nodded.

Soleil stood up and looked at the nuns. They were standing quietly, and Soleil figured that they must have been thanking God that they were alive. "*Danke*," Soleil said, and was answered by a flurry of hands making crosses on the fronts of black-and-white habits.

She turned her head and saw a man walking quickly from the helicopter toward her.

He came and stood in front of Soleil, the wind from the slowing rotors blowing his patch of light-brown hair. She said, "What are you doing here?" in a less-than-pleasant voice.

"Hello, Ms. Tangiere. Is good to see you again," he said in stilted English.

"I'd like to say the same, Vlad," she said warily. "I guess you're looking for Max and your diamonds."

Vladimir Putin said nothing and looked at her carefully. He spread his hands in a shrugging gesture.

Soleil had met Vlad in New York some months back. She didn't really like him then, and now she wasn't in the mood for pleasantries.

"Max is up at the hotel near the top of this mountain. He nearly got killed trying to protect your...your valuable *stuff*." She said it with barely veiled contempt. Then she looked over at the side of the road where Katia had tossed the chamois bag. She chuckled ironically to herself, but a small voice inside told her to cover all her bases. She might as well check.

"Hold on a second," she said to Vlad, turning and walking to the edge of the pavement.

She looked out over the mountains and glacier spreading below her in the glory of the brilliant, morning sun. A thin pillar of black smoke was rising from the wreck of Eddie's Porsche far down in the valley. The world was still there, she said to herself. Beautiful.

She looked down then, over the lip of the road's edge, and there, its little drawstring caught on a small root sticking out of the dirt and hanging over the sheer drop, was the chamois bag. She got on her knees, reached down, and in a moment was back on her feet, the bag dangling from two fingers. She walked slowly to Vlad. "Here," she said, and held it out to him.

He took the bag from her hand, wriggled open the end with his fingers, and looked inside. There, nestled among the ten, rough, uncut diamonds was the microchip.

He looked into her eyes. This woman was really something, he thought. Did she know what was in this little bag? Did she know what she had done, what she'd helped to avoid?

Max was truly lucky. *Da*, today everyone was truly lucky.

For the first time, Soleil saw unvarnished appreciation in the man's small, blue eyes. "Thank you, Soleil," he said.

"Vlad," she said, her voice tight. "These diamonds and that computer thing nearly got Max and me killed. Nothing is worth that. You're supposed to be Max's friend, and I truly hope this is over now, once and for all."

He was lost in thought for a few seconds. Then he said, "Almost." He reached into the little bag with two fingers and pulled out the cracker-sized microchip. He turned it over in his hand once or twice and then put it into his inside coat pocket. *Chorosho.*

He looked at the young Canadian woman and contemplated what the future might hold for her and Max, and more importantly, for himself. He mulled over his next move. Might as well keep it interesting, he said silently to himself.

He took one of Soleil's hands in his, gently placed the bag of diamonds into her palm, and with his two hands, closed her fingers around it. "Is gift," he said. "Once again, people of Soviet Union thank you, Soleil Tangiere."

What? she said to herself. You're kidding.

Soleil pulled her eyes away from the man and turned to Ulrika, who had been trying to secure the crash scene. "How did you find me here?" she asked her.

The inspector pointed to Vladimir. "Herr Putin, here, had contacted my office when his plane landed at the Zurich airport. He was desperate to find you and Max. We discovered that Kurt Ballas had rented a Mercedes through the Baur au Lac Hotel, and I put out a countrywide alert for the car. The Terrace Hotel called us this morning to say that the car was there."

"But how did you find us *here*? On this road?"

She pointed at the motorcycle cop. "When he called in a giant crash with a number of gunshots and bodies and blown-up cars, I figured we should fly here first." She smiled. "I knew it was you."

"Thanks," Soleil said, a bit stung by the irony. She heard a pair of ambulances pushing through the traffic. Good, she thought. Now Yvonne would be safe.

She realized that she'd better call Camille—she'd probably slept through this whole thing. She turned to Ulrika and asked, "Could I call my sister, Camille, up at the hotel on your police phone? I have to tell her what's happened and that Yvonne and I are safe."

"Of course," Ulrika said and motioned for her to follow her back to the helicopter. She leaned in through the open door of the machine and spoke on the police phone for a minute or two, and then handed the receiver to Soleil.

"Terrace Hotel."

"Room 408, please," Soleil said loudly over the noise of the rotors.

"Please hold and I will connect you."

There was a pause and two rings. Then a man answered, "Hello?"

"Kurt?" said Soleil quizzically.

"Hello, Soleil. No, it's not Kurt."

Soleil's eyes went wide, and her heart nearly stopped.

"It's me. Dustin."

23

THE POWER

I guess Kurt went for a morning walk, Camille said to herself as she stretched lazily and got out of bed.

She went into the bathroom to take a shower. At one point, she thought she heard the door to the suite open and close. He was back, she thought, smiling. Always the early riser.

She dried off, wrapped a large, white hotel towel around her, walked into the bedroom, and froze. Dustin was there. His gun was there. And an obviously insane expression on his face was there. She thought her legs were going to give way under her. Where was Kurt?

"Have a seat, Camille," he said.

He's crazy as a loon, she said to herself. And I'm in a lot of trouble.

She sat down on one of the chairs, trying to read his face, and decided that he had no concept of the seriousness of what he was doing. Well, to hell with him. "Still carrying my picture around in your pocket, Sicko?" she said, anger swelling behind her eyes.

"Where did Soleil go?" he asked, ignoring her comment. He stood a few feet in front of her, the gun aimed at the floor between them. "Looks like she killed her Russian friend for that chip. I didn't know she had it in her."

"What?" Camille couldn't keep the word from coming out.

Dustin scratched the back of his head with his free hand. "Yes, *Cami.* I was in the lobby when they brought the body down. Lots of blood." He smiled. "You didn't know, huh?"

No, she didn't know. Max was dead? Camille's heart heaved in her chest, and she felt as if she had taken a body blow. What happened? Where was Soleil? Where was Kurt? Suddenly, the phone by the bed rang. Without taking his eyes off Camille, Dustin walked over and answered after the second ring. "Hello?"

"Kurt?"

"Hello, Soleil. No, it's not Kurt. It's me. Dustin."

He heard an odd whup-whup sound on her end of the phone, but disregarded it and said, "Camille's here. Now, to make a long story short, you have ten minutes to get the chip here or I'm going to shoot her. Promise."

"Twenty!" Soleil said desperately, trying to buy any kind of time.

"Ten. And by the way, Grandma says hello—and goodbye." He hung up the phone, and his eyes bore into Camille's. He shook his head and said, "There's a good chance that I'm the only one who will get out of this alive."

Camille gripped the towel tighter around her and tried hard not to believe him.

It took less than five minutes for the helicopter to climb through the bright sky and finally settle on the hotel's large terrace where just hours ago, the New Year celebration had been in full swing.

Ulrika and Soleil sprinted into the building, leaving Vlad in the helicopter with the pilot. They took the stairs, and when they opened the door at the fourth floor, they were met by the half dozen cops whom Ulrika had mobilized using the helicopter's radio. They had congregated silently near the door to suite 408. Soleil had argued emphatically for Ulrika not to send in the troops, as Dustin was obviously nuts and completely capable of killing her sister, but Ulrika would have none of it.

"He could start killing anyone in that hotel," she had yelled at Soleil as the copter climbed through the Alps. "I can't take that chance."

At the front of the pack of cops in the hallway stood Kurt Ballas in his tan North Face jacket, his face a mask of worry mixed with rage, his room key in hand. When he saw Soleil, he said, "I went out for an hour or so. I know as much as you do."

No, Kurt, Soleil thought to herself. If only you knew the half of it.

Ulrika looked at her watch. It had been eight minutes since Dustin had handed down his ultimatum. The inspector began a hushed and heated strategy meeting with the other cops, but Soleil knew that it would be a fatal mistake for them to rush into the suite with guns blazing. She knew what Dustin wanted.

She quietly walked up to the room door, gently pulled Kurt's room key from his hand, and whispered to him, "Stay here. Keep the cops out."

Before anyone realized what was happening, Soleil had opened the door, stepped into the suite, and closed it behind her. Out of the corner of her eye, Ulrika saw what happened and couldn't believe it. She charged toward the door but ran into Kurt, who held her shoulders. He looked into her eyes and said, "If you've got a way to rescue two people now, instead of one, tell me about it."

Ulrika looked at the closed door and realized that Soleil might never come out of that room alive.

"What happened, Soleil? Cut yourself shaving?" Dustin looked at the blood on her sweater and said to Camille out of the corner of his mouth, "That must be what's left of your pal, the Russian."

Dustin was standing in a corner of the room at least ten feet from Camille, who was still in the chair. Soleil was also a room's length away from the man.

"Where's the chip?" he said to Soleil, his eyes telling her that he had been pushed to the edge of a mental breakdown since she had seen him last. Now his eyes were those of a madman. Not a surprise for the weak coward who left me for dead at Veshkin's mercy, she thought bitterly.

Soleil didn't answer him. She saw the mix of fear and defiance on her older sister's face and made a decision. She looked at Dustin and said, "You want to know how I killed John Clooney, Delores's grandson?"

Dustin was surprised by the out-of-context question and the sudden, strange quality of Soleil's voice. He tilted his head questioningly. Then he tightened his grip on the gun and made sure that Soleil saw that he was ready to shoot Camille.

"I did it with my eyes," she said.

"What?" Dustin couldn't resist asking.

"That's right, Dustin. I didn't have to make a move. I didn't have to say a word." Dustin's eyes stayed glued on Camille, but his brain focused on Soleil's words, which now had an otherworldly cadence to them.

"A man named Winston heard what my eyes were asking him to do," she said evenly. Dustin pulled his eyes off Camille and let them settle on Soleil. She was right, his muddled mind suddenly said: *her eyes...*

Soleil kept talking. "My eyes asked him to throw John Clooney over a railing to his death. These eyes." She pointed at her face.

Dustin was mesmerized, and now he thought that *he* could hear Soleil's eyes talking to him.

"Forty-five stories, Dustin. That's how far John Clooney fell. Can you imagine what he looked like when he hit, Dustin?"

Sweat caused Dustin's forehead to gleam. I can't...I can't let those eyes, with their strange power, keep looking at me. They'll kill me too!

"And all because my eyes told a man what to do." Then she lowered her face an inch and let her eyes do all the talking: "Do you know what *you* have to do now, Dustin?"

Suddenly, Camille, who had been inching out of the chair from the moment Dustin began looking into Soleil's eyes, launched herself at Dustin Magill. She hit him hard and low under his outstretched gun hand with the full force of her body.

The gun went off, shattering a window. Seconds later, the door to the suite flew open. Kurt, Ulrika, and a phalanx of cops piled in. They gasped in unison when they saw Soleil and Camille on top of Dustin. The two sisters were pounding his head repeatedly into the wall behind him.

Camille's towel had come completely off when she lunged at Dustin, but she didn't seem to notice. All the cops did, though, and the sight was sufficiently distracting to allow Camille and Soleil to keep smashing Dustin's head into the wall for a full minute.

Finally, Soleil and Camille looked at each other, at Dustin's unconscious face, and at the large circle of blood on the dented wall behind him. Then they let him drop to the floor. Camille stood up, noticed for the first time that she had nothing on, walked across the room, and quickly wrapped the white towel around her.

"Show's over guys," Kurt said, and rushed to hug Camille. She looked up at him and said, "What about Max?"

"He's fine," said Ulrika, turning to Camille.

Kurt saw relief flood Camille's face.

Soleil glanced down at Dustin, who looked like he wouldn't regain consciousness for days, if ever. Then she looked at Camille in Kurt's arms.

A blanket of silence had descended on the room.

Well, Soleil said to herself, breathing heavily, I have just one more loose end to tie up.

She turned to Ulrika. "I want to go to the chopper."

Vladimir Putin put down the police phone that he was speaking on when he saw Soleil and the inspector coming out of the hotel. He stepped down from the helicopter, ducked his head, and stood waiting for them.

While Ulrika stayed at the helicopter to talk to the pilot, Vladimir and Soleil walked together to the terrace railing.

They stood alone and looked at each other for a minute while the majesty of the snow-covered mountains waited in the background.

Finally, Soleil said, "We still have one more piece of business, Vlad." The light, cold wind tousled her hair, and she pushed a few strands away from her face.

He gave her a noncommittal look. She went on, "I got you your chip back, and I'll bet it's a blockbuster."

"What is 'blockbuster?'" he asked.

"It means important," she said. "And secret. It *is* secret, isn't it?" Her eyes flashed at him.

Yes, Soleil, it is certainly secret, he said to himself. As secret as it gets.

"Now," Soleil continued. "I will give you a gift. And then you will promise to leave Max and me alone." Her eyes blazed. "Forever."

He thought for a moment and then nodded. She continued, "My gift is the name of the person who knows what's on your chip and sent a killer to get it."

This time, Vlad couldn't control his face. What? *Someone knows what's on the chip?*

Reading his face, Soleil said, "That's right. Someone wanted it badly enough to try to kill us for it. Boris Veshkin's intention may have been to sell it to this person, but now there's no way of knowing that. You know what happened to Boris."

Vlad nodded.

She went on. "Someone here in the West wants your microchip badly. *Really* badly."

Finally, Vlad could resist no longer. He leaned toward her and said, "Who?"

Soleil looked at him for almost a full minute, her face telling him clearly that she would hold him to his word.

Forever.

Then she said, "Come closer," and whispered the name in his ear.

24

WHITE SPECK

Through the window, Camille Weston watched the Alps slip by in slow majesty as she and Kurt and the rest of the passengers climbed through ten thousand feet.

A calm voice came over the muted loudspeaker: "This is the captain speaking. Welcome aboard Flight 265 to Chicago O'Hare International Airport. Total flying time is nine hours, twenty-five minutes. Our crew is dedicated to making your flight as comfortable as possible." There was a little "bing" sound. "We've now turned off the 'fasten seat belt' sign, and you're free to move about the cabin. And thank you for flying SwissAir."

Camille turned to Kurt, who gave her a tired but serene look. "Sad to be leaving?" he asked.

She shook her head vaguely. "Yes and no. I'm going to miss Soleil sorely, but that's natural, I guess. Otherwise, I'm happy." She patted his hand. "And besides, I have a life to work on."

"A life with me, I hope." His face was open and calm.

She nodded. They were both quiet for a moment, and then Kurt said, "At the hospital, Max told me that you and Soleil were born on the exact same day. You never told me that."

"Exact same day, seven years apart."

"Max said eleven." He held his hand in front of his mouth to hide the smile.

"That bump on Max's head must have shaken his mouth loose," she said wryly. Inside, she was vastly relieved that Max hadn't suffered permanent brain damage. The doctors had fought a losing battle trying to keep the insistent Russian in a hospital bed, so they had finally agreed to let him leave with Soleil if he wore a tight bandana over his injury.

"Yvonne said she thought Max's white headband was sexy..."

"Un moment, s'il vous plait."

Yvonne Goulet walked unsteadily on her crutches from her kitchen to her apartment door. She had spent only one day in the hospital while they set the small fracture at her ankle, and now she was walking better each day.

Soleil had come to the hospital and offered to stay with her, but when she saw that Yvonne would be able to get around by herself, especially with the sympathetic aid of a number of young male hospital employees, they had said their good-byes.

"I'll be back in a week, maybe two," she had told Yvonne. Her eyes said it might be much longer.

They had hugged and kissed each other's cheeks, and Yvonne said, "Don't get married. Come back here first. Then you can get married—I have a dress all picked out."

"I'll bet you do," Soleil said with a tired smile. "And I'm not getting married. Not anytime soon."

Now Yvonne stood at her apartment door and saw through the peephole that it was the mail carrier. She opened the door and took the package from him. She went back inside the apartment, opened the package, and laughed. It was a gift from Soleil.

A Ken doll, made in the likeness of a very, very young man.

The flight attendant walked by slowly, and Kurt asked her for a beer. He glanced at his watch and resigned himself to their long flight to Chicago.

Camille continued, "I asked Soleil to come visit us in the States, but I'm not holding out much hope. A lot happened to her this year—I mean last year, 1989."

Kurt said, "It was a year of cops, killing, and craziness, that's for sure."

"Speaking of cops, Soleil was lucky and smart to have befriended that police inspector. If it wasn't for her..."

It was a miracle that Inspector Ulrika Sonnenreich hadn't lost her job.

She had risked everything and broken a slew of procedural rules for a woman she barely knew. And she had even let the Russian woman slip through the cracks—a woman who, she figured, had been used and abused enough by men.

Now it was night, and her young daughter slept peacefully in the room next to hers. Ulrika lay in the dark, wondering why she had taken the chance.

Because that woman had cared, she admitted to herself. Soleil had cared.

In this mostly bad, always hard, and generally shitty job of mine, she thought, no one really cares. The boys disguised as men—as cops—didn't understand a single thing about women—in most cases, even about the women who are their wives. And the women despised each other for this small thing or that trivial crap and were afraid to open up, to let someone see into their souls, their hearts.

It seemed like it was that way with everyone nowadays. But not Soleil.

She was ready to give up her freedom, and maybe a lot more, because she cared about *my* plight.

No, that wasn't completely accurate, Ulrika admitted to herself. Soleil cared about an idea—an idea that men should not be allowed to rule women. To intimidate, humiliate, control, or damage women.

She was rare, and it was worth the risk.

One day, Soleil, I'll thank you.

The pretty flight attendant returned with Kurt's Michelob and a paper napkin. She set them down on the little tray table in front of him and gave him a smile. Kurt tapped Camille's arm and said, "The flight attendant reminds me of someone."

Camille had seen her face and said, "She looks like that woman, Katia. Especially with those unusual colored eyes..."

The woman sat on a chair in the center of the empty theater stage. She watched the man carefully with her amber eyes.

"Experience?" he said.

"None."

He looked at her strangely. "So why are you at this audition?"

"Because I am perfect Russian whore-like character with funky accent."

The young director, sitting in the second row of empty seats, laughed. Outside, the sound of the traffic on the Hollywood Freeway was incessant.

"Well, you certainly wouldn't be cast as an angel," he chuckled.

"Hey, *mudak*," Katia Kozh said archly. "At least I am honest."

The director nodded to himself and consulted the clipboard in his lap.

He looked up at her, studied her face, and said, "Yes, I'll give you that."

She narrowed her amber eyes and appraised this young American man, who'd probably never in his life had a problem larger than a flat tire.

"I can see that you're honest," he said. "And quite a devil."

She slowly crossed her legs. "Better an honest devil than a lying angel."

Another flight attendant came by and handed Camille and Kurt single-page menus with some dinner choices.

Once you flew first class, Camille said to herself, there was no going back.

Kurt scanned the little menu and said, "What do you think, Cami? The salmon or the stir fry?"

Her eyes slid over to him and she said, "The salmon, of course. I have no appetite for Chinese food..."

Tiny waves made lapping sounds on the sides of the sampan.

The old boat lay low in the water. An ancient man with a wispy white beard slept in a sitting position in a chair near the bow. He was the lookout.

Ten thousand lights from the hundreds of watercraft, and a million lights from the city of Hong Kong made the night in Victoria Harbor an ever-changing, glittering spectacle.

Eddie Poong sat on one of the two ratty lounge chairs at the other end of the forty-foot boat. On the deck in the middle of the vessel was a low, canvas-covered hut. Eddie watched idly as his brother slowly limped out of the hut and came over to sit next to him in the other lounge chair.

With his left hand, Eddie put a cigarette in his mouth. Then with the same hand, he picked up his lighter from the deck where it had fallen, and he lit up. He would have used his right hand, but that had been shot off and left on the twisting, mountain road in Switzerland. For all he knew, it was still there.

His brother still had both hands, but Yvonne's dead-on shot to his chest had nearly killed him. Both brothers had been taken to a hospital in Lucerne, where Eddie's arm was treated. The bullet that hit Three had been slightly deflected by his breastbone, and the superb Swiss doctors' quick response had saved his life.

When the hospital had determined that they were finally able to travel, they had both been placed on a plane in police custody. When they arrived in Hong Kong, they immediately were arrested.

But this *was* Hong Kong, and they *were* the Poong brothers. The criminal *hongs* and the Triads decreed that the two were worth far more to them if they were free to go about their business and spend the rest of their miserable, dog lives paying off their serious debts.

Strings were pulled, and payoffs were made, and sooner rather than later, the Poong brothers were free men.

Now their fancy office was gone; their gorgeous houses were no more. They sat on their low, plain boat, one of the few possessions that the *hongs* had allowed them to keep, and talked quietly.

They talked about how they would find a way to punish Oscar Menschel, the traitor. They talked about the flying death of Gravva, the buffoon who had put this project on the road to failure. They spoke of Katia the whore, and Boris Veshkin the jackal.

But mostly they discussed Max Stepanov and how he and the woman had outmaneuvered them.

He and Soleil Tangiere.

One day we'll meet again, Eddie's brother said calmly to himself. One day soon.

He gingerly felt the new scar that had formed on his chest exactly three inches below the old one, which had earned him his now-obsolete nickname.

The sampan rocked slightly and made a quiet creaking noise as a small wave passed beneath it.

"What are you thinking about?" Eddie asked, noticing the faraway look on his brother's face and the familiar gold toothpick sticking out of the corner of his mouth.

A vision floated in front of his brother's eyes: a pair of jeans-clad legs wrapped around a roaring, red motorcycle hurtling down an Alpine road.

"What am I thinking about?" responded Four Tit Poong. His eyes narrowed. "The future, Eddie. The future."

Click, click...*Click.*

The voice of the captain came over the loudspeaker to let the passengers know that they should remain in their seats for the next fifteen minutes or so—there was a bit of turbulence in this patch of sky.

Camille looked at Kurt. "Do you think Soleil and Max will be all right now? I asked her more than once, before we left, if she thought that murderous Grandma character was gone for good, and she told me not to think about that anymore. But I can't help it. It's not in my nature to ignore danger like that."

Kurt looked at her kindly and said, "Sometimes the best we can do is just keep our fingers crossed..."

They came for me, and they didn't care.

They didn't care that I was an old woman in a wheel-chair, knocking on death's door.

Delores "Grandma" Clooney looked out the window of the specially outfitted plane. She so preferred traveling on one her Carrington Metals jets, but beggars couldn't be choosers. Imagine! Me, a beggar!

The plane was taxiing up to a terminal under leaden, foreboding skies. A powdery snow started to drift down. A sign with red Cyrillic lettering was secured on the leading edge of the terminal's roof. She turned to the security officer in the seat next to her. "How do you pronounce that again, young man?" she said, pointing to the sign with a nod of her chin.

The man looked past her out the small window and said slowly, "Sher-eh-meht-ye-vo. Is biggest airport in Russia." He smelled like borscht and vodka.

Wonderful, Grandma said to herself, just grand. She had been extradited to what was left of the Soviet Union and accused of conspiracy and spying, of all things. What spying?

The final irony—someone in Russia had believed a lie about me, and I probably know who had whispered that lie.

Well, she ruminated, her mind working faster than any twenty-year-old's. With my age, my connections, and my money, I won't be here long. I'm like a bad old penny—I keep turning up.

And I have a perfectly delightful reason to find my way back.

A wonderful reason: Soleil Tangiere.

She looked out the window at the sign on the terminal once again and suddenly smiled.

At my age, it's nice to have something to look forward to.

They were getting drowsy and there were a lot of hours left to go until they reached Chicago.

Camille stifled a yawn and said, "Let's sleep a little."

Then she looked over at the tall, kind man sitting next to her. "Thanks for being here for me. And for Soleil."

He patted her hand and said softly, "I love you, Camille Tangiere Weston."

I love you too, Kurt, she said with her heart.

The plane flew on, six miles above the Atlantic Ocean, a tiny white speck in the sapphire-blue sky.

• • •

The door closed behind Vladimir Putin.

Now Mikhail Gorbachev, general secretary of the Soviet Union, sat alone in the room behind the huge desk and looked at the electronic chip that the sandy-haired man had set down in front of him before he had walked out. Then he looked at the closed door and thought, That man who just left is the future of the new Russia.

I don't know if I want to be around to see it.

He picked up the microchip, held it in front of his face, and snorted.

Imagine, he said to himself as he peered at this marvel of a brave new technology that he did not understand.

Imagine: on this little wafer, so much information, so much *death.*

How is it possible that it is all here? All the locations, the coordinates, the security codes, the access codes, the arming codes, the firing codes of every primed-and-ready intercontinental ballistic missile in the Soviet arsenal, each tipped with the latest Soviet nuclear warhead.

All any terrorist or rogue state could ever wish for was on that one microchip.

In the wrong hands...

It was too horrifying to contemplate.

He took the cracker-sized chip in both his strong hands and twisted hard until it bent and then loudly broke into two useless pieces.

Chorosho.

25

FAVOR

A gentle wind blew from the lake up the green hill. Bees hummed around the gently rustling flowers that lined the small house's front yard. The midday sunlight was like warm, welcome, golden silk on all it touched.

Zvi heard the expected knock on the door and pushed himself out of his chair. He was seventy-two years old and loved his life in Lake Como. This part of Italy was peaceful and civil, and he had been blessed with its beauty as well as with a good wife for almost forty years.

When Izzy Gutthelf had called him, he was happy to hear from his old friend in America. But after the favor was asked, it had stirred up old memories. He looked down at the faded numbers tattooed on his left wrist, and his happiness gave way to a familiar angst.

Some things never die, he said to himself. You just have to remember to forget them. But he had said to Izzy, of course, anything for you, old friend. And then the young woman had called from Zurich, and he had told her that she would be welcome.

And now at his door was the slim, beautiful woman. With her was a stocky man with dark eyes and a wide, white headband.

"*Per favore*, come in." Zvi ushered them into his small house with an old-fashioned sweep of his arm.

His wife had set tea for them on a small table beneath a window on the north side of the house. When they had settled at the table, she excused herself.

Zvi and Soleil chatted for a while about Izzy and Brenda and New York, and he made Soleil promise to extend his and his wife's greetings and love to them if she went to America.

"I hope I will go there again soon. Maybe this year," said Soleil.

"That would be nice," said Zvi, his keen old eyes liking this quiet young woman and her *fidanzato*, her boyfriend.

After the tea was gone, Zvi put his old, strong hands on the tabletop and said, "So. Let's see what my friend Izzy said you would bring."

Max reached into his pants pocket and pulled out the stone. He released it from its envelope of hard tissue and set it on the table in front of Zvi. The old man looked from the stone to Max and said, "You are Russian?"

"Yes."

Zvi nodded and picked up the crystal. He held it to the light. "Did you weigh this?" he asked.

Soleil shook her head.

Zvi got up slowly, walked out, and came back holding a small, oblong wooden box with a hinged lid. He sat down, opened it, and took out a small balance scale that he held on a string between two fingers. When he gently lifted the string, its two small, metal bowls hung in precise balance from the ends of a short metal arm the length of a pencil.

He placed the diamond crystal in one bowl—it was almost too large to fit—and started piling small, numbered weights into the other. After much adding and removing of ever-smaller weights, the two sides of the scale balanced perfectly.

Zvi put the scale down and said, "One hundred seventeen carats and twenty-five points." He looked at the two young people.

Soleil said, "Zvi, can you tell us, give us an idea, how you would cut this stone?"

He looked at her lovely face with the unusual blue eyes and said, "For you, for Izzy, I can try." He picked up the diamond and turned the stone this way and that in the light. "Something like this can take months to plot—to plan how to get the most from the crystal."

Her eyes encouraged him, and she said, "Just a rough idea would be wonderful. What kind, what shape of finished stone would you cut from it?"

They sat at the table for the better part of fifteen minutes in silence as Zvi turned the stone left and right, up and down, looked at it through his ten-power loupe a hundred times, and let the north light from the window pour into the crystal. As he worked, he made a few calculations and quick little drawings on a small pad.

Finally, he held the crystal up to the light one last time and then gently handed it to Soleil. He looked at Max and said quietly, "This diamond. It is also Russian?"

"Yes."

Zvi nodded. Then he said, "I would cut a single stone, eighty, maybe eighty-five carats. And round—brilliant cut. That's what I would do with this stone. That's what cutters better than I would most likely do," he said with humility.

"This diamond looks close to flawless; it may even be flawless. And the color," he said, eyeing Max. "Like clear Arctic ice."

He looked back at the stone and continued, "And there would be a second stone, maybe fifteen carats, that would be recovered when this diamond is cleaved for the first cut. Also flawless and colorless. Perfect."

Soleil looked deeply into Max's eyes, and then her eyes slid back to look straight into Zvi's. Finally, she said, "Would you do this, Zvi? Would you cut this diamond for us?"

The old man snorted, "Oh, no, I couldn't."

The three sat looking at one another in silence. Finally, Zvi said, "I'm too old—retired. The planning and then the cutting would take three, maybe four months. At least." He looked at the stone again, which Soleil had placed on the table.

Then he thought about his life, about losing his parents to the ovens in the bad years, and about the running and hiding and finally winding up here, in this beautiful place, almost a lifetime ago. He thought about what his life was like when he was the age of the two people sitting across from him. I've been blessed, he reminded himself. He looked carefully at Soleil and Max and pondered.

This diamond, it means much to the two of them, he thought. He could see it in their eyes, in the way they cleaved to each other when they looked at it. There was more to them and this stone than just its monetary value. For a reason he did not know but could see clearly existed, this diamond bonded them together.

He picked up the stone once more and looked at Soleil. Finally, he nodded and said, "I will cut it. For you."

Her smile lit the room and she said, "Thank you, Zvi. It means everything to us that you'll do this. More than you know."

She thought about the day when she was just nineteen and had stumbled down the aisle in the jewelry exchange in the alien and frightening city of New York, bleeding and almost dead and grieving the recent murder of her father. She had been at her wits' and her body's end, and at the mercy of the next bad man who would try to run rough-shod over her. She thought about how Izzy and his wife had taken her, a total stranger, into their home and their lives, no questions asked.

She remembered the silent promise she had made to herself. One day, she had vowed, one day she would repay those two gentle souls in kind, if such a thing were possible.

And now it was, and this was the first step, she said to herself with a quiet determination.

"Zvi," she said, breaking the silence. "Here." She reached into the pocket of her jeans and pulled out a second dia-mond, this one smaller, but of obviously equal quality. She laid it on the table. It must have weighed fifty carats.

She looked at the old man, and a few long, blond hairs fell across her face. "This is for you, Zvi, your payment for cutting the diamond. Promise me you'll use it for good things."

This smaller stone was worth at least two million dollars.

Zvi looked at the stone and then at Max. "You robbed the Hermitage Museum in Leningrad?" he said.

"Close," said Max, and smiled.

Zvi was about to protest and push the smaller stone back at Soleil, but suddenly, he thought no. That would be an insult to her—might hurt her. This small mission she gave to me, and this frozen moment in the river of these two people's lives—may be more precious to them than the stones.

He looked from Max to Soleil and sighed. There is much more to these two than meets the eye. A life force that will never be fully shown to me, and rightly so, that is driving these two young people forward into the future.

So who am I to slow down their destiny?

He reached across the table and grasped Max's right hand and Soleil's left tightly in his old, hardened hands.

"It will be my pleasure," he said.

EPILOGUE

He didn't know what had awakened him in the middle of the night, but then realized it could have been his dream.

He had gone to sleep an hour ago, very, very drunk.

The unrelenting wind and ice balls banged against the room's small, thick window. He shivered and reached his hand around in his bunk until it found the bottle. Squinting in the dark, he brought it up to his face and saw that there was still an inch or two of vodka in it. Good. That was enough.

He lay on his back and drank it down in one long gulp.

What woke me? I can sleep through an air raid or an earthquake. And certainly through another godforsaken ice storm here at the Mir, the frozen asshole of the world.

So what was it?

Then it all came flooding back—it *was* the dream...

In the dream, he was living in someone else's body, seeing through someone else's eyes, feeling through another's skin. He spoke aloud: "Remember the promise?"

"*Da*. Of course," said a silent voice.

Then he looked down and saw, with more than his eyes...

Resting in his arms was the most beautiful woman he had ever seen. Her hair was the gleaming golden silk of the summer sun, and her sapphire eyes gently sparkled with the promise of a secret dawn. Those eyes looked into his soul, and she smiled and kissed him lightly on his lips.

The silent voice said, "My promise to you."

He closed his eyes, smiled contentedly, and muttered, "*Spasibo, Max.*"

Thank you.

Then Arkady rolled over in his bunk and fell finally, peacefully, to sleep.

THE END

THE AUTHOR

Larry Bonner earned degrees in economics and political science from New York University before launching a lifetime career in the precious metals, diamond, and commodities industries.

Following the international success of his debut novel, *Soleil Tangiere,* Bonner has followed with the sequel, *Soleil, Too!*

Larry Bonner has one son, and lives with his wife, two dogs, and a parrot somewhere near Miami.

For more about Soleil Tangiere, visit www.soleiltangiere.com